Discover a real-life love story, from a girlhood crush expressed in ebullient letters, to a mature love channeled into heartstopping verse. This volume presents Emily Dickinson's thirty-six year correspondence with her neighbor, sister-in-law, and muse, Susan Huntington Dickinson.

With insightful commentary, the editors offer a compelling new interpretation of the poet's life and work. This compilation, originally published in 1998, disrupted decades of censorship and misinterpretation. The letters reveal Susan as Emily's closest literary confidante and the love of her life. And Emily herself is transformed from the white-clad recluse of popular imagination into a lively, passionate, witty, and playful woman, writing and loving on her own terms.

Open Me Carefully

EMILY DICKINSON'S
INTIMATE LETTERS TO SUSAN HUNTINGTON DICKINSON

Edited by Ellen Louise Hart & Martha Nell Smith

CHRONICLE BOOKS
SAN FRANCISCO

From *Stories for Romantics: Three Unforgettable Tales of True Love*,
published by Chronicle Books in 2025.

Originally published by Paris Press in 1998.
First Wesleyan University Press edition 2019.

Library of Congress Cataloging-in-Publication Data available.

ISBN 978-1-7972-3570-7

Manufactured in India.

MIX
Paper | Supporting responsible forestry
FSC™ C043100

Series design by Kristen Hewitt.
Design by Lizzie Vaughan and Kelsey Cox.
Typesetting by Frank Brayton.

10 9 8 7 6 5 4 3 2 1

Chronicle books and gifts are available at special quantity discounts to corporations, professional associations, literacy programs, and other organizations. For details and discount information, please contact our premiums department at corporate gifts@chroniclebooks.com or at 1-800-759-0190.

Chronicle Books LLC
680 Second Street
San Francisco, California 94107
www.chroniclebooks.com

CONTENTS

Open Me Carefully is dedicated to the memory of Martha Dickinson Bianchi, Mary Hampson, and to the love of Susan and Emily Dickinson.

PUBLISHER'S NOTE *from the first edition*

Paris Press hopes that this collection of Emily Dickinson's "letters" to Susan Huntington Dickinson helps to enhance and perhaps change your understanding of Emily Dickinson's life as well as her work. Dickinson lived like many of the great writers throughout history: Ensconced in literature, philosophical and spiritual concerns, the natural world, current events, and family, Emily Dickinson managed to integrate solitude into the demands of nineteenth-century responsibility in order to think and to write. She felt deeply and lived her desire, vision, humor, and pain onto the page. Her work was inspired by all the components of daily life, including the deeply intimate and passionate relationship with her friend, neighbor, and sister-in-law, Susan Huntington Dickinson. For thirty-six years, Susan Huntington Dickinson was a primary source of solace, intellectual challenge, and love for Emily Dickinson. It is with great pride that Paris Press offers you a pivotal collection of writings from our most beloved American poet to her most beloved and inspirational companion.

This selection of Emily Dickinson's letters, letter-poems, and poems to Susan Huntington Dickinson is presented as precisely as possible. We have followed the dating, line breaks, spacing, capitalization, spelling, and punctuation of documents as they were compiled and presented to us by Ellen Louise Hart and Martha

Nell Smith, authors of the Introduction, Section Openers, Bridge Notes, and End Notes. We offer our deepest gratitude to these ground-breaking scholars.

Paris Press extends heartfelt thanks to the many individuals and organizations that made the publication of *Open Me Carefully* possible. We are grateful for the guidance and advice of Cathy N. Davidson, Daniel Lombardo, Patricia McCambridge, Ken Wissoker, Eleanor Lazarus, and David Wilensky. For generous financial support we thank Laura Slap Shelton, the Council of Literary Magazines and Presses, the Sonia Raiziss Giop Charitable Trust, the Lydia B. Stokes Foundation, the Massachusetts Cultural Council, the Massachusetts Foundation for the Humanities, and the Xeric Foundation; we are grateful to an anonymous contribution made in memory of EG. Many thanks to Ivan Holmes and Judythe Sieck for their elegant designs, to Jeff Potter for the fine composition of the book, and to Susan Kan and Maryellen Ryan for their hard work and loyalty. Thanks also to Elspeth and Nick Macdonald for use of their quiet retreat during the editing of this book.

—Jan Freeman

INTRODUCTION

In June 1852, Emily Dickinson sent a letter to her friend Susan Huntington Gilbert, who was away from home teaching mathematics at Robert Archer's school for girls in Baltimore, Maryland. The letter was carried and delivered to Susan by Emily's father, Edward Dickinson, on his way to Baltimore to serve as a delegate to the national Whig convention. "Why cant I be a Delegate to the great Whig Convention?" asks Dickinson in the letter's postscript. "Dont I know all about Daniel Webster, and the Tariff, and the Law? Then, Susie, I could see you, during a pause in the session." Placed for Susan to see when she first unfolded the letter is Emily's tender instruction, "open me carefully – "

Over the next four decades, Emily Dickinson would write to Susan more frequently than to any of her other ninety-nine known correspondents, including editor Thomas Wentworth Higginson. The voluminous correspondence with Susan constitutes one of two major bodies of work that Dickinson bequeathed to the world—the other being the more than eight hundred poems that she collected in her handbound manuscript books, or fascicles.

Open Me Carefully presents a selection of this extensive body of correspondence, inviting a dramatic new understanding of Emily Dickinson's life, creative process, and poetry. These intimate letters tell the story of a passionate and sustained attachment between Dickinson and the beloved friend who was her central source of inspiration, love, and intellectual and poetic discourse.

Dickinson's poems, letters, and letter-poems to Susan give us a rare glimpse into the poet's process of writing and revising. They also indicate that Susan, herself a published writer of poems, reviews, essays, and stories, was Emily's primary reader, the recipient of both drafts and finished poems. Yet, in spite of the sheer volume of correspondence between Susan and Emily, and despite compelling evidence of an ongoing literary dialogue between the two women, the relationship between Emily and Susan has been neglected, distorted, and obscured. Whereas pages and pages of academic speculation have been devoted to a mere three letter-drafts that Dickinson wrote to a mysterious real or fictional character identified only as "Master," the correspondence between Dickinson and Susan has received disproportionately little attention.

Audience and Muse, Confidante, Collaborator, and Critic

Emily Dickinson died in 1886, and her poems were not introduced to the reading public until 1890, when editors Thomas Higginson and Mabel Loomis Todd released the first edition of *Poems by Emily Dickinson*. In the hundred years since that first publication, the story of Emily Dickinson and Susan Huntington Dickinson has only gradually emerged in the annals of Dickinson scholarship. In fact, most readers of Dickinson are unaware of the intense and long-lived relationship that was at the very core of the poet's emotional and creative life.

Susan Huntington Gilbert and Emily Elizabeth Dickinson were born within days of each other in December 1830. They may have known each other from girlhood; they certainly knew each other from adolescence; and they had begun to correspond by the age of twenty. Their relationship spanned nearly four decades, and for three of those decades, the women were next-door neighbors. Together, Susan and Emily lived through the vicissitudes of a life closely shared: Susan's courtship, engagement, and eventual marriage to Emily's brother, Austin; Susan and Austin's setting up home next door to the Dickinson Homestead; the births of Susan and Austin's three children, and the tragic death of their youngest son, Gib; anonymous individual publication of at least ten of Dickinson's poems; and the deaths of parents and many friends.

Open Me Carefully includes, for the most part, only Emily Dickinson's side of this correspondence. Nearly all of Susan's letters to Emily were destroyed at the time of the poet's death. This would have been the result of a routine "house cleaning," reflecting the common practice in the nineteenth century to either destroy or return to the senders all letters received by the deceased. That even a handful of Susan's letters to Emily have been preserved, when letters from all other correspondents were irretrievably disposed of, is itself a testament to the vital nature of this correspondence.

A Story Left Untold

The correspondence reproduced in *Open Me Carefully* debunks much of the common Dickinson lore served up for decades by high school literature textbooks, television sitcoms, song lyrics, and literary biographies. According to these tenacious popular legends, Dickinson was an inaccessible, ethereal hermit, too rare for this earthly plane, and probably undone by unrequited love for any or all of several male suitors whose identities have been the stuff of speculation for countless readers.

But why has this important correspondence—which lasted until Dickinson's death in 1886 and preoccupied Susan until her own death in 1913—been relatively ignored, if not suppressed? Emily Dickinson's writings to Susan were certainly not unknown; they have long been recognized as passionately literary, and many scholars have bickered and argued over the nature of Dickinson's obvious devotion to her sister-in-law.

Two cultural factors may have contributed to the discounting of this pivotal relationship. The first is the stereotypical nineteenth-century vision of the "Poetess" as a tortured, delicate woman dressed in virginal white, pining away in seclusion, removed from the vibrant nit, grit, and passion of normal life. It is this stereotype, encouraged by Dickinson's early editors—particularly Mabel Loomis Todd—that has preserved the popular image of Emily Dickinson as the recluse spinster belle of Amherst.

The second factor is the view of intimate female friendships in the nineteenth century. According to this view, women of Dickinson's time often indulged in highly romantic relationships with each other, but these relationships were merely affectionate and patently not sexual. Such same-sex attractions, so the popular wisdom goes, had the character of an adolescent crush rather than a mature erotic love. As this correspondence shows, however, Emily and Susan's relationship surpasses in depth, passion, and continuity the stereotype of the "intimate exchange" between women friends of the period. The ardor of Dickinson's late teens and early twenties matured and deepened over the decades, and the romantic and erotic expressions from Emily to Susan continued until Dickinson's death in May 1886.

The Makings of a Myth

Though details of Emily and Susan's relationship were known to their contemporaries, much of the information about the two women has been passed along through sometimes questionable testimony. The strongest testimonies, and the ones that have been most pivotal in determining the presentation of the relationship until now, have been provided by two controversial sources. The first is Martha

Dickinson Bianchi, Susan's daughter and Emily's niece. Bianchi, who compiled *The Single Hound* (1914) and dedicated it "as a memorial to the love of these 'Dear, dead Women,'" then continued to carry out her mother's plan by presenting extracts from letters in *The Life and Letters of Emily Dickinson* (1924) and *Emily Dickinson Face to Face* (1932). For various unfair and unfounded reasons, many scholars have characterized Bianchi as an always unreliable source. However, we believe otherwise, and we have cited her comments and observations about Susan and Emily throughout this book.

The second source is Mabel Loomis Todd, editor (along with Thomas Higginson) of the first three volumes of Emily's poems. In her desire to hide Susan's central role in Dickinson's writing process, Loomis Todd went to great lengths to suppress any trace of Susan as Emily's primary audience. Much of the reason for this is obvious: the young Mabel Loomis Todd, born the year Susan and Austin wed, had become Austin's mistress; she was the "other woman" to Susan's "wife forgotten."[1] The affair continued until Austin's death in 1895 and was quite public, an inexpressibly painful situation for Susan. Loomis Todd made no mention of Susan when she produced the *Letters of Emily Dickinson* in 1894. There is even evidence in Emily's letters to Austin that someone, probably Loomis Todd, sought to expunge affectionate references to Susan.

When the Dickinson fascicles were turned over to Mabel Loomis Todd, Susan's crucial position as primary audience for Emily's poetry became an inconvenient and irrelevant piece of information that did not jibe with the popular image of a nineteenth-century poetess. To editors of the time, the most marketable image of Dickinson the poet was that of the eccentric, reclusive, asexual woman in white. This mysterious figure necessarily wrote all alone, harboring some "secret sorrow" that no one else could understand or be privy to. There was simply no place in the official Dickinson biography for the revelation of an immediate confidante and audience for her poetry—particularly not one who lived next door. Loomis Todd was therefore willing to play up this "solitary spinster" characterization of Emily Dickinson in her editorial productions, and thus the role of Susan went entirely unmentioned in the earliest publications of Dickinson's works. Loomis Todd even refused Higginson's recommendation that Susan's obituary of Emily (which emphasized that although she kept her own company she was "not disappointed with the world"[2]) serve as the introduction to the 1890 *Poems*. Instead, Loomis Todd used a three-paragraph introduction by Higginson that proclaimed that Emily was "a recluse by temperament and habit,"[3] and hence the mythology of Emily Dickinson, the "recluse of Amherst," was cast.

Susan's Book of Emily's Writings

Between Dickinson's death in 1886 and the first printed volume of her poems four years later, Susan began to work on an inclusive volume of Emily's writings. Seven months after Dickinson's death, Susan submitted to an editor of *The Century* "a poem of Miss Emily Dickinson's on the 'Wind' thinking you might like to print it."[4] That letter's reference to "a novice's attempt at type-writing" shows that Susan was already at work transcribing Emily's poetry. Susan was determined to depict Dickinson in her complexity, making a collection that was "rather more full, and varied"[5] than the conventional presentation in *Poems by Emily Dickinson* (1890). Rather than separating the poems from their original contexts and dividing them into the predictable subjects that audiences of the time expected ("Life, Love, Time & Eternity, and Nature"), Susan wanted to showcase the entire range of Emily's writings: letters, humorous writings, illustrations—in short, everything left out of the Loomis Todd and Higginson edition.

Forty fascicles, or manuscript books, and scores of poems on loose sheets had been found after Dickinson's death, and Emily's sister Lavinia (Vinnie) wanted poems from that trove to be incorporated into a printed volume. Vinnie turned to Susan to accomplish the task. Susan struggled with the problem of making a book from those fascicles, reading through the astonishing production of her friend and marking individual lyrics with initials (D, F, L, N, P, S, W) and "X's" in order to categorize them. In doing this, Susan was not only deferring to Vinnie's wishes but also bowing to Higginson's market judgment that the kind of "more full and varied" volume she had first imagined was "un-presentable."[6] Susan tried to make her book of Emily's writings conform to Vinnie's and Higginson's vision, but she could not accomplish the task because it went against her better judgment, informed by decades of her creative work with Emily. Distracted and grieved both by the loss of Emily and her husband's flagrant affair with Mabel Loomis Todd, Susan moved slowly. Vinnie, growing impatient, demanded that the fascicle poems be returned so that another editor, one who could get the job done more quickly, could work on the project. Though Susan continued to work on designs for her book of Emily's writings until her death in 1913, she returned the fascicle poems to Vinnie, knowing that they would be given to Loomis Todd and edited into an acceptable printed volume that would not amply reflect Emily's genius or her goals as a writer.

Solitary, But Not Removed

Understanding of Dickinson's life and her utterly original and daring poetry has been obscured by a combination of deliberate suppression, easy stereotyping, and convenient but misleading categorization. In *Open Me Carefully*, we see that Emily was not the fragile, childlike, virginal "bride who would never be" writing precious messages about flowers, birds, and cemeteries from the safety and seclusion of her bedroom perch in Amherst, Massachusetts. Dickinson was devoted to her craft, and she was dedicated to integrating poetry into every aspect of her day-to-day life. She was engaged in philosophical and spiritual issues as well as all the complexities of family life and human relationships. She knew love, rejection, forgiveness, jealousy, despair, and electric passion, and she lived for years knowing the intense joy and frustration of having a beloved simultaneously nearby, yet not fully within reach.

While it is true that Dickinson went to extraordinary measures to preserve her privacy, the facts of her solitude have been taken out of context. Like many artists, she needed a great deal of time alone for reading, contemplation, and writing—a requirement that has rarely been questioned when enjoyed by male writers. However, in the case of Dickinson, the need for solitude and contemplation has been interpreted as a pathological reclusiveness and an indication of intense vulnerability and wounding, not as a consciously chosen way of life.

The Subject Matter of Daily Life

Dickinson's most intense and constant relationship moved from "Emilie" to "Emily" and "E." and from "Susie" to "Sue" and "Susan." Focus on any other single correspondent cannot possibly offer the diverse array of insights rendered by scrutiny of these writings to Susan, for no other addressee was as intimate with Emily for as long a period of time, and no other was privy to such a range of her work. The comfort and informality of the correspondence (reflected in the content and in the types of paper used for the missives, as well as by the "rough draft" style of handwriting), reveal the "dailiness" of the intimacy between these two women. Emily did not rely on special occasions such as birthdays, holidays, or deaths to inspire the need for contact; the most ordinary and extraordinary events alike could prompt a poem or letter to Susan. Every aspect of their lives is deemed worthy subject matter in their correspondence, from shared meals and just-read books to personal unveilings about desire and loneliness; from mundane family matters to political situations reported in the newspaper, which both read every day.

Literary and biblical references abound in the correspondence, and many of Emily's favorite writers, such as George Eliot, Elizabeth Barrett Browning, and Shakespeare, are mentioned and quoted. Frequently, characters and situations in novels and plays are referred to in a manner that suggests a "masking" function, implying that Susan and Emily related their secrets through the personalities of literary and biblical characters with whom they were both familiar.

Within the documents, Emily frequently refers to family members, and a Chronology following this Introduction presents the people, places, and important events that the correspondence refers to directly or indirectly. For the most part, Emily writes to Susan from the Homestead in Amherst, Massachusetts, and Susan receives the letters during visits with family members and friends from Manchester, New Hampshire, to Grand Haven, Michigan—but most often the letters travel directly next door, to the Evergreens.

Infused with eroticism, the poetry exchanged between Emily and Susan was part of the texture of their daily life. They simultaneously lived and screened their passion. However much the love between Emily and Susan has been overlooked or diminished by commentators, one thing is clear: the letters and poems are standing proof of a devoted correspondence that has had a profound impact on the history of American literature. Though popular Dickinson lore has veered far from the romantic and intellectual essence of this primary relationship, the work can now, more than a hundred years later, finally speak for itself.

A NOTE ON THE TEXT

In preparing *Open Me Carefully*, there were two main challenges before us. The first was to make a book that, although arising from academic research, would be appealing and informative to the general reader, as well as to Dickinson scholars. The second challenge was how to make a cohesive book that would most effectively relate the human story behind this most generative of literary and emotional unions. Thus, a great deal of thought and effort went into such overarching issues as which principles should serve as a guide to selection of materials to be included; how the chosen writings should then be contextualized; and how the documents should be organized.

A Comfortable, Everyday Correspondence

Even as attention to Dickinson's manuscripts has increased in the past decade, the assumption has been that any knowledge discovered through analyses of the original documents is of primary interest only to specialists. Yet the textual body of the correspondence—Dickinson's manuscripts and all their material facts—forms a powerful witness to Susan's involvement in Emily's writing practices, and is therefore of importance to anyone interested in the life and poetry of Emily Dickinson.

Emily wrote to Susan on different types of paper (graph, scrap, and formal embossed paper of all sizes), while with other correspondents she almost always used more formal, gilt-trimmed stationery, in effect dressing her texts like a gift edition of poetry or a deluxe edition of biblical scripture. Sending writings in one's casual script (as Emily does to Susan), in the handwriting more similar to one's private notes for developing expression, is an act that speaks of trust, familiarity, routine. Using less formal stationery for those writings—scraps of paper lacking gilt edges or elegant embossments—likewise signals the intimacy of comfortable everyday exchange, a correspondence not bound by special occasions, but an everyday writing habit that takes as its subject any element of life, from the monumental death of a loved one to the negligible nuisance of indigestion.

Poems Newly Associated with Susan

Emily's expressions to and about Susan—uttered in pencil and ink, on elegant stationery and on small torn squares of paper—were powerful enough to drive Susan herself to destroy those "too personal and adulatory ever to be printed."[7] Other individuals, most likely Mabel Loomis Todd, erased Susan's name and affectionate references to her; identifying some of these erasures for the first time has enabled us to identify poems not previously known to have been sent to Susan.

Twenty poems and one letter not previously associated with Susan are reproduced in this collection. These include the late 1850s letter to "Susie" discovered in 1992 and the new copy of "The feet of people walking home" addressed to "Darling" (both housed at Amherst College), a new version of "The Overtakelessness / of Those" addressed to "Dollie" (at Princeton), and a new version of "Two – were immortal – / twice – " (at the Morgan Library in New York City). We include manuscripts that editor Thomas W. Johnson did not link to Susan, though material evidence (Susan's markings, paste marks, pinholes, and/or folds) shows that according to his editorial principles, they should have been. We also include drafts of poems. Although Johnson asserted that Dickinson "never sent rough or semifinal drafts to her friends,"[8] we have found drafts we believe were sent to Susan.

For letters and poems that are not actually addressed to Susan, we have a variety of evidence to support our claim that the documents belong in this correspondence, including physical characteristics, paper types, signs of handling, notes written on the manuscripts, transmission and publication history, and work by previous editors.

The Importance of Manuscript Study

Over the past decade, technological advances in textual reproduction—such as photographic representations of the manuscripts and the creation of electronic archives providing digital images of Dickinson's writing—have worked hand in hand with critical advances such as feminist analyses to reveal more clearly Susan's immense importance as a participatory reader of Dickinson's works. *Open Me Carefully* makes use of facsimile reproduction. By studying Emily's writings to Susan in manuscript, readers can examine Dickinson's development from girlhood to advanced middle age, and the parallel maturation in her creative practices. We have made our selections with an eye toward presenting a wide range of textual forms, and in arranging these documents we have emphasized chronology.

All of Dickinson's letters and poems are handwritten, and certain manuscript features—calligraphic orthography, punctuation, capitalization, and line breaks—help to convey meaning. After the late 1850s, Dickinson's letters and poems came to look alike, both with short lines, and rarely any indentation or spacing to separate lines of poetry and lines of prose in a letter. Therefore, in Sections Two, Three, and Four we present Dickinson's line lengths, while previous editors have joined her lines of poetry according to schemes of rhyme and meter and disregarded the lineation of her prose. For consistency, we provide transcriptions, showing line breaks, for Susan's letters of the 1860s. Dickinson does not indent paragraphs in her letters but indicates their start and finish in other ways. In Section One we leave lines of space between passages to represent paragraphing.

Dickinson used the page itself, and the placement of words in relation to embossments, attachments, and margins to convey meaning, and in ways that typography cannot sufficiently transmit. We describe such poetic designs in the End Notes. Other aspects of Dickinson's handwriting which influence our editing and interpretation cannot be fully translated into type.

In reproducing her unusual capitalization, editors' decisions will vary since Dickinson's lower and upper case letters are difficult to distinguish. She generally has four or more sizes of an individual letter in a single piece of work. We call it as we see it, acknowledging that some of the fun of working with this writer's manuscript art, translating it into print, is the pleasure of interpretation and debate. Punctuation is another matter of translation. Dickinson's famous "dashes" are often angled, pointing up or down, curviform or curving with a dot to look like a bird's eye, but for simplicity we show all these "pointings" as short, standard en-dashes, with the exception of one mark that angles up and frequently appears in the later writing. This we translate as an apostrophe, a near approximation, in order to give readers a feel for its pronounced angular difference from other dashes. The calligraphic orthography (unusually shaped "S's," extravagantly crossed "T's," etc.) is described in the corresponding Notes at the back of the book. In our translation of a draft poem, a word that appears in brackets is a word Dickinson crossed out.

Not surprisingly, as Susan's poems echo Emily's in choice of subject, so the physical characteristics of her compositions often reflect Emily's. Any one of these compositional habits may be fairly common, and any one is not enough to argue for significant similarities. But the fact that many of their habits of abbreviation and punctuation mirror one another's is suggestive: like Emily's, Susan's shorthand to reorder words is to place numbers above them to indicate their position in a series (for example, "2" above the word or phrase to be placed second); Susan's quotation marks "sashay" like Emily's, and her dashes are sometimes directed decidedly up or down. Taken all together, and with the fact that in the 1870s and 1880s, Susan begins to space her alphabetic letters as Emily does, such similarities suggest at the very least Susan's intimate familiarity with, and appreciation of, Emily's work.

Descriptions of material elements of the documents, their subsequent handling and publication, are all primary parts of the story of Susan and Emily's writing exchange and are provided in the Notes.

Editions by Thomas H. Johnson and Theodora Ward, and by Ralph W. Franklin incorporate, amend, and sometimes radically revise work of earlier Dickinson editors (Thomas Wentworth Higginson, Mabel Loomis Todd, Millicent Todd Bingham, Martha Dickinson Bianchi, and Alfred Leete Hampson). Our editorial, critical, and biographical presentation also builds on the work of others, most specifically *The Letters of Emily Dickinson* edited by Johnson and Ward. We revise and correct errors in Johnson and Ward's painstaking transcriptions, and impart more information than they about the material elements of the documents, while benefiting from their research and commentary. We also benefit from the research and commentary of literary historian Jay Leyda. *Open Me Carefully* is engaged in a critical conversation with other editorial endeavors, past and present, including those of Ralph W. Franklin, Marta Werner, Edith Wylder, Susan Howe, Sharon Cameron, Jerome McGann, and

Jeanne Holland, and we welcome ongoing discussion and debate about ways of reading and representing Dickinson's manuscripts.

The Question of Genre

Some editors have used genre distinctions as the dominant way of organizing Dickinson's writings, and so the Dickinson corpus has often been divided into separate volumes of poems and letters. *Open Me Carefully* breaks with this method of presentation by integrating various genres in which Dickinson wrote: poems, letters, and the genre identified by Susan as the "letter-poem."[9]

The letter-poem, a category that includes signed poems and letters with poems or with lines of poetry, will be seen here as a distinct and important Dickinson genre. Johnson arranged lines in letters to separate poems and make them look the way we might expect poems to look. We do not do this here. Neither do we divide the correspondence into "Poems to Susan" and "Letters to Susan." Instead, we follow Dickinson's commingling techniques, mindful that conventional notions of genre can limit our understanding of Dickinson's writing practices. Elizabeth Barrett Browning, one of Dickinson's literary heroes, called *Aurora Leigh*, one of Dickinson's favorite works, her "Novel in Verse." We see Dickinson's blending of poetry with prose, making poems of letters and letters of poems, as a deliberate artistic strategy.

The Accuracy of Dating

It is impossible to date and order most of the Dickinson manuscripts with precision, particularly the correspondence of the middle and late periods. Rather than using Johnson's dates, we have attempted to situate each document based on Emily's handwriting, the paper used, and particular references within each missive. These methods of dating result in a grouping of the documents into four categories: 1850 to mid-1850s; mid-1850s to mid-1860s; mid-1860s to mid-1870s; mid-1870s to Dickinson's death on May 15, 1886. With the exception of some early letters, which can be more specifically assigned a month, year, and sometimes even a day, the dating of most individual manuscripts is approximate. Our dating calls into question the supposed gap in the writings from Emily to Susan during 1856 and 1857—a time during which the Dickinson family returned to the Homestead and Austin married and set up home with Susan next door at the Evergreens. Susan's marriage to Austin was no doubt bittersweet for Emily; while it ensured that her dear friend would be close to the family, married life occupied much of Susan's time. But it is obvious that this transition in their lives never put an end to their correspondence. Because we believe that some documents of the mid-1850s may have been destroyed, we do not concur with Johnson and Ward that Emily did not write to Susan during these years; in fact, we regard the gap in previous editions of letters as an editorial construction.

Marks by Other Hands and Other Telling Details

Marks on the manuscripts made by Susan, by her daughter Martha Dickinson Bianchi, and by her children include editing notes, commentary, and signs of household use. Susan marked many poems and letters with an "X" indicating a selection process; she recorded dates and events associated with the writing for editorial purposes, as did Martha Dickinson Bianchi, and she made notes to herself to read various poems to friends. Penciled lines drawn through or beside passages of early letters, also likely to be Susan's editorial markings, resemble lines penciled in books in the Dickinson households, probably made by Susan as she read. On the versos of these manuscripts are word games, shopping lists, mathematical calculations, children's drawings, bearing witness to the fact that these documents had their place in family life. Physical aspects of the manuscripts tell the story of how these letters and poems were delivered, handled, and preserved.

Folds. Rather than placing a letter or a poem in a sealed envelope to be delivered to Susan, most often Dickinson folded the manuscript into thirds or quarters, wrote Susan's name on the verso, and then handed the letter to Susan face-to-face or, alternatively, had a family member (one of the children) or someone who worked in the households carry the letter next door to Susan's house. Of all Dickinson's correspondence to others, only writings to Susan are on very small pieces of paper (11.2 x 12.5 cm.) and when folded, small enough to fit into the pocket of her dress.

The fact that many manuscripts have multiple folds suggests that they were unfolded and refolded in the process of being read and reread by Susan. Some letters were certainly shared with Susan's friends and family members. Since manuscripts in library collections are not stored folded, we can be reasonably sure that a manuscript with worn folds and more than one configuration of folds was handled during Susan's lifetime and that the wear is not the result of handling by scholars. (In contrast, the wear to a sheet's central fold created by paper manufacturers to produce two leaves, four pages, is likely to have resulted from scholarly and editorial handling.)

When a manuscript is not addressed, the fact that it has been folded does not necessarily mean that it was ever sent to a reader. Evidence suggests that Dickinson folded paper before writing on it to avoid writing directly over folds. Thus, in determining which manuscripts were actually sent to Susan, we do not consider the presence of folds alone to be sufficient evidence; there must also be other markings or signs of handling, use, and preservation unique to this correspondence.

The multiple folds and worn folds are consistent with Martha Dickinson Bianchi's statement that Susan read and reread these letters, letter-poems, and poems late in her life as she made preparations with her daughter for an edition of Emily's writings to be published after her death. Folded manuscripts were often pasted into scrapbooks, so the process of unfolding, reading, and refolding would be repeated. The care Susan took in keeping these manuscripts attests to the value she placed on them. When Susan reread the letters and poems pasted down in this way, she would have been recreating the experience of unfolding, opening, and reading them for the first time.

Paste marks. Many manuscripts to Susan were once pasted onto sheets of paper, as indicated by residue remaining on the verso when sheets were removed. Occasionally, pasty fingerprints appear on the manuscripts. In the 1890s, Susan and Martha may have been compiling an edition, or their work may have been done closer to Susan's death in 1913 and the publication of *The Single Hound* in 1914. Some paste marks show traces of blue-ruled sheets, the tablet paper on which Susan and Martha pasted manuscripts and on which Martha recorded information received from her mother about a document. Some manuscripts appear to have been pasted onto sheets of stationery by Susan, perhaps to be placed among loose sheets kept in a scrapbook or notebook.

Pinholes. Many of the manuscripts to Susan show that they once were pinned to some other surface. Pinholes may indicate a variety of uses and handling. Susan pinned manuscripts in scrapbooks. A slip of paper with Susan's name could have been pinned to a poem or letter when it was sent. A folded manuscript may have been pinned inside Dickinson's clothing until she had the opportunity to deliver it to the Evergreens. Or, a sheet may have been pinned to a piece of cloth on a tray or to one covering a gift of bread, candy, or fruit. In addition, before the invention of paper clips, manuscripts were pinned together. The pinholes with traces of rust may mean manuscripts were pinned for a long period of time, stored and preserved.

These salient material facts all argue for embodying Dickinson's most important correspondence, her writings to Susan, in a book all its own. By presenting this most passionate and diverse of all of Dickinson's correspondences, *Open Me Carefully* relates Emily and Susan's devotion to one another and to the craft of poetry. Through all the decades of poems, letters, and letter-poems from Emily to Susan, we are constantly reminded that for these two remarkable women "Poetry" and "Love . . . coeval come."

CHRONOLOGY

December 10, 1830	Birth of Emily Elizabeth Dickinson, daughter of Emily Norcross and Edward Dickinson, sister of Austin Dickinson (b. 1828), in Amherst, Massachusetts.
December 19, 1830	Birth of Susan Huntington Gilbert Dickinson, daughter of Harriet Arms and Thomas Gilbert, the youngest of six children, in Deerfield, Massachusetts.
1832	The Gilbert family moves from Deerfield to Amherst, where Thomas Gilbert becomes proprietor of the Mansion House, an inn and stagecoach stop.
February 28, 1833	Birth of Lavinia (Vinnie) Norcross Dickinson, Emily's sister.
March 1833	Samuel Fowler Dickinson, Emily's grandfather, sells half of the Homestead to General David Mack and moves to Ohio.
late spring 1833	Emily lives with her aunt Lavinia Norcross in Monson, while her mother recuperates from childbirth.

September 7, 1835	Emily begins four years at the district Primary School.
February 13, 1837	Harriet Arms Gilbert, Susan's mother, dies of consumption.
1837	Susan Gilbert and her sister Martha (b. 1829) move to Geneva, New York, to live with their aunt Sophia Arms Van Vranken.
late 1830s–1840s	Susan attends Utica Female Seminary.
January 1838	Edward Dickinson assumes his first term in the Massachusetts General Court.
April 1840	Edward and Emily Norcross Dickinson and their three children move from the Homestead on Main Street to "the Mansion" on South Pleasant Street.
September 1840	Emily and Lavinia Dickinson begin education at Amherst Academy.
December 23, 1841	General Thomas Gilbert, Susan's father, dies.

June 22, 1842	Susan's eldest sister Harriet (b. 1820) and William Cutler are married in Ashfield, Massachusetts, and move to Amherst.
early 1840s–early 1850s	Susan and Martha Gilbert live in Amherst with Harriet and William Cutler as well as in Geneva, New York.
September 1847–August 1848	Emily attends South Hadley Female Seminary (Mount Holyoke College).
fall 1847	Susan attends Amherst Academy for one term.
1850	Emily sends first known letter to Susan.
February 1850	Amherst College *Indicator* prints Emily's "Magnum bonum" Valentine Eve letter.
September 1851–early July 1852	Susan teaches mathematics at Robert Archer's school in Baltimore, Maryland.
February 20, 1852	Emily's first printed poem, "A Valentine," appears in the *Springfield Daily Republican.*
December 17, 1852	Edward Dickinson is elected to Congress, Representative of Tenth Massachusetts District.

March 23, 1853	Susan Gilbert and Austin Dickinson are engaged at the Revere Hotel in Boston.
mid-November 1855	The Dickinson family moves back into the renovated Homestead.
July 1, 1856	Susan and Austin are married in the home of Susan's aunt Sophia Arms Van Vranken in Geneva, New York, then move to the Evergreens, next door to the Homestead.
late 1850s	Emily sends poems regularly to Susan; Emily begins to make her "fascicles" or manuscript books.
1858–1866	Emily publishes eight poems in the *Springfield Republican*, *Drum Beat*, *Round Table*, *Brooklyn Daily Union*, *Boston Post*.
June 19, 1861	Birth of Edward (Ned) Dickinson, Susan and Austin's eldest child.
April 1862	Thomas Wentworth Higginson's "Letter to a Young Contributor" appears as the lead article in the *Atlantic Monthly*.
April 15, 1862	Emily writes to Higginson and sends four poems.

April–November 1864; April–October 1865	
	Emily receives medical care from a Boston ophthalmologist and lives with cousins Fanny and Louise Norcross in Cambridgeport, Massachusetts.
November 29, 1866	Birth of Martha (Mattie) Gilbert Dickinson, Susan and Austin's second child.
spring 1872	Emily and Susan are seen attending church together.
November 5, 1873	Edward Dickinson re-elected to the Massachusetts General Court.
June 16, 1874	Edward Dickinson dies.
June 15, 1875	Emily Norcross Dickinson, Emily's mother, suffers stroke.
August 1, 1875	Birth of Thomas Gilbert (Gib) Dickinson, Susan and Austin's youngest child.
February 8, 1882	Susan introduces Mabel Loomis Todd to Emily's poetry.
November 14, 1882	Emily Norcross Dickinson, Emily's mother, dies.
October 5, 1883	Gib Dickinson, Susan and Austin's youngest child, dies of typhoid fever; Susan and Emily go into seclusion.

May 15, 1886	Emily Elizabeth Dickinson dies from Bright's disease. Susan prepares Emily's body for burial and writes the obituary that appears in the *Springfield Republican*.
December 31, 1886	Susan submits "A Poem of Miss Emily Dickinson's on the 'Wind'" to *The Century*.
November 1890	*Poems by Emily Dickinson*, edited by Mabel Loomis Todd and Thomas Wentworth Higginson, published by Roberts Brothers.
August 16, 1895	Austin Dickinson dies.
May 3, 1898	Ned Dickinson dies of angina.
August 31, 1899	Lavinia Dickinson dies.
May 12, 1913	Susan Huntington Dickinson dies.
1914	*The Single Hound: Poems of a Lifetime*, edited by Martha Dickinson Bianchi, published by Little, Brown and Company.

SECTION ONE

WHY SUSIE!

Early Writings, 1850 to mid-1850s

During the early and mid-1850s, Emily's correspondence to Susan is effusive and filled with puns and references to the act of writing. The first letter that is preserved from Emily to Susan is dated 1850. While it is not certain how Emily and Susan met, it is likely that they were friends by 1847 or 1848. In an 1850 letter to Susan, Emily's brother Austin remarks on the previous Thanksgiving and expresses his happiness when Emily and their sister Lavinia (Vinnie) asked Susan's "family into the circle which had for two or three years been gradually forming."[1] The letters from Emily to Susan and drafts of letters from Austin indicate that Susan is the object of passionate attachment for both brother and sister.

The boundaries of the correspondence from Emily to Susan are defined by what Susan saves rather than by what Emily writes, and it is likely that Emily sends letters to Susan that have not survived. Perhaps Susan begins to keep letters from Emily following the 1850 death of her sister Mary, in childbirth. Or Susan may save Emily's letters when she begins to keep letters from Austin.

In the early years of the correspondence, between 1851 and 1852, Susan moves to Baltimore to teach at Robert Archer's school for girls. Her decision to go away is sudden, and she writes to her brother Dwight, declaring that she has left her "good friends in Amherst actually staring with astonishment."[2] Susan is independent, outspoken, deeply engaged with spiritual concerns, and like Emily, she is committed to pursuing intellectual growth without benefit of continuing education.

Emily's and Susan's impatience and resentment of household duties are nearly identical. In a letter to her friend Samuel Bartlett, Susan says: "I've fairly commenced the Spring siege of sewing, and such quantities of garments and furbelows, to be made, lie stretching away before my crooked needles, I am quite in despair, and continually wondering and fretting, that we are not clothed like the lilies, without any spinning and toiling — I find no time to read or think, and but little to walk — but just go revolving round a spool of 'Coat's cotton' as if it were the grand centre of mental and moral life — "[3]

While Emily sends Susan passionate and playful letters, Austin formally courts Susan, and Emily secretly delivers his letters to her "Darling Sue." In 1853, humor suffuses an edge of envy for Austin's heightened status in the family as an ambitious and "learned" person; having graduated from Amherst College, he now attends Harvard Law School. Although Emily "loves the opportunity to serve those who are mine," she writes to Susan in markedly shaky handwriting, identifying with Miss Julia Mills in *David Copperfield*, whom Dickens describes as "interested in others' loves, herself withdrawn."

The intellectual intimacy between Emily and Susan begins in the early years of their relationship. In her letters to Susan, Emily frequently refers to the novels she is reading and uses various characters as metaphors or codes to relate her feelings about herself and Susan, and comment about friends, relatives, and literary and political luminaries and events.

In early 1853, Susan travels to Manchester, New Hampshire, to visit Mary and Samuel Bartlett, her sister Mary's in-laws. On the return rail trip from Manchester on Wednesday, March 23, Susan arrives in Boston for a tryst with Austin at the Revere Hotel, and the couple becomes engaged. When Susan returns to Amherst, she shares the news with Emily who then writes to Austin: "Oh my dear 'Oliver,' how chipper you must be since any of us have seen you?" and "I hope you have been made happy."[4] In this letter, she blames Austin because Susan seems distracted and absent, and Emily devises punishment: "You deserve, let me see; you deserve hot irons, and Chinese Tartary . . ." She then reminds him how often she is seeing

Susan while he is away at law school and closes with: "Dear Austin, I am keen, but you are a good deal keener, I am something of a fox, but you are more of a hound! I guess we are very good friends tho', and I guess we both love [S]us[ie] just as well as we can."[5] As the brackets indicate, Emily's references to "Susie" have been altered or erased. In another letter written several weeks later beginning, "Do you want to hear from me, Austin?" affectionate references to Susan are erased as well, though kindly references to Lavinia remain untouched. Emily asks Austin, "How long it is since you've been in this state of complacence towards God and our fellow men?" She then follows with, "I think it must be sudden."[6] Facetiously she recommends religious texts to guide Austin in meditating on self-discipline and submission of his will. She hopes that he has "enjoyed" "sanctuary privileges."

In April 1854, Austin, Lavinia, and their mother visit Washington, D.C., where Edward Dickinson is serving as a member of Congress. They arrive on April 7, and stay for several weeks. At this time, Susan lives with Emily, in the company of John Graves, a cousin from nearby Sunderland, who is attending Amherst College. In mid-April, Susan writes to Mary Bartlett saying, "I am keeping house with Emily, while the family are in Washington — We frighten each other to death nearly every night — with that exception, we have very independent times."[7]

Three months later, Susan becomes seriously ill with "nervous fever." Describing Susan's condition to a friend, Emily writes that "every hour possible I have taken away to her." Susan recovers in August and travels to Geneva and Aurora, New York, where she stays with family for nearly three months. Austin, now graduated from Harvard Law School and admitted to the bar, prepares to seek his fortune in the West.

From Aurora, New York, Susan travels to Grand Haven, Michigan, where she stays with her brother Dwight through the early winter. In a letter mapping out her travel plans Susan tells her brother, "I have always felt so like a child the idea of really being married seems absurd enough and if the event ever occurs I think I shall experience a feeling of odd surprise — "[8]

When Susan accuses Austin of interfering with her correspondence with Emily, Austin writes: "As to your deprivation of 'Spiritual converse' with my sister — I Know Nothing — I was aware that you had been in correspondence for some time, but had never had an intimation that the correspondence was at an end — . . . So you will not suspect me of having interfered with your epistolary intercourse with her."[9]

In the letters that follow, Emily and Susan are in their early twenties. Though Emily's feelings of love, desire, and longing for Susan have often been dismissed as a "school-girl crush," the letters resonate with intelligence, humor, and intimacy that cannot be reduced to adolescent flurry.

1

Thursday noon.

Were it not for the weather Susie – my little, unwelcome face would come peering in today – I should steal a kiss from the sister – the darling Rover returned – Thank the wintry wind my dear one – that spares such daring intrusion! Dear Susie – happy Susie – I rejoice in all your Joy – sustained by that dear sister you will never again be lonely. Dont forget all the little friends who have tried so hard to be sisters, when indeed you were alone!

You do not hear the wind blow on this inclement day, when the world is shrugging it's shoulders – your little "Columbarium is lined with warmth and softness," there is no "silence" there – so you differ from bonnie "Alice." I miss one angel face in the little world of sisters – dear Mary – sainted Mary – Remember lonely one – tho, she comes not to us, we shall return to her! My love to both your sisters – and I want so much to see Matty.

Very aff yours, Emily

autumn/winter 1850
In this letter Emily refers to Susan's sister Mary, who died on July 14, 1850. In December, Susan's sister Martha ("Matty") came from Michigan, and the Gilbert family was temporarily reconstituted in the Amherst home of their eldest sister Harriet. The allusion to "Alice" is to Alice Archer of Longfellow's *Kavanagh* (1849) whose

room is "that columbarium lined with warmth, and softness, and silence." Throughout the correspondence, and long before Susan is actually her sister-in-law, Emily addresses Susan as "Sister."

2

Thursday evening

I wept a tear here, Susie – on purpose for you – because this "sweet silver moon" smiles in on me and Vinnie, and then it goes so far before it gets to you – and then you never told me if there was any moon in Baltimore – and how do I know Susie – that you see her sweet face at all? She looks like a fairy tonight, sailing around the sky in a little silver gondola with stars for gondoliers. I asked her to let me ride a little while ago – and told her I would get out when she got as far as Baltimore, but she only smiled to herself and went sailing on.

I think she was quite ungenerous – but I have learned the lesson and shant ever ask her again. To day it rained at home – sometimes it rained so hard that I fancied you could hear it's patter – patter, patter, as it fell upon the leaves – and the fancy pleased me so, that I sat and listened to it – and watched it earnestly. Did you hear it Susie – or was it only fancy? Bye and bye the sun came out – just in time to bid us goodnight, and as I told you sometime, the moon is shining now.

It is such an evening Susie, as you and I would walk and have such pleasant musings, if you were only here – perhaps we would have a "Reverie" after the form of "Ik Marvel," indeed I do not know why it would'nt be just as charming as of that lonely Bachelor, smoking his cigar – and it would be far more profitable as "Marvel" only marvelled, and you and I would try to make a little destiny to have for our own. Do you know that charming man is dreaming again, and will wake pretty soon – so the papers say, with another Reverie – more beautiful than the first?

Dont you hope he will live as long as you and I do – and keep on having dreams and writing them to us – what a charming old man he'll be, and how I envy his grandchildren, little "Bella" and "Paul"! We will be willing to die Susie – when such as he have gone, for there will be none left to interpret these lives of our's.

Longfellow's "golden Legend" has come to town I hear – and may be seen in state on Mr. Adams' bookshelves. It always makes me think of "Pegasus in the pound –" when I find a gracious author sitting side by side with "Murray" and "Wells" and "Walker" in that renowned store – and like him I half expect to hear they have "flown" some morning and in their native ether revel all the day – but for our sakes dear Susie, who please ourselves with the fancy that we are the only poets – and every one else is prose, let us hope they will yet be willing to share our humble world and feed upon such aliment as we consent to do!

You thank me for the Rice cake – you tell me Susie, you have just been tasting it – and how happy I am to send you anything you love – how hungry you must grow before it is noon there – and then you must be faint from teaching those stupid scholars. I fancy you very often descending to the schoolroom with a plump Binomial Theorem struggling in your hand which you must dissect and exhibit to your incomprehending ones – I hope you whip them Susie – for my sake – whip them hard whenever they dont behave just as you want to have them! I know they are very dull – sometimes – from what Mattie says – but I presume you encourage them and forgive all their mistakes. It will teach you patience Susie – you may be sure of that. And Mattie tells me too of your evening carousals – and the funny frights you give in personating the Master – just like you Susie – like you for all the world – how Mr Payson would laugh if I could only tell him, and then those great dark eyes – how they would glance and sparkle! Susie – have all the fun wh' you possibly can – and laugh as often and sing, for tears are plentier than smiles in this little world of our's – only dont be so happy as to let Mattie and me grow dimmer and dimmer and finally fade away, and merrier maids than we smile in our vacant places!

Susie, did you think that I would never write you when you were gone away – what made you? I am sure you know my promise far too well for that – and had I never said so – I should be constrained to write – for what shall separate us from any whom we love – not "hight nor depth["] . . .

October 9, 1851

Susan is now teaching in Baltimore and Emily writes to her frequently. Ik Marvel's (Donald G. Mitchell) Reveries of a Bachelor

(1850) was a bestseller and enjoyed by Emily, Susan, and Austin, as was Longfellow's Golden Legend (1851). Both books celebrate romantic passion and emotional attachment. Lindley Murray, William Harvey Wells, and John Walker were lexicographers and grammarians. In an October 1 letter to Austin, every allusion to "Susie" is erased.

3

Friday forenoon –

Will you let me come dear Susie – looking just as I do, my dress soiled and worn, my grand old apron, and my hair – Oh Susie, time would fail me to enumerate my appearance, yet I love you just as dearly as if I was e'er so fine, so you wont care, will you? I am so glad dear Susie – that our hearts are always clean, and always neat and lovely, so not to be ashamed. I have been hard at work this morning, and I ought to be working now – but I cannot deny myself the luxury of a minute or two with you.

The dishes may wait dear Susie – and the uncleared table stand, <u>them</u> I have always with me, but <u>you</u>, I have "not always," <u>why</u> Susie, Christ hath saints ma<u>nie</u> – and I have <u>few</u>, but thee – the angels shant have Susie – no – no no!

Vinnie is sewing away like a <u>fictitious</u> seamstress, and I half expect some knight will arrive at the door, confess himself a <u>nothing</u> in presence of her loveliness, and present his heart and hand as the only vestige of him worthy to be refused.

Vinnie and I have been talking about growing old, today. Vinnie thinks <u>twenty</u> must be a fearful position for one to occupy – I tell her I dont care if I am young or not, had as lief be thirty, and you, as most anything else. Vinnie expresses her sympathy at my "sere and yellow leaf" and resumes her work, dear Susie, tell me how <u>you</u> feel – ar'nt there days in one's life when to be old dont seem a thing so sad –

I do feel gray and grim, this morning, and I feel it would be a comfort to have a piping voice, and a broken back, and scare little children.

Dont <u>you</u> run, Susie dear, for I wont do any harm, and I do love you dearly tho' I do feel so frightful.

Oh my darling one, how long you wander from me, how weary I grow of waiting and looking, and calling for you; sometimes I shut my eyes, and shut my heart towards you, and try hard to forget you because you grieve me so, but you'll never go away, Oh you never will – say, Susie, promise me again, and I will smile faintly – and take up my little cross again of sad <u>sad</u> separation. How vain it seems to <u>write</u>, when one knows how to feel – how much more near and dear to sit beside you, talk with you, hear the tones of your voice – so hard to "deny thyself, and take up thy cross, and follow me –" give me strength, Susie, write me of hope and love, and of hearts that <u>endured</u>, and great was their reward of "Our Father who art in Heaven." I dont know how I shall bear it, when the gentle spring comes; if she should come and see me and talk to me of you, Oh it would surely kill me! While the frost clings to the windows, and the World is stem and drear; this absence is easier – the

Earth mourns too, for all her little birds; but when they all come back again, and she sings and is so merry – pray, what will become of me? Susie, forgive me, forget all what I say, get some sweet little scholar to read a gentle hymn, about Bethleem and Mary, and you will sleep on sweetly and have as peaceful dreams, as if I had never written you all these ugly things. Never mind the letter Susie, I wont be angry with you if you dont give me any at all – for I know how busy you are, and how little of that dear strength remains when it is evening, with which to think and write. Only want to write me, only sometimes sigh that you are far from me, and that will do, Susie! Dont you think we are good and patient, to let you go so long; and dont we think you're a darling, a real beautiful hero, to toil for people, and teach them, and leave your own dear home? Because we pine and repine, dont think we forget the precious patriot at war in other lands! Never be mournful, Susie – be happy and have cheer, for how many of the long days have gone away since I wrote you – and it is almost noon, and soon the night will come, and then there is one less day of the long pilgrimage. Mattie is very smart, talks of you much, my darling; I must leave you now – "one little hour of Heaven," thank who did give it me, and will he also grant me one longer and more when it shall please his love – bring Susie home, ie! Love always, and ever, and true! Emily –

February 1852
Throughout Emily's letters to Susan, she combines a language of courtly love with terms of spiritual devotion. In 1915, Susan's

daughter Martha Dickinson Bianchi described her Aunt Emily in the Atlantic Monthly, saying: "Her devotion to those she loved was that of a knight for his lady."

4

Wednesday morn

It's a sorrowful morning Susie – the wind blows and it rains; "into each life some rain must fall," and I hardly know which falls fastest, the rain without, or within – Oh Susie, I would nestle close to your warm heart, and never hear the wind blow, or the storm beat, again. Is there any room there for me, or shall I wander away all homeless and alone? Thank you for loving me, darling, and will you "love me more if ever you come home" ! it is enough, dear Susie, I know I shall be satisfied. But what can I do towards you? – dearer you cannot be, for I love you so already, that it almost breaks my heart perhaps I can love you anew, every day of my life, every morning and evening – Oh if you will let me, how happy I shall be!

The precious billet, Susie, I am wearing the paper out, reading it over and o'er, but the dear thoughts cant wear out if they try, Thanks to Our Father, Susie! Vinnie and I talked of you all last evening long, and went to sleep mourning for you, and pretty soon I waked up saying "Precious treasure, thou art mine," and there you were all right, my Susie, and I hardly dared to sleep lest some one steal you away. Never mind the letter, Susie; you have so much to do; just write me every week one line, and let it be, "Emily, I love you," and I will be satisfied! Your own Emily

Upside down on first page

Vinnie's love – Mother's –

In margin on third page

Love to Hattie from us all. Dear Mattie is almost well.

about February 1852
The quote "into each life some rain must fall" is from Longfellow's "The Rainy Day," a poem that Emily and Susan shared with their friends.

5

Sunday morning –

Thank the dear little snow flakes, because they fall today rather than some vain weekday, when the world and the cares of the world would try so hard to keep me from my departed friend – and thank you, too, dear Susie, that you never weary of me, or never tell me so, and that when the world is cold, and the storm sighs e'er so piteously, I am sure of one sweet shelter, one covert from the storm! The bells are ringing, Susie, north, and east, and south, and your own village bell, and the people who love God, are expecting to go to meeting; dont you go Susie, not to their meeting, but come with me this morning to the church within our hearts, where the bells are always ringing, and the preacher whose name is Love – shall intercede there for us!

They will all go but me, to the usual meeting-house, to hear the usual sermon; the inclemency of the storm so kindly detaining me; and as I sit here Susie, alone with the winds and you – I have the old king feeling even more than before, for I know not even the cracker man will invade this solitude, this sweet Sabbath of our's. And thank you for my dear letter, which came on Saturday night, when all the world was still; thank you for the love it bore me, and for it's golden thoughts, and feelings so like gems, that I was sure I gathered them in whole baskets of pearls! I mourn this morning, Susie, that I have no sweet sunset to gild a page for you, nor any bay so blue – not even a little chamber way up in the sky, as your's is, to give me thoughts of heaven, which I would give to you. You know how I must write you, down, down, in the terrestrial – no sunset here, no stars; not even a bit of twilight which I may poetize – and send you! Yet Susie, there will be romance in the letter's ride to you – think of the hills and the dales, and the rivers it will pass over, and the drivers and conductors who will hurry it on to you; and wont that make a poem such as can ne'er be written? I think of you dear Susie, now, I dont know how or why, but more dearly as every day goes by, and that sweet month of promise draws nearer and nearer; and I view July so differently from what I used to – once it seemed parched, and dry – and I hardly loved it any on account of it's heat and dust; but now Susie, month of all the year the best; I skip the violets – and the dew, and the early Rose and the Robins; I will exchange them all for that angry and hot noonday, when I can count the hours and the minutes before you come – Oh Susie, I often think that I will try to tell you how very dear you are, and how I'm watching for you, but the words wont come, tho' the tears will, and I sit down disappointed – yet darling, you know it all – then why do I seek to tell you? I do not know; in thinking of those I love, my reason is all gone from me, and I do fear sometimes that I must make a hospital for the hopelessly insane, and chain me up there such times, so I wont injure you.

Always when the sun shines, and always when it storms, and always always, Susie, we are remembering you, and what else besides remembering; I shall not tell you, because you know!

Were it not for dear Mattie, I dont know what we would do, but she loves you so dearly, and is never tired of talking about you, and we all get together and talk it oer and oer – and it makes us more resigned, than to mourn for you alone.

It was only yesterday, that I went to see dear Mattie, intending in my heart to stay a little while, only a very little one, because of a good many errands which I was going to do, and will you believe it, Susie, I was there an hour – and an hour, and half an hour besides, and would'nt have supposed it had been minutes so many – and what do you guess we talked about, all those hours long – what would you give to know – give me one little glimpse of your sweet face, dear Susie, and I will tell you all – we didn't talk of statesmen, and we didn't talk of kings – but the time was filled full, and when the latch was lifted and the oaken door was closed, why, Susie, I realized as never I did before, how much a single cottage held that was dear to me. It is sweet – and like home, at Mattie's, but it's sad too – and up comes little memory, and paints – and paints – and paints – and the strangest thing of all, her canvass is never full, and I find her where I left her, every time that I come – and who is she painting – Ah, Susie, "dinna choose to tell" – but it is'nt Mr Cutler, and it is'nt Daniel Boon, and I shant tell you any more – Susie, what will you say if I tell you that Henry Root is coming to see me, some evening of this week, and I have promised to read him some parts of all your letters; now you wont care, dear Susie, for he wants so much to hear, and I shant read him anything which I know you would not be willing – just some little places, which will please him so – I have seen him several times lately, and I admire him, Susie, because he talks of you so frequently and beautifully; and I know he is so true to you, when you are far away – We talk more of you, dear Susie, than of any other thing – he tells me how wonderful you are, and I tell him how true you are, and his big eyes beam, and he seems so delighted – I know you would'nt care, Susie, if you knew how much joy it made – As I told him the other evening of all your letters to me, he looked up very longingly, and I knew what he would say, were he enough acquainted – so I answered the question his heart wanted to ask, and when some pleasant evening, before this week is gone, you remember home and Amherst, then know, Loved One – that they are remembering you, and that "two or three" are gathered in your name, loving, and speaking of you – and will you be there in the midst of them? Then I've found a beautiful, new, friend, and I've told him about dear Susie, and promised to let him know you so soon as you shall come. Dear Susie, in all your letters there are things sweet and many about which I would speak, but the time says no – yet dont think I forget them – Oh no – they are safe in the little chest which tells no secrets – nor the moth, nor the rust can reach them – but when the time we dream of – comes, then Susie, I shall bring them, and we will spend hours chatting and chatting of them – those precious thoughts of friends – how I loved them, and how I love them now nothing but Susie herself is half so dear. Susie, I have not asked you if you were cheerful and well – and I cant think why, except that there's something perrennial in those we dearly love, immortal life and vigor; why it seems as if any sickness, or harm, would flee away, would not dare do them wrong, and Susie, while you are taken from me, I class you with the angels, and you know the Bible tells us – "there is no sickness there." But, dear Susie, are you well, and peaceful, for I wont make you cry by saying are you happy? Dont see the blot, Susie. It's because I broke the Sabbath!

Upside down on first page

Susie, what shall I do – there is'nt room enough; not half enough, to hold what I was going to say. Wont you tell the man who makes sheets of paper, that I hav'nt the slightest respect for him!

In margin on first page

And when shall I have a letter – when it's convenient, Susie, not when tired and faint – ever!

In margin on second page

Emeline gets well so slowly; poor Henry; I guess he thinks true love's course does'nt run very smooth –

In margin on third page

Much love from Mother and Vinnie, and then there are <u>some others</u> who do not dare to send –

In margin on fourth page

Who loves you most, and loves you best, and thinks of you when others rest? T'is Emilie –

about February 1852
Precious stones and gold, love's riches, and Susan herself as a jewel become a pattern of imagery that continues throughout Emily's poetry. Her lamentation that she has no "sweet sunset to gild a page for you" may refer to Emily's inability to use gilt-edged stationery to make a gift of her writing. Mr. Cutler is the Amherst merchant, William Cutler, who married Susan's sister Harriet in 1842. In the margin on the second page, Emily refers to Emeline Kellogg and her future husband, Henry Nash. A letter to Austin written at the same time is mutilated when referring to "Susie."

6

Monday morning –

Will you be kind to me, Susie? I am naughty and cross, this morning, and nobody loves me here; nor would you love me, if you should see me frown, and hear how loud the door bangs whenever I go through; and yet it is'nt anger – I dont believe it is, for when nobody sees, I brush away big tears with the corner of my apron, and then go working on – bitter tears, Susie – so hot that they burn my cheeks, and almost schorch my eyeballs, but you have wept such, and you know they are less of anger than sorrow.

And I do love to run fast – and hide away from them all; here in dear Susie's bosom, I know is love and rest, and I never would go away, did not the big world call me, and beat me for not working.

Little Emerald Mack is washing, I can hear the warm suds, splash. I just gave her my pocket handkerchief – so I cannot cry any more. And Vinnie sweeps – sweeps, upon the chamber stairs; and Mother is hurrying round with her hair in a silk pocket handkerchief, on account of dust. Oh Susie, it is dismal, sad and drear eno' – and the sun dont shine, and the clouds look cold and gray, and the wind dont blow, but it pipes the shrillest roundelay, and the birds dont sing, but twitter – and there's nobody to smile! Do I paint it natural – Susie, so you think how it looks? Yet dont you care – for it wont last so always, and we love you just as well – and think of you, as dearly, as if it were not so. Your precious letter, Susie, it sits here now, and smiles so kindly at me, and gives me such sweet thoughts of the dear writer. When you come home, darling, I shant have your letters, shall I, but I shall have yourself, which is more – Oh more, and better, than I can even think! I sit here with my little whip, cracking the time away, till not an hour is left of it – then you are here! And Joy is here – joy now and forevermore!

Tis only a few days, Susie, it will soon go away, yet I say, go now, this very moment, for I need her – I must have her, Oh give her to me!

Mattie is dear and true, I love her very dearly – and Emily Fowler, too, is very dear to me – and Tempe – and Abby, and Eme', I am sure – I love them all – and I hope they love me, but, Susie, there's a great corner still; I fill it with that is gone, I hover round and round it, and call it darling names, and bid it speak to me, and ask it if it's Susie, and it answers, Nay, Ladie, Susie is stolen away!

Do I repine, is it all murmuring, or am I sad and lone, and cannot, cannot help it? Sometimes when I do feel so, I think it may be wrong, and that God will punish me by taking you away; for he is very kind to let me write to you, and to give me your sweet letters, but my heart wants more.

Have you ever thought of it Susie, and yet I know you have, how much these hearts claim; why I dont believe in the whole, wide world, are such hard little creditors – such real little misers, as you and I carry with us, in our bosoms everyday. I cant help thinking sometimes, when I hear about the ungenerous, Heart, keep very still – or someone will find you out!

I am going out on the doorstep, to get you some new – green grass – I shall pick it down in the corner, where you and I used to sit, and have long fancies. And perhaps the dear little grasses were growing all the while – and perhaps they heard what we said, but they cant tell! I have come in now, dear Susie, and here is what I found – not quite so glad and green as when we used to sit there, but a sad and pensive grassie – mourning o'er hopes. No doubt some spruce, young Plantain leaf won its young heart away, and then proved false – and dont you wish none proved so, but little Plantains?

I do think it's wonderful, Susie, that our hearts dont break, every day, when I think of all the whiskers, and all the gallant men, but I guess I'm made with nothing but a hard heart of stone, for it dont break any, and dear Susie, if mine is stony, your's is stone, upon stone, for you never yield any, where I seem quite beflown. Are we going to ossify always, say, Susie – how will it be? When I see the Popes and the Polloks, and the John-Milton Browns, I think we are liable, but I dont know! I am glad there's a big future waiting for me and you. You would love to know what I read – I hardly know what to tell you, my catalogue is so small.

I have just read three little books, not great, not thrilling – but sweet and true. "The Light in the Valley," "Only," and a "House upon a Rock" – I know you would love them all – yet they dont bewitch me any. There are no walks in the wood – no low and earnest voices, no moonlight, nor stolen love, but pure little lives, loving God, and their parents, and obeying the laws of the land; yet read, if you meet them, Susie, for they will do one good.

I have the promise of "Alton Lock" – a certain book, called "Olive," and the "Head of a Family," which was what Mattie named to you. Vinnie and I had "Bleak House" sent to us the other day – it is like him who wrote it – that is all I can say. Dear Susie, you were so happy when you wrote to me last – I am so glad, and you will be happy now for all my sadness, wont you? I cant forgive me ever, if I have made you sad, or dimmed your eye for me. I write from the Land of Violets, and from the Land of Spring, and it would ill become me to carry you nought but sorrows. I remember you, Susie, always – I keep you ever here, and when you are gone, then I'm gone – and we're 'neath one willow tree. I can only thank "the Father" for giving me such as you, I can only pray unceasingly, that he will bless my Loved One, and bring her back to me, to "go no more out forever. " Herein is Love." But that was Heaven – this is but Earth, yet Earth so like to heaven, that I would hesitate, should the true one call away. Dear Susie – adieu! Emilie –

Upside down on first page

Father's sister is dead, and Mother wears black on her bonnet, and has a collar of crape.

In margin on first page

A great deal of love from Vinnie, and she wants that little note.

In margin on second page

Austin comes home on Wednesday, but he'll only stay two days, so I fancy we shant

In margin on third page

go sugaring, as "we did last year." Last year is gone, Susie – did you ever think of that?

In margin on fourth page

Joseph is out south somewhere, a very great way off, yet we hear from him.

April 5, 1852

The reference to "Emerald" distinguishes Mrs. Mack, an Irish woman who works in the Dickinson household, from members of the family of Deacon David Mack. Emily mentions her friend Emily Fowler, and in the margin, she refers to Joseph Lyman, a friend of Emily's and Lavinia's. In Emily's caricatures of friends as literary celebrities, she seems to pun on the names of Alexander Pope and a near-contemporary Scottish divine. The books that are mentioned refer to *The Light in the Valley*, a memorial of Mary Elizabeth Stirling, *Only* and *A House Upon a Rock* by Matilda Anne Mackarness, *Alton Locke* by Charles Kingsley, *Head of a Family* and *Olive* by Dinah Maria Craik, and *Bleak House* by Charles Dickens. In the margins of this letter, Emily also refers to the March 30, 1852, death of her aunt Mary Newman, Edward Dickinson's sister.

7

Sunday afternoon

So sweet and still, and Thee, Oh Susie, what need I more, to make my heaven whole?

Sweet Hour, blessed Hour, to carry me to you, and to bring you back to me, long enough to snatch one kiss, and whisper Good bye, again.

I have thought of it all day, Susie, and I fear of but little else, and when I was gone to meeting it filled my mind so full, I could not find a *chink* to put the worthy pastor; when he said "Our Heavenly Father," I said "Oh Darling Sue"; when he read the 100th Psalm, I kept saying your precious letter all over to myself, and Susie, when they sang – it would have made you laugh to hear one little voice, piping to the departed. I made up words and kept singing how I loved you, and you had gone, while all the rest of the choir were singing Hallelujahs. I presume nobody heard me, because I sang *so small*, but it was a kind of a comfort to think I might put them out, singing of you. I a'nt there this afternoon, tho', because I am here, writing a little letter to my dear Sue, and I am very happy. I think of ten weeks – Dear One, and I think of love, and you, and my heart grows full and warm, and my breath stands still. The sun does'nt shine at all, but I can feel a sunshine stealing into my soul and making it all summer, and every thorn, a *rose*. And I pray that such summer's sun shine on my Absent One, and cause her bird to sing!

You have been happy, Susie, and now are sad – and the whole world seems lone; but it wont be so always, "some days must be dark and dreary"! You wont cry any more, will you, Susie, for my father will be your father, and my home will be your home, and where you go, I will go, and we will lie side by side in the kirkyard.

I have parents on earth, dear Susie, but your's are in the skies, and I have an earthly fireside, but you have one above, and you have a "Father in Heaven," where I have none – and a sister in heaven, and I know they love you dearly, and think of you every day.

Oh I wish I had half so many dear friends as you in heaven – I could'nt spare them now – but to know they had got there safely, and should suffer nevermore – Dear Susie!

I know I was very naughty to write such fretful things, and I know I could have helped it, if I had tried hard enough, but I thought my heart would break, and I knew of nobody here that cared anything about it – so I said to myself, "We will tell Susie about it." You dont know what a comfort it was, and you wont know, till the big cup of bitterness is filled brimfull, and they say, "Susie, drink it!" Then Darling, let me be there, and let me drink the half, and you will feel it all!

I am glad you have rested, Susie. I wish the week had been more, a whole score of days and joys for you, yet again, had it lasted longer, then had you not come so soon and I had been lonelier, it is right as it is! Ten weeks, they will seem short to you – for care will fill them, but to Mattie and me, long. We shall grow tired, waiting, and our eyes will ache with looking for you, and with now and then a tear. And yet we have hope left, and we shall keep her busy, cheering away the time. Only think Susie, it is vacation now – there shall be no more vacation until ten weeks have gone, and no more snow; and how very little while it will be now, before you and I are sitting out on the broad stone step, mingling our lives together! I cant talk of it now tho', for it makes me long and yearn so, that I cannot sleep tonight, for thinking of it, and you.

Yes, we did go sugaring, and remembered who was gone – and who was there last year, and love and recollection brought with them Little Regret, and set her in the midst of us.

Dear Susie, Dear Joseph; why take the best and dearest, and leave our hearts behind? While the Lovers sighed; and twined oak leaves, and the anti enamored ate sugar, and crackers, in the house, I went to see what I could find. Only think of it, Susie; I had'nt any appetite, nor any Lover, either, so I made the best of fate, and gathered antique stones, and your little flowers of moss opened their lips and spoke to me, so I was not alone, and bye and bye Mattie and me might have been seen sitting together upon a high – gray rock, and we might have been heard talking, were anyone very near! And did thoughts of that dear Susie go with us on the rock, and sit there 'tween us twain? Loved One, thou knowest!

I gathered something for you, because you were not there, an acorn, and some moss blossoms, and a little shell of a snail, so whitened by the snow you would think 'twas a cunning artist had carved it from alabaster – then I tied them all up in a leaf with some last summer's grass I found by a brookside, and I'm keeping them all for you.

I saw Mattie at church today, tho' could not speak to her. Friday evening I saw her, and talked with her besides. Oh I do love her – and when you come if we all live till then, it will be <u>precious</u>, Susie. You speak to me of sorrow, of what you have "lost and loved," say rather, of what you have loved and <u>won</u>, for it is <u>much</u>, dear Susie; I can count the big, true hearts by <u>clusters</u>, full of bloom, and bloom amaranthine, because <u>eternal</u>! Emilie –

In margin on first page

I have heard all about the journal, Oh Susie, that you should come to this! I want you to get it bound – at my expense – Susie – so when he takes you from me, to live in his new home, I may have <u>some</u> of you. I am sincere.

In margin on second page

Mother sends her best love to you. It makes her look so happy when I give your's to her. Send it always, Susie, and send your respects to father!

In margin on third page

And much from Vinnie. She was so happy at her note. After she finished reading it, she said, "I dont know but it's wrong, but I love Sue better –

In margin on fourth page

than Jane, and I love her and Mattie better than all the friends I ever had in my life." Vinnie hopes to be like you, and to do as you do.

Upside down, near "Loved One, thou knowest!" on fourth page

Hattie!

late April 1852
Susan is spending ten days of her spring vacation with her friend Harriet Hinsdale, and they are visiting Harriet's sister in Havre de Grace, Maryland. "Dear Joseph" again refers to Joseph Lyman, who recently left Amherst to seek his fortune in the South. Emily links Susan with Joseph because they are both far away. She also refers to her friend Jane Humphrey. As she has done in a previous letter, Emily once again quotes Longfellow's "The Rainy Day": "Some days must be dark and dreary." In offering to share all she owns with Susan, Emily echoes Ruth's words to Naomi from the *Book of Ruth*, a pledge that was frequently included in wedding ceremonies: "Entreat me not to leave thee, or to return from following after thee; for whether thou goest, I will go; and where thou lodgest, I will lodge; thy people *shall be* my people, and thy God my God; where thou diest, will I die, and there will I be buried: the Lord do so to me, and more also *if ought* but death part thee and me." (Ruth 1:16–17)

8

Wednesday –

Precious Sue – Precious Mattie!

All I desire in this life – all I pray for, or hope for in that long life to come!

Dear Mattie just left me, and I stand just where we stood smiling and chatting together a moment ago. Our last words were of you, and as we said Dear Susie, the sunshine grew so warm, and out peeped prisoned leaves, and the Robins answered Susie, and the big hills left their work, and echoed Susie, and from the smiling fields, and from the fragrant meadows came troops of *fairy* Susies, and asked "Is it me"? No, Little One, "Eye hath not seen, nor ear heard, nor can the heart conceive" *my* Susie, whom I love.

These days of heaven bring you nearer and nearer, and every bird that sings, and every bud that blooms, does but remind me more of that garden *unseen*, awaiting the hand that tills it. Dear Susie, when you come, how many boundless blossoms among those silent beds! How I do count the days – how I do long for the time when I may count the *hours* without incurring the charge of Femina insania! I made up the Latin – Susie, for I could'nt think how it went, according to Stoddard and Andrew!

I want to send you *joy*, I have half a mind to put up one of these dear little Robin's, and send him singing to you. I know I would, Susie, did I think he would live to get there and sing his little songs.

I shall keep everything singing tho', until Dear Child gets home – and I shant let anything <u>blossom</u> till then – either.

I have got to go out in the garden now, and whip a CrownImperial for presuming to hold it's head up, until you have come home, so farewell, Susie – I shall think of you at sunset, and at sunrise, again; and at noon, and forenoon, and afternoon, and always, and evermore, till this little heart stops beating and is still. Emilie

about May 1852
Emily refers to the New Testament: "Eye hath not seen, nor ear heard, neither have entered into the heart of man, the things which God hath prepared for them that love him." (I Corinthians 2:9) "Stoddard and Andrew" are Solomon Stoddard and Ethan Allen Andrews, the authors of *A Grammar of the Latin Language for Schools and Colleges*.

9

Friday morning –

They are cleaning house today, Susie, and I've made a flying retreat to my own little chamber, where with affection, and you, I will spend this my precious hour, most precious of all the hours which dot my flying days, and the one so dear, that for it I barter everything, and as soon as it is gone, I am sighing for it again.

I cannot believe, dear Susie, that I have stayed without you almost a whole year long; sometimes the time seems short, and the thought of you as warm as if you had gone but yesterday, and again if years and years had trod their silent pathway, the time would seem less long.

And now how soon I shall have you, shall hold you in my arms; you will forgive the tears, Susie, they are so glad to come that it is not in my heart to reprove them and send them home. I dont know why it is – but there's something in your name, now you are taken from me, which fills my heart so full, and my eye, too. It is not that the mention grieves me, no, Susie, but I think of each "sunnyside" where we have sat together, and lest there be no more, I guess is what makes the tears come. Mattie was here last evening, and we sat on the front door stone, and talked about life and love, and whispered our childish fancies about such blissful things – the evening was gone so soon, and I walked home with Mattie beneath the silent moon, and wished for you, and Heaven. You did not come, Darling, but a bit of Heaven did, or so it seemed to us, as we walked side by side and wondered of that great blessedness which may be our's sometime, is granted now, to some. This union, my dear Susie, by which two lives are one, this sweet and strange adoption wherein we can but look, and are not yet admitted, how it can fill the heart, and make it gang wildly beating, how it will take us one day, and make us all it's own, and we shall not run away from it, but lie still and be happy!

You and I have been strangely silent upon this subject, Susie, we have often touched upon it, and as quickly fled away, as children shut their eyes when the sun is too bright for them. I have always hoped to know if you had no dear fancy, illumining all your life, no one of whom you murmured in the faithful ear of night – and at whose side in fancy, you walked the livelong day; and when you come home, Susie, we must speak of these things.

How dull our lives must seem to the bride, and the plighted maiden, whose days are fed with gold, and who gather pearls every evening; but to the wife, Susie, sometimes the wife forgotten, our lives perhaps seem dearer than all others in the world; you have seen flowers at morning, satisfied with the dew, and those same sweet flowers at noon with their heads bowed in anguish before the mighty sun; think you these thirsty blossoms will now need naught but – dew? No, they will cry for sunlight, and pine for the burning noon, tho' it scorches them, scathes them; they have got through with peace – they know that the man of noon, is mightier than the morning and their life is henceforth to him. Oh, Susie, it is dangerous, and it is all too dear, these simple trusting spirits, and the spirits mightier, which we cannot resist! It does so rend me, Susie, the thought of it when it comes, that I tremble lest at sometime I, too, am yielded up.

Susie, you will forgive me my amatory strain – it has been a very long one, and if this saucy page did not here bind and fetter me, I might have had no end.

I have got the letter, Susie, dear little bud – and all – and the tears came again, that alone in this big world, I am not quite alone. Such tears are showers friend, thro' which when smiles appear, the angels call them rainbows, and mimic them in Heaven.

And now in four weeks more – you are mine, all mine, except I lend you a little occasionally to Hattie and Mattie, if they promise me not to lose you, and to bring you back very soon. I shall not count the days. I shall not fill my cups with this expected happiness, for perhaps if I do, the angels being thirsty, will drink them up – I shall only hope, my Susie, and that tremblingly, for havnt barques the fullest, stranded upon the shore?

God is good, Susie, I trust he will save you, I pray that in his good time we once more meet each other, but if this life holds not another meeting for us, remember also, Susie, that it has no parting more, wherever that hour finds us, for which we have hoped so long, we shall not be separated, neither death, nor the grave can part us, so that we only love! Your Emilie –

In margin on first page

Austin has come and gone; life is so still again; why must the storm have calms?

In margin on second page

I hav'nt seen Root this term, I guess Mattie and I, are not sufficient for him!

In margin on third page

When will you come again, in a week? Let it be a swift week!

In margin on fourth page

Vinnie sends much love, and Mother; and might I be so bold as to enclose a remembrance?

early June 1852

Emily's tone in this letter suggests that she was not aware of the intimacy Susan already shared with Austin. Just four months earlier, Susan had sent Austin a Valentine that included a private joke referring to another young man's gift of chestnuts to Susan, a gift that Susan and Austin ate together. Soon the word in Amherst was that "Austin D. and Susan Gilbert are constant, and the gossips say constantly together."

10

Friday afternoon –

I have but one thought, Susie, this afternoon of June, and that of you, and I have one prayer, only, dear Susie, that is for you. That you and I in hand as we e'en do in heart, might ramble away as children, among the woods and fields, and forget these many fears, and these sorrowing cares, and each become a child again – I would it were so, Susie, and when I look around me and find myself alone, I sigh for you again; little sigh, and vain sigh, which will not bring you home.

I need you more and more, and the great world grows wider, and dear ones fewer and fewer, every day that you stay away – I miss my biggest heart;

my own goes wandering round, and calls for Susie – Friends are too dear to sunder, Oh they are far too few, and how soon they will go away where you and I cannot find them, dont let us forget these things, for their remembrance now will save us many an anguish when it is too late to love them! Susie, forgive me Darling, for every word I say – my heart is full of you, none other than you in my thoughts, yet when I seek to say to you something not for the world, words fail me; If you were here, and Oh that you were, my Susie, we need not talk at all, our eyes would whisper for us, and your hand fast in mine, we would not ask for language – I try to bring you nearer, I chase the weeks away till they are quite departed, and fancy you have come, and I am on my way through the green lane to meet you, and my heart goes scampering so, that I have much ado to bring it back again, and learn it to be patient, till that dear Susie comes. Three weeks – they cant last always, for surely they must go with their little brothers and sisters to their long home in the west!

I shall grow more and more impatient until that dear day comes, for till now, I have only mourned for you; now I begin to hope for you.

Dear Susie, I have tried hard to think what you would love, of something I might send you – I at last saw my little Violets, they begged me to let them go, so here they are – and with them as Instructor, a bit of knightly grass, who also begged the favor to accompany them – they are but small, Susie, and I fear not fragrant now, but they will speak to you of warm hearts at home, and of the something faithful, which "never slumbers nor sleeps" – Keep them 'neath your pillow, Susie, they will make you dream of blue-skies, and home, and the "blessed countrie"! You and I will have an hour with "Edward" and "Ellen Middleton", sometime when you get home – we must find out if somethings contained therein are true, and if they are, what you and me are coming to!

Now farewell, Susie, and Vinnie sends her love, and mother her's, and I add a kiss, shyly, lest there is somebody there!! Dont let them see, <u>will</u> you Susie?
Emilie –

On fourth page

Why cant I be a Delegate to the great Whig Convention? – dont I know all about Daniel Webster, and the Tariff, and the Law? Then, Susie, I could see you, during a pause in the session – but I dont like this country at all, and I shant stay here any longer! "Delenda est" America, Massachusetts and all!

open me carefully –

June 11, 1852
Emily's father Edward Dickinson was a delegate to the national Whig convention, which met in Baltimore on June 16, 1852, and he delivered this letter to Susan. "Delenda est" is Latin for "blot out" or "obliterate" or "erase." Emily fantasizes about returning to childhood, then complains about woman's lower political and social status in nineteenth-century New England.

11

Sunday afternoon –

My Susie's last request; yes, darling, I grant it, tho' few, and fleet the days which separate us now – but six more weary days, but six more twilight evens, and my lone little fireside, my silent fireside is once more full.

"We are seven, and one in heaven," we are three next Saturday, if I have mine and heaven has none.

Do not mistake, my Susie, and rather than the car, ride on the golden wings where you will ne'er come back again – do not forget the lane, and the little cot that stands by it, when people from the clouds will beckon you, and smile at you, to have you go with them – Oh Susie, my child, I sit here by my window, and look each little while down towards that golden gateway beneath the western trees, and I fancy I see you coming, you trip upon the green grass, and I hear the crackling leaf under your little shoe; I hide behind the chair, I think I will surprise you, I grow too eager to see you. I hasten to the door, and start to find me that you are not there. And very, very often when I have waked from sleep, not quite waked, I have been sure I saw you, and your dark eye beamed on me with such a look of tenderness that I could only weep, and bless God for you.

Susie, will you indeed come home next Saturday, and be my own again, and kiss me as you used to?

Shall I indeed behold you, not "darkly, but face to face" or am I fancying so, and dreaming blessed dreams from which the day will wake me? I hope for you so much, and feel so eager for you, feel that I cannot wait, feel that now I must have you – that the expectation once more to see your face again, makes me feel hot and feverish, and my heart beats so fast – I go to sleep at night, and the first thing I know, I am sitting there wide awake, and clasping my hands tightly, and thinking of next Saturday, and "never a bit" of you.

Sometimes I must have Saturday before tomorrow comes, and I wonder if it w'd make any difference with God, to give it to me today, and I'll let him have Monday, to make him a Saturday; and then I feel so funnily, and wish the precious day would'nt come quite so soon, till I could know how to feel, and get my thoughts ready for it.

Why, Susie, it seems to me as if my absent Lover was coming home so soon – and my heart must be so busy, making ready for him.

While the minister this morning was giving an account of the Roman Catholic system, and announcing several facts which were usually startling, I was trying to make up my mind w'h of the two was prettiest to go and welcome you in, my fawn colored dress, or my blue dress. Just as I had decided by all means to wear the blue, down came the minister's fist with a terrible rap on the counter, and Susie, it scared me so, I hav'nt got over it yet, but I'm glad I reached a conclusion! I walked home from meeting with Mattie, and incidentally quite, something was said of you – and I think one of us remarked that you would be here next Sunday; well – Susie – what it was I dont presume to know, but my gaiters seemed to leave me, and I seemed to move on wings – and I move on wings now, Susie, on wings as white as snow, and as bright as the summer sunshine – because I am with you, and so few short days, you are with me at home. Be patient then, my Sister, for the hours will haste away, and Oh <u>so</u> soon!

Susie, I write most hastily, and very carelessly too, for it is time for me to get the supper, and my mother is gone and besides, my darling, so near I seem to you, that I <u>disdain</u> this pen, and wait for a <u>warmer</u> language. With Vinnie's love, and my love, I am once more

Your Emilie –

June 27, 1852

Emily refers to her mother, who is in Boston visiting Austin and probably staying with her sister's family, the Norcrosses. Susan is expected to arrive in Amherst in early July, and Austin is to return at the month's end. Emily refers to Wordsworth's poem "We Are Seven" in the second paragraph, changing two children in heaven to one. The "<u>three</u> next Saturday" will be Susan, Emily, and Vinnie. No written record has been preserved of Susan's homecoming from Baltimore on July 3, nor of Emily's feelings concerning the reunion and Austin's return to Amherst on July 26. How Emily experienced the events of that summer and fall, with Austin and Susan "constantly together" is unclear.

12

Friday noon.

Dear Friend.

I regret to inform you that at 3. oclock yesterday, my mind came to a stand, and has since then been stationary.

Ere this intelligence reaches you, I shall probably be a snail. By this untoward providence a mental and moral being has been swept ruthlessly from her sphere. Yet we should not repine – "God moves in a mysterious way, his wonders to perform, he plants his foot upon the sea, and rides upon the storm," and if it be his will that I become a <u>bear</u> and bite my fellow men, it will be for the highest good of this fallen and perishing world.

If the gentleman in the air, will please to stop throwing snowballs, I may meet you again, otherwise it is uncertain. My parents are pretty well – Gen Wolf is here – we're looking for Major Pitcairn in the afternoon stage.

We were much afflicted yesterday, by the supposed removal of <u>our Cat</u> from time to Eternity.

She returned, however, last evening, having been detained by the storm, beyond her expectations.

I see by the Boston papers that <u>Giddings</u> is up again – hope you'll arrange with Corwin, and have the North all straight.

Fine weather for sledding – have spoken for 52 cord black walnut. We need some paths our way, shant you come out with the team?

Yours till death – Judah

early December 1852

In the second paragraph, Emily quotes William Cowper's "Light Shining Out of Darkness" from memory, altering one line. Edward Dickinson has just been elected to Congress as the Whig candidate, and Emily nicknames his visitors after General Wolfe, who died victorious at Quebec, and Major Pitcairn, who was fatally wounded at Bunker Hill. In 1848, Joshua Reed Giddings broke with the Whigs because the party endorsed the Fugitive Slave Law, which Thomas Corwin, Fillmore's Secretary of the Treasury, also opposed.

13

Thursday afternoon –

The sun shines warm, dear Susie, but the sweetest sunshine's gone, and in that far off Manchester, all my blue sky is straying this winter's afternoon. Vinnie and I are here – just where you always find us when you come in the afternoon to sit a little while – We miss your face today, and a tear fell on my work a little while ago, so I put up my sewing, and tried to write to you. I had rather have talked, dear Susie – it seems to me a long while since I have seen you much – it is a long while Susie, since we have been together – so long since we've spent a twilight, and spoken of what we loved, but you will come back again, and there's all the future Susie, which is as yet untouched! It is the brightest star in the firmament of God, and I look in it's face the oftenest.

I ran to the door, dear Susie – I ran out in the rain, with nothing but my slippers on, I called "Susie, Susie," but you did'nt look at me; then I ran to the dining room window and rapped with all my might upon the pane, but you rode right on and never heeded me.

It made me feel so lonely, that I could'nt help the tears, when I came back to the table, to think I was eating breakfast, and you were riding away – but bye and bye I thought that the same ugly coach which carried you away, would have to bring you back again in but a little while, and the spite pleased me so that I did'nt cry any more till the tear fell of which I told you. And now, my absent One, I am hoping the days away, till I shall see you home – I am sewing as fast as I can, I am training the stems to my flowers, I am working with all my might, so as to pause and love you, as soon as you get home.

How fast we will have to talk then – there will be those farewell gaieties – and all the days before, of which I have had no fact, and there will be your absence, and your presence, my Susie dear, sweetest, and brightest, and best of every and all the themes. It is sweet to talk, dear Susie, with those whom God has given us, lest we should be alone – and you and I have tasted it, and found it very sweet; even as fragrant flowers, o'er which the bee hums and lingers, and hums more for the lingering.

I find it very lonely, to part with <u>one of mine</u>, with mine <u>especially</u>, and the days will have more <u>hours</u> while you are gone away.

They played the trick yesterday – they dupe me again today.

Twelve hours make <u>one indeed</u> – Call it <u>twice</u> twelve, three times twelve, and add, and add, and add, then multiply again, and we will talk about it.

"At Dover dwells George Brown Esq – Good Carlos Finch and David Fryer" – Oh Susie! How much escapes me, mine; whether you reached there safely, whether you are a stranger – or have only just <u>gone home</u> – Whether you find the friends as you fancied you should find them, or dearer than you expected?

All this, and more, Susie, I am eager to know, and I <u>shall</u> know soon, <u>shant</u> I? I love to <u>think</u> I shall.

Oh Susie, Susie, I must call out to you in the old, old way – I must say how it seems to me to hear the clock so silently tick all the hours away, and bring me not my gift – my own, my own!

Perhaps you cant read it, Darling, it is incoherent and blind; but the recollection that prompts it, is very distinct and clear, and reads easily. Susie, they send their love – my mother and my sister – <u>thy</u> mother and thy sister, and the Youth, the Lone Youth, Susie, you know the rest!

Emilie –

Tell me when you write Susie, if I shall send my love to the Lady where you stay!

February 24, 1853
Emily quotes a calendar game included in Longfellow's *Kavanagh*: "At Dover dwells George Brown, Esquire, / Good Christopher Finch, and Daniel Friar." In this game, one could determine on which day the first of every month of the year fell.

14

Saturday morning –

I know dear Susie is busy, or she would not forget her lone little Emilie, who wrote her just as soon as she'd gone to Manchester, and has waited so patiently till she can wait no more, and the credulous little heart, fond even tho' forsaken, will get it's big black inkstand, and tell her once again how well it loves her.

Dear Susie, I have tried so hard to act patiently, not to think unkind thoughts, or cherish unkind doubt concerning one not here, I have watched the stages come in, I have tried to look indifferent, and hum a snatch of tune when I heard Father and Austin coming, and knew how soon they'd bring me a dear letter from you, or I should look in the hat, and find it all empty – and here comes Saturday, and tomorrow the world stands still, and I shall have no message from my dear Susie!

Why dont you write me, Darling? Did I in that quick letter say anything which grieved you, or made it hard for you to take your usual pen and trace affection for your bad, sad Emilie?

Then Susie, you must forgive me before you sleep tonight, for I will not shut my eyes until you have kissed my cheek, and told me you would love me.

Oh it has been so still, since when you went away, nothing but just the ticking of the two ceaseless clocks – swiftly the "Little mystic one, no human eye hath seen," but slowly and solemnly the tall clock upon the mantel – you remember that clock, Susie. It has the oddest way of striking twelve in the morning, and six in the afternoon, just as soon as you come. I am trying to teach it a few of the proprieties of life, now you are gone away, and the poor thing does indeed seem quite obedient, and goes slowly eno', but as soon as you're back again, Susie, it will be the same graceless one it ever used to be, and only gallop with accelerated speed, to make up for resting now.

Dear Susie, it is harder to live alone than it was when you were in Baltimore, and the days went slowly, then – they go e'en slower than they did while you were in the school – or else I grow impatient, and cannot brook as easily absence from those I love. I dont know which it is – I only know that when you shall come back again, the Earth will seem more beautiful, and bigger than it does now, and the blue sky from the window will be all dotted with gold – though it may not be evening, or time for the stars to come.

It is pleasant to talk of you with Austin – and Vinnie and to find how you are living in every one of their hearts, and making it warm and bright there – as if it were a sky, and a sweet summer's noon. Austin has gone this morning – the last little thing I did for him was while they were at breakfast, to write on four envelopes for him to send to you –

It made me smile, Susie, to think how Little Argus was cheated after all – and I smiled again, at thinking of something holier, of something from the skies, come Earthward.

Dear Susie, I dont forget you a moment of the hour, and when my work is finished, and I have got the tea, I slip thro' the little entry, and out at the front door, and stand and watch the West, and remember all of mine – yes, Susie – the golden West, and the great, silent Eternity, forever folded there, and bye and bye it will open it's everlasting arms, and gather us all – all – Good bye, dear Susie – they all send you their love – Emilie –

Susie – will you give my love to Mrs Bartlett, and tell her the fortnight is out next Wednesday, and I thought she m't like to know!

March 5, 1853

Susan's courtship with Austin is intensifying at this time, and Susan is sending him letters. Emily writes to Susan frequently. On March 5, Austin arrived in Cambridge to attend Harvard Law School, and Emily addressed four envelopes for him to send to Susan. "Little mystic one" may be an allusion to "The Life Clock," translated from German and printed in both the *Hampshire Gazette* and *Northampton Courier* in the late 1840s: "There is a little mystic clock, I No human eye hath seen, / That beateth on and beateth on / From morning until e'en."

15

Write! Comrade – write!
On this wondrous sea
Sailing silently,
Ho! Pilot, ho!
Knowest thou the shore
Where no breakers roar –
Where the storm is oer?

In the peaceful west
Many the sails at rest –
The anchors fast –
Thither I pilot thee –
Land Ho! Eternity!
Ashore at last!

Emilie –

March 1853
This is the first poem that Emily is known to have sent to Susan.

16

Dear Susie –

I'm so amused at my own ubiquity that I hardly know what to say, or how to relate the story of the wonderful correspondent. First, I arrive from Amherst, then comes a ponderous tome from the learned Halls of Cambridge, and again by strange metamorphosis I'm just from Michigan, and am Mattie and Minnie and Lizzie in one wondering breath –

Why, dear Susie, it must'nt scare you if I loom up from Hindoostan, or drop from an Appenine, or peer at you suddenly from the hollow of a tree, calling myself King Charles, Sancho Panza, or Herod, King of the Jews – I suppose it is all the same.

"Miss Mills," that is, Miss Julia, never dreamed of the depths of my clandestiny, and if I stopped to think of the figure I was cutting, it would be the last of me, and you'd never hear again from your poor Jeremy Bentham –

But I say to my mind, "tut, tut," "Rock a bye baby" conscience, and so I keep them still!

And as for the pulling of wool over the eyes of Manchester, I trust to the courtesy of the Recording Angel, to say nothing of that. One thing is true, Darling, the world will be none the wiser, for Emilie's omnipresence, and two big hearts will beat stouter, as tidings from me come in. I love the opportunity to serve those who are mine, and to soften the least asperity in the path which ne'er "ran smooth," is a delight to me. So Susie, I set the trap and catch the little mouse, and love to catch him dearly, for I think of you and Austin – and know it pleases you to have my tiny services. Dear Susie, you are gone – One would hardly think I had lost you to hear this revelry, but your absence insanes me so – I do not feel so peaceful, when you are gone from me –

All life looks differently, and the faces of my fellows are not the same they wear when you are with me. I think it is this, dear Susie; you sketch my pictures for me, and 'tis at their sweet colorings, rather than this dim real that I am used, so you see when you go away, the world looks staringly, and I find I need more vail – Frank Peirce thinks I mean berage vail, and makes a sprightly plan to import the "article," but dear Susie knows what I mean. Do you ever look homeward, Susie, and count the lonely hours Vinnie and I are spending, because that you are gone?

Yes, Susie, very lonely, and yet is it very sweet too to know that you are happy, and to think of you in the morning, and at eventide, and noon, and always as smiling and looking up for joy – I could not spare you else, dear Sister, but to be sure your life is warm with such a sunshine, helps me to chase the shadow fast stealing upon mine – I knew you would be happy, and you know now of something I had told you.

There <u>are</u> lives, sometimes, Susie – Bless God that we catch faint glimpses of his brighter Paradise from <u>occasional</u> Heavens <u>here</u>!

Stay, Susie; yet <u>not</u> stay! I cannot spare your sweet face another hour more, and yet I want to have you gather more sheaves of joy – for bleak, and waste, and barren, are most of the fields found here, and I want you to <u>fill</u> the <u>garner</u>. <u>Then</u> you may come, dear Susie, and from our silent home, Vinnie and I shall meet you. There is much to tell you, Susie, but I cannot bring the deeds of the rough and jostling world into that sweet inclosure; they are fitter <u>fonder, here</u> – but Susie, I do bring you a Sister's fondest love – and gentlest tenderness; little indeed, but "a'," and I know you will not refuse them. Please remember me to your friend, and write soon to your lonely – Emilie –

Upside down on first page

Vinnie sends you her love – She would write, but has hurt her hand – Mother's love too – Oh Susie!

March 12, 1853
Emily refers to Austin as the philosopher and jurist Jeremy Bentham. Julia Mills is the close friend of Dora Spenlow in *David Copperfield*. Erasures of affectionate references to "Susie" continue in Emily's letters to Austin of this period. On March 23, Susan and Austin become engaged.

17

It's hard to wait, dear Susie, though my heart is there, and has been since the sunset, and I knew you'd come I'd should have gone right down, but Mother had been at work hard, as it was Saturday, and Austin had promised to take her to Mrs Cobb's, as soon as he got home from Palmer – then she wanted to go, and see two or three of the neighbors, and I wanted to go to you, but I thought it would be unkind – so not till tomorrow, Darling – and all the stories Monday – except short sketches of them at meeting tomorrow night. I have stories to tell – very unusual for me – a good many things have happened – Love for you Darling – How can I sleep tonight? Ever Emilie –

So precious, my own Sister, to have you here again. Somebody loves you more – or I were there this evening –

Mother sends her love – She spoke of it this morning, what a day Susie would have –

about October 1853
There are few existing letters from Emily to Susan for the next eight months. During this time Emily writes frequently to Austin in Cambridge, sending him news from home and often elaborating on time spent with Susan. Her tone is generally cheerful as she and all of the Dickinsons welcome Susan into the family as Austin's future wife, and Emily and Susan see each other nearly every day.

18

Sabbath Day –

I'm just from meeting, Susie, and as I sorely feared, my "life" was made a "victim." I walked – I ran – I flew – I turned precarious corners – One moment I was not – then soared aloft like Phoenix, soon as the foe was by – and then anticipating an enemy again, my soiled and drooping plumage might have been seen emerging from just behind a fence, vainly endeavoring to fly once more from hence. I reached the steps, dear Susie – I smiled to think of me, and my geometry, during the journey there – It would have puzzled Euclid, and it's doubtful result, have solemnized a Day.

How big and broad the aisle seemed, full huge enough before, as I quaked slowly up – and reached my usual seat!

In vain I sought to hide behind your feathers – Susie – feathers and Bird had flown, and there I sat, and sighed, and wondered I was scared so, for surely in the whole world was nothing I need to fear – Yet there the Phantom was, and though I kept resolving to be as brave as Turks, and bold as Polar Bears, it did'nt help me any. After the opening prayer I ventured to turn around. Mr Carter immediately looked at me – Mr Sweetser attempted to do so, but I discovered nothing, up in the sky somewhere, and gazed intently at it, for quite a half an hour. During the exercises I became more calm, and got out of church quite comfortably. Several roared around, and, sought to devour me, but I fell an easy prey to Miss Lovina Dickinson, being too much exhausted to make any farther resistance.

She entertained me with much sprightly remark, until our gate was reached, and I need'nt tell you Susie, just how I clutched the latch, and whirled the merry key, and fairly danced for joy, to find myself at home! How I did wish for you – how – for my own dear Vinnie – how for Goliah, or Samson – to pull the whole church down, requesting Mr Dwight to step into Miss Kingsbury's, until the dust was past!

Prof Aaron Warner, late propounder of Rhetoric to youth of Amherst College, gave us the morning sermon. Now Susie, you and I, admire Mr Warner, so my felicity, when he arose to preach, I need not say to you. I will merely remark that I shall be much disappointed if the Rev Horace Walpole does'nt address us this evening.

You can see how things go, dear Susie, when you are not at home. If you stay another Sunday I hav'nt any doubt that the "Secretary of War" will take charge of the Sabbath School – yet I would not alarm you!

The singing reminded me of the Legend of "Jack and Gill," allowing the Bass Viol to be typified by Gill, who literally tumbled after, while Jack – i e the choir, galloped insanely on, "nor recked, nor heeded" him.

Dear Sister, it is passed away, and you and I may speak of dear things, and little things – some of our trifles Susie – There's Austin – he's a trifle – and trifling as it is that he is coming Monday, it makes my heart *[ink blot covers "beat"]* faster – Vinnie's a trifle too – Oh how I love such trifles. Susie, under that black spot, technically termed a blot, the word beat may be found – My pen fell from the handle – occasioning the same, but life is too short to transcribe or apologize – I dont doubt Daniel Webster made many a blot, and I think you said, you made one, under circumstances quite aggravating! But of Austin and Vinnie – One is with me tomorrow noon, and I shall be so happy –

The one that returns, Susie, is dearer than "ninety and nine" that did not go away.

To get you all once more, seems vague and doubtful to me, for it would be so dear. Did you ever think, Susie, that there had been no grave here? To me there are three, now. The longest one is Austin's – I must plant brave trees there, for Austin was so brave – and

Susie, for you and Vinnie I shall plant each a rose, and that will make the birds come.

Sister, I hav'nt asked if you got to Manchester safely, if all is happy, and well, and yet I'm sure it is – if it were not, you would have told me. Susie, the days and hours are very long to me, but you must not come back until it is best and willing.

Please remember me to your friends, with respect and affection, leaving only affection for you –

from your own Emily –

In margin on first page

Remember the hint, Susie!

In margin on third page

Mother asks if I've given her love.

January 15, 1854

Susan is away visiting her sister's in-laws, Mary and Samuel Bartlett, in Manchester, New Hampshire, and Austin is due home almost immediately for a six week stay. Professor Aaron Warner resigned from Amherst College because the trustees did not give him the opportunity to rebut criticisms of his work.

19

Monday evening.

Susie – it is a little thing to say how lone it is – anyone can do it, but to wear the loneness next your heart for weeks, when you sleep, and when you wake, ever missing something, <u>this</u>, all cannot say, and it baffles me.

I could paint a portrait which would bring the tears, had I canvass for it, and the scene should be <u>solitude</u>, and the figures – solitude – and the lights and shades, each a solitude.

I could fill a chamber with landscapes so lone, men should pause and weep there; then haste grateful home, for a loved one left. Today has been a fair day, very still and blue. Tonight, the crimson children are playing in the West, and tomorrow will be colder.

In all I number you. I want to think of you each hour in the day. What you are saying – doing – I want to walk with you, as seeing yet unseen. You say you walk and sew alone. I walk and sew alone. I dont see much of Vinnie – she's mostly, dusting stairs!

We go out very little – once in a month or two, we both set sail in silks – touch at the principal points, and then put into port again – Vinnie cruises about some to transact the commerce, but coming to anchor, is most that I can do. Mr and Mrs Dwight are a sunlight to me, which no night can shade, and I still perform weekly journeys there, much to Austin's dudgeon, and my sister's rage.

I have heard it said "persecution kindles" – think it kindled me! They are sweet and loving, and one thing, dear Susie, always ask for you. Sunday Afternoon – I left you a long while Susie, that is, in pen and ink – my heart kept on. I was called down from you to entertain some company – went with a sorry grace, I fear, and trust I acted with one. There is a tall – pale snow storm stalking through the fields, and bowing here, at my window – shant let the fellow in!

I went to church all day in second dress, and boots. We had such precious sermons from Mr Dwight. One about unbelief, and another Esau. Sermons on unbelief ever did attract me. Thanksgiving was observed throughout the state last week! Believe we had a Turkey, and two kinds of Pie. Otherwise, no change. Father went Thanksgiving night. Austin goes tomorrow, unless kept by storm. He will see you, Darling! What I cannot do. Oh could I! We did not attend the Thanksgiving "Soiree" – owing to our sadness at just parting with father –

Your sister will give particulars.

Abby is much better – rode horseback every day until the snow came, and goes down street now just like other girls – Abby seems more gentle, more affectionate, than she has.

Eme Kellogg wonders she does not hear from you. I gave your message to her, and bring you back the same. Eme is still with Henry, tho' no outward bond has as yet encircled them. Edward Hitchcock and baby – and Mary, spent Thanksgiving here. I called upon Mary – she appears very sweetly, and the baby is quite becoming to her. They all adore the baby.

Mary inquired for you with a great deal of warmth, and wanted to send her love when I wrote.

Susie – had that been you – well – well! I must stop, Sister. Things have wagged, dear Susie, and they're wagging still. "Little Children, love one another." Not all of life to live, is it, nor all of death to die.

In margin on first page

Susie – we all love you – Mother – Vinnie – me. Dearly!

Upside down on first page

I have not heard from Mat for months. "They say that absence conquers." It has vanquished me.

In margin on second page

Your Sister Harriet is our most intimate friend.

In margin on third page

Mother and Vinnie send their love. Austin must carry his.

In margin on fourth page

The last night of the term, John sent his love to you.

November 27 to December 3, 1854
Thanksgiving night, Edward Dickinson returns to Washington for the second session of the thirty-third Congress. On December 4, Austin departs for Chicago and Grand Haven, Michigan to visit his future brothers-in-law. He returns to Amherst at the beginning of the new year, 1855, and Susan stays in Michigan until late February. John is Emily's cousin, John Graves, an Amherst College student. The letter's last line refers to the last two lines of a stanza from James Montgomery's hymn, "O where shall rest be found": "'Tis not the whole of life to live; Nor all of death to die."

20

Sabbath Day.

I am sick today, dear Susie, and have not been to church. There has been a pleasant quiet, in which to think of you, and I have not been sick eno' that I cannot write to you. I love you as dearly, Susie, as when love first began, on the step at the front door, and under the Evergreens, and it breaks my heart sometimes, because I do not hear from you. I wrote you many days ago – I wont say many weeks, because it will look sadder so, and then I cannot write – but Susie, it troubles me.

I miss you, mourn for you, and walk the Streets alone – often at night, beside, I fall asleep in tears, for your dear face, yet not one word comes back to me from that silent West. If it is finished, tell me, and I will raise the lid to my box of Phantoms, and lay one more love in; but if it lives and beats still, still lives and beats for <u>me</u>, then say me <u>so</u>, and I will strike the strings to one more strain of happiness before I die. Why Susie – think of it – you are my precious Sister, and will be till you die, and will be still, when Austin and Vinnie and Mat, and you and I are marble – and life has forgotten us!

Vinnie and I are going soon – either this week or next – father has not determined. I'm sure I cannot go, when I think that you are coming, and I would give the whole world if I could stay, instead.

I cant believe you are coming – but when I think of it, and tell myself it's so, a wondrous joy comes over me, and my old fashioned life capers as in a dream. Sue – I take the words of that Sweet Kate Scott, I have never seen – and say "it is too blissful." I never will be "so busy" when you get back to me, as I used to be. I'll get "my spinning done," for Susie, it steals over me once in a little while, that as fingers fly and I am so busy, a far more wondrous Shuttle shifts the subtler thread, and when <u>that's</u> web is spun, <u>indeed</u> <u>my</u> spinning will be done. I think with you, dear Susie, and Mat by me again, I shall be still for joy. I shall not fret or murmur – shall not care when the wind blows, shall not observe the storm – "Such, and so precious" are you.

Austin told me about you when he came from the West – though many little things I wanted most to know, he "had not noticed." I asked him how you looked, and what you wore, and how your hair was fixed, and what you said of me – his answers were quite limited – "you looked as you always did – he did'nt know what you wore – never did know what people wore – you said he must tell me everything," which by the way dear Child, he has not done to this day, and any portion of which, I would savor with joy, might I but obtain it. Vinnie inquired with promptness "if you wore a Basque" – "it seemed to him," he said, "you did have on a black thing."

Ah Susie – you must train him 'twill take full many a lesson in the fashion plate, before he will respect, and speak with proper deference of this majestic garment. I have some new clothes, Susie – presume I shall appear like an embarrassed Peacock, quite unused to its plumes. Dear Susie – you will write to me when I am gone from home – Affy, Emilie –

Upside down on first page

Mother and Vinnie send much love – they will be delighted to see you. My dearest love to Mat.

In margin on first page

I asked Austin if he had any messages – he replied he –

In margin on second page

had not! The good for nothing fellow! I presume he will

In margin on third page

fill a fools Cap with protestations to you, as soon

In margin on fourth page

as I leave the room! Bats think Foxes have no eyes – Ha Ha!!

late January 1855
Emily's early 1855 letter makes clear how all-consuming her love for Susan is, and how enamored Emily is of Susan's appearance. Emily's frustration is obvious, since Austin has "sanctuary privileges" and can see Susan when he wishes, yet he appears to be oblivious of his good fortune. The "step at the front door" where "love first began" is a reference to the house on South Pleasant Street in which the Dickinsons lived from 1840 to 1855. Sometimes called the "Mansion," this house is no longer standing.

21

Wednesday morning.

Sweet and soft as summer, Darlings, maple trees in bloom and grass green in the sunny places hardly seems it possible this is winter still; and it makes the grass spring in this heart of mine and each linnet sing, to think that you have come.

Dear Children – Mattie – Sue for one look at you, for your gentle voices, I'd exchange it all. The pomp – the court – the etiquette – they are of the earth – will not enter Heaven.

Will you write to me – why hav'nt you before? I feel so tired looking for you, and still you do not come. And you love me, come soon – this is not forever, you know, this mortal life of our's. Which had you rather I wrote you – what I am doing here, or who I am loving *there*?

Perhaps I'll tell you both, but the "last shall be first, and the first last." I'm loving you at home – I'm coming every hour to your chamber door. I'm thinking when awake, how sweet if you were with me, and to talk with you as I fall asleep, would be sweeter still.

I think I cannot wait, when I remember you, and that is *always*, Children. I shall love you more for this sacrifice.

Last night I heard from Austin – and I think he fancies we are losing sight of the things at home – Tell him "not so," Children – Austin is mistaken. He says we forget "the Horse, the Cats, and the geraniums" – have not remembered Pat – proposes to sell the farm and move west with mother – to make boquets of my plants, and send them to his friends – to come to Washington in his Dressing gown and mortify me and Vinnie.

Should be delighted to see him, even in "dishabille," and will promise to *notice* him whenever he will come. The *cats* I will confess, have not so absorbed my attention as they are apt at home, yet do I still remember them with tender emotion; and as for my sweet flowers, I shall know each leaf and every bud that bursts, while I am from home. Tell Austin, never fear! My thoughts are far from idle, concerning e'en the *trifles* of the world at home, but all is jostle, here – scramble and confusion, and sometimes in writing home I cant stop for detail, much as I would love. Vinnie met the other evening, in the parlor here a certain Mr Saxton, who inquired of her for his Amherst cousins. Vinnie told him joyfully, all she knew of you, and another evening, took me down to him.

We walked in the hall a long while, talking of you, my Children, vieing with each other in compliment to those we loved so well. I told him of you both, he seemed very happy to hear so much of you. He left Washington yesterday morning. I have not been well since I came here, and that has excused me from some gaieties, tho' at that, I'm gayer than I was before. Vinnie is asleep this morning – she has been out walking with some ladies here and is very tired. She says much of you – wants so much to see you. Give my love to your sister – Kiss Dwightie for me – my love for Abbie and Eme, when you see them, and for dear Mr & Mrs Dwight.

On top of first page

Tell Mother and Austin they need'nt flatter themselves we are forgetting them – they'll find themselves much mistaken before long. We think we shall go to Philadelphia next week, tho' father has'nt decided. Eliza writes most every day, and seems

In margin on second page

impatient for us. I dont know how long we shall

In margin on third page

stay there, nor how long in New York. Father has not de[ci]

In margin on fourth page

ded. Shant you write, when this gets to you? Affy – E –

Washington, February 28, 1855

Susan received this letter when she returned to Amherst from Michigan. Emily and Lavinia are in Washington for three weeks, from mid-February until early March. From there they travel to Philadelphia to visit their cousins the Colemans. Eliza Coleman, two years younger than Emily, became a close friend when the girls were in their midteens. "Dwightie," to whom Emily sends a kiss, is the youngest child of Susan's sister Harriet Cutler, with whom Susan and Martha are living.

By 1855, Susan and Austin had been engaged for more than a year. Yet it would be another sixteen months before they married and settled in the Evergreens. There Susan would live next door to Emily for the next thirty years.

SECTION TWO

SUE, DEAR SUE, SWEET SUE, SISTER

Early Middle Writings, mid-1850s to mid-1860s

Between the mid-1850s and mid-1860s, Emily's correspondence to Susan unequivocally acknowledges that their emotional, spiritual, and physical communion is vital to her creative insight and sensibilities. In fact, Emily will call Susan "imagination" itself.

During this period, the structure of their lives changes dramatically. The Dickinson family moves from the "Mansion" on South Pleasant Street in Amherst back to the renovated Homestead on Main Street.

Susan's engagement to Austin lasts three years, and the wedding, having been postponed by Susan on several occasions, finally takes place at the house of Susan's aunt Sophia Arms Van Vranken in Geneva, New York, on July 1, 1856. Austin is the only Dickinson in attendance. No letters exist from the period of the wedding, a fact that seems surprising given Emily's previous attentiveness. Not even a letter of congratulations remains. Again, it is possible that letters or letter-poems from this period were written, sent, and destroyed or lost. With financial assistance from Susan's brothers, Edward Dickinson builds the Evergreens, next door to the Homestead, and Susan and Austin settle there and raise their family.

In the late 1850s, Emily begins making her manuscript books, or fascicles. This common nineteenth-century practice enabled people to create their own special collections of favorite poems, essays, or stories. In fact, several years earlier, Susan had compiled a fascicle, including works by writers such as James Russell Lowell, Julia A. Fletcher, and Edgar Allan Poe. Emily's fascicles differ, however, because they are comprised of her own poems, and they total forty separate books at the time of her death in 1886.

During the period when Emily begins to gather her poems into fascicles, she writes three missives, now known as the "Master" letters, to a fictional or real addressee(s). Emily also places three love poems to "Dollie" (Susan's nickname) in her manuscript books. These "Dollie" poems are deeply romantic and erotic, and it is unclear whether Emily ever actually gives them to Susan, or if Susan receives them and destroys them because they are "too personal and adulatory ever to be printed."[1] Emily does send two letter-poems addressed "Dollie" to Susan, and they appear in the following pages. Emblematic of the ongoing passion Emily feels for Susan, these documents reflect an ardor that is sustained throughout Susan's engagement to Austin and the unavoidable shift in Susan's availability once she undertakes her wifely duties.

After Susan moves to the Evergreens, she becomes immersed in social engagements, entertaining a wide range of literary and political figures over the next twenty years, including essayist and philosopher Ralph Waldo Emerson, novelist Harriet Beecher Stowe, landscape architect Frederick Olmsted, and abolitionist and suffragist Wendell Phillips. Emily attends many of the Evergreens gatherings, but she secludes herself more often and devotes her energies and time to writing and contemplation.

From the late 1850s on, Emily shares her poems with Susan, regularly sending drafts and inviting feedback. It is likely that this relationship is reciprocal, and that Susan sends Emily her own poems for critiques as well. One example of this process is preserved in the following exchange of various versions of Emily's poem "Safe in their Alabaster Chambers."

Throughout this period, Susan sends a selection of Emily's poems to various newspapers and magazines for printing, and she writes excitedly of "our Fleet" when the *Springfield Republican* prints what is probably her own poem, "The Shadow of Thy Wing," just below a version of "Safe in their Alabaster Chambers." Over the next several years, Emily publishes eight poems in *Drum Beat*, *Round Table*, the *Brooklyn Daily Union*, the *Springfield Republican*, and the *Boston*

Post. In April 1862, *Atlantic Monthly* editor, Thomas Wentworth Higginson, publishes "Letter to a Young Contributor," and Emily sends him the first of many letters, along with four poems.

Emily spends several months in the Boston area in 1864 and 1865. During these eight- and seven-month periods, she receives medical care for her eyes and lives with her cousins Louise (Loo) and Fanny Norcross in a boarding house in Cambridgeport.

By the mid-1860s, Emily has written over a thousand poems. Susan has given birth to her son Ned (b. 1861) and her daughter Martha (b. 1866). Emily's correspondence to Susan continues to reflect on a great array of subjects, from the ordinary details of life in the Homestead and the Evergreens households to monumental spiritual considerations, literature, and the birth of Susan's first child. Some of the missives are playful while others indicate the strain of profound differences of opinion between the two women. Emily's writings to Susan expand from conventional letters to what Susan refers to as "letter-poems" as she later compiles her book of Emily's writings. These "letter-poems" are letters that look and sound like poems; they are also poems addressed to Susan that read like letters, or messages. During this time, Emily appears to take the calligraphic design and placement of the text on the page more and more into account. To show this gradual transformation, the missives in the following three sections of *Open Me Carefully* replicate many characteristics of Emily's placement of words and lines on the page as closely as possible.

While Dickinson's expressions of love for Susan mature over the decades, they do not become less intense, and the transformation from early exuberance to the direct, often humorous, and contemplative tone in these middle letters reflects the magnitude of Emily's passion and respect for her beloved friend.

22

Tuesday morning –

Sue – you can go or stay – There is but one alternative – We differ often lately, and this must be the last.

You need not fear to leave me lest I should be alone, for I often part with things I fancy I have loved, – sometimes to the grave, and sometimes to an oblivion rather bitterer than death – thus my heart bleeds so frequently that I shant mind the hemorrhage, and I only add an agony to several previous ones, and at the end of day remark – a bubble burst!

Such incidents would grieve me when I was but a child, and perhaps I could have wept when little feet hard by mine, stood still in the coffin, but eyes grow dry sometimes, and hearts get crisp and cinder, and had as lief burn.

Sue – I have lived by this.

It is the lingering emblem of the Heaven I once dreamed, and though if this is taken, I shall remain alone, and though in that last day, the Jesus Christ you love, remark he does not know me – there is a darker spirit will not disown it's child.

Few have been given me, and if I love them so, that for <u>idolatry</u>, they are removed from me – I simply murmur <u>gone</u>, and the billow dies away into the boundless blue, and no one knows but me, that one went down today. We have walked very pleasantly – Perhaps this is the point at which our paths diverge – then pass on singing Sue, and up the distant hill I journey on.

I have a Bird in spring
Which for myself doth sing –
The spring decoys.
And as the summer nears –
And as the Rose appears,
Robin is gone.

Yet do I not repine
Knowing that Bird of mine
Though flown_
Learneth beyond the sea
Melody new for me
And will return.

Fast in a safer hand
Held in a truer Land
Are mine_
And though they now depart,
Tell I my doubting heart
They're thine.

In a serener Bright,
In a more golden light
I see
Each little doubt and fear,
Each little discord here
Removed.

Then will I not repine,
Knowing that Bird of mine
Though flown
Shall in a distant tree
Bright melody for me
Return.

E –

mid-1850s
"The Jesus Christ you love, remark he does not know me" suggests that the differences expressed in this letter may have been over spiritual matters. While Emily would soon remove herself from the ceremonies of organized religion altogether, Susan struggled with the place of orthodoxy in her life. Known to honor certain religious conventions, Susan once assured her brothers that she only wrote letters on the Sabbath in the case of overriding necessity. For Emily, who kept the Sabbath "staying at Home," the pomp and pageantry of High Church was as foreign as "Firmament to Fin." As late as September 1898, Susan considered converting to Catholicism.

23

A slash of Blue –
A sweep of Gray –
Some scarlet patches
on the way,
Compose an Evening Sky –
A little purple – slipped
between –

Some Ruby Trowsers
hurried on –
A Wave of Gold –
A Bank of Day –
This just makes out
the M<u>orning</u> Sky –

1850s

This is one of several poems from which the address "Sue" was later erased.

24

Dear Susie – I send
you a little air –
The "Music of the Spheres."
They are represented above
as passing thro' the sky.

mid-1850s

This may be an example of a letter-poem inspired by the elaborate poetry games that Emily and Susan play throughout their correspondence. On this missive, written in her more casual "rough draft" hand, Emily sketches ascending musical notations and clouds, perhaps joking about the "Pythagorean maxim" to "avoid eating beans, which cause flatulence" that Melville refers to in *Moby Dick*. She may also be teasing Susan, the math teacher, about Pythagoreanism, or poking fun at her own style of writing, of feeding people on air.

25

These are the days when Birds come back –
A very few – a Bird or two –
To take a final look.

These are the days when skies resume
The old – old Sophistries of June –
A blue and gold mistake.

Oh fraud that cannot cheat the Bee –
Almost thy plausibility
Induces my belief.

Till ranks of seeds their witness bear –
And swiftly thro' the altered air
Hurries a timid leaf.

Oh Sacrament of summer days !
Oh Last Communion in the Haze
Permit a child to join.

Thy sacred emblem to partake –
Thy consecrated bread to take
And thine immortal wine!

1850s

Emily's poem echoes a poem by Susan, "There are three months of the Spring," suggesting a call-and-response relationship in their writing life.

26

Besides the Autumn poets sing
A few prosaic days
A little this side of the snow
And that side of the Haze.
A few incisive Mornings –
A few ascetic Eves –
Gone – Mr Bryant's "Golden Rod"
And Mr Thomson's "Sheaves."
Still, is the bustle in the brook –
Sealed, are the spicy valves –
Mesmeric fingers softly touch
The Eyes of many Elves –
Perhaps a squirrel may remain –
My sentiments to share –
Grant me Oh Lord a
sunny mind –
Thy windy will to bear!

Emilie –

1850s

Letter-poems take a variety of forms, including signed poems. In this letterpoem, Emily refers to poems by William Cullen Bryant, who lived in nearby Cummington, and the Scottish poet James Thomson. The address "Sue" was erased from the verso.

27

Pigmy Seraphs – gone astray –
Velvet people from Vevay –
Belles from some lost summer
day–
Bees exclusive Coterie –
Paris could not lay the fold
Belted down with Emerald!
Venice could not show a cheek
Of a tint so lustrous meek.
Never such an Ambuscade
As of briar and leaf displayed
For my little damask maid.
I had rather wear her grace
Than an Earl's distinguished
face –
I had rather dwell like her
Than be Duke of Exeter –
over –
Next page

Royalty eno' for Me
To subdue the Bumblebee.

Emily –

1850s
Previous editors have not noted that this poem was addressed to Susan.

28

Thursday Eve

Susie –

You will forgive me, for I never visit. I am from the fields, you know, and while quite at home with the Dandelion, make but sorry figure in a Drawing – room – Did you ask me out with a bunch of Daisies, I should thank you, and accept – but with Roses – "Lilies" – "Solomon" himself – suffers much embarrassment! Do not mind me Susie – If I do not come with feet, in my heart I come – talk the most, and laugh the longest – stay when all the rest have gone – kiss your cheek, perhaps, while those honest people quite forget you in their Sleep!

Thank you for your frequent coming, and the flowers you bring – thank you for the glad laugh, which I heard this morning, tho' I did not see you.

I will keep them all till I reach my other Susie, whose sweet face you bring afresh, every day you come.

Affy –

Emilie –

late 1850s

To describe her place in society, Emily draws on a mock hierarchy of flowers—daisies at the bottom, roses and lilies at the top. Throughout this correspondence, she uses the symbols of the rose and the lily to represent Susan and herself. She identifies with King Solomon and his riches, and her description of her own social interaction when her heart is so inclined—"talking the most and laughing the longest"—will be echoed decades later by her niece, who declared that with an appreciative audience her "Aunt Emily [would] talk more and funnier."

29

Sunday.

I hav'nt any paper, dear, but faith continues firm – Presume if I met with my "deserts," I should receive nothing. Was informed to that effect today by a "dear pastor." What a privilege it is to be so insignificant! Thought of intimating that the "Atonement" was'nt needed for such atomies! I think you went on Friday. Some time is longer than the rest, and some is very short. Omit to classify Friday – Saturday – Sunday! Evenings get longer with the Autumn – that is nothing new! The Asters are pretty well. "How are the other blossoms?" "Pretty well, I thank you."

Vinnie and I are pretty well. Carlo – comfortable – terrifying man and beast, with renewed activity – is cuffed some – hurled from piazza frequently, when Miss Lavinia's "flies" need her action elsewhere.

She has the "patent action," I have long felt!

I attended church early in the day. Prof Warner preached. Subject – "little drops of dew."

Este[y] took the stump in the afternoon. Aunt Sweetser's dress would have startled Sheba. Aunt Bullard was not out – presume she stayed at home for "self examination." Accompanied by father, they visited the grave yard, after services. These are stirring scenes! Austin supped with us. "Appears well." Ah – Dobbin – Dobbin – you little know the chink which your dear face makes.

We would'nt mind the sun, dear, if it did'nt set – How much you cost – how much Mat costs – I will never sell you for a piece of silver. I'll buy you back with red drops, when you go away. I'll keep you in a casket – I'll bury you in the garden – and keep a bird to watch the spot – perhaps my pillow's safer – Try my bosom last – That's nearest of them all, and I should hear a foot the quickest, should I hear a foot – The thought of the little brown plumes makes my eye awry. The pictures in the air have few visitors.

You see they come to their own and their own do not receive them, "Power and honor" are here today, and "dominion and glory"! I shall never tell!

You may tell, when "the seal" is opened; Mat may tell when they "fall on their faces" – but I shall be lighting the lamps then in my new house – and I cannot come.

God bless you, if he please! Bless Mr John and Mrs Mat – Bless two or three others!

I wish to be there – Shall I come? If I jump, shall you catch me. Hav'nt the conceit to jump! Vinnie is asleep – and must dream her message. Good night, little girls!

Since there are two varieties, we will say it softly – Since there are snowier beds, we'll talk a little every night, before we sleep in these!

Love Emilie –

September 26, 1858
In late September, Susan went to Geneva, New York, to visit her sister Martha, now wife of John Williams Smith. "Aunt Sweetser" and "Aunt Bullard" are Edward Dickinson's sisters, in town for a Dickinson family reunion. Emily's dog Carlo, possibly a Newfoundland, was first mentioned in an 1850 Valentine spoof, so the dog is now at least eight years old. Allusions in the third paragraph from the end are to Revelation 7:11: "And all the angels stood round about the throne, and *about* the elders and the four beasts, and fell before the throne on their faces, and worshipped God." Captain Dobbin is the steadfast, devoted lover of Amelia Sedley in Thackeray's V*anity Fair*.

30

One Sister have I in our house –
And one, a hedge away.
There's only one recorded,
But both belong to me.

One came the road that I came –
And wore my last year's gown –
The other as a bird her nest,
Builded our hearts among.

She did not sing as we did –
It was a different tune –
Herself to her a Music
As Bumble bee of June.

Today is far from Childhood –
But up and down the hills
I held her hand the tighter –
Which shortened all the miles –

And still her hum
The years among,
Deceives the Butterfly;
Still in her Eye
The Violets lie
Mouldered this many May.

I spilt the dew –
But took the morn –
I chose this single star
From out the wide night's numbers –
Sue _ forevermore!

Emilie –

late 1850s
Written after Austin and Susan took up residence in the Evergreens, this letter-poem is torn above the folding crease on the third page. The tear is probably not a mutilation unless it signals Susan's removal of expressions "too personal and adulatory to be printed." However, the fascicle version of this poem was entirely inked over. It is quite possible that someone (probably Mabel Loomis Todd) found this poem's unabashed expression of affection offensive and tried to blot it out. This mutilation parallels those in the earlier letters, as well as the erasure of "Sue" as the addressee of erotic verses such as "Her breast is fit for pearls."

31

Darling.
The feet of people walking home –
With gayer Sandals go –
The Crocus, till she rises
The Vassal of the snow –

The lips at Hallelujah
Long years of practise bore –
Till bye and bye, these Bargmen
Walked singing, on the shore –

Pearls are the Diver's farthings –
Extorted from the Sea_
Pinions – the Seraph's wagon
Pedestrian once – as we –

Night is the Morning's Canvas –
Larceny_Legacy –
Death, but our rapt attention
To Immortality –

My figures fail to tell me
How far the Village lies
Whose Peasants are the Angels –
Whose Cantons dot the skies –

My Classics vail their faces –
My faith that dark adores –
Which from its' solemn Abbeys

Such Resurrection pours –

Lovingly,

Emilie –

late 1850s
With both households well established and prospering, Emily sends many poems to Susan, some as messages, and some for her evaluation and critical response. During this time, the poet was making her manuscript books, or fascicles, and she had begun a significant lifelong relationship with another recipient of many poems, Samuel Bowles, editor of the *Springfield Republican*. Bowles and his wife Mary were also friends of Susan and Austin, who probably met him in the mid-1850s when Bowles began to cover the Amherst College commencements. The *Republican* was considered one of the most influential newspapers in the country. Both Dickinson households read the paper every day, and Emily often comments on the news in the notes she sends to Susan.

32

Frequently the woods are pink –
Frequently are brown.
Frequently the hills undress
Behind my native town.
Oft a head is crested
I was wont to see –
And as oft a cranny
Where it used to be –
And the Earth_ [world_] they tell me –
On it's Axis turned!

Wonderful Rotation!
By but Twelve performed!

late 1850s
As neighbors, the two women often passed notes and poems in face-to-face encounters, the folded paper small enough to tuck handily into a pocket. Emily frequently sends Susan poems that she also shares with other readers. Yet she comfortably offers Susan drafts, like this one, in addition to finished poems. Here "world" is crossed out and "Earth" inscribed above it.

33

There is a word
Which bears a sword
Can pierce an armed man –
It hurls it's barbed syllables
And is mute again –
But where it fell
The Saved will tell
On patriotic day,
Some Epauletted Brother
Gave his breath away!

Wherever runs the breathless sun –
Wherever roams the day –
There is it's noiseless onset –
There is it's victory!

Behold the keenest marksman –
The most accomplished shot!

Time's sublimest target
Is a soul "forgot"!

Emily–

late 1850s

34

Thro' lane it lay – thro' bramble –
Thro' clearing, and thro' wood –
Banditti often passed us
Upon the lonely road –
The wolf came peering curious –
The owl looked puzzled down –
The Serpent's satin figure
Glid stealthily along –
The tempests touched our garments –
The Lightning's poinards gleamed –
Fierce from the crag above us
The hungry Vulture screamed –
The Satyr's fingers beckoned –
The Valley murmured "Come" –
These were the mates –
This was the road
These Children fluttered home.

"Emily – "

late 1850s
The "hungry Vulture" may refer to Kate Anthon, a lifelong friend of

Susan's whom Emily refers to as "Condor Kate" in a letter written a few years later.

35

My Wheel is in the dark.
I cannot see a spoke –
Yet know it's dripping feet
Go round and round.

My foot is on the Tide –
An unfrequented road
Yet have all roads
A "Clearing" at the end.

Some have resigned the Loom –
Some – in the busy tomb
Find quaint employ.
Some with new – stately feet
Pass royal thro' the gate
Flinging the problem back, at you and I.

late 1850s

36

I never told the buried gold
Upon the hill that lies –
I saw the sun, his plunder done –
Crouch low to guard his prize –

He stood as near
As stood you here –
A pace had been between –
Did but a snake bisect the brake
My life had forfeit been.

That was a wondrous booty –
I hope 'twas honest gained –
Those were the fairest ingots
That ever kissed the spade.

Whether to keep the secret –
Whether to reveal –
Whether while I ponder
Kidd may sudden sail –

Could a shrewd advise me
We might e'en divide –
Should a shrewd betray me –
"Atropos" decide_

late 1850s
"Atropos" refers to one of the three Fates in Greek mythology.

37

The morns are meeker than they were –
The nuts are getting brown –
The berry's cheek is plumper –
The Rose is out of town –

The Maple wears a gayer scarf –
The field – a Scarlet gown –
Lest I sh'd seem old fashioned
I'll put a trinket on!

Emilie –

late 1850s

A yellowed ribbon that once held a flower is woven through this letter-poem. The paper is cut so that the ribbon, precisely trimmed, does not cover the text of the poem.

38

"Navy" Sunset!

The guest is gold and Crimson –
An Opal guest, and gray –
Of Ermine is his doublet –
His Capuchin gay –
He comes to town at nightfall –
He stops at every door –
Who looks for him at morning –
I pray him too – explore
The Lark's pure territory –
Or, the Lapwing's shore!

Emilie –

late 1850s

39

A little over Jordan,
As Genesis record,
An Angel and a Wrestler
Did wrestle long and hard.

Till, morning touching mountain,
And Jacob waxing strong,
The Angel begged permission
To breakfast and return.

Not so, quoth wily Jacob
And girt his loins anew,
"Until thou bless me, stranger!"
The which acceded to:

Light swung the silver fleeces
Peniel hills among,
And the astonished Wrestler
Found he had worsted God!

late 1850s

Whatever the religious differences between Emily and Susan, the image of the biblical figures Jacob and the angel would have resonated profoundly for both of them. Throughout the correspondence, biblical characters and events are often emblematic of Emily's internal and external observations. As Susan's daughter, Martha Dickinson Bianchi, put it, "her [Aunt Emily's] mind dared earth and heaven," and "apocrypha and apocalypse met in her."

40

“Sown in dishonor”?
Ah’ Indeed!
May this dishonor be?
If I were half so fine, myself,
I’d notice nobody!

“Sown in corruption”?
By no means!
Apostle is Askew!
Corinthians 1.15. narrates
A Circumstance, or two!

late 1850s

The quotations refer to the New Testament: “So also is the resurrection of the dead. It is sown in corruption; it is raised in incorruption: It is sown in dishonor; it is raised in glory; it is sown in weakness; it is raised in power.” (1 Corinthians 15:42–43)

41

Some Rainbow coming from the Fair!
Some Vision of the World Cashmere
I confidently see!
Or else a Peacock’s purple train
Feather by feather – on the plain –
Fritters itself away!

The dreamy Butterflies bestir!
Lethargic pools resume the whirr

Of last year's sundered tune –
From some old Fortress on the Sun
Baronial Bees march – one by one –
In murmuring platoon!

The Robins stand as thick today
As flakes of snow did, yesterday –
On fence, and roof – and twig –
The Orchis binds her feather on
For her old lover – Don the Sun.
Revisiting the Bog.

over –

Without Commander_Countless – still –
The Regiments of Wood and Hill
In bright detachments stand!
Behold! Whose Multitudes are these?
The Children of whose Turbaned seas –
Or what Circassian Land!

Emily.

Dear Sue –
I havnt "paid you an attention" for some time.

Girl.

late 1850s

42

Success is counted sweetest
By those who ne'er succeed.
To comprehend a nectar
Requires sorest need.
Not one of all the purple Host
Who took the flag today
Can tell the definition so Clear
of Victory–
As he defeated – dying –
On whose forbidden Ear
The distant strains of triumph
Burst agonized and Clear.

late 1850s
This was first printed during the Civil War in the *Brooklyn Daily Union*. It is likely that Susan passed the poem along to the editor Reverend Richard Salter Storrs, who was a guest at the Evergreens. In 1878 Helen Hunt Jackson, a writer and close friend of Emily's, included this poem in the collection *A Masque of Poets*, without identifying the poet. Many readers attributed it to Ralph Waldo Emerson.

43

Ambition cannot find him!
Affection does'nt know
How many leagues of Nowhere

Lie between them now!
Yesterday, undistinguished!
Eminent Today
For our mutual honor,
Immortality!

late 1850s

A small cut in the paper suggests that Emily attached a ribbon or a flower to this poem.

44

Low at my problem bending –
Another problem comes –
Larger than mine – Serener –
Involving statelier sums –
I check my busy pencil,
My Ciphers steal away '
Wherefore my baffled fingers
Thine Extremity?

late 1850s

45

A throe upon the features –
A hurry in the breath –
An extacy of parting
Denominated Death.
An anguish at the mention

Which when to patience grown,
I've known permission given
To rejoin it's own.

late 1850s
Dickinson repeatedly attempted to capture the moment of death in her poems.

46

Who never lost, is
unprepared
A Coronet – to find.
Who never thirsted,
Flagons, and Cooling Tamarind.
Who never climbed the
weary league –
Can such a foot Explore
The purple Territories
On Pizarro's shore?
How many legions overcome –
The Emperor will say?
How many Colors taken
over–

new page

On Revolution Day?
How many Bullets bearest?
Hast thou the Royal Scar!
Angels! Mark "Promoted"

On this soldier's brow!

Emily–

late 1850s

During the late 1850s, Dickinson's integration of letter writing and poetry begins to affect the form of her poems. Many that she sends to Susan are in her rough-draft handwriting, and presented in a single stanza, suggesting that the poems are works-in-progress.

47

She died at play '
Gambolled away
Her lease of spotted hours,
Then sank as gaily as a Turk
Upon a Couch of flowers.

Her ghost strolled softly o'er the hill
Yesterday, and today.
Her vestments as the silver fleece –
Her countenance, as spray,

Emily '

late 1850s

48

Exultation is the going
Of an inland soul to sea,
Past the houses – past the headlands –
Into deep Eternity ,

Bred as we, among the mountains,
Can the sailor understand
The divine intoxication
Of the first league out from land?

late 1850s

49

Our lives are Swiss,
So still – so cool –
Till some odd afternoon
The Alps neglect their curtains
And we look further on.
Italy stands the other side.
While like a guard between –
The solemn Alps.
The siren Alps
Forever intervene.

late 1850s

In her literary play, Emily often appears to allude to Elizabeth Barrett Browning, "that Foreign Lady" whom she associated with Italy and who "enchanted" her so.

50

Her breast is fit for pearls,
But I was not a "Diver" –
Her brow is fit for thrones
But I have not a crest,
Her heart is fit for <u>home</u> –
I – a Sparrow – build there
Sweet of twigs and twine
My perennial nest.

Emily–

1850s

This poem, and the following one, are written in pencil, in Emily's rough-draft hand. "Sue" was carefully erased from the verso. In Mabel Loomis Todd's 1894 edition of *Letters*, she placed this poem in the Samuel Bowles correspondence, suggesting that Emily had sent "Her breast is fit for pearls" to Samuel in honor of his wife, Mary. Loomis Todd may well have been attempting to make Emily's correspondence with Mary Bowles look more extensive, since Dickinson wrote the Bowleses few joint letters. By falsely attributing the poem, Loomis Todd accomplished two objectives: she disguised a love poem to Susan, and she made Emily's correspondence to Bowles (with whom she is said to have been in love) appear more inclusive of his wife.

51

As Watchers hang upon the East,
As Beggars revel at a feast

By savory Fancy spread –
As brooks in deserts babble sweet
On ear too far for the delight,
Heaven beguiles the tired.
As that same watcher, when the East
Opens the lid of Amethyst
And lets the morning go –
That Beggar, when an honored Guest,
Those thirsty lips to flagons pressed,
Heaven to us, if true.

Emilie –

late 1850s

52

The sun kept stooping – stooping – low –
The Hills to meet him – rose –
On his part – what Transaction!
On their part – what repose!

Deeper and deeper grew the stain
Upon the window pane –
Thicker and thicker stood the feet
Until the Tyrian

Was crowded dense with Armies –
So gay – so Brigadier –
That I felt martial stirrings
Who once the Cockade wore –

Charged – from my Chimney Corner –
But nobody was there!

Emily–

late 1850s

53

Except to Heaven – she is nought.
Except for Angels – lone.
Except to some wide-wandering Bee –
A flower superfluous – blown.

Except for winds – provincial –
Except for Butterflies
Unnoticed as a single dew
That on the Acre lies –

The smallest Housewife in the grass –
Yet take her from the lawn
And somebody has lost the face
That made Existence – Home –

Emily.

early 1860s

54

The Bumble of a Bee –
A Witchcraft, yieldeth me.
If any ask me "Why – "
 'Twere easier to die
 Than tell!

The Red upon the Hill
Taketh away my will –
If Anybody sneer,
 Take care, for God is near –
 That's All!

The Breaking of the Day –
Addeth to my Degree –
If any ask me "how" –
Artist who drew me so –
Must tell!

Emily '

early 1860s

55

Just lost, when I was saved!
Just heard the world go by!
Just girt me for the onset with eternity,
When breath drew back,

And on the other side
I heard recede the disappointed tide!

Therefore, as one returned, I feel,
Odd secrets of "the Line" to tell!
Some sailor skirting novel shores –
Some pale "reporter" from the awful doors
Before the Seal!

Next time to stay!
Next time the things to see
By ear unheard,
Unscrutinized by eye –
Next time to tarry,
While the ages steal –
Tramp the slow centuries,
And the cycles wheel!

early 1860s
First published in the *Independent* on March 12, 1891, and titled "Called Back," this is among the poems that Susan submitted for publication shortly after Emily's death.

56

Will Susan – please lend
Emily – "Life in the Iron Mills" –
and accept Blossom

from Emily –

spring 1861
Here, Emily requests Susan's copy of the April 1861 issue of the Atlantic Monthly, which contained Rebecca Harding Davis's *Life in the Iron Mills*.

57

Is it true, dear Sue?
Are there two?
I should'nt like to come
For fear of joggling Him!
If you could shut him up
In a Coffee Cup,
Or tie him to a pin
Till I got in –
Or make him fast
To "Toby's" fist
Hist! Whist! I'd come!

Emily –

about June 19, 1861
This letter-poem was written after the birth of Susan's first child, Edward (Ned). In earlier published versions, "If you could shut him up" is mistranscribed as "If I could shut him up . . . ," inaccurately suggesting that Emily was jealous of the newborn. "Toby" is the cat, and "Coffee Cup" may playfully refer to Susan's love of coffee.

58

from Susan

Emily –
All's well–

Never mind Emily – to-morrow
will do just as well – Don't bother –
I'm "not an hard master" – You
know Maggie is out, and I don't like
to leave my fold – There were two or
three little things I wanted to talk
with you about without witnesses
but to-morrow will do just as
well – Has girl read Republican?
It takes as long to start our
Fleet as the Burnside.

March 1862

On March 1, 1862, the *Springfield Republican* printed an early version of "Safe in their Alabaster Chambers" entitled "The Sleeping." It is likely that the poem printed in the *Republican* beneath "The Sleeping," entitled "The Shadow of Thy Wing," was written by Susan. Both poems were published anonymously. In one of the few surviving letters from Susan to Emily, Susan excitedly inscribes the greeting, "All's well" in one quarter of the fold, and then compares their mutual enterprise—making their poetry known to the public—to the Civil War general Burnside's siege and the capture of Roanoke Island in February 1862.

59

The Sleeping.
Safe in their alabaster chambers,
Untouched by morning,
 And untouched by noon,
Sleep the meek members of the Resurrection,
 Rafter of satin, and roof of stone.

Light laughs the breeze
In her castle above them,
 Babbles the bee in a stolid ear,
Pipe the sweet birds in ignorant cadences:
 Ah! What sagacity perished here!
Pelham Hill, June, 1861.

March 1, 1862
This is Emily's poem that Susan refers to reading in the *Springfield Republican.*

60

Safe in their Alabaster Chambers,
Untouched by Morning –
And untouched by Noon –
Lie the meek members of
the Resurrection –
Rafter of Satin – and Roof of
Stone –

Grand go the Years – in the
Crescent – above them –
Worlds scoop their Arcs –
And Firmaments – row –
Diadems – drop – and Doges –
Surrender –
Soundless as dots – on a
Disc of Snow –

Perhaps this verse would
please you better – Sue –

Emily '

about 1861
Emily sends Susan another version of the poem, and appends a note showing that Susan is familiar with the poem and does not like the second verse.

61

from Susan

I am not suited
dear Emily with the second
verse – It is remarkable as the
chain lightening that blinds us
hot nights in the Southern sky
but it does not go with the
ghostly shimmer of the first verse
as well as the other one – It just

occurs to me that the first verse
is complete in itself it needs
no other, and can't be coupled –
Strange things always go alone – as
there is only one Gabriel and one
Sun – You never made a peer
for that verse, and I guess you[r]
kingdom does'nt hold one – I
always go to the fire and get warm
after thinking of it, but I never
can again – The flowers are sweet
and bright and look as if they
would kiss one – ah, they expect
a humming-bird – Thanks for
them of course – and not thanks
only recognition either – Did it
ever occur to you that is all there
is here after all – "Lord that I
may receive my sight"_
Susan is tired making bibs for
her bird her ring-dove – he will
paint my cheeks when I am old
to pay me–

Sue –

about 1861
This rare sample of a correspondence, marked "Pony Express," from Susan to Emily may have been preserved because it was sent back to Susan with another draft of the poem, and then kept by Susan's daughter Martha. Susan refers to a second stanza of "Safe in their Alabaster Chambers," which may be the one printed in the

Republican, or another version that Emily bound into an early fascicle. A decade later, Thomas Higginson's paraphrase of Emily's definition of poetry echoes Susan's note: "If I read a book [and] it makes my whole body so cold no fire ever can warm me I know that is poetry."

62

Is this, frostier?

Springs – shake the Sills –
But – the Echoes – stiffen –
Hoar – is the Window – and
numb – the Door –
Tribes of Eclipse – in Tents
of Marble –
Staples of Ages – have
buckled – there –

Dear Sue –
Your praise is good –
to me – because I know
it knows – and suppose –
it means –
Could I make you and
Austin – proud – sometime – a
great way off – 'twould give
me taller feet –
Here is a crumb – for the
"Ring dove"– and a spray '
for his Nest, a little while

ago – just – "Sue"–

Emily'

about 1861
Susan's daughter, Martha Dickinson Bianchi, attached a note to the folder that contained this poem: "In reply to Mamma's criticism of one stanza – " After Emily's death, when Susan was compiling her book of Emily's writings, she jotted down Emily's words of thanks from memory, "'If some day far off I / should make you glad I / should have taller feet' Emily."

63

from Susan

Private
I have intended to
write you Emily to-day but the
quiet has not been mine I send
you this, lest I should seem to
have turned away from a kiss –
If you have suffered this past
summer I am sorry I
Emily bear a sorrow that I
never uncover – – If a nightingale
sings with her breast against
a thorn, why not we [!]
When I can, I shall write —

Sue–

early 1860s
This message probably accompanied a gift of some sort—"I send you this." Martha Dickinson Bianchi described her mother and her aunt watching and waiting for a few private moments in a day when they could talk, deliver letters face-to-face, and exchange favored reading materials. These exchanges usually took place in the "Northwest Passage," the back hallway of the Homestead.

64

The face I carry with
me – last –
When I go out of Time –
To take my Rank – by – in
the West –
That face – will just be thine –

I'll hand it to the Angel –
That – Sir – was my Degree –
In Kingdoms – you have heard
the Raised –
Refer to – possibly .

He'll take it – scan it – step
aside –
Return – with such a Crown
As Gabriel – never capered at –
And beg me put it on –

And then – he'll tum me round

and round –
To an admiring sky –
As One that bore her Master's name –
Sufficient Royalty!

1860s

This poem, associated with the fascicles, has the address "Sue" erased from the verso.

65

Could I – then –
shut the door –
Lest my beseeching
face – at last –
Rejected – be – of Her?

early 1860s

66

When Etna
basks and purrs
Naples is more
afraid
Than when she
shows her Garnet Tooth –
Security is loud –

1862 or later
Emily refers to Mount Etna in eastern Sicily, the highest active volcano in Europe.

67

Savior! I've no one else
to tell –
And so I trouble <u>thee</u>.
I am the one forgot
thee so –
Dost thou remember
me?
Nor, for myself, I
came so far –
That were the little
load –
I brought thee the
imperial Heart
I had not strength
to hold –
The Heart I carried
in my own –
Till mine too heavy
grew–
Yet – strangest – <u>heavier</u>
since it went –
Is it too large for
<u>you</u>?

early 1860s

68

Blazing in Gold – and
Quenching – in Purple!
Leaping – like Leopards – [in] to
the Sky –
Then – at the feet of the
old Horizon –
Laying it's spotted face – to die!

Stooping as low as the
kitchen window –
Touching the Roof –
And tinting the Barn –
Kissing it's Bonnet to
the Meadow–
And the Juggler of
Day – is gone!

early 1860s

Susan's copy of this poem was "lost," though it is likely that she sent it to the editors of the *Republican* or *Drum Beat* where it was printed in 1864. Emily's cousin Perez Cowan, a student at Amherst College from 1862 to 1866, transcribed this poem from memory in an 1891 letter, noting that Susan had given it to him when he was in Amherst. This indicates that Susan was transcribing Emily's poems and giving them as gifts from an early date.

69

Dear Sue –
I'm thinking
on that other morn –
When Cerements – let
go –
And Creatures – clad
in Victory –
Go up – by two – and
two!

Emily.

early 1860s

70

Dear Sue.
Your – Riches –
taught me – poverty!
Myself, a "Millionaire"
In little – wealths – as
Girls can boast –
Till broad as "Buenos Ayre" –
You drifted your Dominions –
A Different – Peru –
And I esteemed – all –
poverty–
For Life's Estate – with you!

Of "Mines" – I little know –
my self–
But just the names – of Gems –
The Colors – of the
Commonest–
And scarce of Diadems –
So much – that did
I meet the Queen –
Her glory – I should know –
But this – must be a
different Wealth –
To miss it – beggars – so!

I'm sure 'tis "India" – all
day–
To those who look on
you –
Without a stint – without
a blame –
Might I – but be the Jew!
I know it is "Golconda" –
Beyond my power to
dream –
To have a smile – for
mine – each day –
How better – than a Gem!

At least – it solaces –
to know–
That there exists – a Gold –

Altho' I prove it, just
in time –
Its' distance – to behold!
Its' far – far – Treasure – to
surmise –
And estimate – the Pearl –
That slipped – my simple fingers –
thro'
While yet – a Girl –
at School!

Dear Sue –
You see I remember –
Emily.

early 1860s

71

I reason –
Earth is short –
And Anguish – absolute –
And many – hurt –
But, what of that?
I reason –
We should
die –
The best – Vitality –
Could not excel Decay –
But – What of that?
I reason –

That in "Heaven" –
Somehow – it will be even –
Some new Equation – given –
But – what of that!

early 1860s

As Emily increasingly copies poems into manuscript books, she includes more poems in letters, and sends poems as letters, using the arrangement of lines on the page to reflect the content of her messages and observations.

72

Sue –
Give little Anguish –
Lives will fret –
Give Avalanches –
And they'll slant –
Straighten – look cautious
for their Breath –
But make no syllable –
like Death –
Who only shows his
Marble Disc –
Sublimer sort – than
Speech –
Emily –

early 1860s

73

I send two Sunsets –
Day and I – in com –
petition – ran –
I finished Two, and
several Stars
While He – was making
One –
His own is ampler –
but as I
Was saying to a friend –
Mine – is the more
Convenient
To Carry in the Hand ,

Emily –

1860s

74

For Largest Woman's
Heart I knew –
'Tis little I can do –
And yet the Largest
Woman's Heart
Could hold an Arrow – too –
And so, instructed by
my own,

I tenderer, turn me to.

Emily.

early 1860s

75

It sifts from Leaden
Sieves –
It powders all the Wood.
It fills with Alabaster
Wool
The Wrinkles of the Road –

It makes an Even
Face
Of Mountain, and of
Plain –
Unbroken Forehead
from the East
Unto the East again –

It reaches to the Fence –
It wraps it Rail by Rail
Till it is lost in Fleeces –
It deals Celestial Vail

To Stump, and Stack –
and Stem –
A Summer's Empty Room –

Acres of Joints, where
Harvests were,
Recordless, but for them –

It Ruffles Wrists
of Posts
As Ankles of a
Queen –
Then stills it's Artisans –
like Ghosts –
Denying they have been –

Emily –

early 1860s

76

Her – "last Poems" –
Poets ended –
Silver perished with her
Tongue –
Not on Record bubbled
Other –
Flute, or Woman, so
divine –
Not unto its' Summer –
Morning
Robin – uttered – half – the
tune –
Gushed too free for the

Adoring –
From the Anglo-Florentine –
Late – the Praise –
'Tis dull – conferring
On a Head too high
to crown –
Diadem – or Ducal Showing –
Be its' Grave – sufficient
Sign –
Yet, if We – No Poet's
Kinsman –
Suffocate – with easy Wo –
What and if Ourself
a Bridegroom –
Put Her down – in Italy?

Emily –

early 1860s
Emily sends this letter-poem to Susan after the death of Elizabeth Barrett Browning, whom she and Susan deeply admired.

77

Defeat – whets Victory –
they say –
The Reefs in Old
Gethsemane –
Endear the Coast –
beyond !
'Tis Beggars – Banquets –

can define –
'Tis Parching – vitalizes
Wine –
Faith bleats – to
understand !

Emily '

early 1860s

78

Nature – sometimes
sears a Sapling –
Sometimes – scalps
a Tree –
Her Green People
recollect it –
When they do not
die –
Fainter Leaves – to
further Seasons
Dumbly testify –
We – who have
the Souls
Die oftener – not
so vitally –

Emily.

early 1860s

79

Distance – is not
the Realm of Fox
Nor by Relay of
Bird
Abated – Distance is
Until thyself, Beloved

Emily '

early 1860s
Susan remembered this letter-poem when making notes for her book of Emily's writings. On a sheet of paper are: "'A spring of intellectuality [?]' – Pater" and "'Distance! Tis till thyself, Beloved' – E." It is likely that she was writing down her favorite first lines or aphorisms.

80

He fumbles at your Soul
As Players at the Keys
Before they drop full
Music on –
He stuns you by degrees –
Prepares your brittle Nature
For the Etherial Blow
By fainter Hammers –
further heard –
Then nearer – Then so slow
Your Breath has time to

straighten –
Your Brain – to bubble Cool –
Deals – One – imperial –
Thunder bolt –
That scalps your
naked Soul –

When Winds take Forests
in their Paws –
The Universe – is still –

Emily.

early 1860s

81

There came a Day at Summer's full,
Entirely for me –
I thought that such was for the Saints,
Where Resurrections – be –

The Sun, as common, went abroad,
The flowers, accustomed, blew,
As if no sail the solstice passed
That maketh all things new –

The time was scarce profaned, by speech –
The symbol of a word
Was needless, as at Sacrament,
The Wardrobe – of our Lord –

Each was to
Each – the Sealed
Church,
Permitted to commune
this – time –
Lest we too awkward
show
At Supper of "the Lamb"

The Hours slid past – as Hours will,
Clutched tight, by greedy hands –
So faces on two Decks, look back,
Bound to opposing lands –

And so when all the time had leaked,
Without external sound
Each bound the Other's Crucifix –
We gave no other Bond –

Sufficient troth, that we should rise –
Deposed – at length, the Grave –
To that new Marriage,
Justified – through Calvaries of Love –

1862

This poem was later titled "Renunciation" by Susan. Omitting the fourth stanza, she submitted it to *Scribner's Magazine* after Emily's death, and the poem was published in August 1890. After the publication Emily's sister, Lavinia, who had a fascicle copy of the poem, objected to Susan's presumption. However, Susan maintained that she had the right to publish any poems that Emily had sent to her.

This poem was also among the work that Emily sent to Thomas Higginson in 1862.

82

Essential Oils are
wrung –
The Attar from the
Rose
Is not expressed
by Suns – alone –
It is the gift of
Screws –
The General Rose
decay –
While this – in
Lady's Drawer
Make Summer, when
the Lady lie
In Spiceless Sepulchre.

Emily –

early 1860s

83

I showed her Hights
she never saw –
"Would'st climb," I said?
She said – "Not so" –

"With me –" I said –
With me?
I showed her Secrets –
Morning's Nest –
The Rope the Nights
were put across –
And now – "Would'st
have me for a Guest"?
She could not find her Yes –

And then, I brake
My life – And Lo,
A Light, for her,
did solemn glow,
The larger, as her
face withdrew –
And could she, further,
"No"?

Emily –

early 1860s
Emily changes the pronouns in another version of this poem, which she included in the fascicles: "He showed me Hights I / never saw – ."

84

The difference between
Despair
And Fear, is like

the One
Between the instant
of a Wreck
And when the
Wreck has been.
The Mind is
smooth –
No Motion – Contented
as the Eye
Upon the Forehead
of a Bust –
That knows it
cannot see.

Emily '

1860s

85

Like Some Old fashioned
Miracle
When Summertime is done –
Seems Summer's Recollec –
tion
And the Affairs of June
As infinite Tradition
As Cinderella's Bays –
Or little John – of
Lincoln Green –
Or Blue Beard's

Galleries –

Her Bees have a fictitious Hum –
Her Blossoms, like
a Dream –
Elate us – till we
Almost weep –
So plausible – they seem –

Her Memories like
Strains – Review –
When Orchestra is
dumb –
The Violin in Baize
replaced –
And Ear – and Heaven –
numb –

Emily –

early to mid-1860s

86

The Soul unto itself
Is an imperial friend –
Or the most agonizing Spy
An Enemy – could send –
Secure against it's own –
No treason it can fear –
Itself – it's Sovereign – of itself

The Soul should stand in awe –

Emily –

mid-1860s
The address, "Sue," was erased from the verso of this letter-poem.

87

The Soul's Superior
instants
Occur to Her – alone –
When friend – and
Earth's occasion
Have infinite withdrawn –

Or She – Herself – as
cended
To too remote a Hight
For lower Recognition
Than Her Omnipotent –

This Mortal Abolition
Is seldom – but as fair
As Apparition – subject
To Autocratic Air –

Eternity's disclosure
To favorites – a few –
Of the Colossal
  Substance

Of Immortality

Emily.

mid-1860s

88

Ah' Teneriffe!
Retreating Mountain!
Purples of Ages – pause
for you.

Sunset – reviews her Sapphire
Regiment –
Day – drops you her Red
Adieu!

Still – Clad in your Mail
of ices –
Thigh of Granite – and
thew – of Steel –
Heedless – alike – of pomp –
or parting

Ah' Teneriffe!
I'm kneeling – still –

Emily '

mid-1860s

"Teneriffe" is the volcanic island in the Canary Islands, and most likely refers to the poetic and painterly portrayals of Elizabeth Barrett Browning, John Ruskin, and Byron.

89

"Nature" is what
we See –
The Hill – the
Afternoon –
Squirrel – Eclipse –
the Bumble bee –
Nay – Nature is
Heaven –
Nature is what
we hear –
The Bobolink – the Sea –
Thunder – the
Cricket –
Nay – Nature is
Harmony –
Nature is what
we know –
Yet have no art
to say –
So impotent Our
Wisdom is
To her Simplicity

Emily

mid-1860s

90

No Romance sold
unto
Could so enthrall
a Man
As the perusal of
His Individual One –
'Tis Fiction's – to dilute
to Plausibility
<u>Our</u> Novel – When 'tis
small enough
To Credit – 'Tis'nt true!

Emily –

mid-1860s

91

One need not be
a Chamber – to be
Haunted –
One need not
be a House –
The Brain has
Corridors – surpassing
Material Place –

Far safer, of a
Midnight Meeting
External Ghost
Than its' interior
Confronting –
That Cooler Host –

Far safer, through
an Abbey gallop,
The Stones a'chase –
Than Unarmed,
One's a'self encounter –
In lonesome Place –
Ourself behind
Ourself, Concealed –
Should startle most –
Assassin hid in
Our Apartment
Be Horror's least

The Body – borrows
a Revolver –
He bolts the Door –
O'erlooking a
Superior Spectre –
Or More –

Emily –

mid-1860s

92

Excuse me – Dollie –

The Love a Child can
show – below –
Is but a Filament – I
know –
Of that Diviner – Thing –
That faints upon the face
of Noon –
And smites the Tinder
in the Sun –
And hinders – Gabriel's – Wing!

'Tis This – in Music –
hints – and sways –
And far abroad – on
Summer Days –
Distils – uncertain – pain –
'Tis This – afflicts us
in the East –
And tints the Transit
in the West –
With Harrowing – Iodine!

'Tis This – invites – appalls –
endows –
Flits – glimmers – proves –
dissolves –
Returns – suggests – convicts –
enchants –

Then – flings in Paradise!

Emily –

mid-1860s
Emily refers to Susan using her nickname, "Dollie."

93

The Overtakelessness
of Those
Who have accom –
plished Death –
Majestic is to Me
beyond
The Majesties of
Earth –
The Soul her
"Not at Home"
Inscribes upon the
Flesh,
And takes a fine
aerial gait
Beyond the Writ
of Touch –

Emily –

mid-1860s
This poem, a previously unpublished version, is addressed to "Dollie" on the verso.

94

Least Bee that
Brew –
A Honey's worth
The Summer multiply –
Content Her smallest
fraction help

mid-1860s

This poem was handled extensively by Susan and her children. There is a game on the verso, which the children played by drawing sets of boxes in rows and entering letters that spelled their names. One of the names is "Matty Dickinson," Susan's second child, Martha, born in 1866. These marks suggest that some years after Susan received this poem it was being used by her children. Pinholes in the manuscript suggest that this occurred as Susan was working on her scrapbooks.

95

To be alive, is
power –
Existence – in itself –
Without a further
function –
Omnipotence – Enough –
To be alive and
Will –

'Tis able as a God –
The Further of
Ourselves, be What –
Such being Fin
itude?
Emily '

1860s

96

Nor myself to Him,
by accent
Forfeit probity.
Weariness of Him, were
quainter
Than Monotony
Knew a particle, of
Space's
Vast society –
Neither if He visit other –
Do He dwell or nay
Know I – just instinct
esteem Him
Immortality – Emily.

mid-1860s

These lines constitute the last two and a half stanzas of the fascicle version of Emily's poem, "Conscious am I in my Chamber."

97

Content of fading
is enough for me
Fade I unto Divinity –
And Dying – Lifetime – ample
as the eye
Her least attention raise
on Me.

mid-1860s

98

Ungained – it may be
By a Life's low Venture –
But then
Eternity enable the
endeavoring
Again –
    Springfield

mid-1860s

It is possible that Emily's signature, "Springfield," may refer to their mutual friend Samuel Bowles, editor of the *Springfield Republican*, or it may refer to the newspaper itself and the publication of her poems.

99

Soil of Flint, if
Steady tilled –
Will refund the Hand –
Seed of Palm, by
Lybian Sun
Fructified in Sand –

Emily –

mid-1860s

100

Two – were immortal –
twice –
The privilege of few –
Eternity – obtained – in
Time –
Reversed – Divinity –
That Our ignoble
Eyes
The Quality – perceive
Of Paradise Superlative –
Thro' Their – Comparative.

mid-1860s

101

I could not drink
it, Sue,
Till you had tasted
first –
Though cooler than
the Water – was
The Thoughtfulness of
Thirst,

Emily.

mid-1860s

102

Sweet Sue,
There is
no first, or last,
in Forever –
It is Centre, there,
all the time –
To believe – is enough,
and the right of
supposing –
Take back that
"Bee" and "Buttercup" –
I have no Field
for them, though

for the Woman
whom I prefer,
Here is Festival –
When my Hands
are Cut, Her
fingers will be
found inside –
Our beautiful Neigh
bor "moved" in May –
It leaves an
Unimportance.
Take the Key to
the Lily, now, and
I will lock the Rose –

1864

In February 1864, Emily went to Boston to consult an ophthalmologist. In late April, she returned to Boston for eye treatments and stayed until November. During these seven months she lived with her Norcross cousins, ages twentytwo and sixteen, in a boarding house in Cambridgeport. Loo and Fannie had been orphaned by the death of their father in 1863, and their mother, Mrs. Dickinson's sister Lavinia, in 1861. The "beautiful Neigh- / bor" refers to Nathaniel Hawthorne who died on May 19, 1864. Emily suggests that his "moving" is unimportant because his spirit thrives in his literary productions. The "Lily" and the "Rose" have special significance in the spiritual, erotic exchange between Emily and Susan. These, not the daisy, are now the signature flowers in the correspondence, and they measure a shift in dynamics, a maturation of the bond between the two women. Emily regularly identifies or otherwise connects the lily (faith) and the rose (blood, beauty, and love) with Susan.

103

at Centre of
the Sea –
I am glad Mrs.
Gertrude lived –
I believed she
would – Those that
are worthy of Life
are of Miracle,
for Life is Miracle,
And Death, as
harmless as a Bee –
except to those
who run_
It would be best to
see you – it would
be good to see the
Grass, and hear the
Wind blow the wide
way in the Orchard –
Are the Apples
ripe – Have the
Wild Geese crossed –
Did you save the
seed to the
Pond Lily?
Love for Mat, and
John, and the
Foreigner – And
kiss little Ned

in the seam in
the neck, entirely
for Me –
The Doctor is
very kind –
I find no Enemy –
Till the Four o'Clocks
strike Five, Loo
will last, she says.
Do not cease, Sister.
Should I turn in
my long night, I should
murmur "Sue"?

Emily.

September 1864
References to the "Doctor" and "Loo" suggest that this is another letter-poem that Emily sends to Susan while she is in the Boston area undergoing medical treatments for her eye condition. "Mrs. Gertrude" refers to Susan's friend Gertrude Vanderbilt, who was wounded by a gunshot when she came to the rescue of her maid, who was being attacked by a former suitor. "Mat" is Susan's sister Martha, and "John" is her brother-in-law.

104

The Soul selects
her own Society
Then shuts the
Door

To her divine
Majority
Present no more –

on verso
Love reckons by
itself – alone –
"As large as I" –
relate the Sun
To One who never
felt it blaze –
Itself is all the
like it has –

mid-1860s
The handwriting used for both poems is from the mid-1860s; however, one is in ink and one in pencil, suggesting that they were probably written at different times. The numerous folds of this manuscript indicate that the sheet was passed back and forth between Susan and Emily.

105

So set its' Sun in
Thee
What Day be dark
to me –
What Distance, far,
So I the Ships
may see
That touch, how

seldomly,
Thy Shore?

Emily.

mid-1860s

106

Her Grace is all
she has,
And that, so
least displays,
One Art, to
recognize, must be,
Another Art, to
praise –

Emily '

mid-1860s

107

We pass, and
she abides.
We conjugate
Her Skill.
While She – creates

and federates
Without a syllable,

mid-1860s

108

The Luxury to
apprehend
The Luxury 'twould
be
To look at Thee
a single time
An Epicure of Me
In whatsoever
Presence makes
Till for a further
food
I scarcely recollect
to starve
  So first am I
supplied –
The Luxury to
meditate
The Luxury it was
To banquet on
thy Countenance
A Sumptuousness
bestows
On plainer Days,

whose Table, far
As Certainty – can see –
Is laden with a
single Crumb –
The Consciousness –
of Thee.

Emily.

mid-1860s

109

Given in Marriage
unto Thee
Oh thou Celestial
Host –
Bride of the
Father and the
Son,
Bride of the
Holy Ghost.

Emily –

mid-1860s

110

Dear Sue –
Unable are the
Loved – to die –
For Love is immortality –
Nay – it is Deity –

Emily.

March 1865
This letter-poem was sent to Susan after the death of her sister, Harriet Cutler, on March 16, 1865. This is one of the many instances in which Emily's poems are bestowed as spiritual gifts for Susan's solace.

111

Sister,
We both are
Women, and there
is a Will of God –
Could the Dying
confide Death,
there would be no
Dead – Wedlock
is shyer than Death.
Thank you for
Tenderness –
I find it is the only

food that the Will
takes, nor that
from general fingers.
I am glad you go –
It does not remove
you. I seek you
first in Amherst,
then turn my
thoughts without
a Whip – so well
they follow you –
An Hour is a Sea
Between a few, and me –
With them would Harbor
be –

early December 1865
It is likely that Susan is visiting her sister Martha Smith in Geneva, New York, when Emily writes this letter-poem. Martha's two-year-old daughter, named Susan, died on November 2. This may also refer to the December 2 death of Emily and Susan's friend Susan Phelps.

112

Ample make this Bed.
Make this Bed
with Awe –
In it, wait till
Judgment Break
Excellent, and Fair –

Be it's Mattress
straight –
Be it's Pillow
round-
Let no Sunrise'
Yellow noise
Interrupt this
Ground –

mid-1860s

113

You must let me
go first, Sue,
because
I live in the Sea
always and know
the Road –
I would have drowned
twice to save
you sinking, dear,
If I could only
have covered your
Eyes so you would'nt
have seen the Water –

mid-1860s
On a slip of paper attached to this letter-poem is a note by Martha Dickinson Bianchi: "One of the first scraps sent over – ." However, Emily had been writing to Susan for approximately

fifteen years. It is possible that Susan's daughter misdated the note to protect her mother and aunt from public scrutiny of their intimate correspondence.

114

The Missing All –
prevented Me
From missing minor
Things '
If nothing larger
than a World's
Departure from a
Hinge,
Or Sun's extinction –
be observed –
'Twas not so large
that I
Could lift my Forehead
from my work
For Curiosity –

Emily.

mid-1860s

115

Gratitude – is not
the mention

Of a Tenderness,
But its' still
appreciation
Out of Plumb of
Speech.

Emily '

mid-1860s

116

The Dust behind
I strove to join
Unto the Disk
before –
But Sequence
ravelled out of
Sound
Like Balls upon
a Floor –

mid-1860s

117

Except the smaller
size
No Lives are Round –
These – hurry to a Sphere –

And show – and end –

The Larger – slower grow –
And later hang –
The Summers of Hesperides
Are long –

Emily –

mid-1860s
In Greek mythology, "Hesperides" refers to the Daughters of the West, who, with the aid of a dragon, watch over the Garden of the Golden Apples at the western end of the earth. Pencil scratches cover the front and back of this letter-poem. Drawings of a little cow or dog are probably by Susan's son Ned, who was five or six at the time.

118

Perception of an
Object costs
Precise the Objects'
loss –
Perception in itself
a Gain
Replying to its'
Price –
The Object Absolute –
is nought –
Perception sets it
fair
And then upbraids

a Perfectness
That situates
so far.

Emily –

mid-1860s

119

The Definition of
Beauty, is
That Definition
is none –
Of Heaven, Easing
Analysis,
Since Heaven
and He
Are One.

Emily –

mid-1860s

Emily changes "Beauty" to "Melody" and uses the lines "The Definition of Melody – is – / That Definition is none –" in the poem, "By my Window have / I for Scenery." The repetition of lines throughout this literary liaison shows how central revision or re-seeing is to Emily's creative process as she contemplates beauty, despair, love, neighborly affiliations, madness, desire—indeed, as she ponders all of life's experiences.

SECTION THREE

THE INCIDENTS OF LOVE

Late Middle Writings, mid-1860s to mid-1870s

From the mid-1860s to the mid-1870s, the collaborative nature of the literary, emotional bond is evident, for Emily's correspondence with Susan continues to include letter-poems, poems, and poems-in-progress. Many of the following missives include allusions to shared literary pleasures coupled with references to Emily and Susan's involvement in family concerns and in the daily business of their households. By the early 1870s, it is often the children and the household servants who carry the messages from Emily in the Homestead to Susan, next door.

The writings of this period call into question the biographical commonplace that Emily did not see Susan for years at a time. In fact, the contact between the two is deeply intimate and sustained. The letter-poems allude to unkempt appearance, shared cups of coffee, and private interludes, which Susan's daughter Martha described as taking place in the back hallway of the Homestead. Not only were the two regularly in each other's company at home, they were occasionally together in public. Flora White, a friend of Martha Dickinson Bianchi, remembered meeting Emily in the spring of 1872 at the Congregational Church, where Susan was a member. She described Susan seating Emily, remarking that Susan's quiet words to her beloved friend "seemed smilingly protective."[1]

During the 1860s and 1870s, the relationship between Emily and Susan deepens, matures, and solidifies. Both Emily and Susan have several correspondents with whom they exchange letters and poems, and discuss books and the details of their daily lives. However, no other correspondence of Emily's approaches that to Susan for its sheer volume, duration, and diversity. Many of the messages to Susan remain informal, inspired by emotion, an observation, a household concern, and the basic need to communicate in the most ordinary way with the object of love, comfort, and intellectual and creative inspiration.

As indicated in the Notes at the end of *Open Me Carefully*, in addition to sending poems to Susan, Emily sends work to Thomas Wentworth Higginson, Samuel Bowles, Elizabeth Holland, Fanny and Loo Norcross, Helen Hunt Jackson, and others. However, we can only assume that a love poem sent to the beloved has a very different impact from a version of the same poem sent to a friend or an editor.

A number of the following documents are written on scrap paper, which indicates the level of comfort and informality between the two women. Susan's "X's" and other notations are usually placed on the verso of a letter-poem or poem, and signal her editorial work as she later compiles her book of Emily's writings. Pinholes can be seen on the paper, suggesting that the messages are conveyed inside clothing or perhaps attached to gifts of bread, cake, fruit, or preserved in one of Susan's scrapbooks. Unlike letters and poems that Emily sends to other recipients, those preserved by Susan are often worn, suggesting Susan's numerous readings and re-readings. On the verso of one of the poems in this section ("The Crickets / sang"), Susan wrote a pair of stanzas of her own.

During the early 1870s, Austin replaces Edward Dickinson as treasurer of Amherst College, and Edward is elected to the General Court of Massachusetts. Susan takes annual autumn vacations with her children to visit her sister Martha and her brother-in-law John Smith in Geneva, New York. Susan also travels to Swampscott, Massachusetts, in the summer of 1873, and Emily writes to her there as the family vacations at the beach. As is evident throughout the correspondence, Emily's love and desire for Susan, and her playfulness with her, continue in the various stages of their lives. In one letter sent to Swampscott, Emily compares her feelings for Susan with Dante's passionate love of Beatrice, Jonathan Swift's love of Stella, and Mirabeau's love of Sophie de Ruffey.

On June 16, 1874, while serving a term in the State Legislature, Emily's father collapses and dies in his room at a Boston hotel. The following year, on the eve of the first anniversary of his death, Emily's mother suffers a debilitating stroke, requiring that Lavinia and Emily take over the household responsibilities for the Homestead as well as nurse their mother. Because no letters or letter-poems to Susan reflect on the death of Emily's father and the illness of her mother, it is likely that Emily and Susan speak face-to-face about these profound events, and that throughout these trying times Susan consoles Emily in person. Two months after Emily's mother falls ill, Susan gives birth to her third child, Gilbert (Gib).

120

Title divine, is mine.
The Wife without
the Sign –
Acute Degree
Conferred on Me –
Empress of Calvary –
Royal, all but the
Crown –
Betrothed, without
the Swoon
God gives us Women –
When You hold
Garnet to Garnet –
Gold – to Gold –
Born – Bridalled –
Shrouded –
In a Day –
Tri Victory –
"My Husband" –
Women say
Stroking the Melody –
Is this the Way –

Emily –

mid-1860s

121

It passes and we
stay.
A quality of loss
Affecting our
Content
As Trade had
suddenly encroached
Upon a Sacrament

Emily.

mid-1860s
Emily uses these lines to end her poem, "A Light exists in Spring." This poem appears to have been sent to Susan as a message as well as for her critical evaluation.

122

The Crickets
sang
And set the
Sun
And Workmen
finished One by
One
Their Seam the
  Day upon –

The low Grass
loaded with the
  Dew
The Twilight
stood, as Strangers
 do
With Hat in
Hand, polite and
new
To stay as if,
or go –

A Vastness, as
a Neighbor, came,
A Wisdom, without
Face, or Name,
A Peace, as
Hemispheres at
Home
And so the
Night became –

Emily '

on verso in pencil, by Susan

 I was all ear
And took in strains that
 might create a seal
Under the lids of death

upside down

Despair is treason
 toward Man
And blasphemy
 to Heaven.

mid-1860s
Emily and Susan found one another's work mutually inspirational.

123

We do not know the time
we lose –
The awful moment is
And takes its' fundamental
place
Among the Certainties –

A firm appearance still
inflates
The card – the chance –
the friend –
The spectre of solidities
 Whose substances are sand –

mid-1860s

124

[The] A Diamond on
[A]
the Hand
To Custom Common
grown
Subsides from its'
significance
The Gem were
best unknown '
Within a Seller's
Shrine
How many sight
and sigh
And cannot, but
for
are mad with fear
That any other buy.
Lest some one else
should
Lest Richer People
buy –

late 1860s

This poem and the next are among the drafts sent to Susan, indicating that the exchange in the creation of "Safe in their Alabaster Chambers" was indeed routine.

125

I fit for them –
I seek the Dark
Till I am thorough
fit.
The labor is a sober
one
With the austerer
sweet ' an – this '
With this sufficient
Sweet

That abstinence of mine
me
produce
A purer food for them,
if I succeed,
If not I had
The transport of
the Aim.

late 1860s

126

Going is less, Sister,
long gone from you,
yet We who take
all with Us, leave

not much behind '
Busy missing you '
I have not tasted
Spring – Should
there be other Aprils,
We will perhaps dine –

Emily '

late 1860s
It is possible that Emily writes this when Susan travels to Stamford, Connecticut, in April 1868 to visit her friends Joseph and Laura Lyman, authors of *The Philosophy of Housekeeping*.

127

Susan's Idolater keeps
a Shrine for Susan.

late 1860s

128

Dear Sue'
Just say one
word,
"Emily has not
grieved me"
Sign your name
to that and

I will wait for
the rest –

late 1860s

The text of this letter-poem continues onto the verso, with the address, "Sue." When the sheet is unfolded, it appears that Susan has signed her name to this agreement.

129

That my
sweet Sister
remind me
to thank her
for herself
is valuablest.

Emily '

late 1860s

130

The murmuring of
Bees, has ceased
But murmuring of
some
Posterior, prophetic,
Has simultaneous come.
The lower metres

of the Year
When Nature's laugh
is done
The Revelations of
the Book
Whose Genesis was June.
Appropriate Creatures
to her Change
The Typic Mother
sends
As Accent fades
to interval
With separating
Friends
Till what we
speculate, has been
And thoughts we
will not show '
More intimate with
us become
Than Persons,
that we know.

Emily.

late 1860s

131

There is another Loneliness
That many die without,

Nor want or friend occasions it,
Or circumstance or lot.

But nature sometimes, sometimes thought
And who so it befall
Is richer than could be divulged;
By mortal numeral.

late 1860s

132

A Mine there is
no Man would own
But must it be
conferred,
Demeaning by
Exclusive Wealth
A Universe beside –

Potosi never to
be spent
But hoarded in
the Mind
What Misers
wring Their
hands Tonight
For Indies in
the Ground!

Emily '

late 1860s
Emily refers to the Bolivian city "Potosi" and the East "Indies," which were associated with great wealth. In December 1868, Samuel Bowles was arrested for libel and jailed for a night, while his friends rallied for him. Two days later, Emily's father Edward wrote a letter to Bowles saying that he would rather have been there that night "than to have owned the mines of Potosi."

133

Exhiliration is the Breeze
That lifts us from
the Ground
And leaves us in
another place
Whose statement is
not found –

Returns us not,
but after time
We soberly descend
A little newer for
the term
Upon Enchanted Ground –

Best Witchcraft is
Geometry
To the Magician's Mind –
His Ordinary Acts

are feats
To thinking of mankind .

late 1860s

The arrangement of these poems, separated with a line, resembles pages in the fascicles where Emily draws lines between poems. Susan does the same in manuscript copies of her own poems. Here Emily sends a sheet with drafts for Susan's evaluation.

134

The things of
which we want
the proof are those
we knew before –

late 1860s

135

Dont do such
things, dear Sue –
The "Arabian
Nights" unfit
the Heart for
its' Arithmetic –

Emily –

late 1860s

136

Too cold is this
To warm with Sun –
Too stiff to bended
be,
To joint this Agate
were a work – feat –
Outstaring Masonry-
Defying – Appalling – Abashing
Beyond machinery –

How went the Agile
Kernel out
Contusion of the Husk
Nor Rip, nor wrinkle
indicate
But just an Asterisk.

late 1860s

137

Rare to the Rare – .
Her sovreign People
Nature knows as
well
And is as fond
of signifying

As if fallible –

Emily –

late 1860s

138

The Frost of
Death was on the
Pane,
"Secure your Flower"
said he.
Like Sailors
fighting with a Leak
We fought
Mortality.

Our passive Flower
we held to Sea –
  To Mountain,
To the Sun –
Yet even on his
Scarlet shelf
To crawl the
Frost begun –

We pried him
back
Ourselves we
wedged

Himself and her
between.
Yet easy as the
narrow Snake
He forked his
way along

Till all her
helpless beauty
bent
And then our
wrath begun –
We hunted him
to his Ravine
We chased him
to his Den –

We hated Death
and hated Life
And nowhere
was, to go –
Than Sea and
continent there
is
A larger – it
is Woe

Emily –

late 1860s
This was among the poems that Susan copied, which suggests that she planned to include it in her book of Emily's writings or that she intended to send it to a friend or an editor for printing.

139

The Duties of the
Wind are few,
To cast the ships
at Sea,
Establish March,
the Floods escort
And usher Liberty.

Emily –

late 1860s
Martha Dickinson Bianchi pasted this poem onto the half-title page of *The Single Hound* when she presented the book to her friend Laura Scull of Langhorne, Pennsylvania. Her inscription reads: "To Laura – In memory of our Immortals – with Martha's love – 1914."

140

To pile like
Thunder to
its' close
Then crumble
grand away

While Everything
created hid
This – would
be Poetry –

Or Love – the
two coeval come –
We both and
neither prove –
Experience either
and consume –
For None see
God and live –

Emily

1866 or later
Susan copied "None see God and live" into one of her journals.

141

A Spider sewed
at Night
Without a Light
Upon an Arc of
White.

If Ruff it was
of Dame
Or Shroud of Gnome
Himself himself

inform '

Of Immortality
His Strategy
Was Physiognomy.

Emily.

late 1860s
"Physiognomy" is the attempt to understand the character and spiritual qualities of an individual through the study of facial features. Martha Dickinson Bianchi made a point of mentioning that during the years when Susan and Emily were in their thirties, "My Mother was blessedly busy in her home," and one could see "Aunt Emily's light across the snow in the Winter gloaming, or burning late when she remained up all night, to protect her plants from chill." For "days and even weeks," the light was a "mute greeting between them supplemented only by their written messages." Emily sent or recited this poem to Loo and Fanny Norcross, and the Norcross sisters then sent the poem to Thomas Higginson.

142

The Face we
choose to miss –
Be it but for
a Day
As absent as
a Hundred
Years,

When it has rode
away '

on verso, in Susan's handwriting

The face we
 choose to miss
Be it but for
  a day
As absent as
A hundred years
When it has
 rode away –

Emily.

late 1860s
In a penciled note, Susan's daughter Martha Dickinson Bianchi wrote: "The other side is Aunt Emily's own original m.s. This side is a copy in my mother's hand – ."

143

Safe Despair
it is that
raves –
Agony is
frugal –
Puts itself
severe away
For its' own

perusal –
Garrisoned no
Soul can be
In the front
of Trouble –
Love is one –
not aggregate –
Nor is Dying
double –

Emily.

1866 or later

144

To take away our
Sue leaves but a
lower World, her
firmamental quality
our more familiar
Sky.
It is not Nature –
dear, but those
that stand for
Nature.
The Bird would be
a soundless thing
without Expositor.
Come Home and
see your Weather.

The Hills are full
of Shawls, and I
am going every
Day to buy myself
a Sash.
Grandma moans for
Neddie, and Austin's
face is soft as
Mist when he
hears his name.
Tell "Dexter" I
miss his little
team.
I humbly try to fill
your place at the
Minister's, so faint
a competition, it
only makes them
smile.
Mattie is stern and
lovely_literary, they
tell me – a graduate
of Mother Goose
and otherwise ambi-
tious.
We have a new
man whose name
is Tim.
Father calls him
"Timothy" and the
Barn sounds like
the Bible.

Vinnie is still on
her "Coast Survey"
and I am so
hurried with Parents
that I run all
Day with my Tongue
abroad, like a
Summer Dog.
Tell Mattie for me
glad little Girl
is safe, and
congratulate minor
little Girl on her
priceless Mama.
Susan's

Emily.

autumn 1869
During the fall of 1869, Susan is visiting her sister Martha in Geneva, New York. Emily refers to her sister Lavinia ("Vinnie"), who is in Boston through the autumn. "Mattie" is Susan's three-year-old daughter, Martha. The "minor / little Girl" refers to Susan's infant niece, Elizabeth Throop Smith. The minister Emily alludes to is probably J.L. Jenkins, pastor of Amherst's Congregational Church.

145

The Props assist the
House
Until the House is

built
And then the Props
withdraw
And adequate, erect,
The House support
itself
And cease to recollect
The Augur and the
Carpenter –
Just such a retrospect
Hath the perfected
Life –
A past of Plank
and Nail
And slowness – then
the Scaffolds drop
Affirming it a Soul.

Emily.

late 1860s

146

I bet with every
Wind that blew
Till Nature
in chagrin
  Employed a
Fact to visit
me

And scuttle
my Balloon –

late 1860s to 1870s

147

My Sue –
Loo and
Fanny will come
tonight, but need
that make a
difference?
Space is as the
Presence –

A narrow Fellow
in the Grass
Occasionally rides –
You may have
met him?
Did you not
His notice instant is –

The Grass divides
as with a Comb –
A Spotted Shaft
is seen,
And then it closes
at your Feet

And opens
further on_

He likes a
Boggy Acre_
A Floor too
cool for Corn_
But when a
Boy and Barefoot
I more than
once at Noon

Have passed
I thought a
Whip Lash
Unbraiding in the
Sun
When stooping
to secure it
It wrinkled
and was gone_

Several of
Nature's People
I know and they
know me
I feel for
them a transport
Of Cordiality

But never met
this Fellow

Attended or
alone
Without a
tighter Breathing
And Zero at
the Bone.

Emily.

about 1870

Loo and Fanny, Emily's cousins, are arriving in Amherst for a visit. The poem that Emily includes here was printed in the *Springfield Daily Republican* on February 14, 1866. It is possible that Emily now sends Susan the poem to replace the copy that Susan sent to the newspaper. From this letter-poem, it is clear that the two women are seeing each other face-to-face. In a letter postmarked March 17, 1866, Emily worried that Higginson would come across the poem in the *Republican* and think that she had been duplicitous concerning her intentions not "to print."

148

Who were
"the Father and
the Son"
[I] We pondered
when a Child –
And what had
they to do with
[me] us
And when [in]
[Terror] portentous told

With inference [alarming] appalling
By [Distance] Childhood fortified
[Through Accents
terrible as Death
To one that
never died]
[I] We thought, at
least they are
no worse
Than they have
been described.

Who are "the
Father and the
Son"
Did [I] we demand
Today
"The Father
and the Son"
himself
Would doubtless
[Answer me] specify –

But had they
[had] the felicity [readiness]
When [I] we desired
to know,
We better
Friends had
been, perhaps,
1 3
Than time to

4   2
be ensue –

We start – to
learn that We
believe
But once –
Entirely –
Belief, it does
not fit so well
When altered
frequently –

We blush,
that Heaven
if We [behold –] achieve
Event ineffable –
We shall
have shunned
until Ashamed
To own the
Miracle –

1870 or later

This ink draft has many penciled changes and is further documentation of Emily and Susan working over poems.

149

Best Witchcraft
is Geometry

To a Magician's
eye –

Emily –

early 1870s
This is a revision of a portion of a letter-poem sent to Susan in the late 1860s. The paper includes a cut that was probably intended for a flower. On the back of the letter is a shopping list written by Susan, which includes "ink" and "satin ribbon."

150

Oh Matchless
Earth , We
underrate the
chance to
dwell in Thee

early 1870s
Susan quotes these lines in a letter she writes to the *Springfield Republican* in 1906.

151

We meet
no Stranger
but Ourself

early 1870s

152

Were not Day
of itself memo-
rable, dear Sue's
remembrance would
make it so

Emily.

early 1870s

153

The Wind begun to
knead the Grass
As Women do a Dough –
He flung a Hand full
at the Plain
A Hand full at the Sky.
The Leaves unhooked
themselves from Trees
And started all abroad –
The Dust did scoop
itself like Hands
And throw away the
Road –
The Wagons
quickened on the Streets
The Thunders gossiped
low

The lightning showed
a Yellow Head
And then a livid Toe –
The Birds put up
the Bars to Nests
The Cattle flung to
Barns
Then came one
drop of Giant Rain
        And then as if
the Hands
That held the Dams
had parted hold
The Waters Wrecked
the Sky
But Overlooked my
Father's House
Just Quartering a Tree

Emily –

early 1870s

154

Lest any doubt
that we are glad
that they were born
Today
Whose having lived
is held by us

in noble Holiday
Without the date,
like Consciousness
or Immortality '

Emily '

early 1870s
In *Face to Face*, Martha Dickinson Bianchi notes that this was sent "To Sue with flowers on her birthday."

155

Trust is better
than Contract, for
One is still, but
the other moves.

Emily '

early 1870s

156

Has All – a
codicil?

Emily –

early 1870s

157

To see you
unfits for staler
meetings.
I dare not
risk an intemperate
moment before
a Banquet of
Bran.

early 1870s

158

To miss you, Sue,
is power.
The stimulus
of Loss makes
most Possession
mean.
To live lasts
always, but to
love is firmer
than to live.
No Heart that
broke but further
went than
Immortality.
The Trees keep

House for you
all Day and
the Grass looks
chastened.
A silent Hen
frequents the
place with
superstitious
Chickens – and
still Forenoons
a Rooster knocks
at your outer
Door.
To look that
way is Romance.
The Novel "out,"
pathetic worth
attaches to the
Shelf.
Nothing has gone
but Summer, or
no one that you
knew.
The Forests
are at Home –
the Mountains
intimate at
Night and arrogant
at Noon, and
lonesome Fluency
abroad, like
suspending Music.

Of so divine
a Loss
We enter but
the Gain,
Indemnity for
Loneliness
That such a
Bliss has been.
Tell Neddie
that we miss
him and cherish
"Captain Jinks."
Tell Mattie
that Tim's Dog
calls Vinnie's Pussy
names and I dont
discourage him.
She must come
Home and chase
them both and
that will make
it square.
For Big Mattie
and John, of
course a strong
remembrance.
I trust that
you are warm.
I keep your
faithful place.
Whatever throng
the Lock is

firm upon your
Diamond Door.

Emily.

September 1871
"Captain Jinks" refers to the horse marines in a popular song, and apparently was Emily's nickname for Ned, who enjoyed the family's horses. "Big Mattie" is Susan's sister, Martha Smith, and "John" is Martha's husband.

In the early 1870s, Ned, nearly ten, and Mattie, almost five, were old enough to travel and vacation with Susan. July 1871 was a difficult month: both children had the measles, and Ned, suffering from physical weakness and general ill health, was being treated by a doctor in Springfield, Massachusetts. Mary Bowles, who hosted Susan during these visits, reported in a letter to her son that "poor little Ned is having a hard time & does not look really so hale as when he was here last – and he does his best to keep up . . . they come down next week and I told Mrs D – that she had better bring Mattie with her and stay a little time for she too looked used up." Early in the fall the children accompanied Susan on her annual trip to Geneva, New York, to visit their aunt and uncle.

159

A prompt – executive
Bird is the Jay –
Bold as a Bailiff's
Hymn –
Brittle and Brief
in quality –

Warrant in every
Line –

Sitting a Bough
like a Brigadier
Confident and straight –
Much is the mien
of him in March
As a Magistrate –

Emily –

early 1870s
Susan also found blue jays a worthy topic for her own poems and wrote about a jay's "low loving notes" in "Amor" (1884).

160

My God – He sees
thee –
Shine thy best –
Fling up thy
Balls of Gold
Till every Cubit
play with thee
And every Crescent
hold –
Elate the Acre
at his feet –
Upon his Atom
swim –

Oh Sun, but
just a Second's
right
In thy long
Race with him!

Emily '

early 1870s

161

When I hoped,
I feared –
Since I hoped
I dared
Everywhere alone
As a Church
remain –
Spectre cannot
harm
Serpent cannot
charm
He is Prince of
Harm
Who hath suffered
him.

Emily '

early 1870s

162

Our Own
possessions,
though Our Own –
'Tis well to
hoard anew –
Remembering
the Dimensions
Of Possibility.

Emily –

early 1870s

163

Of Death
the Sharpest
function
That just
as we discern
The Excellence
defies us
Securest gathered
then
The Fruit
perverse to
plucking
But leaning

to the Sight
With the
Extatic limit
Of unobtained
Delight.

early 1870s

164

Sister
    Our parting
was somewhat
interspersed and
I cannot con-
clude which
went.
I shall be
cautious not to
so as to miss
no one.
Vinnie drank
your Coffee
and has looked
a little like you
since, which
is nearly a
comfort.
Austin has had
two calls and
is very tired _

One from
Professor Tyler,
and the other
from Father.
I am afraid
they will call
here.
Bun has run
away _
Disaffection_
doubtless – as to
the Supplies.
Ned is a better
Quarter Master
than his vagrant
Papa.
The little Turkey
is lonely and
the Chickens
bring him to call.
His foreign
Neck in familiar
Grass is quaint
as a Dromedary.
I suppose the
Wind has
chastened the
Bows on Mattie's
impudent Hat
and the Sea
presumed as
far as he dare

on her Stratified
Stockings.
If her Basket
wont hold the
Boulders she
picks, I will
send a Bin.
Ned is much
lamented and
his Circus Airs
in the Rowen
will be doubly
sweet.
Bela Dickinson's
son is the only
Basso remaining.
It rains every
pleasant Day now
and Dickens'
Maggie's Lawn
will be green
as a Courtier's.
Love for your
Brother and
Sister _ please_
and the dear
Lords.
Nature gives
her love –
Twlight touches
Amherst with
his yellow Glove.
Miss me

sometimes, dear –
Not on most
occasions, but
the Seldoms
of the Mind.

Emily –

early 1870s
During summer months, Emily writes to Susan as Susan vacations with her family. This letter may have been sent to Long Branch, New Jersey, or to Swampscott, Massachusetts, where the next letter was sent.

165

Part to whom
Sue is precious
gave her a note
Wednesday, but as
Father omitted the
"Ocean House"
presume it is
still groping in
the Swampscott
Mail –
We remind her
we love her –
Unimportant fact,
though Dante
did'nt think so,
nor Swift, nor

Mirabeau.
Could Pathos
compete with
that simple
statement
"Not that we
loved him but
that he loved
us"?

Emily –

summer 1873

Emily refers to Dante's passionate love of Beatrice, Jonathan Swift's love of Stella, and Mirabeau's love of Sophie de Ruffey. The closing quotation is from 1 John 4:10: " . . . not that we loved God, but that he loved us."

166

The Butterfly
in honored Dust
Assuredly will lie
But none will
man's
pass the Catacomb
So chastened as
the Fly –

Emily '

mid-1870s

Emily probably intended this poem for her niece's and nephew's pleasure as well as for Susan's.

167

Without the
annual parting
I thought to
shun the
Loneliness that
parting ratifies.
How artfully
in vain!
Your Coffee cooled un
touched except
by random
Fly.
A one Armed
Man conveyed
the flowers.
Not all my
modest schemes
have so perverse
a close.
My love to
"Captain Jenks"
who forbore
to call.
If not too
uncongenial
to the Divine

Will, a Kiss
also for
Mattie.
"God is a
jealous God."
I miss the
Turkey's quaint
face – once
my grave
Familiar, also
the former
Chickens, now
forgotten Hens.
"Pussum" cries
I hear, but
it is too
select a grief
to accept solace.
Tell Mattie
Tabby caught
a Rat and it
ran away.
Grandpa caught
it and it
stayed.
He is the best
Mouser.
The Rabbit
winks at me
all Day, but
if I wink
back, he

shuffles a
Clover.
What Rowen
he leaves,
Horace will
pick for the
Cow.
This is the
final Weather.
The transport
that is not
postponed is
is stopping
with us all.
But Subjects
hinder talk.
Silence is all
we dread.
There's Ransom
in a Voice –
But Silence
is Infinity.
Himself have
not a face.

Love for
John and
Mattie.
Sister.

autumn 1873
Letters from this period show that Emily and Susan are in the habit

of having coffee together. Susan is now visiting her sister Martha in Geneva, New York, as she did most autumns. In the quotation, Dickinson paraphrases Exodus: "I the Lord thy God am a jealous God." (20:5)

168

Dear Sue –
I would
have liked to
be beautiful and
tidy when you
came –
You will excuse
me, wont you,
I felt so sick.
How it would
please me if
you would come
once more, when
I was palatable.

Emily

mid-1870s

169

Had this one
Day not been ,

Or could it
cease to be
How smitten ,
how superfluous ,
Were every
other Day !

Lest Love
should value
less
What Loss
would value
more
Had it the
stricken privi –
lege ,
It cherishes
before.

Emily.

mid-1870s

170

Dear Sue '
It is
sweet you
are better .
I am greedy
to see you.

Your note was
like the Wind.
The Bible
chooses that
you know to
define the
Spirit .

A Wind that
rose though
not a Leaf
In any Forest
stirred,
But with
Itself did cold
engage
Beyond the
realm of Bird.

A Wind
That woke
a lone Delight
Like Separation's
Swell –

mid-1870s

171

Trifles – like
Life – and

the Sun, we
Acknowledge
in Church,
but the Love
that demeans them , having
no Confede –
rate , dies
without a
Term .

Emily'

mid-1870s

172

Never mind
dear –
Trial as a
Stimulus far
exceeds Wine
though it would
hardly be
prohibited as a
Beverage.

Emily.

mid-1870s

173

Two Lengths
has every Day –
It's absolute
extent
And Area
superior
By Hope or
 Horror lent –

Eternity will
be
Velocity or
Pause
At Fundamental
Signals
From Fundamental
Laws.

To die is
not to go
On Doom's
consummate
Chart
No Territory
new is Staked –
Remain thou
as thou Art .

mid-1870s

Emily penciled a draft of the second stanza of this poem on the triangular flap of an envelope: "Eternity will / be / Velocity or Pause / Precisely as / the Candidate / Preliminary / was – / character." Martha Dickinson Bianchi notes that Susan kept this piece pinned to her workbox.

174

I think that the Root of
the Wind is Water –
It would not sound
so deep
Were it a Firmamental
Product –
Airs no Oceans keep –
Mediterranean intonations –
To a Current's Ear –
There is a maritime
conviction
In the Atmosphere –

1870s

175

Not One by
Heaven defrauded
stay –
Although he seem
to steal

He restitutes in
some sweet way
Secreted in his will –

1870s

176

To lose what we
never owned
might seem an
eccentric Bereavement
but Presumption
has its' Affliction
as actually as
Claim –

Emily

mid-1870s

177

The incidents of
Love
Are more than
its' Events –
Investment's best
Expositor

Is the minute
Per Cents –

Emily –

mid-1870s

SECTION FOUR

TO BE SUSAN IS IMAGINATION

Late Writings, mid-1870s to May 1886

From the mid-1870s until Emily's own death on May 15, 1886, the correspondence from Emily to Susan features dramatic personal statements and remarkable manuscript art. The quotations at the beginning of this section raise intriguing questions of literary identity. Single-line messages from various Shakespeare plays may be part of parlor or calendar games or they may indicate Emily's use of characters as diverse as Anthony and Horatio to convey her deepest desires to Susan. Certainly, the numerous letter-poems and poems that Emily sends to Susan during the end of Emily's life discount the popular claim that the two women had nothing to do with each other in these final years. The following writings feature many allusions to seeing and hearing Susan in the flesh, and they testify to her taking care of Emily during her illness.

The period begins shortly after the birth of Susan's youngest child Gib, and it reaches a tragic climax when the child dies from typhoid fever on October 5, 1883, at the age of eight. Susan's daughter Martha makes it clear that Emily's total seclusion occurs after—not before—Gib's death, which corrects the standard account that October 1883 is the only time Emily ventures to see Susan. According to Martha, Emily visits Susan and her niece and nephews regularly, and she is a distinct presence across the great lawn, either as a light burning late into the night or as a figure waving from the window. Martha describes her Aunt Emily as the "confederate in every contraband desire, the very Spirit of 'Never, Never Land.'"[1]

A few weeks after Gib's death, Austin begins an affair with Mabel Loomis Todd, who moved to Amherst with her husband in 1881. Originally a friend of Susan's, Mabel never meets Emily face-to-face, but she later presents herself as an authority on Emily's life and work and becomes the first editor of a printed volume of Dickinson's poetry. In fact it is Mabel Loomis Todd who sets in motion many of the fallacies that have since become Dickinson legend.

After the death of her son, Susan goes into seclusion, overwhelmed with grief. Emily also removes herself from public contact at this time, yet she continues to console Susan through her writing, her devotion and love as palpable as always.

This period in Emily's correspondence to Susan is marked by numerous other losses, beginning with the 1877 death of Elizabeth Lord, family friend and visitor to the Dickinson houses, and the 1878 death of Samuel Bowles, editor of the *Springfield Republican*. J.G. Holland, family friend, publisher and editor of *Scribner's*, dies in October 1881, and Emily's friend and spiritual confidant Charles Wadsworth dies in April 1882. In November of the same year, Emily's mother, Emily Norcross Dickinson, dies. Then in March 1884, Emily loses her friend Judge Otis Phillips Lord, and her literary friend and correspondent Helen Hunt Jackson dies in August 1885.

Austin suffers from malaria in 1883, and Emily falls ill immediately after Gib's death. Her health deteriorates in 1884, and she is eventually diagnosed with kidney ailments known as Bright's disease. Over the next year, she moves in and out of remission, and it is Susan who nurses Emily through her last days. In grief and illness, Emily writes profusely, and the letter-poems and poems she sends to Susan are profound, passionate, and encoded with feelings, memories, and literary allusions.

On May 15, 1886, Emily Dickinson dies at home. In the hours that follow, Susan prepares Emily's body for burial. She then writes an obituary for the *Springfield Republican* publicly declaring her admiration and love for her friend, neighbor, and sister-in-law, whom she will quote as a literary authority for the rest of her life. In her tributary essay, Susan presents Emily as a writer as well as a compassionate human being, and she pays homage to her originality, her brilliance, and her devotion to those she loved.

178

"Egypt – thou
knew'st " –

mid-1870s
Emily and Susan circulate literary quotations as commentary on events and relationships. Here Emily borrows from Shakespeare, using a line from Antony's speech to Cleopatra (III, xi, 56–61):

> Egypt, thou knew'st too well,
> My heart was to thy rudder tied by the strings,
> And thou shouldst tow me after. O'er my spirit
> Thy full supremacy thou knew'st, and that
> Thy beck might from the bidding of the gods
> Command me.

This may be part of a game based on their mutual love for Shakespeare, or from a daily Shakespeare calendar.

179

"For Brutus,
as you know,
was Caesar's
Angel."

mid-1870s
Again Emily quotes Shakespeare, this time using lines from

Julius Caesar (III, ii, 183). Emily once wrote to an editor at the *Springfield Republican*: "He has found his Future who has found Shakespeare."

180

"Doth forget
that ever
he heard
the name
of Death."

mid-1870s
These are lines from Shakespeare's *Coriolanus* (III, i, 256–258):

His heart's his mouth:
What his breast forges, that his tongue must vent;
And, being angry, does forget that ever
He heard the name of death.

In this speech, Menenius Agrippa defends his friend Coriolanus. Emily's "talking in Shakespeare" reflects the literary consecration of her relationship with Susan.

181

Emily and all
that she has
are at Sue's
service , if of

any comfort
to Baby.
Will send
Maggie , if you
will accept
her –

Sister –

early August 1875
At the age of forty-four, Susan gives birth to her third child, Thomas Gilbert Dickinson (Gib). This letter-poem celebrates his arrival on August 1, 1875. "Maggie" is Margaret Maher. Born in Ireland in 1841, Maggie began working for the Dickinsons in 1869. She was especially protective of and trusted by Emily.

182

Only Woman
in the World ,
Accept a
Julep '

mid-1870s

183

A little
Madness in
the Spring

Is wholesome
even for the
King '
But God be
with the Clown –
Who ponders
this tremendous
scene,
This whole
Experiment of
Green,
As if it
were his own!

mid-1870s

184

Thank you,
dear, for the
"Eliot"
She is the
Lanc to thc
Indies , Columbus
was looking for.

Emily '

1870s
Emily thanks Susan for George Eliot's latest novel, *Daniel Deronda*.

In a letter to Thomas Higginson, Emily writes that "'Sue' smuggled it under my Pillow."

185

Not when we know,
the Power accosts,
The Garment of
Surprise
Was all our timid
Mother wore
At Home – in
Paradise –

mid-1870s

186

The Rat
is the
concisest
Tenant.
He pays no
Rent .
Repudiates
the Obligation –
On Schemes
Intent

Balking our
Wit
To Sound
or Circumvent
Hate cannot
harm
A Foe so
reticent –
Neither Decree
prohibit him
Lawful as
Equilibrium.

mid-1870s

187

"Faithful to
the End"
Amended
From the
Heavenly
Clause
Constancy with
a Proviso
Constancy
Abhors –

mid-1870s

188

Susan knows
she is a Siren –
and that at a
word from her,
Emily would
forfeit Righteousness –
Please excuse
the grossness
of this Morning –
I was for a
moment disarmed –
This is the
World that opens
and shuts, like
the Eye of the
Wax Doll –

1876 or later

189

The healed Heart
shows it's shallow
scar
With confidential
moan –
Not mended by
Mortality

Are Fabrics truly
torn –
To go its'
convalescent way
So shameless is
to see
More genuine
were Perfidy
Than such
Fidelity-

1876 or later

190

'Tis not the
swaying frame
we miss '
It is the
steadfast Heart,
That had it
beat a thousand
years,
With Love alone
had bent,
It's fervor the
Electric Oar,
That bore it
through the Tomb,
Ourselves, denied
the privilege,

Consolelessly
presume –

1876 or later

The top two-thirds of the first leaf of this poem is cut away. It is possible that Susan may have removed something she considered too confidential, or that she may have placed lines of verse in one of her scrapbooks.

191

The Treason
of an Accent
Might vilify
the Joy –
To breathe –
corrode the
rapture
Of Sanctity
to be –

mid-1870s

192

The long sigh
of the Frog
Upon a Summer's
Day
Enacts intoxication
Upon the Revery –

But his receding
Swell
Substantiates a Peace
That makes the
Ear inordinate
For corporal
release –

mid-1870s

193

The ignominy
to receive – is
eased by the
reflection that
interchange of
infamies – is
either's Antidote.

Emily.

mid-1870s

194

Sue – This
is the last
flower –

To wane
without
disparagement
In a dissembling
hue
That will not
let the Eye
decide
If it abide
or no
is Sunset's –
perhaps – only. Emily

mid-1870s

195

To own a
Susan of
my own
Is of itself
a Bliss –
Whatever
Realm I
forfeit, Lord,
Continue
me in this!

Emily.

late 1870s

196

But Susan is
a Stranger yet –
The Ones who
cite her most
Have never scaled
her Haunted House
Nor compromised
her Ghost –

To pity those who
know her not
Is helped by the
regret
That those who
know her know
her less
The nearer her
they get –

Emily –

late 1870s

197

My Maker –
let me be
Enamored most
of thee –

But nearer
this
I more should
miss –

late 1870s

198

March is
the Month
of Expectation.
The Things
we do not
know –
The Persons
of prognostication
Are coming
now -
We try to
show becoming
firmness –
But pompous
Joy
Betrays us, as
his first
Betrothal
Betrays a
Boy.

—

late 1870s

199

Crisis is sweet and
yet the Heart
Upon the hither side
Has Dowers of Prospective
Surrendered by the Tried –
Withheld to the arrived

Upside down

Witheld to the arrived –
Defamed – denied

In margin beside preceding lines

To Denizen denied
Inquire of the proudest
fullest
Rose closing
Triump
Which rapture – Hour –
Moment
she preferred
And she [would] will point
undoubtedly
tell you sighing – answer

The Transport of the

Bud – rapture rescinded
To her surrendered Bud

The Hour of her Bud –
session of
And she will point you
longingly
fondly – sighing
receding
To her rescinded Bud
Departed –
Receipted Bud
Expended

late 1870s

200

(115)
The inundation of
the Spring
+ Enlarges every
Soul – +submerges
It sweeps the
tenement – [or s] away
But leaves the
Water whole –

In which the
Soul at first
+ estranged – + alarmed
Seeks +faintly for
its' Shore – + softly
But acclima- gropes

ted – pines no more
For [its'] Peninsula –
    that
+ submerged –

+ [seeks furtive
    For its' shore]

sideways, on bottom right

Loses sight
Of aught
    aught Peninsular –

late 1870s
Plus signs and various alternatives for her final word choice indicate Emily's writing and revision process. Once again, the exchange of drafts suggests that Emily works on poems in various stages with Susan, showing unfinished work and welcoming Susan's reactions and feedback.

201

Where we
owe but a
little, we pay.
Where we
owe so much
it defies
Money, we
are blandly

insolvent.
Adulation is
inexpensive
Except to him
who accepts
it.
It has cost
him – Himself.

Emily.

late 1870s

202

I must wait
a few Days
before seeing
you – You are
too momentous.
But remember
it is idolatry,
not indifference.

Emily.

late 1870s

203

Susan –
      Whoever blesses,
you always
bless – the last –
and often made
the Heaven of
Heavens – a sterile
Stimulus –
Cherish Power –
dear –
Remember that
stands in the
Bible between the
Kingdom and
the Glory, because
it is wilder
than either of
them –

    Emily –

late 1870s

204

Susan –
      The sweetest
acts both exact

and defy, gratitude,
so silence is all
the honor there is –
but to those who
[c]an estimate silence,
it is sweetly
enough –
In a Life that
stopped guessing,
you and I should
not feel at home

late 1870s

This letter-poem is torn at the bottom of the second leaf, and it is likely that the signature was removed by Susan to offer as a gift or to paste into a scrapbook, a common practice in the nineteenth century.

205

To the faithful
Absence is
condensed presence.
To others, but
there <u>are</u> no
others –

late 1870s

206

Sue – to be
lovely as you
is a touching
Contest, though
like the Siege
of Eden, impracticable,
Eden never
capitulates –

Emily '

1876 or later

207

Susan – I dreamed
of you, last
night, and send
a Carnation to
indorse it
Sister of Ophir –
Ah Peru –
Subtle the Sum
That purchase
you –

1876 or later

In this late handwriting, Emily's "Y" looks like an "S," so that "you" in the second and final lines looks like "Sou," or Sue. "Ophir" is a biblical land rich in gold and precious stones (1 Kings 10:11).

208

In petto –

A Counterfeit –
a Plated Person –
I would not be –
Whatever Strata
of Iniquity
My Nature underlie –
Truth is good
Health – and
Safety, and the
Sky.
How meagre, what
an Exile – is a Lie,
And Vocal – when
we die –
Lothrop –

late 1870s

Emily signs this letter-poem "Lothrop," referring to the Amherst minister, Charles Dexter Lothrop, who was accused of domestic abuse by his three daughters. "In petto" means "in confidence." Both Susan and Austin were involved with the events of this case from 1876 through 1879, supporting the claims of the daughters and defending Samuel Bowles and the *Republican*'s reporting of the case. Emily speaks in the voice of the perpetrator, who was later excommunicated from the First Congregational Church in Amherst.

209

Sister spoke
of Springfield –
The beginning of
"Always" is more
dreadful than
the close – for
that is sustained
by flickering
identity –
His nature was
Future –
He had not yet
lived –
David's route was
simple – "I shall
go to him" –

Emily '

January 1878
"Springfield" refers to Samuel Bowles, who died on January 16, 1878. Emily sent this letter-poem to Susan after the funeral of their dear friend. In it she alludes to the Book of Samuel in the Old Testament, when, after the death of his son, David says: "But now he is dead, wherefore should I fast? can I bring him back again? I shall go to him, but he shall not return to me." (2 Samuel 12:23)

210

Those not live
yet
Who doubt to
live again –
"Again" is of
a twice
But this – is one –
The Ship beneath
the Draw
Aground – is he?
Death – so – the Hyphen
of the Sea –
Deep is the
Schedule
Of the Disk
to be –
Costumeless Consciousness,
That is he –

Easter.

late 1870s

Susan wrote "To read to friends" at the bottom of this letter-poem. Susan's interest in sharing Emily's poetry with others included the introduction of Emily's work to Mabel Loomis Todd, the editor of the first printed volume of Emily's poetry and Austin's lover. In an 1882 diary entry, written one year before the affair with Austin began, Loomis Todd jotted, "Went in the afternoon to Mrs. Dickinson's. She read me some strange poems by Emily Dickinson. They are full of power."

211

So gay a
Flower
Bereaves the
Mind
As if it were
a Woe –
Is Beauty an
Affliction – then?
Tradition
ought to know –

late 1870s

212

Emily is sorry for
Susan's Day –
To be singular
Under plural
circumstances , is
a becoming heroism –
Opinion is a
flitting thing,
But Truth , outlasts
the Sun –
If then we cannot
own them both –

Possess the oldest
One –

Emily '

late 1870s

213

So sorry for
Sister's hardships –
"Make me thy
wrack when I come
back, but spare
me when I gang."

Emily '

late 1870s

214

Mrs Delmonico's
things were very
nice – Art has
a "Palate," as well
as an Easel –
Susan breaks
many Commandments,
but <u>one</u> she obeys –

"Whatsoever ye do,
do it unto the
Glory" –
Susan will be
saved –
Thank her –

Emily –

late 1870s
For Emily, Susan's delectable dinners make it seem as if Delmonico's, a fashionable New York restaurant, is right next door. The reference to Paul's injunction, "Whether therefore ye eat, or drink, or whatsoever ye do, do all to the glory of God" (1 Corinthians 10:31), uses New Testament rhetoric to describe the heights of taste achieved by Susan's dinners. The recipes that are among Susan's papers describe "A February Dinner" that includes "Caviar & toast, bermuda onion / Oysters on half-shell; horseradish; brown bread & butter / Clear soup, with noodle puffs / Timbales of salmon w/mayonnaise hearts / Creamed celery in cheese shell / Crown roast of lamb w/ French peas; potato hearts / Ginger sherbet / Breast of roast duck w/ orange slices & dressed chicory / Large ice-cream heart w/frozen roses; fancy cakes / Brie cheese, toasted wafers; coffee."

215

Susan –
A little overflowing
word
That any, hearing,

had inferred
For Ardor or
for Tears,
Though Generations
pass away,
Traditions ripen
and decay,
As eloquent
appears –

Emily –

late 1870s

216

The Sweets of
Pillage, can be known
To no one but
the Thief –
Compassion for
Integrity
Is his divinest
Grief –

1876 or later

It is likely that Emily sends this poem to Susan and to her niece and nephews, especially Ned. In the fall of 1880, Ned becomes a student at Amherst College, and pursues a partial course of study while living at home due to protracted health problems, including general weakness and epilepsy. Emily sends him several poems and notes during this time, including one in which she teases him about "that Pie you stole – well, this is that Pie's brother."

217

The Moon upon
her fluent Route
Defiant of a Road –
The Star's
Etruscan Argument
Substantiate a God –

If Aims impel
these Astral Ones
The ones allowed
to know
Know that which
makes them as
forgot

As Dawn
forgets them –
Now –

1870s to 1880s

218

The Devil – had he
fidelity

Would be the best
friend –
Because he has
ability –
But Devils cannot
mend –
Perfidy is the
Virtue
That would but he
resign
The Devil – + without
question
Were thoroughly
divine
– so amended –
were durably divine –

late 1870s to 1880s

219

That Susan
lives – is a
Universe which
neither going
nor coming
could displace –

---

spring 1880
During the spring of 1880, Susan and Austin are both unwell. Austin is suffering from malaria, a disease that he has already succumbed to twice, and Susan is described by a friend as "unstrung and nervous." To regain her strength, she travels to Providence, Rhode Island, for a two-week stay, and then she meets Austin and Ned in Boston. It is likely that Emily sends this letter-poem to Susan upon her return to Amherst.

220

Susan is a
vast and sweet
Sister, and
Emily hopes to
deserve her,
but not now –

Written sideways on top of page

Thanks
for the
profligate
little Box
that lacked
only
Cigars.

early 1880s

221

"Thank you"
ebbs – between us,
but the Basis
of thank you,
is sterling and
fond –

Emily'

early 1880s

222

Susan – I would
have come out
of Eden to open
the Door for you
if I had known
you were there.
You must knock
with a Trumpet
as Gabriel does,
whose Hands are
small as yours –
I knew he knocked
and went away –

I did'nt dream
that you did –

Emily'

early 1880s
Emily refers to the archangel Gabriel. Martha Dickinson Bianchi pointed out that her aunt sometimes addressed her mother as "You from whom I never run away." By apologizing for not being able to see Susan on one occasion, Emily suggests that there are other occasions when she will see her, indicating that Emily and Susan enjoyed face-to-face contact until the end of Emily's life.

223

Memoirs of Little
Boys that live –
"Were'nt you chasing
Pussy," said Vinnie
to Gilbert?
"No – she was chasing
herself" –
"But was'nt she
running pretty
fast"? "Well, some
slow and some
fast" said the
beguiling Villain –
Pussy's Nemesis
quailed –
Talk of "hoary

Reprobates"!
Your Urchin is
more antique in
wiles than the
Egyptian Sphinx –
Have you noticed
Granville's Letter
to Lowell?
"Her Majesty" has
contemplated you,
and reserves
her decision!

Emily'

early 1880s
Emily presents a playful exchange between her sister Lavinia and her youngest nephew, Gib, while alluding to James Russell Lowell, who served as minister to England in 1880, the year in which the second Earl of Granville took over the Foreign Office.

224

Susan.
To thank one
for Sweetness, is
possible, but for
Spaciousness, out
of sight –
The Competition of
Phantoms is

On separate page

inviolate –

Emily'

early 1880s

225

"Boast not"
myself "of Tomorrow"
for I "knowest
not what a"
Noon "may bring
forth" –

early 1880s
Emily adapts an exhortation from Solomon in the Old Testament: "Boast not thyself of tomorrow; for thou knowest not what a day may bring forth." (Proverbs 27:1) "Noon" or "day" often signifies a climactic event throughout Emily's letters and poems. It is possible that the phrases in this letter poem are part of a word game that Emily and Susan are in the midst of playing or that the phrases represent a playful encoding of desire.

226

It was like
a breath from

Gibraltar to hear
your voice again,
Sue – Your
impregnable
syllables need
no prop, to stand –
The Loaf
for Ned, I will
send Wednesday
evening, unless
he prefer before –
If he would,
let him whisper
to me –

Emily'

early 1880s

227

How inspiriting
to the clandestine
Mind those Words
of Scripture,
"We thank thee
that thou hast
hid these things" –

Candor – my
tepid friend –

Come not to
play with me –
The Myrrhs, and
Mochas, of the
Mind
Are it's
iniquity –

Emily'

1880s

Though Emily rejects formal religion, she frequently uses the language of the Old Testament and the New Testament in a metaphorical way, to express social commentary as well as emotional and spiritual observations. This letter-poem alludes to Matthew (11:25): "At that time Jesus answered and said, I thank thee, O Father, Lord of heaven and earth, because thou hast hid these things from the wise and prudent, and hast revealed them unto babes."

228

I send My
Own, two answers –
Not one of
them so spotless
nor so strong
as her's – Sinew
and Snow in
one –
Thank her for
all the promise –

I shall perhaps
need it –
Thank her
dear power
for having come,
An Avalanche
of Sun! Emily –

1880s

This letter-poem echoes Emily's poem "I send Two Sunsets," which she wrote in the 1860s, twenty years earlier.

229

Dear Sue –
With the
Exception of
Shakespeare, you
have told me of
more knowledge
than any one living –
To say that sincerely
is strange praise –

early 1880s

230

Had "Arabi"
only read

Longfellow, he'd
have never been
caught –
Khedive.

"Shall fold their
Tents like the
Arabs, and as
silently steal
away" ———

September 1882
"Arabi" refers to the Egyptian rebel Ahmed Arabi Pasha, who was defeated at Tel-el-Kebir, on September 13, 1882. Khedive served as the Turkish viceroy of Egypt from 1867 to 1914. Emily uses Longfellow's "The Day Is Done" to comment on current events.

231

No Brigadier
throughout the
year
So civic as the
Jay –
A Neighbor and
a Warrior too –
With shrill felicity
Pursuing Winds
That censure us

A Febuary Day –
The Brother of
the Universe
Was never blown
away –
The Snow and
he are intimate –
I've often seen
them play
When Heaven looked
upon us all
With such severity
I felt apology
were due to
an insulted Sky
Whose pompous
frown was nutriment
To their Temerity –
The Pillow of
this daring Head
Is pungent
Evergreens –
His Larder – terse
and Militant –
Unknown – refreshing
things –
His Character
a Tonic,
His Future a
Dispute –
Unfair an
Immortality

That leaves
this Neighbor
out___

Emily '

spring 1883

232

Will my great
Sister accept
the minutiae of
Devotion, with ti-
midity that it is
no more?
Susan's Calls are
like Antony's
Supper –
"And pays his
Heart for what
his Eyes eat,
only ' "

Emily '

1880s

The quotation from Shakespeare depicts the moment when Enobarbus describes Antony gazing with longing at Cleopatra: "And for his ordinary, pays his heart, / For what his eyes eat only." (*Antony and Cleopatra*, II, ii, 225–226)

233

To be Susan
is Imagination,
To have been
Susan, a Dream –
What depths
of Domingo
in that torrid
Spirit!

Emily '

1880s

Emily refers to Santo Domingo, well-known for its rum and for the bloody slave revolt that ushered in the nineteenth century.

234

Dear Sue –
The Vision
of Immortal
Life has been
fulfilled –
How simply at
the last the
Fathom comes!
The Passenger
and not the
Sea, we find

surprises us –
Gilbert rejoiced
in Secrets –
His Life was
panting with them –
With what menace
of Light he cried
"Dont tell, Aunt
Emily"! Now my
ascended Playmate
must instruct me.
Show us, prattling
Preceptor, but the
way to thee!
He knew no
niggard moment –
His Life was
full of Boon –
The Playthings of
the Dervish were
not so wild
as his –
No Crescent was
this Creature –
He traveled from
the Full –
Such soar, but
never set –
I see him in
the Star, and
meet his sweet
velocity in every-

thing that flies –
His Life was
like the Bugle,
which winds
itself away,
his Elegy an
Echo – his Requiem
Ecstacy –
Dawn and
Meridian in one.
Wherefore would
he wait, wronged
only of Night,
which he left
for us –
Without a spec-
ulation, our
little Ajax
spans the whole –
Pass to thy
Rendezvous of
Light,
Pangless except
for us,
Who slowly ford
the Mystery
Which thou hast
leaped across!

Emily –

October 1883

On October 5, 1883, Susan and Austin's seven-year-old son Gib dies from typhoid fever. Devastated by the death, Susan secludes herself for over a year and does not leave her home. Emily retreats as well. In an attempt to assuage the family's grief, Susan's other children, Martha and Ned, stop speaking their brother's name aloud.

235

Perhaps the
dear, grieved
Heart would
open to a
flower, which
blesses unre-
quested , and
serves without
a Sound.

Emily.

early October 1883

236

Dear Sue –
A Promise
is firmer than
a Hope, although
it does not hold
so much –

Hope never knew
Horizon –
Awe is the first
Hand that is
held to us –
Hopelessness in it's
first Film has not
leave to last –
That would
close the Spirit,
and no
intercession could
do that –
Intimacy with
Mystery, after great
Space, will usurp
it's place –
Moving on in
the Dark like
Loaded Boats
at Night, though
there is no
Course, there is
Boundlessness –
Expanse cannot
be lost –
Not Joy, but
a Decree
Is Deity –
His Scene,
Infinity –
Whose rumor's

Gate was shut
so tight
Before my Beam
was sown,
Not even a
Prognostic's push
Could make
a Dent thereon –
The World
that thou hast
opened
Shuts for thee,
But not alone,
We all have
followed thee –
Escape more
slowly
To thy Tracts
of Sheen –
The Tent is
listening,
But the Troops
are gone!

Emily –

early October 1883

237

Climbing to
reach the
costly Hearts
To which he
gave the worth,
He broke them,
fearing punishment
He ran away
from Earth –

Emily –

October 1883

238

The Heart
has many Doors –
I can but
knock –
For any sweet
"Come in"
Impelled to
hark –
Not saddened
by repulse,
Repast to me
That somewhere,

there exists,
Supremacy –

Emily –

late 1883

239

Thank Sister
with love, and
reserve an Apart –
ment for two
Cocks in the
Cocks
Thanksgiving plan –
ning –
Mattie is almost
with you –
The first section
of Darkness is
the densest, Dear,
After that, Light
trembles in –
You asked would
I remain?
Irrevocably, Susan –
I know no
other way –
Ether looks
dispersive, but

try it with
a Lever –

Emily –

late November 1883

240

Twice, when
I had Red
Flowers out,
Gilbert knocked,
raised his sweet
Hat, and asked
if he might
touch them –
Yes, and take
them too, I said,
but Chivalry
forbade him,
Besides, he
gathered Hearts,
not Flowers –
Some Arrows
slay but whom
they strike,
But this slew
all <u>but</u> him,
Who so
appareled his

Escape,
Too trackless
for a Tomb –

Emily –

late 1883 to early 1884

241

Dear Sue –
I was
surprised, but
Why? Is she
not of the
lineage of the
Spirit? I knew
she was beauti-
ful – I knew she
was royal, but
that she was
hallowed, how
could I surmise,
who had scarcely
seen her since
her deep Eyes
were brought in
your Arms to her
Grandfather's '
Thanksgiving?
She is a strange

trust – I hope
she may be saved –
Redemption Mental
precedes Redemp-
tion Spiritual.
The Madonna
and Child
descend from
the Picture '
while Creation
is kneeling
before the Frame –
I shall keep the
secret –

Emily –

about 1882
This letter-poem may refer to poems sent to Emily that were written by Susan's daughter, Martha.

242

Dear Sue –
Your little
mental gallantries
are sweet as
Chivalry, which
is to me a
shining Word
though I dont

know its meaning –
I sometimes re-
member we are
to die, and
hasten toward
the Heart which
how could I woo

In margin on right side

in a rendezvous where there

In margin on left side

is no Face? Emily –

1880s

243

I felt it no
betrayal, Dear –
Go to my Mine
as to your own,
only more
unsparingly –
I can scarcely
believe that the
Wondrous Book
is at last to
be written, and

it seems like
a Memoir of
the Sun, when
the Noon is
gone –
You remember
his swift way
of wringing and
flinging away
a Theme, and
others picking it
up and gazing
bewildered after
him, and the
prance that
crossed his Eye
at such times
was unrepeatable –
Though the
Great Waters
sleep,
That they are
still the Deep,
We cannot doubt –
No Vacillating
God
Ignited this
Abode
To put it out –

I wish I could
find the

Warrington Words,
but during
my weeks of
faintness, my
Treasures were
misplaced, and
I cannot find
them – I think
Mr Robinson
Had been left
alone, and
felt the opinion
while others were
gone –

Remember, Dear,
an unfaltering
<u>Yes</u> is my
only reply to
your utmost
question –

With constancy,

Emily '

about 1884
The "Wondrous Book," "Memoir of the Sun," refers to biographer George S. Merriam's *The Life and Times of Samuel Bowles* (1885). With "Go to my Mine / as to your own," Emily tells Susan that she does not mind that Merriam was given access to personal information about their friend Samuel Bowles, for which Emily was a source.

This letter-poem shows that Emily continues to mourn and celebrate Bowles' life. She meditates on the words of William S. Robinson (known as "Warrington" in the *Springfield Republican*): "This life is so good, that it seems impossible for it to be wholly interrupted by death."

244

Dear Sue –
One of
the sweetest
Messages I ever
received, was,
"Mrs Dickinson
sent you this
Cardinal Flower,
and told me
to tell you
she thought
of you."
Except for
usurping your
Copyright –
I should
regive the
Message, but
each Voice
is it's own –

Emily –

1880s

245

That any
Flower should
be so base
as to stab
my Susan,
I believe un
willingly –
"Tasting the
Honey and
the Sting", should
have ceased
with Eden –
Choose Flowers
that have no
Fang, Dear –
Pang is the
Past of Peace –

Sister –

about 1884
It is possible that this letter-poem refers to Austin's ongoing affair with Mabel Loomis Todd, which began less than three months after Gib's death. Mabel had been Susan's friend.

246

Morning
might come
by Accident –
Sister –
Night comes
by Event –
To believe the
final line of
the Card would
foreclose Faith –
Faith is Doubt.

Sister –
Show me
Eternity , and
I will show
you Memory –
Both in one
package lain
And lifted
back again –

Be Sue, while
I am Emily –
Be next, what
you have ever
been, Infinity –

1880s

247

No Words
ripple like
Sister's –
Their Silver
genealogy is
very sweet
to trace –
Amalgams
are abundant,
but the lone
student of
the Mines
adores Alloyless
things –

Emily–

1880s

248

Tell the Susan
who never
forgets to be
subtle , every
Spark is
Numbered –

The farthest
Thunder that
I heard
Was nearer
than the Sky,
And rumbles
still,
Though torrid
Noons
Have lain
their Missiles
by –

Emily –

1880s
This letter-poem reflects the nineteenth century belief in electricity and its frictions as a life force.

249

Who is it seeks
my Pillow Nights,
With plain in-
specting face.
"Did you" or
"Did you not,"
to ask'
'Tis "Conscience,"
Childhood's

Nurse –

With Martial
Hand she
Strokes the
Hair
Upon my
Wincing Head –
"All" Rogues
"shall have
their part in"
what –
The Phosphorus
of God –

mid-1880s

Here Emily alludes to the New Testament scripture – "But the fearful, and unbelieving and the abominable, and murderers, and whoremongers, and sorcerers, and idolators, and all liars, shall have their part in the lake which burneth with fire and brimstone: which is the second death." (Revelation 21:8)

250

Dear Sue –
I could
send you no
Note so sweet
as the last words of
your Boy –
"You will look

after Mother"?

Emily '

summer 1885
Emily probably writes this note just before Ned leaves to vacation at Lake Placid in the Adirondacks. By this time Emily's final illness, called Bright's disease, is in remission. She is very ill in the fall of 1884, recovers later that year, and is well through the summer of 1885.

251

The World
hath not
known her, but
I have known
her, was the
sweet Boast
of Jesus –
The small Heart
cannot break –
The Ecstasy of
it's penalty
solaces the
large –
Emerging from
an Abyss, and
re-entering it '
that is Life,
is it not,
Dear?

The tie between
us is very
fine, but a
Hair never
dissolves.

Lovingly '

Emily '

late 1885
Emily falls ill again in November 1885. This letter-poem suggests that even death cannot disengage Emily from Susan nor Susan from Emily.

252

Dear Sue –
The Supper
was delicate
and strange –
I ate it with
compunction
as I would
eat a Vision –
The Blossoms
only were too
hearty – those
I saved for
the Birds –
How tenderly

I thank you –
I often hope
you are better –
Beneath the
Alps the
Danube runs –

late 1885

A section of this manuscript is torn away. Attached to this letter-poem is a note from Susan on blue-ruled paper, which says, "Signature Taken out to give a begging friend." The practice of giving signatures as gifts was common in the nineteenth century. This signature, from one of Emily's late letters, would have been a particularly precious offering from Susan.

253

I was
just writing
these very
words to you,
"Susan fronts
on the Gulf
Stream," when
Vinnie entered
with the Sea –
Dare I touch
the Coincidence?
Do you remem-
ber what whis-
pered to

"Horatio"?

Emily –

1886
Emily conveys her feelings to Susan through the innuendo of Shakespeare's *Hamlet*, when Horatio hears rumors of war and ill fortune.

254

How lovely
every Solace!
This long,
short, penance
"Even I regain
my freedom
with a Sigh"

Emily –

early 1886
According to Susan's daughter Martha, this letter-poem is "One of the latest." Emily quotes the final lines of Lord Byron's "The Prisoner of Chillon." Throughout Emily's final illness, Susan is her constant caretaker. Martha Dickinson Bianchi described the months before Emily's death: "The rest of the winter was spent in the country with books and music, still consciously making adjustment of being a family of four not five; and though Susan was giving us the happiest times in reach, we realized that she was not only far from strong herself, but under a shadow of apprehension about Aunt Emily. We carried the little notes back and forth as we always had."

CODA

Emily Dickinson lost consciousness on May 13th or 14th and died a little after 6:00 in the evening on May 15, 1886. The cause of death was diagnosed as Bright's disease resulting in kidney failure.

A neighbor and friend of the Dickinsons who was with Lavinia when Emily died gave her son the following account: "Just after dinner Vinnie sent over word — if I could come over I might see Miss Emily — and very glad was I of the privilege — She looked more like her brother than her sister, with a wealth of auburn hair and a very spirituelle face — She was robed in white — with a bunch of violets at her throat . . . . Sue & Emily were friends from girlhood and Vinnie was perfectly satisfied that Sue should arrange everything knowing it would be done lovingly as well as tastefully."

It is no surprise that it was Susan who swaddled Emily's body for burial, "arranged violets and a pink cypripedium at Emily's throat and covered her white casket with violets and ground pine," and "lined the grave with boughs."[1] Susan wrote the following commemorative paragraphs within hours of Emily's last breath. Printed in the *Springfield Republican*, Susan's obituary, "Miss Emily E. Dickinson of Amherst," publicly voiced her regard for her beloved friend. Susan's memoir portrays a strong, brilliant, and loving woman given to a life of thinking and writing, and fully involved with her family, her household, and the community in which she lived.

MISS EMILY E. DICKINSON OF AMHERST

The death of Miss Emily E. Dickinson, daughter of the late Edward Dickinson, at Amherst on Saturday, makes another sad inroad on the small circle so long occupying the old family mansion. It was for a long generation overlooked by death, and one passing in and out there thought of old-fashioned times, when parents and children grew up and passed maturity together, in lives of singular uneventfulness unmarked by sad or joyous crises. Very few in the village, except among older inhabitants, knew Miss Emily personally, although the facts of her seclusion and her intellectual brilliancy were familiar Amherst traditions. There are many houses among all classes, into which her treasures of fruit and flowers and ambrosial dishes for the sick and well were constantly sent, that will forever miss those evidences of her unselfish consideration, and mourn afresh that she screened herself from close acquaintance. As she passed on in life, her sensitive nature shrank from much personal contact with the world, and more and more turned to her own large wealth of individual resources for companionship, sitting thenceforth, as some one said of her, "in the light of her own fire." Not disappointed with the world, not an invalid until within the past two years, not from any lack of sympathy, not because she was insufficient for any mental work or social career — her endowments being so exceptional — but the "mesh of her soul," as Browning calls the body, was too rare, and the sacred quiet of her own home proved the fit atmosphere for her worth and work. All that must be inviolate. One can only speak of "duties beautifully done"; of her gentle tillage of the rare flowers filling her conservatory, into which, as into the heavenly Paradise, entered nothing that could defile, and which was ever abloom in frost or sunshine, so well she knew her subtle chemistries; of her tenderness to all in the home circle; her gentlewoman's grace and courtesy to all who served in house and grounds; her quick and rich response to all who rejoiced or suffered at home, or among her wide circle of friends the world over. This side of her nature was to her the real entity in which she rested, so simple and strong was her instinct that a woman's hearthstone is her shrine.

Her talk and her writings were like no one's else, and although she never published a line, now and then some enthusiastic literary friend would turn love to larceny, and cause a few verses surreptitiously obtained to be printed. Thus, and through other natural ways, many saw and admired her verses, and in consequence frequently notable persons paid her visits, hoping to overcome the protest of her own nature and gain a promise of occasional contributions, at least, to various magazines. She withstood even the fascination of Mrs. Helen Jackson, who earnestly sought her co-operation in a novel of the No Name series, although one little poem somehow strayed into the volume of verse which appeared in that series. Her pages would ill have fitted even so attractive a story as "Mercy Philbrick's Choice," unwilling though a large part of the literary public were to believe that she had no part in it. "Her wagon was hitched to a star" — and who could ride or write with such a voyager? A Damascus blade gleaming and glancing in the sun was her wit. Her swift poetic rapture was like the long glistening note of a bird one hears in the June woods at high noon, but can never see. Like a magician she caught the shadowy apparitions of her brain and tossed them in startling picturesqueness to her friends, who, charmed with their simplicity and homeliness as well as profundity, fretted that she had so easily made palpable the tantalizing fancies forever eluding their bungling, fettered grasp. So intimate and passionate was her love of Nature, she seemed herself a part of the high March sky, the summer day and bird-call. Keen and eclectic in her literary tastes, she sifted libraries to Shakespeare and Browning; quick as the electric spark in her intuitions and analyses, she seized the kernel instantly, almost impatient of the fewest words by which she must make her revelation. To her life was rich, and all aglow with God and immortality. With no creed, no formalized faith, hardly knowing the names of dogmas, she walked this life with the gentleness and reverence of old saints, with the firm step of martyrs who sing while they suffer. How better note the flight of this "soul of fire in a shell of pearl" than by her own words?—

> Morns like these, we parted;
> Noons like these, she rose;
> Fluttering first, then firmer,
> To her fair repose.

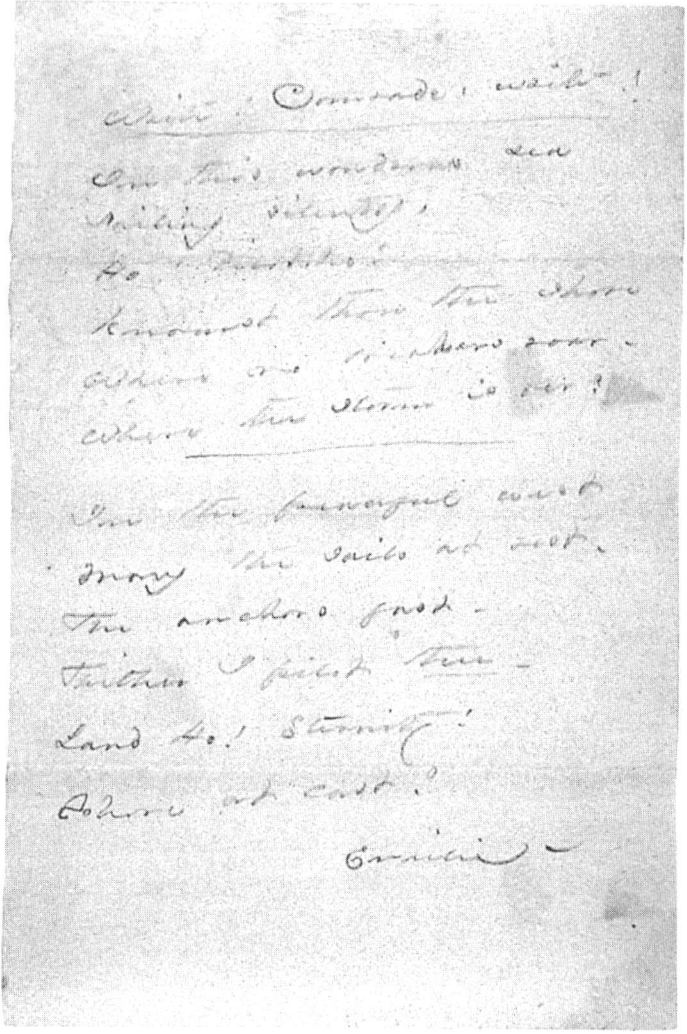
Write! Comrade – write!
On this wondrous sea
Sailing silently,
Ho! Pilot, ho!
Knowest thou the shore
Where no breakers roar –
Where the storm is o'er?

In the peaceful west
Many the sails at rest –
The anchors fast –
Thither I pilot thee –
Land Ho! Eternity!
Ashore at last!

Emilie –

Write! Comrade – write! *March 1853* (15):44

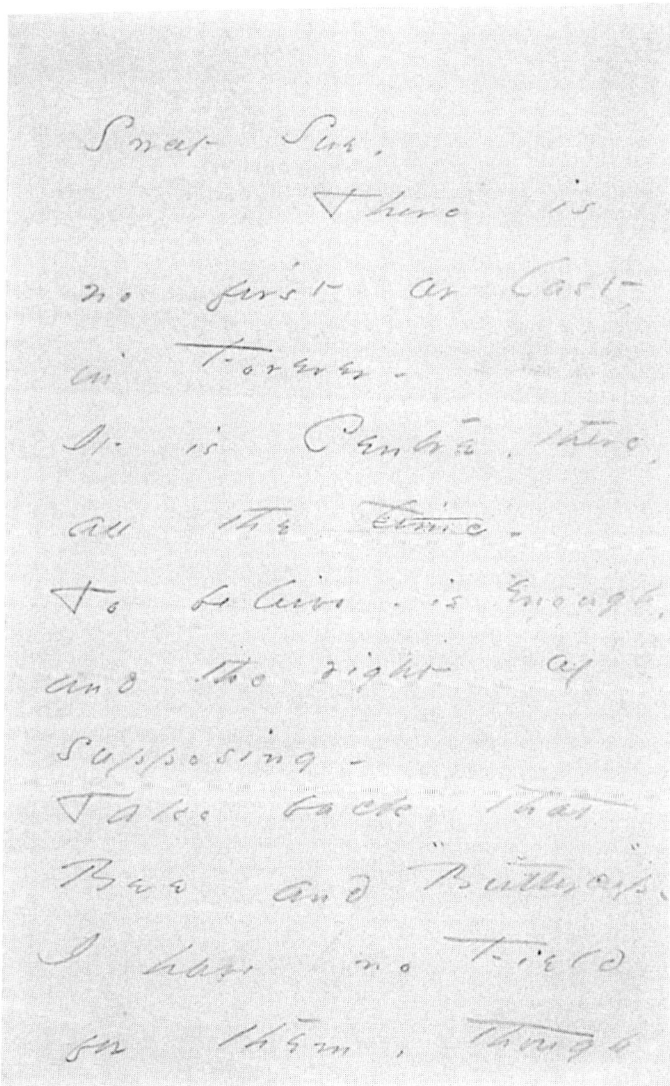
Sweet Sue,
There is
no first, or Last,
in Forever -
It is Centre, there,
all the time -
To believe - is enough,
and the right of
supposing -
Take back that
"Bee" and "Buttercups" -
I have no Field
for them, though

Sweet Sue, / There is / no first, or last, *1864* (102):130

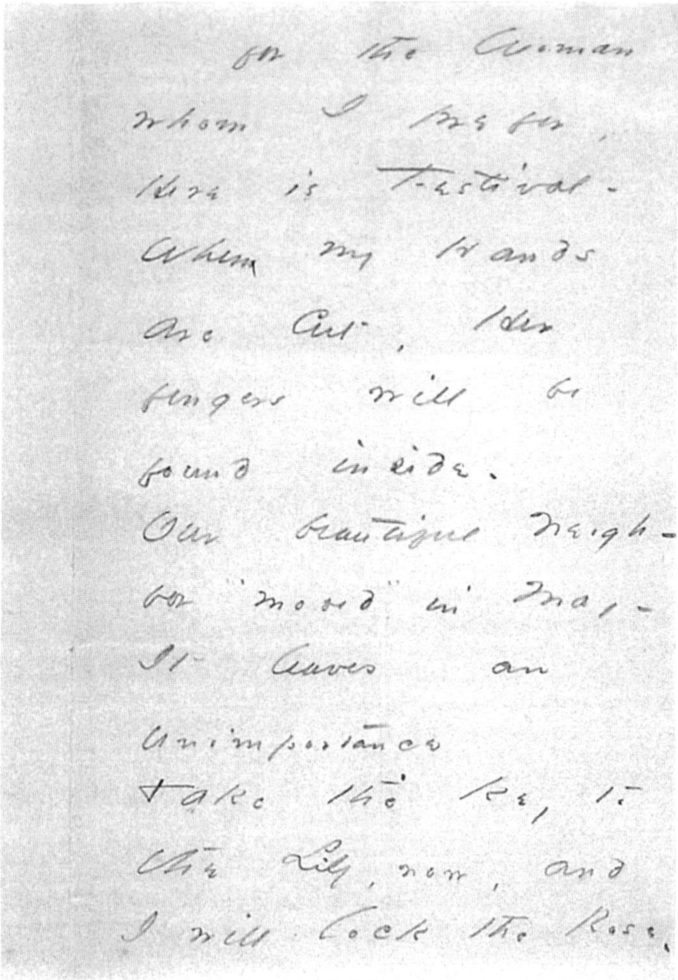
for the Woman
whom I prefer,
Here is Festival -
When my Hands
are Cut, Her
fingers will be
found inside.
Our beautiful Neigh-
bor "moved" in May -
It leaves an
Unimportance
Take the Key to
the Lily, now, and
I will lock the Rose,

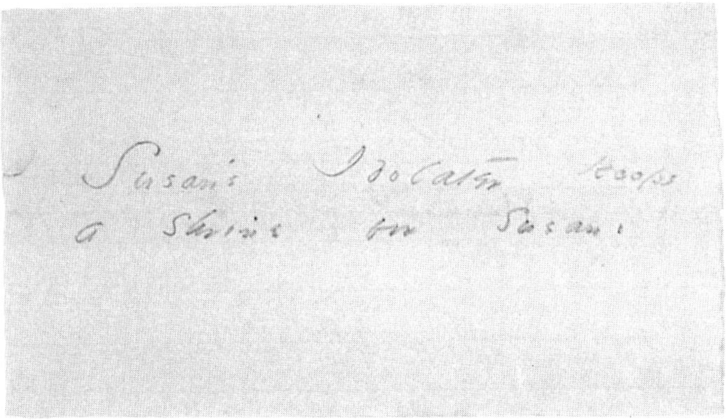
Susan's Idolater keeps
a Shrine for Susan.

Susan's Idolater keeps / a Shrine for Susan. *late 1860s* (127):156

I must wait / a few Days *late 1870s* (202):220

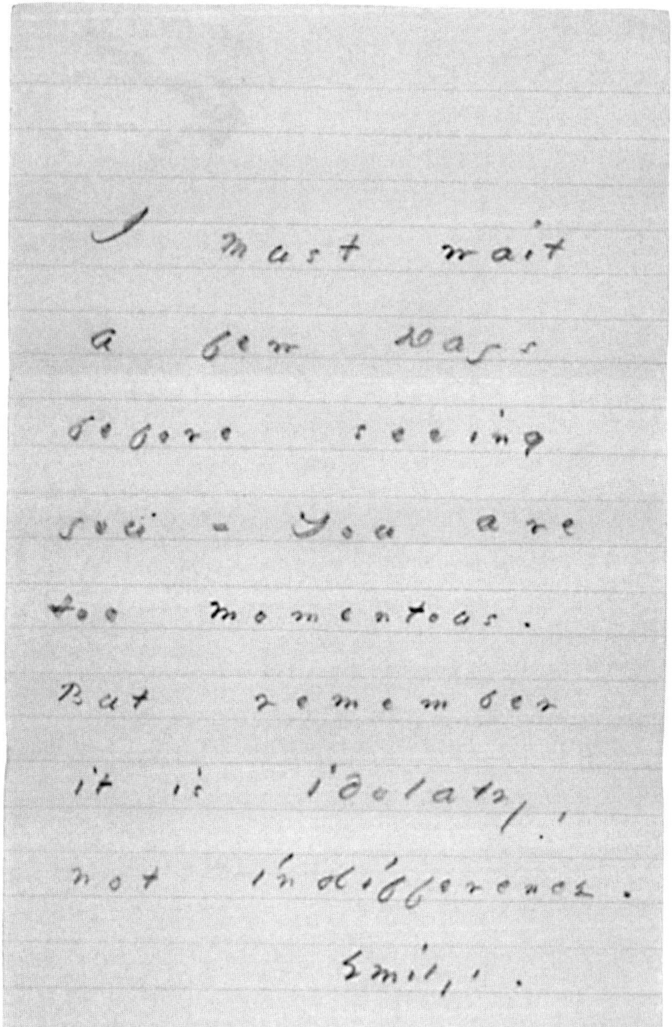
I must wait
a few Days
before seeing
you - You are
too momentous.
But remember
it is idolatry,
not indifference.
Emily.

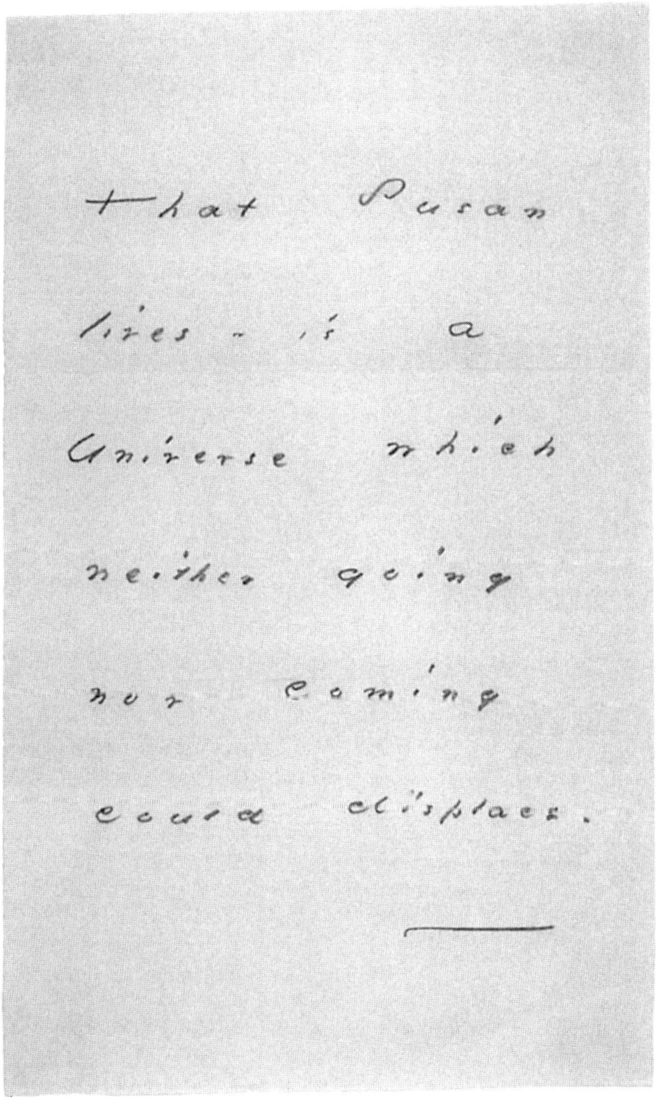
That Susan
lives – is a
Universe which
neither going
nor coming
could displace.

That Susan / lives – is a / Universe *spring 1880* (219):232

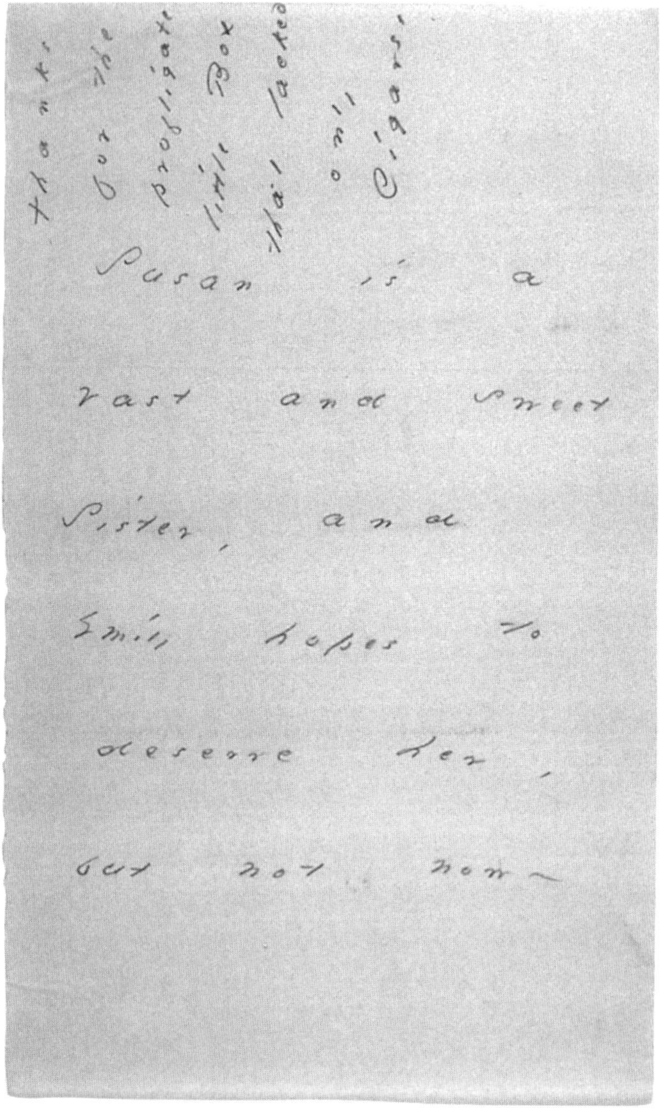

Susan is a
vast and sweet
Sister, and
Emily hopes to
deserve her,
but not now –

Susan is a / vast and sweet / Sister, *early 1880s* (220):232

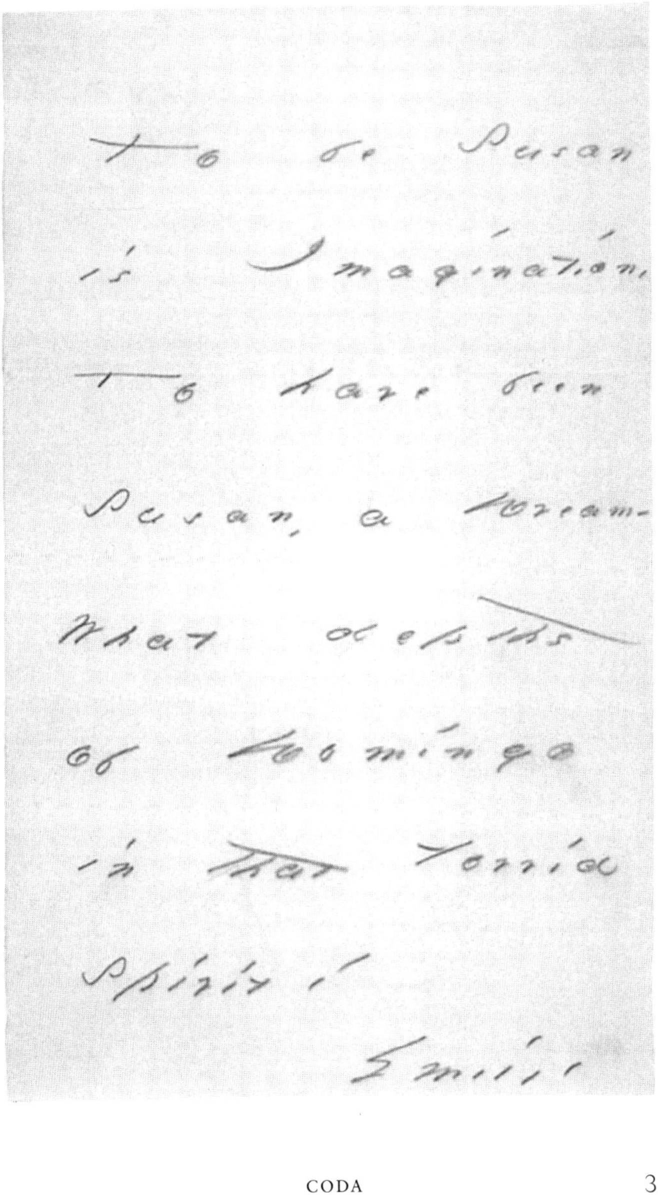

To be Susan
is Imagination,
To have been
Susan, a Dream -
What depths
of Domingo
in that torrid
Spirit!
Emily

To be Susan / is Imagination, *1880s* (233):242

KEY TO MATERIALS

SYMBOLS USED TO IDENTIFY MANUSCRIPTS

A	Manuscripts at Amherst College will be indicated by this initial and the library catalog number.
"Annals"	Dickinson, Susan. "Annals of the Evergreens." Box 9. Dickinson Papers. Houghton Library, Harvard University, Cambridge, Massachusetts.
Brown	Manuscripts and other documents in the Martha Dickinson Bianchi Collection, John Hay Library, Brown University, Providence, Rhode Island.
H	Manuscripts at the Houghton Library, Harvard University, Cambridge, Massachusetts, will be indicated by this initial and the library catalog letter and/or number.
Morgan	Manuscripts at the Morgan Library, New York, New York.
Princeton	Manuscripts at the Princeton University Library, Princeton, New Jersey.
Smith	Manuscripts at the Neilson Library, Smith College, Northampton, Massachusetts.
Yale	Manuscripts at the Beinecke Library, Yale University, New Haven, Connecticut.

ABBREVIATIONS OF FREQUENTLY CITED SOURCES

AB	Bingham, Millicent Todd. *Ancestors' Brocades: The Literary Debut of Emily Dickinson.* New York: Harper & Brothers Publishers, 1945.
CP	Bianchi, Martha Dickinson and Alfred Leete Hampson, editors. *The Complete Poems of Emily Dickinson.* Boston: Little, Brown, 1924.
FF	Bianchi, Martha Dickinson. *Emily Dickinson Face to Face: Unpublished Letters With Notes and Reminiscences.* Boston: Houghton Mifflin Publishers, 1932.
L	Johnson, Thomas H. and Theodora Ward, editors. *The Letters of Emily Dickinson.* Cambridge: Belknap Press of Harvard University Press, 1958. References to this edition will use this initial and give the number assigned by Johnson.
LL	Bianchi Martha Dickinson. *The Life and Letters of Emily Dickinson.* Boston: Houghton Mifflin, 1924.
P	Johnson, Thomas H., editor. *The Poems of Emily Dickinson.* Cambridge: Belknap Press of Harvard University Press, 1955. References to this edition will use this initial and give the number assigned by Johnson.
PF	This refers to the Prose Fragments printed in Volume III, *Letters* (911–929). Citations will use these initials and give Johnson's number.
SH	Bianchi, Martha Dickinson, editor. *The Single Hound: Poems of a Lifetime.* Boston: Little, Brown and Company, 1914.
YH	Leyda, Jay. *The Years and Hours of Emily Dickinson.* New Haven and London: Yale University Press, 1960.

NOTES

Citations for the following Houghton call numbers should be translated as follows:

H80b	MS Am 1118.3 (80b)
H L2	MS Am 1118.4 (L2)
HB1	MS Am 1118.5 (B1)
H SH	EDR 1.3.18
H ST	bMS Am 1118.95 Box 12
H Box 8	bMS Am 1118.95 Box 8
Photostats	MS Am 1118.99b

Watermarks and embossments are described using symbols from the Houghton Library's Manuscript Condition Survey. Our special thanks to Jana Dambrogio for compiling these facts about the manuscripts and their present state.

INTRODUCTION

1. H L20; L 93.
2. *Springfield Republican* May 18, 1886; *Writings by Susan Dickinson*, ed. Smith et al. Dickinson Electronic Archives.
3. iii.
4. Letter to Richard Watson Gilder, December 31, 1886.
5. Letter to Higginson, December 1890.
6. December 1890 letter.
7. H Lowell Autograph; 14 March 1891 to William Hayes Ward; *Writings by Susan Dickinson.*
8. *Poems* 1568n.
9. H Lowell Autograph, 8 February 1891; *Writings by Susan Dickinson.*

SECTION ONE NOTES

1 YH I, 183.
2 YH I, 212.
3 YH 1:267.
4 A 596, L 109.
5 A 597, L 110.
6 A 608, L 128, A 597, L 119.
7 YH 1:302-303.
8 YH 1:315.
9 YH 1:316.

1. Ink, gilt-edged, embossed "PARIS" (I). "Susie Gilbert" on verso, and "Read – No" penciled in Susan's handwriting, probably much later. That notation may indicate a decision not to read this letter to friends at a gathering in her home or not to include this letter in her book of Emily's writings. [H B131, L 38. *FF* 186–187.]
2. Ink, one sheet, four pages, end of letter may be missing. Coffee stains (rings of mug) are on manuscript, perhaps from Susan. Text of every paragraph has faint penciled lines, as if someone (presumably Susan) were reading and marking passages for editorial purposes. A calligraphic "g" in "hight" underlines the first part of the word in the "last" sentence (last of the surviving holograph). Ellipsis indicates end of letter may be missing. Thomas Johnson omits "left" from the line, "for there will be none left to interpret . . ." [H L5, L 56. *FF* 205–208.]
3. Ink, one sheet, four pages, multiple folds, faint lines across text. "G's" in "ugly things" dramatically underline letters preceding them. Johnson omits the article "a" before "a broken back." [H L10, L 73. *FF* 182–184, in part.]
4. Ink, one sheet, four pages, folded in half. "Susie" on verso, and "No" in Susan's handwriting. Johnson creates a final paragraph from the marginalia. [H L22, L 74.]
5. Ink, blue paper, embossed "J Prout / Stationer/ Worcester" (JFJ), multiple folds. "Chuck" or "Church" penciled in Susan's handwriting across the last page. Here and on other letters "Chuck" may mean that Susan has not selected a letter or a section to read or to include in her book of Emily's writings. There is a blot of ink

where Emily writes, "Dont see the blot." Exclamation mark after "him" after upside-down marginalia is inverted. A letter written to Austin Dickinson at the same time, beginning, "I will write while they've gone to meeting," erases or cuts away all references to Susan. Johnson omits "would" in the first sentence: "when the world and the cares of the world would try so hard . . ." and he records "did'nt" rather than "didn't." He forms a paragraph from the marginalia and places it after the signature. [H L9, L 77. *FF* 177–181, in part.]

6. Ink, embossed "Paris" (SFHBP), faint pencil marks across paragraphs, folded in half, then in thirds, very worn. In the first paragraph, last sentence, Johnson mistakenly transcribes "much" instead of "such," and at the end of the letter he regularizes Dickinson's one quotation mark for two quotations in: " . . . forever . " Herein . . . ." [H L13, L 85. *FF* 197–200, in part.]
7. Ink, embossed "Superfine" (SFHBP), folded in half, then in thirds, and worn. Faint pencil lines in Susan's handwriting cross the body of text; "Baltimore" at end of first sentence; and "Chuck" or "Church" across the text of the first two sentences. Johnson omits the article "a" from "where I have <u>none</u> – and a <u>sister</u> . . ." [H L18, L 88. *LL* 20, three sentences in part; *FF* 213–215, in part.]
8. Ink, small sheet, folded in thirds, bottom third torn away. Johnson omits "little" from the last sentence, "till this little heart . . . ." [H B173, L 92. *LL* 27, in small part, and altered.]
9. Ink, embossed "Paris" (SFHBP), one sheet, four pages, folded in half, then in thirds. "Dont" and "CFS" or "CPS" are scribbled across paragraph beginning "God is good, Susie." Emily's handwriting is noticeably different. Underlinings are very wavy, calling attention to themselves. Johnson mistranscribes Dickinson's "This union, my dear Susie, by which two lives are one" as "These unions"; he prints "if that great blessedness" instead of Emily's "of that great blessedness"; in the last paragraph before the signature Johnson prints "it had no parting," rather than "it has no parting more"; he transcribes "gather" as "gathers" and omits the word "me" from "if they promise me not to lose you." [H L20, L 93. *LL* 43, in part.]
10. Ink, no embossment, one sheet, four pages, lightly ruled, folded in thirds, pinholes, holes on each third similar to some of those made

on the fascicles for binding. Addressed "Miss Susan H. Gilbert. / 40-Lexington St. / Baltimore. / Md-" "May want again," in Susan's or Martha Dickinson Bianchi's handwriting just above the address. A pencil line down the left side of text on the third leaf marks the passage from "Dear Susie, I have tried hard" to "never slumbers nor sleeps"; and a heavier line on the left side of the postscript marks "Why cant I be a Delegate." Johnson transcribes "fears" as "years" in the first paragraph. [H L2, L 94. *FF* 215–217, in part.]

11. Ink, no embossment, one sheet, four pages, folded into rectangles. Penciled lines across the final three paragraphs. Dashes dramatically point down. Johnson mistranscribes "I'd" for "I'll" in the sixth paragraph. [H L7, L 96, *FF* 217–219, in part.]
12. Ink, gilt-edged, no embossment, two sheets torn precisely down left side, making small leaves, multiple folds, pinholes, and rust marks from paper clips. [H B176, L 97. *LL* 55, in part, with changes.]
13. Ink, embossed XSTR, multiple folds, quite worn. Lines penciled across paragraphs from "It made me feel so lonely" to "At Dover"; "Manchester" (where Susan was visiting) penciled above the date. "T's" in this letter have an extraordinary flair, and most of the dashes are noticeably longer than in previous missives. "X" on verso in Susan's handwriting. [H L16, L 102. *FF* 220–223, in part, with changes.]
14. Ink, no embossment, one sheet, four pages, folded in rectangles. Lines penciled across second, fifth, sixth, and eighth paragraph. In the first paragraph, Emily uses "it" to refer to her emotional "heart" in a way that recalls her use of "it" in the "Master" letter Johnson calls the third and Franklin designates as the second. [H L8, L 103. *FF* 188–189, in part.]
15. Pencil, no embossment, a torn half sheet, folded in fourths, paste marks. Line between stanzas drawn by Emily, which parallels Susan's practice of putting lines between stanzas in her own poems. The dash after "Comrade" points up to the right, heightening the excited, exclamatory tone of the heading's command. Susan transcribed this poem twice. There is another version of this poem in the fascicles. [H B73, H ST 23e, H ST 24, P 4. *Poems* (1896) 200, titled "Eternity"; *LL* 78–79.]

16. Ink, embossed, one sheet, four pages, folded in half, then in thirds. Handwriting is markedly shaky. Lines penciled through all paragraphs. Johnson mistranscribes "shadow" in the sixth paragraph as "shadows." [H L4, L 107. *FF* 190–192, in part.]
17. Pencil, embossed with capitol building (CNGRSS), "Congress" printed, folded in thirds, very worn, paste marks. "Susie" on verso. [H B152, L 135. *FF* 220, in part.]
18. Ink, embossed (BTH), folded in thirds, penciled lines across last five paragraphs. Over paragraph beginning "To get you all once more," "Shyness" penciled in Susan's handwriting. Emily's handwriting is noticeably shaky, and an ink blot appears over the word "beat" in the seventh paragraph. Johnson omits the clause "I flew –" from the second sentence. [H L19, L 154. *LL* 31, in part, with changes.]
19. Ink, embossed (SLP), blue-ruled, one sheet, two leaves, folded in rectangles. Lines penciled across most paragraphs; "Chuck" or "Church" penciled across the fifth paragraph. Johnson transcribes "good" instead of "great" in the next to last paragraph. [H L6, L 176. *FF* 211–213, in part.]
20. Ink, embossed (SLP), one sheet, two leaves, blue-ruled, rust marks from paper clips. Illegible note in Susan's handwriting, perhaps "Last" (?), penciled in the upper margin of first page, and penciled lines cross paragraphs. Johnson forms final paragraph with the marginalia following the signature. [H L1, L 177. *LL* 33–34, in small part; *FF* 200–202 in part.]
21. Ink, embossed (SLP), one sheet, two leaves, blue-ruled, folded in rectangles, lines penciled through paragraphs. "Washington" in Susan's handwriting on top of the first page and across lines in sixth paragraph beginning "Vinnie met the other evening." The envelope, addressed by Edward Dickinson "Miss Susan H. Gilbert. / Amherst. / Mass," has been torn open, sealing wax is still attached, and bears paste marks on the verso, indicating preservation in a scrapbook. [H L14, L 178. *FF* 202–205, in part.]

SECTION TWO NOTES

1 H Lowell Autograph, 14 March 1891 to William Hayes Ward, *Writings by Susan Dickinson*, ed. Smith et al.

22. Ink, gilt-edged, embossed coat of arms (SMLY), one sheet, four pages, multiple folds, poem on pages 3 and 4, with corners turned to be inserted into scrapbook. Handwriting appears shaky. "Young" is penciled in Susan's handwriting on fourth page, "X" on verso. [H L17, P 5, L 173. *FF* 181–182, poem but not the letter; *Letters* (1894) 162; (1931) 159, *LL* 188, prose variant of the second stanza serves as the concluding paragraph in a "Late Autumn, 1853" letter to Josiah and Elizabeth Holland (dated "early 1854" in *LH* 38).]
23. Pencil, gilt, embossed "Paris" (A), writing on first of four pages, folded in thirds. "Sue" erased from verso. Another version of the poem is in the fascicles. [A 663, P 204. *UP* 46.]
24. Pencil, no embossment, neatly torn (8 x 13.5 cm.), folded in quarters, paste marks. "Susie" on verso. "Send this back to me" in pen in Susan's handwriting of the 1860s, suggesting that she and Emily passed this note back and forth. [H B75, L 134. *FF* 185.]
25. Pencil, gilt, lightly blue-ruled, embossed (FNP), writing on first of four pages, folded in thirds. Address erased from verso. Two other versions of this poem were written; one is included in the fascicles. [A 654, P 130 (handwriting like that of "A poor – torn Heart"). Printed as "October" in *Drum Beat* (11 March 1864); as "Indian Summer" in *Poems* (1890) 100–101.]
26. Pencil, gilt, embossed (FNP), blue-ruled, writing on first of four pages, folded in thirds. "Sue" erased from verso. Another version of this poem is in the fascicles. [A 655, P 131. First and third stanzas in Frederick H. Hitchcock, *The Handbook of Amherst, Massachusetts* (1891); *Poems* (1891) 173 titled "November."]
27. Ink, embossed "Paris," gilt-edged, two leaves, folded in thirds. "Sue" on verso, which Johnson does not note. This poem is divided into stanzas in the fascicle copy. [A 634, P 138. *Poems* (1891) 124, as "My Rose."]
28. Ink, two leaves, blue-ruled, folded in thirds, "Susie" on the verso. "Letter from Emily Dickinson to Sue Dickson," written by an unknown hand, is in ink on verso. [A 70.]

29. Ink, embossed (V), one sheet, four pages, multiple folds. "Church" or "Chuck" written on top of first leaf. [H L3, L 194. *LL* 28–29, in part.]
30. Ink, on two blue-ruled leaves, pinholes. "X" in Susan's handwriting on verso. Earlier editions delete the heading and alter the signature to "Emily." [H *SH* 1, P 14. *SH* 1–2.]
31. Ink, writing on three pages of two-leaf sheet, multiple folds. Addressed "Susie" on verso. "E.D." penciled in unknown hand on first page. The "I" in "Immortality" is scripted with flourish at an angle so that the letter looks as if it is wearing a fancy hat. There are three other versions of this poem, two in the fascicles. [A 71, P 7. *SH* 90–91.]
32. Ink, blue-ruled, no embossment, half sheet torn at left, folded in thirds, pinholes. "F's" are crossed with flourish. "Earth" is raised above the line because Dickinson originally wrote "world," which she crossed out. Another version of this poem is in the fascicles. [H 255, P 6. *Poems* (1891) 157.]
33. Ink, blue-ruled paper, no embossment, half sheet torn at left, multiple folds, with many stains. "Sue" in pencil on verso. [H 349, P 8. *Poems* (1896) 83, titled "Forgotten."]
34. Ink, no embossment, on two-thirds of half sheet folded in quarters. Marked with "X" and "E" in Susan's handwriting. Another version of this poem is included in the fascicles. [H 359, P 9. *CP* (1924) 297–298.]
35. Ink, no embossment, on half sheet torn at left, folded in thirds, many stains. Another version of this poem is in the fascicles. [H 291, P 10. *SH* 19.]
36. Ink, gilt-edged, embossed "Crown," folded in rectangles. Two dots in "sail," and the ending dash is elongated. Another version of this poem is in the fascicles. [H 273, P 11. *SH* 48–49.]
37. Ink, blue-ruled, no embossment, half sheet, carefully torn at left, multiple folds. "X" in Susan's handwriting on verso. The "T's" are all crossed extravagantly. Another version of this poem is in the fascicles. [H 344, P 12. *Poems* (1890) 102, titled "Autumn."]
38. Ink, embossed wreath (FNP), half sheet, bottom third is partially torn away, folds very worn, pinholes. "Sue –" on verso. Dash after "Crimson" points down. Envelope from "The National Arts Club / 15 Gramercy Park / New York N.Y." has Bianchi's notes for the

book of Emily's writings. Another version of this poem is in the fascicles. [H 387, P 15. *FF* 185.]

39. Manuscript to Susan is "lost"; text reproduced from *The Single Hound*. "Signor" penciled on the surviving manuscript (first poem in Fascicle 7) is in Emily's handwriting of much later date. In the fascicles, Susan marked a poem with a similar theme—"Musicians wrestling Everywhere!" [H 289, P 157, marked by Susan with a "P." P 59. *SH* 110; *New England Quarterly*, XX (1947) 148.]
40. Pencil, gilt-edged, embossed "Paris" (A), one sheet, two leaves, folded in thirds, pinholes. "Sue" on verso. Another version of this poem is in the fascicles. [H 321, P 62. *SH* 105.]
41. Ink, no embossment, two leaves. "Sue" on verso, crossed-out "C" in Susan's handwriting, multiple folds and two incisions in vertical fold as if for an attachment. Punctuation has a sportive kick to it: "Period" on exclamation at end of first line appears to be a comma turned on its side. Another version of this poem is in the fascicles. [H 319, P 64. *Poems* (1890) 76–77, titled "Summer's Armies."]
42. Pencil, embossed (FNP), blue-ruled on half sheet torn at left, folded in thirds, pinholes, top corners folded over, as if for insertion in a scrapbook. Another version of this poem is in the fascicles and a copy was sent to Higginson in July 1862. [H B189, P 67. *Brooklyn Daily Union*, 27 April 1864; *A Masque of Poets*, ed. Helen Hunt Jackson (1878); *Poems* (1890) 13.]
43. Pencil, blue-ruled, no embossment, torn upper half of sheet, folded in half "X" on verso in Susan's handwriting. "Y's" written with flourish. Corners folded as if for insertion in a scrapbook. Another version of this poem is in the fascicles. [H 233, P 68. *SH* 113.]
44. Pencil, gilt-edged, embossed (FNP), blue-ruled, half sheet torn at left, folded in thirds, pinholes on top. Dashes more exaggerated, scooped (as in that after "Like you –" in "Master" letter). The cross of the "T" in the last line almost underlines "my" in preceding line. Dickinson changed "Thy pe" to "Thy" to "Thine," and crossed out "pe." [H 286, P 69. *SH* 86.]
45. Pencil, gilt-edged, embossed (FNP), half sheet torn at left, folded in thirds. Marked with "P" by Susan. Another version of this poem is in the fascicles. [H 239, P 71. *Poems* (1891) 226.]

46. Ink, gilt-edged, embossed "Paris" (A), half sheet torn at left, folded in thirds, pinholes. "X" in pencil in Susan's handwriting on verso. Bold "Y" in "Emily" spans the entire word. Another version of this poem is in the fascicles. [H 377, P 73. *Poems* (1891) 29, titled "Triumphant."]
47. Pencil, faintly embossed "Holyoke Co." (X), half sheet torn at left, folded in thirds. The "Y" in "Away" is scrawled so boldly that it extends between "of"and "spotted" in the following line. Pencil "X" and triangle on verso in Susan's handwriting, including a list: "Remember Mister / Austins Hold / *[illegible]* Waltzes – Labitax / Bobolink Polka / Remember(?)." [H 310, P 75. *SH* 38; *CP* 269–270.)
48. Pencil, no embossment, half sheet torn at left. Addressed "Sue" on verso, with "X" in pencil in Susan's handwriting. Descending and differently shaped arcs, perhaps of "E" and "Y" in "Emily," make it appear that signature was torn away. Johnson does not note that this manuscript is addressed to "Sue." There is another version in the fascicles. [H 254, P 76. *Poems* (1890) 116, titled "Setting Sail."]
49. Pencil, gilt-edged, embossed (FNP), two leaves, multiple folds. "P" and "X" on verso in Susan's handwriting. Another version of this poem is in the fascicles. [H 305, P 80, late 1850s. *Poems* (1896) 55, titled "Alpine Glow."]
50. Pencil, gilt, embossed (FNP), blue-ruled, multiple folds, pinholes. There is another version in the fascicles. "Sue" erased from verso. [A 651, P 84 (handwriting like that of "A poor – torn Heart"). *Letters* (1894) 215; Letters (1931) 202–203; *LL* 253.)
51. Pencil, gilt, embossed, lightly blue-ruled, writing on first of four pages, folded in thirds, pinholes. "Sue" erased from verso. Another version of this poem is in the fascicles. [A 653, P 121. BM 216.]
52. Pencil, embossed oval (stationery and handwriting like that of earlier pencil manuscripts at AC), half sheet, folded in thirds, torn at left, signs of wear and use. The dash after "charged" in last stanza points down, and the tail on the "Y" in "Emily" arches toward the signature. "X" in Susan's handwriting on verso. Another version of this poem is in the fascicles. [Morgan Library, MA 1488, P 152. *BM* 23.]
53. Pencil, gilt-edged, embossed (FNP), two leaves, folded in thirds. "Y" in signature scoops and cradles "Emily." "Sue" on verso, as is

"Printed" in Susan's handwriting. Another version of the poem in fascicles. [H 251, P 154. *Poems* (1890) 142.]

54. Ink, embossed queen's head (Q), two leaves, blue-ruled, folded in thirds, pinholes. "Sue" on verso, and "X" in Susan's handwriting. There is another version in the fascicles. [H B195, P 155. *Poems* (1890) 71.)
55. Another version of this poem is in the fascicles. [P 160. First published in the *Independent*, XLIII, using Susan's holograph (see *AB* 145–146). Also published in *Poems* (1891) 85–86, with same title.)
56. Pencil, embossed (FNP), gilt, two leaves, blue-ruled, folded in thirds, paste marks. "Sue" on verso, and "X" in Susan's handwriting. Paste marks reveal that this letter was mounted in a scrapbook. [H B133, L 231.]
57. Ink, small sheet torn to size, bottom has been torn away, missing as of June 20, 1963. Photostat confirms that Susan's note at the bottom of the letter-poem reads: "1860 – written on Ned's birth-day - / Toby was the cat –." Johnson mistranscribes "I" for "you" in the line "If you could shut him up." "1860" may refer to the decade, since Ned was born in 1861. [H B140, P 218. *L* 232, *L* 53.]
58. Ink, no embossment, folded in quarters, last line and reassurance to Emily on verso. [H B94. Johnson, *Emily Dickinson* 117; *Rowing in Eden* 181.]
59. Susan's copy, now "lost," was most likely sent to the newspaper for printing. Another version is in the fascicles. [*Springfield Republican* (March 1, 1862).]
60. Pencil, gilt-edged, embossed (FNP), blue-ruled, paste marks. Another version is in the fascicles, and yet another was sent in Emily's first letter to Higginson. [H B74c, L 238.]
61. Ink, embossed with queen's head (Q), paste marks. "Emily –" and "Pony Express" (lower left corner) on verso. [H B74b, L 238, P 216.]
62. Ink, gilt-edged, embossed (FNP). Folded in thirds, pinholes. Another version is in the fascicles. [H B74a; L 238, P 216n; Susan's transcription is in H Box 9.]
63. Pencil, on Queen's head stationery. "Private" angles up to the right and the dash beside "kiss" angles down to the right. A little square of paper is scissored away beneath the words "If you have suffered this

past / summer I am sorry *[square excision]* I" and "a thorn, why not we [!]" Scissorings are partially angled across the document. Though a word appears to have been cut out from the first incision, none is excised by this second in which the pieces on either side of the cut fit together perfectly. The shape of the second is cut to excise the last sentence and mimics the mark we use for long division. The cuts are probably the result of a letter opener or some editing process to place writings in scrapbooks. [H Box 8.]

64. Ink, blue-ruled, embossed "G." and "T.," folded in thirds. Franklin has placed this in Fascicle 19. "Sue –" erased from verso. [A 80–7, P 336. *BM* 177.]
65. Pencil, gilt-edged, embossed (FNP), two leaves, paste marks. "Sue" on verso with calligraphic extravagance, inscribed in large handwriting, with wide spacing between words, and written in the middle third of the page. [H B125, L 239, P 220.]
66. Pencil, embossed "A Pirie & Sons 1862" (Y), half sheet torn at left, folded in thirds and then multiple folds, pinholes. "X" in Susan's handwriting on verso. [H 374, P 1146. *SH* 9.]
67. Ink, gilt-edged, embossed "Paris" (A), two leaf sheet, corner folded over and pinned. "*SH*D's copy" and "5" penciled in top right-hand corner. Another version of this poem is in the fascicles. [H 309, P 217. *London Mercury*, XIX (February 1929), 358; FP 188.]
68. Two other versions: one in the fascicles, one sent to Higginson. [H 127a, P 228, (copy to Susan "lost"). Titled "Sunset" in three printings during Dickinson's lifetime: *Springfield Daily Republican*, 30 March 1864; *Springfield Weekly Republican*, 2 April 1864; *Drum Beat*, 29 February 1864.]
69. Ink, on two-thirds of half sheet, torn on right and bottom, folded in half, stains, paste marks. Last six lines repeat last part of "'Tis Anguish grander than Delight," which is dated "about 1865" by Johnson, though this letter-poem appears to have been sent to Susan earlier. [H B191, P 984 (last ll.). *SH* 96.]
70. Ink, gilt-edged, embossed (Q), four page sheet and poem continues onto the fourth page, rectangular folds. "X" and "60–70" in Susan's handwriting on verso, probably indicating the decade of the poem's writing. "This book" in Bianchi's handwriting. There are two other

versions, one in the fascicles and one sent to Thomas Higginson in July 1862. [H B44, L258, P 229. *FF* 228, with poem omitted.]

71. Ink, on faintly embossed paper, half sheet torn at left, folded in thirds. "X" penciled in Susan's handwriting on verso. Another version is in the fascicles. [H 274, P 301. *Poems* (1890) 134, *CP* 313.]

72. Ink, half sheet torn at left, rectangular folds. "P" on verso. Another version is in the fascicles. [H 256, P 310.]

73. Ink, no embossment, half sheet torn at left, folded in thirds, paste marks. "Sue" on verso, and "X" in pencil in Susan's handwriting, as is "with gay flowers" and "Sent with very rich flowers." Another version of this poem is in the fascicles. [H B154, P 308, *SH* 60.]

74. Ink, half sheet torn at left, folded in thirds, paste marks. Addressed "Sue" on verso, and "X" in pencil in Susan's handwriting. "L" in "Largest" is noticeably large. There is another version in the fascicles. [H B28, P 309, *FF* 263.]

75. Ink, two leaves, no embossment, folded in thirds, pinholes, signs of everyday use (impressions from scribbling). Word choice and lineation is dramatically different from the copy bound in the fascicle and the other two versions. [H 278, P 311. *Poems* (1891) 174–175, titled "The Snow."]

76. Ink, two half sheets. There are two other versions, one in the fascicles. [P 312, 1935 photostat. *SH* 94.]

77. Ink, embossed (Q), half sheet torn at left, folded in thirds. "Sue" on verso. [H 246, P 313 (last stanza only). *Poems* (1891), 46–47, entire poem titled "Too Much."]

78. Ink, gilt-edged, embossed "Paris" (I), two leaves, folded in thirds. Pencil "X" in Susan's handwriting on verso. Another version is in the fascicles. [H 292, P 314. *BM* 245.]

79. Pencil, embossed "Paris" (I), gilt, two leaves, folded in thirds. Writing on first page, centered on page. "X" in Susan's handwriting on verso. [Morgan Library, MA 1357, P 1155. *SH* 126.]

80. Ink, half sheet torn at left, folded in quarters, pinholes, paper clip impressions. "Sue" and text on verso. Another version of this poem is in the fascicles. [H 262, P 315. *Poems* (1896) 86.]

81. Susan's copy is "lost," but may be that located at Amherst College by Marget Sands. There is another version in the fascicles and a

copy was sent to Higginson. [A 457, P 322. *Scribner's Magazine*, VIII (August 1890), 240; *Poems* (1890) 58–59; *CP* (1924) 152–153.]

82. Ink, gilt, embossed "Paris" (I), half sheet torn at left, multiple folds. "P" on verso. Another version is in the fascicles. [H 249, P 675, *Poems* (1891) 210.]

83. Ink, gilt-edged, embossed "Paris" (A), multiple folds. "X" in Susan's hand on verso. Another version of this poems in the fascicles. [H 276, P 446. *SH* 132.]

84. Pencil, gilt-edged, embossed "Paris" (I), folded in thirds, two leaves. "Sue" on verso, and "X" in Susan's handwriting on verso. Another version of this poem is in the fascicles. [H 330, P 305. *SH* 26; *LL* 195–196.]

85. Ink, embossed (V), folded in thirds, paper clip impressions. The dash after "Hum" slants down. Emily wrote "Combined Girl" on the middle third of the verso, as if it were a title or an address. "X" penciled in Susan's handwriting on verso. Another version of this poem is in the fascicles. [H B178, P 302, *SH* 65.]

86. Ink, torn at the right and bottom, folded in half vertically, then horizontally in thirds. "Sue" erased from verso. One version of this poem was sent to Higginson, another is in the fascicles. [A 690, P 683. *Poems* (1891) 37.]

87. Ink, two leaves, embossed (V), folded in thirds. "Dash" after "seldom" curves, with dot above, appearing as a kind of bird's eye. "Sue" on verso. [H 350, P 306. *SH* 35, concluding part I.]

88. Ink, embossed oval shield (E), blue-ruled, half sheet torn at left, folded in thirds. "Sue" on verso. Another version of this poem is in the fascicles. [H 226, P 666. *SH* 37.]

89. Ink, gilt-edged, embossed "Paris" (I), half sheet torn at left, multiple folds. "X" in Susan's handwriting on verso. Another version of this poem is in the fascicles. [H 293, P 668. *SH* 36.]

90. Ink, gilt-edged, embossed "Paris" (I). Two leaves. "Sue" on verso, inked with inch-long descending arc. Another version of this poem is in the fascicles. [H 296, P 669. *SH* 14.]

91. Ink, gilt-edged, embossed "Paris" (I), four pages. "X" penciled in Susan's handwriting on verso. Another version of this poem is in

the fascicles. [H 304, P 670. *Poems* (1891) 214–215, titled "Ghosts." Facsimiles of holographs of this poem, *Harvard Library Bulletin*, VII (1953) 260–261.]

92. Ink, two leaves, manuscript has not been folded. "Du-" on top of sheet. Another version of this poem is in the fascicles. [A 635, P 673. *FP* 147.]

93. Embossed "Paris" (I). Gilt-edged, two leaves, folded in thirds. "Dollie" on verso. The other version of this poem is a transcript made by Susan. [Princeton, H ST 22d, P 1691. *SH* 97.]

94. Ink, embossed "Paris" (I), small square torn at left and on bottom (bottom third of manuscript removed, possibly excising last line, "The Amber Quantity –" and other writing), numerous pinholes. Another version is in the fascicles. [H B180, P 676, *BM* 70.]

95. Ink, gilt, embossed "Paris" (I), two leaves, folded in thirds, pinholes. Part of signature and/or postscript is torn off. "X" in Susan's handwriting on verso. Another version of this poem is in the fascicles. [H 362, P 677, *SH* 11.]

96. Pencil, gilt, embossed "Paris" (I), half sheet torn at left, folded in thirds. [H 297, P 679 (last two and a half stanzas of "Conscious am I in my Chamber").]

97. Pencil draft, partial sheet torn on top and left, folded in half and then again. [H 242, P 682 (last ll. of "'Twould ease – a Butterfly").]

98. Pencil, gilt, embossed "Paris" (I), half sheet torn at right, multiple folds. [H 368, P 680 (last stanza of "Each Life converges to some Centre –."]

99. Gilt, embossed "Paris" (I), half sheet torn at left, tear in manuscript, multiple folds. "X" in Susan's handwriting. [H 316, P 681.]

100. Ink, small sheet (11.2 x 12.5 cm.) torn at left and on bottom, folded in half. Dash after "Superlative" emphatically directed down. Franklin dates this handwriting around 1863. The fascicle copy is broken into stanzas, but, typically, the copy to Susan is not. Johnson did not know of this manuscript. Here this poem is associated with Susan for the first time. [Morgan Library, MA 1641, variant of Fascicle 38, P 800, *BM* 199.]

101. Pencil, gilt-edged, embossed "Paris" (I), half sheet torn at left, folded and refolded, paste marks. "Sue" on verso, and "X" penciled in Susan's handwriting. [H B 139, P 818, L 287. *FF* 270.]

102. Pencil, gilt-edged, embossed “Paris” (I), four pages, multiple folds, paste marks. [H B56, L 288. *FF* 267.]
103. Pencil, embossed “Paris” (I), four pages, folded in rectangles. [H B179, L 294. *FF* 231 and 266–267, excerpts only.]
104. Ink, gilt-edged, embossed “Paris” (I). [H B163b, P 303. *Poems* (1890) 26, titled “Exclusion.” Verso: Pencil, gilt-edged, embossed “Paris” (I).] Johnson does not note that these two poems are back-to-back on a half sheet torn at left. [H B163a, P 826. *SH* 122.]
105. Pencil, gilt-edged, embossed “Paris” (I), half sheet torn at left, folded in thirds. “Sue” penciled on verso. Another version of this poem is in the fascicles. [H 315, P 808. *SH* 138. Susan sent out two transcripts of this poem.]
106. Pencil, gilt-edged, embossed “Paris” (I), four pages, folded in thirds. “X” and an exaggerated “E” in Susan’s handwriting on verso. Another version of this poem is in the fascicles. [H 264, P 810. *SH* 135.]
107. Pencil, embossed “Paris” (I), half sheet torn at left, folded in quarters. Stanza upside down on the sheet (thus “Paris” is at bottom left instead of at top left). “170 x 15” multiplied on verso, presumably by Susan. Another version of this poem is in the fascicles. [H 371, P 811. *BM* 51.]
108. Pencil, gilt-edged, embossed “Paris” (I), four pages, folded in thirds. “Sue” penciled on verso, and “X” in Susan’s handwriting. Luxurious spacing between words and lines. There are three other versions of this poem, one of which was sent to Higginson. Another version is in the fascicles. [H 341, P 815. *SH* 119.]
109. Pencil, gilt-edged, embossed “Paris” (I), four pages, multiple folds. “X” in Susan’s handwriting on verso. Another version of this poem is in the fascicles. [H 257, P 817. *Poems* (1896) 145.]
110. Pencil, no embossment, half sheet torn at left, folded in quarters, paste marks, paper clip impressions. “Sue –” on verso and “C” inked in Susan’s handwriting on verso. [H B18, P 809, L 305. Published by Bianchi in *Atlantic Monthly,* CXV (1915) 40; *FF* 263.]
111. Pencil, gilt-edged, embossed “Paris” (I), four pages, multiple folds, paste marks. “Sue –” on verso. [H B78, L 312, P 825. *AM* CXV (1915) 37, in part; *LL* 49, in part; *FF* 236, in part.]

112. Pencil, gilt-edged, embossed "Paris" (I), writing on first and third pages of four, folded in thirds. Children's scribblings, probably Ned's, are prominent on the verso. There are three other versions, including one sent to Higginson. [A 699, P 829. *Poems* (1891) 207, as "A Country Burial."]
113. Pencil, gilt-edged, embossed "Paris" (I), half sheet torn at left, folded in quarters, paste marks, paper clip marks. "Sue." penciled on verso. [H B162, L 306. *LL* 100, in part; *FF* 270.]
114. Pencil, gilt-edged, embossed "Paris" (I), folded in quarters, half sheet torn at left. Asterisk-like mark on top of page (recto), slightly to the right. "3" also on recto. "Sue" on verso, and "X" in Susan's handwriting. Another version of this poem is in the fascicles. [H 342, P 985. *SH* 23; *LL* 195.]
115. Pencil, gilt-edged, embossed "Paris" (I), on half sheet with bottom third torn off, paste marks. These lines, with a second stanza, are in the fascicles. [H B53, P 989. *FF* 227.]
116. Ink, gilt-edged, embossed "Paris" (I), leaf carefully torn from sheet down right side, folded in thirds. Variant of second stanza is in loose sheets Franklin calls "sets." [H 331, P 992.]
117. Ink, gilt-edged, embossed "Paris" (I), two leaves, folded in thirds, pencil marks on recto and verso, drawings of animals on verso. There are precise triangular cuts between the first two lines of the second stanza. There are two other versions: one sent to Higginson and one in the fascicles. [H 250, P 1067. In *Atlantic Monthly*, LXVIII (October 1891) 451, in article by Higginson about their correspondence; Letters (ed. 1894) 312; (ed. 1931) 282; also *LL* 268–269; *SH* 5; *New England Quarterly*, XX (1947) 16.]
118. Ink, gilt-edged, embossed "Paris" (I), four pages, folded in thirds. "Sue –" in ink on verso, and "X" penciled in Susan's handwriting. Another version is in the fascicles. [H B192, P 1071. *SH* 16.]
119. Ink, gilt-edged, embossed "Paris" (I), two leaves, folded in thirds. "X" penciled in Susan's handwriting on verso. Another version is in the fascicles. [H 328, P 988. *LL* 49; *New England Quarterly*, XX (1947) 46.]

SECTION THREE NOTES

1 YH 11, 186.

120. Ink, gilt-edged, embossed "Paris" (I), two leaves, folded in quarters. Illegible penciled words in Susan's handwriting: "Mr Sayed" or "W Soced" or "Saved"? Another version of this poem was probably sent to Samuel Bowles. [H 361, P 1072. *LL* 49–50; *CP* 176–177.)
121. Pencil, gilt-edged, embossed "Paris" (I), half sheet torn at left, folded in thirds. [H 277, P 812. *Poems* (1896) 103–104.)
122. Ink, gilt-edged, embossed "Paris" (I), writing on first, second, third pages, folded in thirds. "X" in Susan's handwriting beneath second of Susan's poems. Two other versions of this poem exist: one that is signed and included among Emily's ungathered poems, and another in the fascicles. [H 325, P 1104. *Poems* (1896) 130, titled "Evening."]
123. Pencil, blue-ruled, no embossment, two-thirds leaf torn at top and right, folded in half, paste marks. "X" and "Read with [illegible]" in Susan's handwriting on verso. [H B159, P 1106. *FF* 264.]
124. Pencil draft, half sheet torn at right, no embossment, multiple folds. First "A" is crossed out, "The" written in and crossed out, "A" written in again. [H 223, P 1108. *FF* 244.]
125. Pencil, embossed wreath (W?), sheet torn in half, blue-ruled, folded in quarters, pinholes. [H 271, P 1109. *SH* 88.]
126. Pencil, scrap paper torn at left and bottom, folded in quarters, pinholes, paste marks. "Sue." penciled on verso. [H B135, L 324. *AM* CXV (1915) 37, in part; *LL* 57, in part; *FF* 237, in part.]
127. Pencil, torn at bottom, folded in half, paste marks. Two lines are centered on the page. "X" penciled in Susan's handwriting on verso. [H B71, L 325. *FF* 247.]
128. Pencil on small sheet, no embossment, folded in quarters. "Sue" penciled in one quarter of verso. [H B80, L 327. *FF* 264.]
129. Pencil, gilt-edged, embossed "Paris" (A), four pages, folded in quarters, paste marks. Text is centered in the middle of the first page. [H B97, L 328.]
130. Pencil, gilt-edged, embossed "Paris" (A), four pages, folded in thirds. "X" in Susan's handwriting on verso. There is another version in the

fascicles. [H 345, P 1115. First stanza only in Frederick H. Hitchcock, ed., *The Handbook of Amherst, Massachusetts* (Amherst, 1891) 21; first two quatrains in *Poems* (1896) 136, titled "Aftermath"; *CP*, without stanza divisions; all four stanzas in *New England Quarterly*, XX (1947) 26.]

131. This is a reproduction of Bianchi's version of the poem, which presumably follows the copy that Emily sent to Susan, now lost. There is another pencil draft of the poem. [P 1116. *SH* 20; *LL* 195.]

132. Pencil, gilt, embossed "Paris" (I), folded in thirds. Writing on first and third of four pages. Scribblings on verso, as is "X" in Susan's handwriting; bottom third also has mathematical calculations. [H 234, P 1117. *FF* 240.]

133. Pencil, single white sheet embossed "P & S" (JP), blue-ruled, folded in rectangles, as if for an envelope, pinholes through all four folds. "X" on verso, as is "Parts gone" in Susan's handwriting. [H 252a, P 1118. *SH* 13.]

134. Pencil, blue-ruled, third of sheet torn at left and bottom, multiple folds, paste marks. Text is centered on the page. "Sue" on verso. [H B20, L 334. *LL* 62.]

135. Pencil, gilt-edged, embossed "Paris" (A), one sheet, paste marks. "Sue '" penciled on verso. [H B70, L 335. *LL* 62.]

136. Pencil draft, no embossment, one leaf graph paper, torn at left, folded in thirds. "X" in Susan's handwriting on verso. [H 366, P 1135. *SH* 82.]

137. Pencil, half sheet, torn at left, folded in thirds. "X" in Susan's handwriting on verso. [L 336, P 1139, Smith College. *Daily Hampshire Gazette*, 18 December 1952.]

138. Pencil, gilt-edged stationery embossed "Paris" (I), four pages, multiple folds. "X" in Susan's handwriting on verso. There is also a transcript by Susan (H ST 15a). [H 335, P 1136. *BM* 54.]

139. Pencil, folded in half, pasted onto the half-title page of a copy of *The Single Hound* once owned by Laura Scull of Langhorne, Pennsylvania. Bianchi has inscribed the copy: "To Laura – In memory of our Immortals – with Martha's love – 1914." This verse is the first stanza of a four-stanza poem among the ungathered writings. [P 1137, first stanza, privately owned, *SH* 54.]

140. Ink, watermark "A Pirie & Sons / 1866" (Y), two leaves, folded in thirds. "X" penciled in Susan's handwriting on verso. [H 364, P 1247. *SH* 147.]
141. Pencil, gilt-edged, embossed "Paris" (I), four pages, folded in thirds. "Sue." on verso, which also has a "P" in Susan's handwriting. [H 238, P 1138. *Poems* (1891) 147, titled "The Spider."]
142. Pencil, graph paper, multiple folds. Glued on a leaf with Susan's transcript on blue-ruled paper (embossed AMB), to which Susan has added Emily's signature. [H 333, P 1141. *SH* 144; *LL* 197.]
143. Ink, watermark "A Pirie & Sons 1866" (Y), paper clip marks, bottom two-thirds of second leaf are cut away, folded in thirds. Dashes after "one" and "aggregate" point down. [H 308, P 1243. *SH* 143; *LL* 197.]
144. Ink, four pages, folded in rectangles, pinholes on central fold as if for binding. [H B185, L 333. *FF* 239–240, in part.]
145. Pencil, gilt-edged, embossed "Paris" (I), two leaves, folded in thirds. "X" in Susan's handwriting on verso. There is another version in the fascicles. [H 347, P 1142. *SH* 28.]
146. Pencil, gilt-edged, two-thirds of a leaf, folded in half. "X" in Susan's handwriting on verso. Dickinson's small "b" and "f" are often nearly indistinguishable, and that is the case here. Dash after "Balloon" points down. [H 268, P 1215. *SH* 32.]
147. Ink, embossed "A Pirie & Sons" (Y). Another version of the poem is in the fascicles. [H B193, P 986, L 378. *FF* 231–232.
148. Ink with all changes in pencil, white paper embossed "A Pirie & Sons / 1870" (Y), ruled, folded in quarters. Dashes after "Child," "[behold," and "ineffable"] point down. "X" in Susan's handwriting on bottom right of verso. [H 378, P 1258. *SH* 116–117.]
149. Pencil, torn at right and bottom, folded in quarters, paste marks. On verso a shopping list in Susan's handwriting: "[S?L? wake or word ending in 'll'] Ink, Satin Ribbon, Young's Druggist." [H B23, P 1158 (first two lines), L 350. *FF* 145 and 242.]
150. Pencil, embossed "Paris" (A), half sheet torn at left, multiple folds, paste marks; stains on verso. "X" in Susan's handwriting on verso. Susan quotes this in "When Autumn Began," review letter "To the

Editor of the Republican" by S.H.D. of "Autumn's Divine Beauty Begins" (August 2, 1906; Brown St. A 126). [H B49, L 347. *FF* 238.]

151. Pencil, small sheet torn to size at right and bottom, paste marks. Text is centered on the page. "X" in Susan's handwriting on verso. [H B57, L 348. *FF* 259.]
152. Pencil, embossed "Paris" (I), gilt, half sheet torn at left, folded in thirds, paste marks. "X" in Susan's handwriting on verso. [H B8, L 349. *FF* 241.]
153. Pencil, gilt-edged, embossed "Paris" (I), folded in thirds. "2" in red pencil on upper right of recto, full sheet plus half sheet torn at left. "Sue" on verso, as is "X" in Susan's handwriting; "in *[unintelligible] Poems*" on recto, which likely refers to the poem's printing in Loomis Todd and Higginson's second volume of Dickinson's verse and is Susan's editorial note as she worked on her book of Emily's writings. Versions of this poem were sent to Thomas Higginson, Elizabeth and Josiah Holland, and an unknown recipient. Other versions are in the ungathered poems. [H 356, P 824. *Poems* (1891) 158–159, titled "A Thunder-Storm."]
154. Pencil, gilt-edged, embossed "Paris" (A), half sheet torn at left, folded, as if for an envelope, paste marks. [H B33, P 1156, L 356. *FF* 225.]
155. Pencil, embossed profile (D), two leaves, paste marks. [H B107, L 365. *FF* 254.]
156. Pencil, gilt-edged, embossed "Paris" (I), two leaves, folded in thirds, paste marks. "Sue." on verso. "A" on "All" is emphatically large, and there is extended spacing between letters. [H B182, L 366. *LL* 62.]
157. Pencil, gilt edged, embossed "Paris" (I), half sheet torn at left, folded in quarters, paste marks. Text is centered on the page and words are widely spaced. "Sue." on verso. [H B10, L 346. *LL* 65.]
158. Ink, full sheet plus half sheet torn at left, folded in quarters, paper clip marks. [H B184, P 1179, L 364. *FF* 233–234, in part. The poem made out of the lines "Of so divine / a Loss . . . Bliss has been" is in *SH* 145; *LL* 197–198.]
159. Pencil, embossed with "Crown" (J), four pages, folded in thirds. "X" in Susan's handwriting on verso. [H 235, P 1177. *SH* 71. Two other

versions of this poem are in the groups of unbound poems found after Dickinson's death (Sets 7 & 11).]

160. Pencil, gilt-edged, embossed "Paris" (I), two leaves, multiple folds, pinholes as if flowers were attached. [H 290, P 1178. *FF* 229.]

161. Pencil, gilt-edged, embossed "Paris" (I), two pages, folded in thirds. "Sue –" on verso. Emily sent one version of this poem to Thomas Higginson in 1871; another version is in the fascicles. [H 375, P 1181. *Poems* (1891), 65.]

162. Ink, embossed "A Pirie & Sons" (Y), half sheet torn at left, folded in quarters. "X" in Susan's handwriting on verso. Emily includes these lines in a letter to Higginson written about the same time. [H 306, P 1208. Lines to Higginson in *Letters* (ed. 1894) 316; (ed. 1931) 290; *LL* 277.]

163. Ink, embossed "A Pirie & Sons" (Y, 1866), two leaves, folded in thirds. Exaggerated spacing between letters and words. Another version of this poem was sent to Higginson; additional version in the fascicles. [H 302, P 1209. *Letters* (ed. 1894) 316–317, *Poems* (ed. 1931) 301–302; (ed. 1931) 290; also in *LL* 277, 323–324, 304, printed as though it were part of a letter written in 1876; *SH* 30; *CP* 266; *FP* 197.]

164. Ink, embossed "A Pirie & Sons 1870" (Y), full sheet plus half sheet torn at left, folded in thirds, paper clip and paste marks, "125" penciled on recto of first leaf. [H B150, L 392. *LL* 63, ending only; *FF* 234–235, in part.]

165. Pencil, graph paper, no embossment, two leaves, multiple folds, paste marks. [H B95, L 393. *AM* CXV (1915) 37, in part; *FF* 235, in part.]

166. Pencil, no embossment, two-thirds of a leaf, torn at left and bottom, folded in quarters. [H 324, P 1246. *AM* CXV (1915) 38; *LL* 60.]

167. Ink, embossed "A Pirie & Sons 1871" (Y), two leaves plus half sheet torn at left, folded in thirds. Exaggerated crossing of "T's," as well as wide spacing. [H B123, L 397, P 1251. *FF* 232–233.]

168. Ink, embossed "A Pirie & Sons" (Y), half sheet torn at left, folded in quarters, paste marks. [H B153, L 383. *FF* 267.]

169. Ink, embossed "A Pirie & Sons / 1871" (Y), two leaves, folded in quarters. "X" penciled in Susan's handwriting on verso. Here spacing

between letters is so exaggerated that the comma appears separated from the word it follows. [H 261, P 1253. *SH* 139.]

170. Ink, no embossment, two half sheets scissored and torn at left, folded in thirds, paper clip marks. Page appears to have been cut off, possibly omitting last two lines included in other versions: "Restored in Arctic Confidence / To the Invisible –" Emily sent a version of this letter-poem to Higginson; two other versions are among the ungathered poems and drafts. [H B190, P 1259, L 407. *FF* 256–257; *Letters* (ed. 1931 only) 307.]
171. Ink, no embossment, two leaves, folded in thirds, paste marks. "X" pen ciled in Susan's handwriting on verso. Wide spacing between lines as well as words; at this point, all the "T's" are crossed with exaggeration, spanning words. [H B99, L 427. *FF* 247.]
172. Ink, no embossment, half sheet torn at left, folded in thirds, paste marks. [H B38, L 428. *LL* 87.]
173. Ink, embossed "A Pirie & Sons / 1862" (Y), two leaves, folded in quarters. Dashes after "Day," "lent," and "Staked" point down. "O.K." penciled in Susan's handwriting on verso. [H 367, B 3, P 1295. *SH* 34, *LL* 196–197.]
174. Pencil, no embossment, two-thirds of a large leaf, torn at top, blue-ruled, multiple folds. "Top" printer's margin of paper is at bottom of draft. "X" in Susan's handwriting on verso. [H 280, P 1302. *SH* 56.]
175. Pencil, same paper as 174 (H 280) (blue-ruled), no embossment, roughly torn on bottom, about two-thirds of a leaf, folded in half, corners are folded, most likely for inserting in a scrapbook. "X" in Susan's hand writing on verso. [H 299, P 1303. *SH* 89]
176. Pencil, no embossment, on rectangle of note paper (blue-ruled) torn at left and bottom, folded in quarters, pinholes. "X" in Susan's handwriting on verso. [H B6, L 429. *LL* 62.]
177. Pencil, embossed "A Pirie & Sons / 1870" (Y), multiple folds, pinholes, paste marks. "X" in Susan's handwriting on verso. [H B160, P 1248. *SH* 141.]

SECTION FOUR NOTES

1 *SH* vi.

178. Pencil, no embossment, small rectangle torn at right and bottom, folded in half, paste marks. [H B25, L 430. *FF* 237. Susan's card is in H Box 9.]
179. Pencil, no embossment, half sheet, torn at left, folded in quarters, pinholes, paste marks. [H B34, L 448. *FF* 245.]
180. Ink, no embossment, two leaves, folded in thirds, pinholes. [H B168, L 484. *FF* 255.]
181. Heavy pencil, no embossment, two leaves, multiple folds, paste marks. [H B42, L 443. *FF* 244.]
182. Pencil, torn at right and bottom, folded in half, paste marks. [H B76, L 447. *FF* 246.]
183. Pencil, no embossment, two leaves, folded in thirds. "X" in Susan's handwriting on verso. Another version was sent to Elizabeth Holland. [H 229, P 1333. *SH* 40; *LH* (1951) 106.]
184. Ink, half sheet, torn at left, folded in thirds, pinholes, paste marks. Marks on page and appears to have been used as ink blotter. Dashes are written with wavy flair. [H L25, L 456. *AM* CXV (1915) 40; *FF* 237, with facsimile.]
185. Heavy pencil, blue-ruled, no embossment, torn at left and bottom, folded in quarters. "X" in Susan's handwriting on verso. [H 300, P 1335. *Poems* (1896) 93 (first stanza only), titled "Dreams"; *SH* 101 (second stanza only, reproducing copy to Susan), apparently following Dickinson's scheme for lineation; *New England Quarterly*, XX (1947) 44, using the version in the fascicle.]
186. Ink, embossed "A Pirie & Sons / 1862" (Y), two leaves, folded in quarters. Marked with "P." Susan made a transcript of this poem, probably from this copy. A different version of this poem was sent to Higginson. [H 348, P 1356. *Poems* (1891) 156, titled "The Rat."]
187. Pencil. There are at least three other versions of this poem, including one which was sent to Higginson. Other versions are divided into two stanzas. [P 1357, privately owned.]

188. Heavy pencil, watermark "Weston's Linen / 1876" (T), two leaves, folded in quarters, paste marks. A version of this poem was included in a letter to Higginson, with a reference to "the Hope that opens and shuts, like the eye of the Wax Doll." [H B11, L 554. *LL* 62, in part.]

189. Pencil, watermark "Weston's Linen 1876" (T), text on first and third of four pages, folded in thirds. Red pencil marks "1–" on first page, upper right-hand corner. [H 337, P 1440. *SH* 146.]

190. Ink, on stationery, watermark "Weston's Linen 1876" (T), two leaves and folded into thirds. On second leaf, "were" is written sideways next to "With Love alone / had bent, / It's fervor the." "X" in Susan's handwriting on verso. [H 360, P 1597. *FF* 268.]

191. Ink, no embossment, half sheet torn at left, multiple folds. "Y" wraps "vilify" in the third line. A version of this poem was sent to Higginson. [H 355, P 1358. *Letters* (ed. 1931 only) 297 (version to Higginson). *SH* 127.]

192. Heavy pencil, graph paper, no embossment, two leaves, folded in thirds. "X" penciled in Susan's handwriting on verso. [H 340, P 1359. *SH* 58.]

193. Heavy pencil, print-like, embossed "Paris" (A), half sheet torn at left, folded in half, then in thirds, pinholes, paste marks. "X" with "Prose" beneath penciled in Susan's handwriting on verso. [H B96, L 467. *FF* 242.]

194. Ink, no embossment, half sheet torn at left, folded in quarters, paste marks. *Letters* and words widely spaced. Emily sent a two-stanza version of this letter-poem to Josiah Holland, and she sent a single-stanza version in a letter to Higginson. Another single-stanza version is among the ungathered poems. [H B54, L 480. *FF* 265.]

195. Ink, no embossment, two leaves, folded in thirds, paste marks. "1860–70" penciled in Susan's handwriting on verso. [H B4, P 1401, L 531. *FF* 243.]

196. Heavy pencil, half sheet torn at left, multiple folds, paste marks. There is an alternate draft version of the last stanza at AC. Loomis Todd transcribed a six-stanza poem. [H B62, P 1400, L 530. *FF* 260. Similar to last two stanzas of "What mystery pervades a well" in

Poems (1896) 117–118, titled "A Well" (with second stanza omitted); lines are printed in *AB* 337; complete poem is printed in *New England Quarterly*, XX (1947) 23–24.]

197. Pencil, watermark "Weston's Linen" (T), half sheet torn at left, folded in thirds, pinholes, paste marks. Two other versions of this poem are included among the ungathered poems. [H B13, P 1403. *Atlantic Monthly*, CXV (1915) 39; *LL* 61.]

198. Ink, no embossment, two leaves, folded in thirds, paper clip marks. "X" penciled in Susan's handwriting on verso. Two drafts exist. [H 287, P 1404. *SH* 53.]

199. Pencil, blue-ruled, no embossment, extensive revisions, half sheet torn at left, folded in thirds. [H 244, P 1416. *SH* 129.]

200. Pencil draft on thin brown paper (scrap paper), no embossment, torn at right, folded in half, very worn. "Miss L Dickinson" and "10c" in unknown handwriting on verso. Number in parentheses is on top of draft. [H 338, P 1425. *SH* 123.]

201. Ink, no embossment, two leaves, folded in thirds, paste marks. "X" and "Special" in Susan's handwriting on verso. [H B93, L 541. *LL* 62, in part; *FF* 241, in part.]

202. Heavy pencil, on blue-ruled paper, embossed capitol (O), half sheet torn at left, folded in thirds. Envelope addressed "Susan – ," elaborately lettered, with paste marks. [H B181, L 581. *LL* 57.]

203. Pencil, no embossment, two leaves, folded in thirds, pinholes, paste marks. Elaborate lettering. [H B37, L 583. *LL* 62, in part.]

204. Heavy pencil, watermark "Weston's / Linen / 1876" (T), two leaves, folded in thirds, bottom of second leaf torn away, paste marks. [H B55, L 586. *LL* 62; *FF* 255.]

205. Pencil, watermark "Weston's Linen 18??" (T), half sheet torn at left, folded in thirds. Susan made a transcript of these lines. [Yale, Za Dickinson 1, L 587. *AM* CXV (1915) 37; *LL* 57.]

206. Heavy pencil, watermark "Weston's / Linen / 1876" (T), half sheet torn at left with bottom third removed, folded in half, paste marks. [H B50, L 584. *FF* 264, with facsimile reproduction.]

207. Pencil, watermark "Weston's / Linen / 1876" (T), two leaves, folded in quarters, pinholes, paste marks, dramatic calligraphy. "Susan –"

on verso. Dash after "you" is elongated and pointed down. Another version of the poem is among the ungathered poems. Emily sent a version of this letter-poem to Sarah Tuckerman in December 1880, following the death of her friend Elihu Root, a professor at Amherst College. [H B32, P 1366, L 585. *LL* 79; *FF* 243.]

208. Pencil, no embossment, two leaves, folded in thirds, paper clip impressions, paste marks. "X" in Susan's handwriting on verso. The "L's" in "Lie" and in "Lothrop" are scored with particular flourishes, perhaps to call attention to the "Lying Culprit." Bianchi's note accompanies the letter-poem: "After the 'Lothrop Case' in which a local pious fraud was exposed." [H B157, P 1453. *LL* 91, with signature altered to "Pecksniff."]

209. Heavy pencil, half sheet, torn at left, folded in quarters, paste marks. [H B82, L 534. *FF* 254.]

210. Pencil, no embossment, two leaves, folded in thirds. "To read to friends" in Susan's handwriting on verso. "Y" in "Hyphen" is a straight line (/), crossing of "T" in "Easter" extends from one end of the word to the other. [H 358, P 1454. *FF* 267–268.]

211. Pencil, graph paper, no embossment, two leaves, folded in thirds. "X" in Susan's handwriting on verso. [H 314, P 1456. *SH* 21.]

212. Heavy pencil, watermark "Weston's / Linen / 1876" (T), half sheet torn at left, multiple folds, pinholes, paste marks. "Susan –" on verso. [H B26, P 1455, L 625. *LL* 62, prose part only; poem, *LL* 57.]

213. Pencil, watermark "Weston's / Linen / 1876" (T), a half sheet torn at left, folded in quarters, pinholes. [H B169, L 624. *FF* 240.]

214. Pencil, watermark "Weston's / Linen / 1876" (T), two leaves, multiple folds, paste marks. "Susan." on verso. [H B48, L 626. *FF* 243.]

215. Pencil, no embossment, two leaves, folded in thirds. "Susan" on verso. [H 230, P 1467. *LL* 80; *CP* 311.]

216. Pencil, "Weston's / Linen / 1876" (T), half sheet torn at left, folded in quarters, pinholes. [H 353, P 1470. *SH* 109.]

217. Pencil, watermark "Irish Linen / Fabric" (U), text on first and third of four pages, folded in quarters. "X" in Susan's handwriting on verso. Another version was prepared for an unknown recipient. [H 343, P 1528. *SH* 64.]

218. Pencil, brown graph paper, no embossment, two-thirds of leaf torn at top and left, text on recto and verso, folded in half. "Devil–" and "X" penciled in Susan's handwriting on bottom half of verso. [H 329, P 1479. *SH* 99.]

219. Pencil, watermark "Weston's / Linen / 1876" (T), half sheet torn at left, folded in thirds, paste marks, bold script. [H B141, L 636. *FF* 247.]

220. Pencil, watermark "Weston's / Linen / 1876" (T), half sheet torn at left, folded in thirds, paste marks. [H B7, L 660. *FF* 241.]

221. Pencil, half sheet torn at left, folded in thirds, paste marks. "Susan ' " on verso. [H B43, L 661. *FF* 260.]

222. Pencil, no embossment, half sheet torn at left, folded in thirds, paste marks. [H B63, L 662. *LL* 65.]

223. Pencil, "Weston's / Linen / 1876" (T), two leaves, folded in thirds, paste marks. [H B72, L 664. *AM* CXV (1915) 37–38; *LL* 58.]

224. Pencil, embossed "Paris" (I), two leaves, folded in thirds, paste marks. [H B138, L 707. *FF* 237.]

225. Pencil, half sheet torn at left, watermark "Weston's / Linen / 1876," folded in thirds, pinholes, paste marks. Notes, scribbles, lists of phrases, as well as the address "40 Lafayette St." penciled in unknown hand(s) over most of the verso. [Yale, Za Dickinson 1, L 708. *LL* 62.]

226. Pencil, no embossment, two leaves, folded in thirds, paste marks. "Susan –" on fold. [H B89, L 722. *LL* 79, in part; *FF* 241, in part.]

227. Pencil, watermark "Weston's / Linen / 1876" (T), two leaves, folded in thirds, paste marks. "X" and tiny "x" and "1–" in Susan's handwriting on verso. [H B119, L 853, P 1537. *AM* CXV (1915) 39; *LL* 61 (with L 580).]

228. Pencil, no embossment, two leaves, folded in thirds, paste marks. [H B188, L 755. *FF* 265–266.]

229. Photograph indicates that the sheet has been torn across bottom of leaf, and folded into thirds. Photograph of verso shows paste marks. [Photostat H B2, L 757. Manuscript now missing. *LL* 64; *FF* 176.]

230. Pencil, watermark "Weston's / Linen / 1876" (T), on small (4 x 4 in.) leaf cut at right and bottom, folded in half, pinholes, paste marks. "X" in Susan's handwriting on verso. [H B12, L 768. *FF* 242.]

231. Pencil, watermark “Irish Linen / Fabric” (U), one full sheet plus one half sheet torn at left, folded in thirds. “Wanting” in Susan’s handwriting on verso, perhaps Susan’s suggested title or her note that this sheet had been separated from the rest. There are other versions of this poem among the ungathered poems, and one was sent to Higginson. [H 294, P 1561. *Atlantic Monthly*, LXVIII (October 1891) 454, titled “The Blue Jay,” in Higginson’s article about her letters and poems; *Poems* (1891) 176–177, also titled “The Blue Jay.”]
232. Pencil, watermark “Weston’s / Linen / 1876” (T), three-quarters of leaf torn at top and left, folded in thirds, paste marks. Addressed “Susan” on fold, with an elaborate “S.” [H B24, L 854. *FF* 242–243, altered.]
233. Pencil, “The American Paper Company,” half sheet torn at left, folded in thirds, paste marks. Calligraphy features large, bold letters. [H B51, L 855. *FF* 237.]
234. Pencil, watermark “Pure Irish Linen” (PIL), onion skin, two two-leaf sheets, multiple folds. Envelope torn at end, with paste marks. [H B79, L 868, P 1564. *LL* 85; *AM* CXV (1915) 42; *Letters* (ed. 1931) 319.]
235. Pencil, watermark “Weston’s / Linen / 1881” (T), two leaves, folded in thirds, stains. [H L50, L 869.]
236. Pencil, watermark “Irish Linen / Fabric” (U), two sheets, writing on first and third pages of each sheet, multiple folds, paste marks. Lines in this letter, beginning “Whose rumor’s / Gate” and ending “a Dent theron,” appear in five other versions: letters sent to Maria Whitney, Charles Clark, and three drafts found among the ungathered poems. Johnson makes a poem from some of these lines, beginning “Expanse cannot be lost.” [H B91, L 871, L 872, P 1576, P 1588. *LL* 87, prose only.]
237. Pencil, watermark “Linen Record” (LR), half sheet torn at right, folded in thirds. A version was sent to Higginson. [H 385, P 1566. *Letters* (ed. 1931 only) 321.]
238. Pencil, watermark “Weston’s / Linen / 1876” (T), two leaves, folded in thirds. [H 386, P 1567.]
239. Pencil, no embossment, two leaves, folded in thirds, paste marks. [H B 67, L 874. *FF* 263.]

240. Pencil, two leaves, folded in thirds, paste marks. [H B145, P 1565, L 938, (compare with *PF* 49). *FF* 259.]
241. Pencil, watermark "The American Linen Paper" (TALP), two leaves, folded in quarters, pinholes, paper clip, and paste marks. "1882" in Susan's handwriting on verso. [H B102, *L* 886. *LL* 54, in part; *FF* 171, in part.]
242. Pencil, half sheet torn at left, folded in thirds, paste marks. [H B77, *L* 856. *LL* 79, in part.]
243. Pencil, watermark "The American Linen Paper" (TALP), two two-leaf sheets, folded in thirds, both sheets with paste marks. Four other versions of this poem exist: one was sent to Benjamin Kimball, a friend of Otis Lord, and three others are among the ungathered poems. [H B158, *L* 908, P 1599. *LL* 82, four lines; *LL* 296; *FF* 266, in part; similar message to a Mrs. Cooper in *Letters* (ed. 1894) 392; (ed. 1931) 381.]
244. Pencil, no embossment, two leaves, folded in thirds, paste marks. [H B144, *L* 909. *FF* 264.]
245. Pencil, watermark "Weston's / Linen / 1876" (T), two leaves, folded in thirds, paste marks. [H B106, L 911. *FF* 249, in part.]
246. Pencil, watermark "Linen Record" (?LNNRCD), two leaves, folded in thirds, paste marks. [H B90, L 912. *LL* 87.]
247. Pencil, watermark "Weston's / Linen / 1876" (T), folded in thirds, pin holes, paste marks. [H B134, L 913. *FF* 243.]
248. Pencil, two leaves, no embossment, folded in thirds, paste marks. There are two other versions of the poem. [H B108, L 914, P 1581. *FF* 265.]
249. Pencil, two leaves, multiple folds, pinholes. "Susan –" on verso, and "X" in Susan's handwriting. [H 376, P 1598. *SH* 106.]
250. Pencil, half sheet, torn at left, folded in thirds, paste marks. [H B41, L 999. *FF* 262.]
251. Pencil, two leaves, folded in thirds, paste marks. [H B148, L 1024. *LL* 63, in part; *FF* 270, in part.]
252. Pencil, watermark "RCRD 1881," two leaves, folded in thirds, paste marks. [H B66, L 1025. *FF* 269.]

253. Pencil, watermark "RCRD 1881," two leaves, folded in thirds, pinholes, paste marks. [H B65, L 1028. *FF* 242.]
254. Pencil, "Weston's / Linen / 1876," half sheet torn at left, folded in thirds, paste marks. With Bianchi's note, "One of the latest." [H B128, L 1029. *FF* 269.]

CODA

1 *FF* 61.

ACKNOWLEDGMENTS

In October 1986, we took a long walk beneath the sweet mountains of Northern California and realized that we had been dreaming the same book separately for several years. Since that time, we have been dreaming and making the book together that you now hold in your hand, and our first thanks must go to our perspicacious and deft editor, Jan Freeman. Without her faith in the project and understanding of its depth and breadth, there would be no volume to open carefully.

We especially thank Leslie Morris, Curator of Manuscripts in the Harvard College Library; without her conscientious assistance and that of the Houghton Library staff, this book would not have been possible. And we thank John Lancaster, Special Collections Curator, and staff at the Amherst College Library, and Mark Brown, Curator, and staff of Special Collections, Brown University Library, as well as Barton St. Armand for access to papers in the The Barton Levi St. Armand Collection of Dickinson Family Papers. We are also grateful to the curators and staff at the archives and special collections at Yale University, Princeton University, Smith College, and the Morgan Library in New York. Ellen Louise Hart is grateful to the Houghton Library for a Stanley J. Kahrl Fellowship that enabled her to complete much of the research for this volume. For early support of research that led to *Rowing in Eden* and this volume, Martha Nell Smith gratefully acknowledges the American Council of Learned Societies and the National Endowment for the Humanities. And, for enabling that research to continue, the General Research Board of the University of Maryland. And we are thankful to the Massachusetts Foundation for the Humanities for a generous grant which helped usher this volume into print.

The work of Ralph Franklin and Thomas H. Johnson, and the collegial advice of Ralph Franklin, deserve special mention. For her enthusiastic support and editorial insights, we thank Marta Werner. Numerous friends and colleagues have believed in this project's importance and possibility, and for their unstinting support we thank Vivian Pollak, Margaret Dickie, Polly Longsworth, Dan Lombardo, Sandra Gilbert, Susan Stanford Friedman, Katie King, Deb Price, Bart St. Armand, Jerome McGann, Ruth Stone, and Alicia Ostriker. Ellen Louise Hart is indebted to friends, family members, and colleagues for their interest in this project, and wishes to thank Priscilla W. Shaw and Theresa Louise McRae for their wisdom and long-term support. And for her enthusiasm, incisive critiques, endlessly generative discussions, as well as for her fulfillment of a promise to render a joke a day to realize Emily Dickinson's beatitude—blessed are those that play—Martha Nell Smith is ever and devotedly indebted to Marilee Lindemann.

SELECTED BIBLIOGRAPHY

Bennett, Paula. *Emily Dickinson: Woman Poet*. Iowa City: University of Iowa Press, 1990.

Bianchi, Martha Dickinson. *Emily Dickinson Face to Face: Unpublished Letters* With Notes and Reminiscences. Boston: Houghton Mifflin, 1932.

—. *The Life and Letters of Emily Dickinson*. Boston: Houghton Mifflin, 1924.

—. "Selections from the Unpublished *Letters* of Emily Dickinson to Her Brother's Family." *Atlantic Monthly* XV (1915): 35–42.

—, ed. *The Single Hound: Poems of a Lifetime*. Boston: Little, Brown and Co., 1914.

—, and Alfred Leete Hampson, eds. *The Complete Poems of Emily Dickinson*. Boston: Little, Brown and Co., 1924.

—, and Alfred Leete Hampson, eds. *Further Poems of Emily Dickinson*. Boston: Little, Brown and Co., 1929.

—. "Life Before Last: Reminiscences of a Country Girl," eds. Barton St. Armand and Martha Nell Smith.

Bingham, Millicent Todd. *Ancestors' Brocades: The Literary Debut of Emily Dickinson*. New York: Harper & Brothers Publishers, 1945.

—. *Emily Dickinson: A Revelation*. New York: Harper & Brothers Publishers, 1954.

—. *Emily Dickinson's Home: Letters of Edward Dickinson and His Family*. New York: Harper & Brothers Publishers, 1955.

Cameron, Sharon. *Choosing Not Choosing: Dickinson's Fascicles*. Chicago & London: University of Chicago Press, 1992.

Crumbley, Paul. *Inflections of the Pen: Dash and Voice in Emily Dickinson.* Lexington: University Press of Kentucky, 1997.

Dandurand, Karen. "Another Dickinson Poem Published in Her Lifetime." *American Literature* 54 (1982): 434–437.

—. "New Dickinson Civil War Publications." American Literature 56.1 (1984): 17–27.

Dickie, Margaret. *Lyric Contingencies: Emily Dickinson and Wallace Stevens*. Philadelphia: University of Pennsylvania Press, 1991.

Dickinson, Emily Elizabeth. Dickinson Papers. Amherst College Library, Amherst, MA. Houghton Library, Harvard University, Cambridge, MA. Library of Congress, Washington, D.C. Morgan Library, New York, NY. Neilson Library, Smith College, Northampton, MA. Princeton University Library, Princeton, NJ. Beinecke Library, Yale University, New Haven, CT.

Dickinson, Susan. Dickinson Papers. Boxes 9, 10, 12. Houghton Library, Harvard University, Cambridge, MA. Martha Dickinson Bianchi Collection, John Hay Library, Brown University, Providence, RI.

Dobson, Joanne. *Dickinson and the Strategies of Reticence: The Woman Writer in Nineteenth-Century America.* Bloomington & Indianapolis: Indiana University Press, 1989.

Eberwein, Jane. *Dickinson: Strategies of Limitation.* Amherst: University of Massachusetts Press, 1985.

Erskine, John. "The Dickinson Feud," *The Memory of Certain Persons.* Philadelphia & New York: J.B. Lippincott Co., 1947.

Ezell, Margaret J.M. and Katherine O'Brien O'Keeffe, eds. *Cultural Artifacts and the Production of Meaning: The Page, the Image, and the Body.* Ann Arbor: University of Michigan Press, 1994.

Faderman, Lillian. "Emily Dickinson's *Letters* to Sue Gilbert." *The Massachusetts Review* 18.2 (1977): 197–225.

—. *Surpassing the Love of Men: Romantic Friendship and Love Between Women From the Renaissance to the Present.* New York: William Morrow and Co., Inc., 1981.

Farr, Judith. *I Never Came to You in White.* Boston & New York: Houghton Mifflin, 1996.

—. *The Passion of Emily Dickinson*. Cambridge, MA & London: Harvard University Press, 1992.

Franklin, R.W., *The Editing of Emily Dickinson: A Reconsideration*. Madison, Milwaukee & London: University of Wisconsin Press, 1967.

—. "The Emily Dickinson Fascicles," *Studies in Bibliography* 36 (1983): 1–20.

—. ed. *The Manuscript Books of Emily Dickinson*. Cambridge: Belknap Press of Harvard University Press, 1980.

—, ed. *The Master Letters of Emily Dickinson*. Amherst: Amherst College Press, 1986.

Fuller, Jamie. *The Diary of Emily Dickinson*. San Francisco: Mercury House, 1993.

Gilbert, Sandra Caruso Mottola and Susan Dreyfuss David Gubar. "Ceremonies of the Alphabet: Female Grandmatologies and the Female Autograph," *The Female Autograph: Theory and Practice of Autobiography From the Tenth to the Twentieth Century*, ed. Domna C. Stanton. Chicago & London: University of Chicago Press, 1987.

Grabher, Gudrun, Roland Hagenbuchle, Cristanne Miller, eds. *The Emily Dickinson Handbook*. Amherst: University of Massachusetts Press, 1998.

Grahn, Judy. *The Highest Apple: Sappho and The Lesbian Poetic Tradition*. San Francisco: Spinsters Ink, 1985.

Halpin, K.D. and Kate Nugent. *EMILY unplugged*. Northampton, MA: Sleeveless Theatre, Inc., 1995-.

Hart, Ellen Louise. "New Approaches to Editing Emily Dickinson." Diss., University of California, Santa Cruz, 1996.

—. "New Light on Manuscripts Addressed to 'Sue.'" *The Emily Dickinson International Society Bulletin* 8.2 (1996): 14–15, 23.

—. "The Elizabeth Whitney Putnam Manuscripts and New Strategies for Editing Emily Dickinson's *Letters*." *Emily Dickinson Journal* 4.1 (1995): 44–74. http://www.colorado.edu/EDIS/journal/articles/IV.1.Hart.html

—. "The Encoding of Homoerotic Desire: Emily Dickinson's *Letters* and *Poems* to Susan Dickinson, 1850–1886." *Tulsa Studies in Women's Literature* 9.2 (1990): 251–272.

Holland, Jeanne. "Scraps, Stamps, and Cutouts: Emily Dickinson's Domestic Technologies of Publication," *Cultural Artifacts and the Production of Meaning*, eds. Margaret J.M. Ezell and Katherine O'Brien O'Keeffe. Ann Arbor: University of Michigan Press, 1994.

Horan, Elizabeth. "To Market: The Dickinson Copyright Wars." *The Emily Dickinson Journal* V.1 (1996): 88–120. http://www.colorado.edu/EDIS/journal/articles/V.1.Horan.html

Howe, Susan. *My Emily Dickinson.* Berkeley: North Atlantic Books, 1985.

—. *The Birth-mark: Unsettling the Wilderness in American Literary History.* Hanover & London: Wesleyan University Press, 1993.

—. "Women and Their Effect in the Distance." *Ironwood* 28 (1986): 58–91.

Johnson, Thomas H. and Theodora Ward, eds. *The Letters of Emily Dickinson.* Cambridge: Belknap Press of Harvard University Press, 1958.

—, ed. *The Poems of Emily Dickinson.* Cambridge: Belknap Press of Harvard University Press, 1955.

Kauffman, Linda. *Discourses of Desire: Gender, Genre, and Epistolary Fictions.* Ithaca & London: Cornell University Press, 1986.

Leyda, Jay. *The Years and Hours of Emily Dickinson.* 2 vols. New Haven & London: Yale University Press, 1960.

Longsworth, Polly. *Austin & Mabel: The Amherst Affair and Love Letters of Austin Dickinson and Mabel Loomis Todd.* New York: Holt, Rinehart, Winston, 1984.

—. *Emily Dickinson: A Letter.* Amherst: The Friends of the Amherst College Library, 1992.

Love, Harold. *Scribal Publication in Seventeenth-Century England.* Oxford: Clarendon Press, 1993.

Luce, William. *The Belle of Amherst.* Boston: Houghton Mifflin, 1976.

McGann, Jerome. *Black Riders: The Visible Language of Modernism.* Princeton: Princeton University Press, 1993.

. "Composition as Explanation (of Modern and Postmodern Poetries)," *Cultural Artifacts and the Production of Meaning*, eds. Margaret J.M. Ezell and Katherine O'Brien O'Keeffe. Ann Arbor: University of Michigan Press, 1994.

—. "The Rationale of Hypertext." Institute for Advanced Technology in the Humanities (IATH), University of Virginia, 1993.

Miller, Cristanne. *Emily Dickinson: A Poet's Grammar.* Cambridge, MA & London: Harvard University Press, 1987.

Mudge, Jean McClure. "Emily Dickinson and 'Sister Sue.'" *Prairie Schooner* 52 (1978): 90–108.

Ostriker, Alicia. *Stealing the Language: The Emergence of Women's Poetry in America*. Boston: Beacon Press, 1986.

Patterson, Rebecca. "Elizabeth Browning and Emily Dickinson," *Educational Leader* 20.1 (1956): 21–48.

—. *Emily Dickinson's Imagery*, ed. Margaret H. Freeman. Amherst: University of Massachusetts Press, 1979.

—. *The Riddle of Emily Dickinson*. Boston: Houghton Mifflin, 1951.

Petrino, Elizabeth A. *Emily Dickinson and Her Contemporaries: Women's Verse in America 1820-1885*. Hanover & London: University Press of New England, 1998.

Pollak, Vivian. *Dickinson: The Anxiety of Gender*. Ithaca & London: Cornell University Press, 1984.

St. Armand, Barton Levi. *Emily Dickinson and Her Culture: The Soul's Society*. Cambridge: Cambridge University Press, 1984.

Sands, Marget. "Re-reading the *Poems*: Editing Opportunities in Variant Versions," *The Emily Dickinson Journal* V.2 (1996): 139–147.

Sewall, Richard. *The Life of Emily Dickinson*, 2 vols. New York: Farrar, Straus, Giroux, 1974. Reprint. Harvard University Press, 1994.

Smith, Martha Nell. "Editing Emily Dickinson's Manuscripts," *The Emily Dickinson Handbook*, eds. Gudrun Grabher, Roland Hagenbuchle, and Cristanne Miller. Amherst: University of Massachusetts Press, 1998.

—. "The Poet as Cartoonist," *Comic Power in Emily Dickinson*, eds. Suzanne Juhasz, Cristanne Miller, and Martha Nell Smith. Austin: University of Texas Press, 1993.

—. *Rowing in Eden: Rereading Emily Dickinson*. Austin: University of Texas Press, 1992.

—. "Suppressing the Books of Susan in Emily Dickinson," *Cultural Correspondences: Essays on Epistolary Writing*, eds. Amanda Gilroy and Wil Verhoeven. Charlottesville: University Press of Virginia, 1998.

—, with Ellen Louise Hart, Laura Lauth, Lara Vetter, and Marcy Tanter, eds. *Writings by Susan Dickinson*. Dickinson Electronic Archives. *http://jefferson.village.virginia.edu/dickinson/susan*

Swanson, Don R. "Undiscovered Public Knowledge." *Library Quarterly* 56 (1986): 103–118.

Walker, Cheryl. *The Nightingale's Burden: Women Poets and American Culture Before 1900*. Bloomington: Indiana University Press, 1982.

Werner, Marta. *Emily Dickinson's Open Folios: Scenes of Reading, Surfaces of Writing*. Ann Arbor: University of Michigan Press, 1995.

Wolff, Cynthia Griffin. *Emily Dickinson.* New York: Alfred A. Knopf, 1986.

Wylder, Edith. *The Last Face: Emily Dickinson's Manuscripts.* Albuquerque: University of New Mexico Press, 1971.

INDEX OF FIRST LINES

INDEX OF NAMES AND SUBJECTS

C

H

I

J

K

L

M

N

O

P

Q

R

T

U

V

W

ELLEN LOUISE HART teaches for the Writing Program, the Educational Opportunity Program, and the Literature Department at the University of California, Santa Cruz. She is the author of articles on editing Dickinson that have appeared in *The Emily Dickinson International Society Bulletin*, *Emily Dickinson Journal*, *An Emily Dickinson Encyclopedia*, *Tulsa Studies in Womens Literature*, *The Womens Review of Books*, and *The Heath Anthology of American Literature*.

MARTHA NELL SMITH is professor of English at the University of Maryland, College Park. She is the author of many articles on Emily Dickinson, as well as of *Rowing in Eden*, *Rereading Emily Dickinson* (University of Texas Press, 1992); she is co-author of the *Comic Power in Emily Dickinson* (University of Texas Press, 1993) and coordinator of the *Dickinson Electronic Archives* project.

KATE FORRESTER is an illustrator and hand-lettering artist based by the sea in Brighton, England. She works predominantly in the publishing industry, adorning book covers with her intricate hand-drawn words and swirling, organic illustrations. Forrester is also known for her packaging designs, branding, patterns, and large-scale murals for international clients—mainly in the United States and Europe. She is also, of course, a hopeless romantic!

On a dreary February afternoon, Lotty Wilkins stumbles upon an advertisement in the newspaper: "To Those who Appreciate Wistaria and Sunshine. Small mediaeval Italian Castle on the shores of the Mediterranean to be Let Furnished for the month of April. Necessary servants remain. Z, Box 1000, *The Times*."

Together with three other women—a religious do-gooder, a world-weary socialite, and a prickly widow—Mrs. Wilkins sets off for a transformative journey. The ladies' month in Italy is indeed enchanting, as the castle seems to work a kind of magic on all four of them. Amongst the profusion of flowers and sunshine, each woman is able to open her heart to love again—whether rekindling a marriage gone cold, finding a new partner, or discovering the beauty of found family.

Elizabeth von Arnim's gem of a novel is funny and heartfelt, offering readers their own escape to springtime in Italy.

The Enchanted April

ELIZABETH VON ARNIM

CHRONICLE BOOKS
SAN FRANCISCO

From *Stories for Romantics: Three Unforgettable Tales of True Love*, published by Chronicle Books in 2025.

Library of Congress Cataloging-in-Publication Data available.

ISBN 978-1-7972-3570-7

Manufactured in India.

FSC www.fsc.org MIX Paper | Supporting responsible forestry FSC™ C043100

Series design by Kristen Hewitt.
Design by Lizzie Vaughan and Kelsey Cox.
Typesetting by Frank Brayton.

10 9 8 7 6 5 4 3 2 1

Chronicle Books LLC
680 Second Street
San Francisco, California 94107
www.chroniclebooks.com

CONTENTS

CHAPTER 1

It began in a Woman's Club in London on a February afternoon—an uncomfortable club, and a miserable afternoon—when Mrs. Wilkins, who had come down from Hampstead to shop and had lunched at her club, took up *The Times* from the table in the smoking-room, and running her listless eye down the Agony Column saw this:

To Those who Appreciate Wistaria and Sunshine.
Small mediaeval Italian Castle on the shores of the
Mediterranean to be Let Furnished for the month of April.
Necessary servants remain. Z, Box 1000, *The Times*.

That was its conception; yet, as in the case of many another, the conceiver was unaware of it at the moment.

So entirely unaware was Mrs. Wilkins that her April for that year had then and there been settled for her that she dropped the newspaper with a gesture that was both irritated and resigned, and went over to the window and stared drearily out at the dripping street.

Not for her were mediaeval castles, even those that are specially described as small. Not for her the shores in April of the Mediterranean, and the wistaria and sunshine. Such delights were only for the rich. Yet the advertisement had been addressed to persons who appreciate these things, so that it had been, anyhow, addressed too to her, for she certainly appreciated them; more than anybody knew; more than she had ever told. But she was poor. In the whole world she possessed of her very own only ninety pounds, saved from year to year, put by carefully pound by pound, out of her dress allowance. She had scraped this sum together at the suggestion of her husband as a shield and refuge against a rainy day. Her dress allowance, given her by her father, was £100 a year, so that Mrs. Wilkins's clothes were what her husband, urging her to save, called modest and becoming, and her acquaintance to each other, when they spoke of her at all, which was seldom for she was very negligible, called a perfect sight.

Mr. Wilkins, a solicitor, encouraged thrift, except that branch of it which got into his food. He did not call that thrift, he called it bad housekeeping. But for the thrift which, like moth, penetrated into Mrs. Wilkins's clothes and spoilt them, he had much praise. "You never know," he said, "when there will be a rainy day, and you may be very glad to find you have a nest-egg. Indeed we both may."

Looking out of the club window into Shaftesbury Avenue—hers was an economical club, but convenient for Hampstead, where she lived, and for Shoolbred's, where she shopped—Mrs. Wilkins, having stood there some time very drearily, her mind's eye on the Mediterranean in April, and the wistaria, and the enviable opportunities of the rich, while her bodily eye watched the really extremely horrible sooty rain falling steadily on the hurrying umbrellas and splashing omnibuses, suddenly wondered whether perhaps this was not the rainy day Mellersh—Mellersh was Mr. Wilkins—had so often encouraged her to prepare for, and whether to get out of such a climate and into the small mediaeval castle wasn't perhaps what Providence had all along intended her to do with her savings. Part of her savings, of course; perhaps quite a small part. The castle, being mediaeval, might also be dilapidated, and dilapidations were surely cheap. She wouldn't in the least mind a few of them, because you didn't pay for dilapidations which were already there; on the contrary—by reducing the price you had to pay they really paid you. But what nonsense to think of it . . .

She turned away from the window with the same gesture of mingled irritation and resignation with which she had laid down *The Times*, and crossed the room towards the door with the intention of getting her mackintosh and umbrella and fighting her way into one of the overcrowded omnibuses and going to Shoolbred's on her way home and buying some soles for Mellersh's dinner—Mellersh was difficult with fish and liked only soles, except salmon—when she beheld Mrs. Arbuthnot, a woman she knew by sight as also living in Hampstead and belonging to the club, sitting at the table in the middle of the room on which the newspapers and magazines were kept, absorbed, in her turn, in the first page of *The Times*.

Mrs. Wilkins had never yet spoken to Mrs. Arbuthnot, who belonged to one of the various church sets, and who analyzed, classified, divided and registered the poor; whereas she and Mellersh, when they did go out, went to the parties of impressionist painters, of whom in Hampstead there were many. Mellersh had a sister who had married one of them and lived up on the Heath, and because of this alliance Mrs. Wilkins was drawn into a circle which was highly unnatural to her, and she had learned to dread pictures. She had to say things about them, and she didn't know what to say. She used to murmur, "Marvelous," and feel that it was not enough. But nobody minded. Nobody listened. Nobody took any notice of Mrs. Wilkins. She was the kind of person who is not noticed at parties. Her clothes, infested by thrift, made her practically invisible; her face was non-arresting; her conversation was reluctant; she was shy. And if one's clothes and face and conversation are all negligible, thought Mrs. Wilkins, who recognized her disabilities, what, at parties, is there left of one?

Also she was always with Wilkins, that clean-shaven, fine-looking man, who gave a party, merely by coming to it, a great air.

Wilkins was very respectable. He was known to be highly thought of by his senior partners. His sister's circle admired him. He pronounced adequately intelligent judgments on art and artists. He was pithy; he was prudent; he never said a word too much, nor, on the other hand, did he ever say a word too little. He produced the impression of keeping copies of everything he said; and he was so obviously reliable that it often happened that people who met him at these parties became discontented with their own solicitors, and after a period of restlessness extricated themselves and went to Wilkins.

Naturally Mrs. Wilkins was blotted out. "She," said his sister, with something herself of the judicial, the digested, and the final in her manner, "should stay at home." But Wilkins could not leave his wife at home. He was a family solicitor, and all such have wives and show them. With his in the week he went to parties, and with his on Sundays he went to church. Being still fairly young—he was thirty-nine—and ambitious of old ladies, of whom he had not yet acquired in his practice a sufficient number, he could not afford to miss church, and it was there that Mrs. Wilkins became familiar, though never through words, with Mrs. Arbuthnot.

She saw her marshaling the children of the poor into pews. She would come in at the head of the procession from the Sunday School exactly five minutes before the choir, and get her boys and girls neatly fitted into their allotted seats, and down on their little knees in their preliminary prayer, and up again on their feet just as, to the swelling organ, the vestry door opened, and the choir and clergy, big with the litanies and commandments they were presently to roll out, emerged. She had a sad face, yet she was evidently efficient. The combination used to make Mrs. Wilkins wonder, for she had been told by Mellersh, on days when she had only been able to get plaice, that if one were efficient one wouldn't be depressed, and that if one does one's job well one becomes automatically bright and brisk.

About Mrs. Arbuthnot there was nothing bright and brisk, though much in her way with the Sunday School children that was automatic; but when Mrs. Wilkins, turning from the window, caught sight of her in the club she was not being automatic at all, but was looking fixedly at one portion of the first page of *The Times*, holding the paper quite still, her eyes not moving. She was just staring; and her face, as usual, was the face of a patient and disappointed Madonna.

Obeying an impulse she wondered at even while obeying it, Mrs. Wilkins, the shy and the reluctant, instead of proceeding as she had intended to the cloakroom and from thence to Shoolbred's in search of Mellersh's fish, stopped at the table and sat down exactly opposite Mrs. Arbuthnot, to whom she had never yet spoken in her life.

It was one of those long, narrow refectory tables, so that they were quite close to each other.

Mrs. Arbuthnot, however, did not look up. She continued to gaze, with eyes that seemed to be dreaming, at one spot only of *The Times*.

Mrs. Wilkins watched her a minute, trying to screw up courage to speak to her. She wanted to ask her if she had seen the advertisement. She did not know why she wanted to ask her this, but she wanted to. How stupid not to be able to speak to her. She looked so kind. She looked so unhappy. Why couldn't two unhappy people refresh each other on their way through this dusty business of life by a little talk—real, natural talk, about what they felt, what they would have liked, what they still tried to hope? And she could not help thinking that Mrs. Arbuthnot, too, was reading that very same advertisement. Her eyes were on the very part of the paper. Was she, too, picturing what it would be like—the color, the fragrance, the light, the soft lapping of the sea among little hot rocks? Color, fragrance, light, sea; instead of Shaftesbury Avenue, and the wet omnibuses, and the fish department at Shoolbred's, and the Tube to Hampstead, and dinner, and to-morrow the same and the day after the same and always the same . . .

Suddenly Mrs. Wilkins found herself leaning across the table. "Are you reading about the mediaeval castle and the wistaria?" she heard herself asking.

Naturally Mrs. Arbuthnot was surprised; but she was not half so much surprised as Mrs. Wilkins was at herself for asking.

Mrs. Arbuthnot had not yet to her knowledge set eyes on the shabby, lank, loosely-put-together figure sitting opposite her, with its small freckled face and big gray eyes almost disappearing under a smashed-down wet-weather hat, and she gazed at her a moment without answering. She *was* reading about the mediaeval castle and the wistaria, or rather had read about it ten minutes before, and since then had been lost in dreams—of light, of color, of fragrance, of the soft lapping of the sea among little hot rocks . . .

"Why do you ask me that?" she said in her grave voice, for her training of and by the poor had made her grave and patient.

Mrs. Wilkins flushed and looked excessively shy and frightened. "Oh, only because I saw it too, and I thought perhaps—I thought somehow—" she stammered.

Whereupon Mrs. Arbuthnot, her mind being used to getting people into lists and divisions, from habit considered, as she gazed thoughtfully at Mrs. Wilkins, under what heading, supposing she had to classify her, she could most properly be put.

"And I know you by sight," went on Mrs. Wilkins, who, like all the shy, once she was started plunged on, frightening herself to more and more speech by the sheer sound of what she had said last in her ears. "Every Sunday—I see you every Sunday in church—"

"In church?" echoed Mrs. Arbuthnot.

"And this seems such a wonderful thing—this advertisement about the wistaria—and—"

Mrs. Wilkins, who must have been at least thirty, broke off and wriggled in her chair with the movement of an awkward and embarrassed schoolgirl.

"It seems *so* wonderful," she went on in a kind of burst, "and—it is such a miserable day . . ."

And then she sat looking at Mrs. Arbuthnot with the eyes of an imprisoned dog.

"This poor thing," thought Mrs. Arbuthnot, whose life was spent in helping and alleviating, "needs advice."

She accordingly prepared herself patiently to give it.

"If you see me in church," she said, kindly and attentively, "I suppose you live in Hampstead too?"

"Oh yes," said Mrs. Wilkins. And she repeated, her head on its long thin neck drooping a little as if the recollection of Hampstead bowed her, "Oh yes."

"Where?" asked Mrs. Arbuthnot, who, when advice was needed, naturally first proceeded to collect the facts.

But Mrs. Wilkins, laying her hand softly and caressingly on the part of *The Times* where the advertisement was, as though the mere printed words of it were precious, only said, "Perhaps that's why *this* seems so wonderful."

"No—I think *that's* wonderful anyhow," said Mrs. Arbuthnot, forgetting facts and faintly sighing.

"Then you *were* reading it?"

"Yes," said Mrs. Arbuthnot, her eyes going dreamy again.

"Wouldn't it be wonderful?" murmured Mrs. Wilkins.

"Wonderful," said Mrs. Arbuthnot. Her face, which had lit up, faded into patience again. "Very wonderful," she said. "But it's no use wasting one's time thinking of such things."

"Oh, but it *is*," was Mrs. Wilkins's quick, surprising reply; surprising because it was so much unlike the rest of her—the characterless coat and skirt, the crumpled hat, the undecided wisp of hair straggling out. "And just the considering of them is worth while in itself—such a change from Hampstead—and sometimes I believe—I really do believe—if one considers hard enough one gets things."

Mrs. Arbuthnot observed her patiently. In what category would she, supposing she had to, put her?

"Perhaps," she said, leaning forward a little, "you will tell me your name. If we are to be friends"—she smiled her grave smile—"as I hope we are, we had better begin at the beginning."

"Oh yes—how kind of you. I'm Mrs. Wilkins," said Mrs. Wilkins. "I don't expect," she added, flushing, as Mrs. Arbuthnot said nothing, "that it conveys anything to you. Sometimes it—it doesn't seem to convey anything to me either. But"—she looked round with a movement of seeking help—"I *am* Mrs. Wilkins."

She did not like her name. It was a mean, small name, with a kind of facetious twist, she thought, about its end like the upward curve of a pugdog's tail. There it was, however. There was no doing anything with it. Wilkins she was and Wilkins she would remain; and though her husband encouraged her to give it on all occasions as Mrs. Mellersh-Wilkins she only did that when he was within earshot, for she thought Mellersh made Wilkins worse, emphasising it in the way Chatsworth on the gate-posts of a villa emphasises the villa.

When first he suggested she should add Mellersh she had objected for the above reason, and after a pause—Mellersh was much too prudent to speak except after a pause, during which presumably he was taking a careful mental copy of his coming observation—he said, much displeased, "But I am not a villa," and looked at her as he looks who hopes, for perhaps the hundredth time, that he may not have married a fool.

Of course he was not a villa, Mrs. Wilkins assured him; she had never supposed he was; she had not dreamed of meaning . . . she was only just thinking . . .

The more she explained the more earnest became Mellersh's hope, familiar to him by this time, for he had then been a husband for two years, that he might not by any chance have married a fool; and they had a prolonged quarrel, if that can be called a quarrel which is conducted with dignified silence on one side and earnest apology on the other, as to whether or no Mrs. Wilkins had intended to suggest that Mr. Wilkins was a villa.

"I believe," she had thought when it was at last over—it took a long while—"that *anybody* would quarrel about *anything* when they've not left off being together for a single day for two whole years. What we both need is a holiday."

"My husband," went on Mrs. Wilkins to Mrs. Arbuthnot, trying to throw some light on herself, "is a solicitor. He—" She cast about for something she could say elucidatory of Mellersh, and found: "He's very handsome."

"Well," said Mrs. Arbuthnot kindly, "that must be a great pleasure to you."

"Why?" asked Mrs. Wilkins.

"Because," said Mrs. Arbuthnot, a little taken aback, for constant intercourse with the poor had accustomed her to have her pronouncements accepted without question, "because beauty handsomeness—is a gift like any other, and if it is properly used—"

She trailed off into silence. Mrs. Wilkins's great gray eyes were fixed on her, and it seemed suddenly to Mrs. Arbuthnot that perhaps she was becoming crystallized into a habit of exposition, and of exposition after the manner of nursemaids, through having an audience that couldn't but agree, that would be afraid, if it wished, to interrupt, that didn't know, that was, in fact, at her mercy.

But Mrs. Wilkins was not listening; for just then, absurd as it seemed, a picture had flashed across her brain, and there were two figures in it sitting together under a great trailing wistaria that stretched across the branches of a tree she didn't know, and it was herself and Mrs. Arbuthnot—she saw them—she saw them. And behind them, bright in sunshine, were old gray walls—the mediaeval castle—she saw it—they were there . . .

She therefore stared at Mrs. Arbuthnot and did not hear a word she said. And Mrs. Arbuthnot stared too at Mrs. Wilkins, arrested by the expression on her face, which was swept by the excitement of what she saw, and was as luminous and tremulous under it as water in sunlight when it is ruffled by a gust of wind. At this moment, if she had been at a party, Mrs. Wilkins would have been looked at with interest.

They stared at each other; Mrs. Arbuthnot surprised, inquiringly, Mrs. Wilkins with the eyes of some one who has had a revelation. Of course. That was how it could be done. She herself, she by herself, couldn't afford it, and wouldn't be able, even if she could afford it, to go there all alone; but she and Mrs. Arbuthnot together . . .

She leaned across the table. "Why don't we try and get it?" she whispered.

Mrs. Arbuthnot became even more wide-eyed. "Get it?" she repeated.

"Yes," said Mrs. Wilkins, still as though she were afraid of being overheard. "Not just sit here and say 'How wonderful,' and then go home to Hampstead without having put out a finger—go home just as usual and see about the dinner and the fish just as we've been doing for years and years and will go on doing for years and years. In fact," said Mrs. Wilkins, flushing to the roots of her hair, for the sound of what she was saying, of what was coming pouring out, frightened her, and yet she couldn't stop, "I see no end to it. There is no end to it. So that there ought to be a break, there ought to be intervals—in everybody's interests. Why, it would really be being unselfish to go away and be happy for a little, because we would come back so much nicer. You see, after a bit everybody needs a holiday."

"But—how do you mean, get it?" asked Mrs. Arbuthnot.

"Take it," said Mrs. Wilkins.

"Take it?"

"Rent it. Hire it. Have it."

"But—do you mean you and I?"

"Yes. Between us. Share. Then it would only cost half, and you look so—you look exactly as if you wanted it just as much as I do—as if you ought to have a rest—have something happy happen to you."

"Why, but we don't know each other."

"But just think how well we would if we went away together for a month! And I've saved for a rainy day, and I expect so have you, and this *is* the rainy day—look at it—"

"She is unbalanced," thought Mrs. Arbuthnot; yet she felt strangely stirred.

"Think of getting away for a whole month—from everything—to heaven—"

"She shouldn't say things like that," thought Mrs. Arbuthnot. "The vicar—" Yet she felt strangely stirred. It would indeed be wonderful to have a rest, a cessation.

Habit, however, steadied her again, and years of intercourse with the poor made her say, with the slight though sympathetic superiority of the explainer, "But then, you see, heaven isn't somewhere else. It is here and now. We are told so."

She became very earnest, just as she did when trying patiently to help and enlighten the poor. "Heaven is within us," she said in her gentle low voice. "We are told that on the very highest authority. And you know the lines about the kindred points, don't you—"

"Oh yes, I know *them*," interrupted Mrs. Wilkins impatiently.

"The kindred points of heaven and home," continued Mrs. Arbuthnot, who was used to finishing her sentences. "Heaven is in our home."

"It isn't," said Mrs. Wilkins, again surprisingly.

Mrs. Arbuthnot was taken aback. Then she said gently, "Oh, but it is. It is there if we choose, if we make it."

"I do choose, and I do make it, and it isn't," said Mrs. Wilkins.

Then Mrs. Arbuthnot was silent, for she too sometimes had doubts about homes. She sat and looked uneasily at Mrs. Wilkins, feeling more and more the urgent need of getting her classified. If she could only classify Mrs. Wilkins, get her safely under her proper heading, she felt that she herself would regain her balance, which did seem very strangely to be slipping all to one side. For neither had she had a holiday for years, and the advertisement when she saw it had set her dreaming, and Mrs. Wilkins's excitement about it was infectious, and she had the sensation, as she listened to her impetuous, odd talk and watched her lit-up face, that she was being stirred out of sleep.

Clearly Mrs. Wilkins was unbalanced, but Mrs. Arbuthnot had met the unbalanced before—indeed she was always meeting them—and they had no effect on her own stability at all; whereas this one was making her feel quite wobbly, quite as though to be off and away, away from her compass points of God, Husband, Home, and Duty—she didn't feel as if Mrs. Wilkins intended Mr. Wilkins to come too—and just for once be happy, would be both good and desirable. Which of course it wasn't; which certainly of course it wasn't. She, also, had a nest-egg, invested gradually in the Post Office Savings Bank, but to suppose that she would ever forget her duty to the extent of drawing it out and spending it on herself was surely absurd. Surely she couldn't, she wouldn't ever do such a thing? Surely she wouldn't, she couldn't ever forget her poor, forget misery and sickness as completely as that? No doubt a trip to Italy would be extraordinarily delightful, but there were many delightful things one would like to do, and what was strength given to one for except to help one not to do them?

Steadfast as the points of the compass to Mrs. Arbuthnot were the great four facts of life: God, Husband, Home, Duty. She had gone to sleep on these facts years ago, after a period of much misery, her head resting on them as on a pillow; and she had a great dread of being awakened out of so simple and untroublesome a condition. Therefore it was that she searched with earnestness for a heading under which to put Mrs. Wilkins, and in this way illumine and steady her own mind; and sitting there looking at her uneasily after her last remark, and feeling herself becoming more and more unbalanced and infected, she decided *pro tem*, as the vicar said at meetings, to put her under the heading Nerves. It was just possible that she ought to go straight into the category Hysteria, which was often only the antechamber to Lunacy, but Mrs. Arbuthnot had learned not to hurry people into their final categories, having on more than one occasion discovered with dismay that she had made a mistake; and how difficult it had been to get them out again, and how crushed she had been with the most terrible remorse.

Yes. Nerves. Probably she had no regular work for others, thought Mrs. Arbuthnot; no work that would take her outside herself. Evidently she was rudderless—blown about by gusts, by impulses. Nerves was almost certainly her category, or would be quite soon if no one helped her. Poor little thing, thought Mrs. Arbuthnot, her own balance returning hand in hand with her compassion, and unable, because of the table, to see the length of Mrs. Wilkins's legs. All she saw was her small, eager, shy face, and her thin shoulders, and the look of childish longing in her eyes for something that she was sure was going to make her happy. No; such things didn't make people happy, such fleeting things. Mrs. Arbuthnot had learned in her long life with Frederick—he was her husband, and she had married him at twenty and was now thirty-three—where alone true joys are to be found. They are to be found, she now knew, only in daily, in hourly, living for others; they are to be found only—hadn't she over and over again taken her disappointments and discouragements there, and come away comforted?—at the feet of God.

Frederick had been the kind of husband whose wife betakes herself early to the feet of God. From him to them had been a short though painful step. It seemed short to her in retrospect, but it had really taken the whole of the first year of their marriage, and every inch of the way had been a struggle, and every inch of it was stained, she felt at the time, with her heart's blood. All that was over now. She had long since found peace. And Frederick, from her passionately loved bridegroom, from her worshipped young husband, had become second only to God on her list of duties and forbearances. There he hung, the second in importance, a bloodless thing bled white by her prayers. For years she had been able to be happy only by forgetting happiness. She wanted to stay like that. She wanted to shut out everything that would remind her of beautiful things, that might set her off again longing, desiring . . .

"I'd like so much to be friends," she said earnestly. "Won't you come and see me, or let me come to you sometimes? Whenever you feel as if you wanted to talk. I'll give you my address"—she searched in her handbag—"and then you won't forget." And she found a card and held it out.

Mrs. Wilkins ignored the card.

"It's so funny," said Mrs. Wilkins, just as if she had not heard her, "but I *see* us both—you and me—this April in the mediaeval castle."

Mrs. Arbuthnot relapsed into uneasiness. "Do you?" she said, making an effort to stay balanced under the visionary gaze of the shining gray eyes. "Do you?"

"Don't you ever see things in a kind of flash before they happen?" asked Mrs. Wilkins.

"Never," said Mrs. Arbuthnot.

She tried to smile; she tried to smile the sympathetic yet wise and tolerant smile with which she was accustomed to listen to the necessarily biased and incomplete views of the poor. She didn't succeed. The smile trembled out.

"Of course," she said in a low voice, almost as if she were afraid the vicar and the Savings Bank were listening, "it would be most beautiful—most beautiful—"

"Even if it were wrong," said Mrs. Wilkins, "it would only be for a month."

"That—" began Mrs. Arbuthnot, quite clear as to the reprehensibleness of such a point of view; but Mrs. Wilkins stopped her before she could finish.

"Anyhow," said Mrs. Wilkins, stopping her, "I'm sure it's wrong to go on being good for too long, till one gets miserable. And I can see you've been good for years and years, because you look so unhappy"—Mrs. Arbuthnot opened her mouth to protest—"and I—I've done nothing but duties, things for other people, ever since I was a girl, and I don't believe anybody loves me a bit—a bit—the b-better—and I long—oh, I long—for something else—something else—"

Was she going to cry? Mrs. Arbuthnot became acutely uncomfortable and sympathetic. She hoped she wasn't going to cry. Not there. Not in that unfriendly room, with strangers coming and going.

But Mrs. Wilkins, after tugging agitatedly at a handkerchief that wouldn't come out of her pocket, did succeed at last in merely apparently blowing her nose with it, and then, blinking her eyes very quickly once or twice, looked at Mrs. Arbuthnot with a quivering air of half humble, half frightened apology, and smiled.

"Will you believe," she whispered, trying to steady her mouth, evidently dreadfully ashamed of herself, "that I've never spoken to any one before in my life like this? I can't think, I simply don't know, what has come over me."

"It's the advertisement," said Mrs. Arbuthnot, nodding gravely.

"Yes," said Mrs. Wilkins, dabbing furtively at her eyes, "and us both being so—"—she blew her nose again a little—"miserable."

CHAPTER 2

Of course Mrs. Arbuthnot was not miserable—how could she be, she asked herself, when God was taking care of her?—but she let that pass for the moment unrepudiated, because of her conviction that here was another fellow-creature in urgent need of her help; and not just boots and blankets and better sanitary arrangements this time, but the more delicate help of comprehension, of finding the exact right words.

The exact right words, she presently discovered, after trying various ones about living for others, and prayer, and the peace to be found in placing oneself unreservedly in God's hands—to meet all these words Mrs. Wilkins had other words, incoherent and yet, for the moment at least, till one had had more time, difficult to answer—the exact right words were a suggestion that it would do no harm to answer the advertisement. Non-committal. Mere inquiry. And what disturbed Mrs. Arbuthnot about this suggestion was that she did not make it solely to comfort Mrs. Wilkins; she made it because of her own strange longing for the mediaeval castle.

This was very disturbing. There she was, accustomed to direct, to lead, to advise, to support—except Frederick; she long since had learned to leave Frederick to God—being led herself, being influenced and thrown off her feet, by just an advertisement, by just an incoherent stranger. It was indeed disturbing. She failed to understand her sudden longing for what was, after all, self-indulgence, when for years no such desire had entered her heart.

"There's no harm in simply *asking*," she said in a low voice, as if the vicar and the Savings Bank and all her waiting and dependent poor were listening and condemning.

"It isn't as if it *committed* us to anything," said Mrs. Wilkins, also in a low voice, but her voice shook.

They got up simultaneously—Mrs. Arbuthnot had a sensation of surprise that Mrs. Wilkins should be so tall—and went to a writing-table, and Mrs. Arbuthnot wrote to Z, Box 1000, *The Times*, for particulars. She asked for all particulars, but the only one they really wanted was the one about the rent. They both felt that it was Mrs. Arbuthnot who ought to write the letter and do the business part. Not only was she used to organizing and being practical, but she also was older, and certainly calmer; and she herself had no doubt too that she was wiser. Neither had Mrs. Wilkins any doubt of this; the very way Mrs. Arbuthnot parted her hair suggested a great calm that could only proceed from wisdom.

But if she was wiser, older, and calmer, Mrs. Arbuthnot's new friend nevertheless seemed to her to be the one who impelled. Incoherent, she yet impelled. She appeared to have, apart from her need of help, an upsetting kind of character. She had a curious infectiousness. She led one on. And the way her unsteady mind leaped at conclusions—wrong ones, of course; witness the one that she, Mrs. Arbuthnot, was miserable—the way she leaped at conclusions was disconcerting.

Whatever she was, however, and whatever her unsteadiness, Mrs. Arbuthnot found herself sharing her excitement and her longing; and when the letter had been posted in the letter-box in the hall and actually was beyond getting back again, both she and Mrs. Wilkins felt the same sense of guilt.

"It only shows," said Mrs. Wilkins in a whisper, as they turned away from the letter-box, "how immaculately good we've been all our lives. The very first time we do anything our husbands don't know about we feel guilty."

"I'm afraid I can't say I've been immaculately good," gently protested Mrs. Arbuthnot, a little uncomfortable at this fresh example of successful leaping at conclusions, for she had not said a word about her feeling of guilt.

"Oh, but I'm sure you have—I *see* you being good—and that's why you're not happy."

"She shouldn't say things like that," thought Mrs. Arbuthnot. "I must try and help her not to."

Aloud she said gravely, "I don't know why you insist that I'm not happy. When you know me better I think you'll find that I am. And I'm sure you don't mean really that goodness, if one could attain it, makes one unhappy."

"Yes, I do," said Mrs. Wilkins. "Our sort of goodness does. We have attained it, and we are unhappy. There are miserable sorts of goodness and happy sorts—the sort we'll have at the mediaeval castle, for instance, is the happy sort."

"That is, supposing we go there," said Mrs. Arbuthnot restrainingly. She felt that Mrs. Wilkins needed holding on to. "After all, we've only written just to ask. Anybody may do that. I think it quite likely we shall find the conditions impossible, and even if they were not, probably by to-morrow we shall not want to go."

"I *see* us there," was Mrs. Wilkins's answer to that.

All this was very unbalancing. Mrs. Arbuthnot, as she presently splashed through the dripping streets on her way to a meeting she was to speak at, was in an unusually disturbed condition of mind. She had, she hoped, shown herself very calm to Mrs. Wilkins, very practical and sober, concealing her own excitement. But she was really extraordinarily moved, and she felt happy, and she felt guilty, and she felt afraid, and she had all the feelings, though this she did not know, of a woman who has come away from a secret meeting with her lover. That, indeed, was what she looked like when she arrived late on her platform; she, the open-browed, looked almost furtive as her eyes fell on the staring wooden faces waiting to hear her try and persuade them to contribute to the alleviation of the urgent needs of the Hampstead poor, each one convinced that they needed contributions themselves. She looked as though she were hiding something discreditable but delightful. Certainly her customary clear expression of candor was not there, and its place was taken by a kind of suppressed and frightened pleasedness, which would have led a more worldly-minded audience to the instant conviction of recent and probably impassioned lovemaking.

Beauty, beauty, beauty . . . the words kept ringing in her ears as she stood on the platform talking of sad things to the sparsely attended meeting. She had never been to Italy. Was that really what her nest-egg was to be spent on after all? Though she couldn't approve of the way Mrs. Wilkins was introducing the idea of predestination into her immediate future, just as if she had no choice, just as if to struggle, or even to reflect, were useless, it yet influenced her. Mrs. Wilkins's eyes had been the eyes of a seer. Some people were like that, Mrs. Arbuthnot knew; and if Mrs. Wilkins had actually seen her at the mediaeval castle it did seem probable that struggling would be a waste of time. Still, to spend her nest-egg on self-indulgence— The origin of this egg had been corrupt, but she had at least supposed its end was to be creditable. Was she to deflect it from its intended destination, which alone had appeared to justify her keeping it, and spend it on giving herself pleasure?

Mrs. Arbuthnot spoke on and on, so much practiced in the kind of speech that she could have said it all in her sleep, and at the end of the meeting, her eyes dazzled by her secret visions, she hardly noticed that nobody was moved in any way whatever, least of all in the way of contributions.

But the vicar noticed. The vicar was disappointed. Usually his good friend and supporter Mrs. Arbuthnot succeeded better than this. And, what was even more unusual, she appeared, he observed, not even to mind.

“I can’t imagine,” he said to her as they parted, speaking irritably, for he was irritated both by the audience and by her, “what these people are coming to. *Nothing* seems to move them.”

“Perhaps they need a holiday,” suggested Mrs. Arbuthnot; an unsatisfactory, a queer reply, the vicar thought.

“In February?” he called after her sarcastically.

“Oh no—not till April,” said Mrs. Arbuthnot over her shoulder.

“Very odd,” thought the vicar. “Very odd indeed.” And he went home and was not perhaps quite christian to his wife.

That night in her prayers Mrs. Arbuthnot asked for guidance. She felt she ought really to ask, straight out and roundly, that the mediaeval castle should already have been taken by some one else and the whole thing thus be settled, but her courage failed her. Suppose her prayer were to be answered? No; she couldn’t ask it; she couldn’t risk it. And after all—she almost pointed this out to God—if she spent her present nest-egg on a holiday she could quite soon accumulate another. Frederick pressed money on her; and it would only mean, while she rolled up a second egg, that for a time her contributions to the parish charities would be less. And then it could be the next nest-egg whose original corruption would be purged away by the use to which it was finally put.

For Mrs. Arbuthnot, who had no money of her own, was obliged to live on the proceeds of Frederick’s activities, and her very nest-egg was the fruit, posthumously ripened, of ancient sin. The way Frederick made his living was one of the standing distresses of her life. He wrote immensely popular memoirs, regularly, every year, of the mistresses of kings. There were in history numerous kings who had had mistresses, and there were still more numerous mistresses who had had kings; so that he had been able to publish a book of memoirs during each year of his married life, and even so there were great further piles of these ladies waiting to be dealt with. Mrs. Arbuthnot was helpless. Whether she liked it or not, she was obliged to live on the proceeds. He gave her a dreadful sofa once, after the success of his Du Barri memoir, with swollen cushions and soft, receptive lap, and it seemed to her a miserable thing that there, in her very home, should flaunt this re-incarnation of a dead old French sinner.

Simply good, convinced that morality is the basis of happiness, the fact that she and Frederick should draw their sustenance from guilt, however much purged by the passage of centuries, was one of the secret reasons of her sadness. The more the memoired lady had forgotten herself, the more his book about her was read and the more free-handed he was to his wife; and all that he gave her was spent, after adding slightly to her nest-egg—for she did hope and believe that some day people would cease to want to read of wickedness, and then Frederick would need supporting—on helping the poor. The parish flourished because, to take a handful at random, of the ill-behavior of the ladies Du Barri, Montespan, Pompadour, Ninon de l'Enclos, and even of learned Maintenon. The poor were the filter through which the money was passed, to come out, Mrs. Arbuthnot hoped, purified. She could do no more. She had tried in days gone by to think the situation out, to discover the exact right course for her to take, but had found it, as she had found Frederick, too difficult, and had left it, as she had left Frederick, to God. Nothing of this money was spent on her house or dress; those remained, except for the great soft sofa, austere. It was the poor who profited. Their very boots were stout with sins. But how difficult it had been. Mrs. Arbuthnot, groping for guidance, prayed about it to exhaustion. Ought she perhaps to refuse to touch the money, to avoid it as she would have avoided the sins which were its source? But then what about the parish's boots? She asked the vicar what he thought, and, through much delicate language, evasive and cautious, it did finally appear that he was for the boots.

At least she had persuaded Frederick, when first he began his terrible successful career—he only began it after their marriage;

when she married him he had been a blameless official attached to the library of the British Museum—to publish the memoirs under another name, so that she was not publicly branded. Hampstead read the books with glee, and had no idea that their writer lived in its midst. Frederick was almost unknown, even by sight, in Hampstead. He never went to any of its gatherings. Whatever it was he did in the way of recreation was done in London, but he never spoke of what he did or whom he saw; he might have been perfectly friendless for any mention he ever made of friends to his wife. Only the vicar knew where the money for the parish came from, and he regarded it, he told Mrs. Arbuthnot, as a matter of honor not to mention it.

And at least her little house was not haunted by the loose-lived ladies, for Frederick did his work away from home. He had two rooms near the British Museum, which was the scene of his exhumations, and there he went every morning, and he came back long after his wife was asleep. Sometimes he did not come back at all. Sometimes she did not see him for several days together. Then he would suddenly appear at breakfast, having let himself in with his latchkey the night before, very jovial and good-natured and free-handed and glad if she would allow him to give her something—a well fed man, contented with the world; a jolly, full blooded, satisfied man. And she was always gentle, and anxious that his coffee should be as he liked it.

He seemed very happy. Life, she often thought, however much one tabulated was yet a mystery. There were always some people it was impossible to place. Frederick was one of them. He didn't seem to bear the remotest resemblance to the original Frederick. He didn't seem to have the least need of any of the things he used to say were so important and beautiful—love, home, complete communion of thoughts, complete immersion in each other's interests. After those early painful attempts to hold him up to the point from which they had hand in hand so splendidly started, attempts in which she herself had got terribly hurt and the Frederick she supposed she had married was mangled out of recognition, she hung him up finally by her bedside as the chief subject of her prayers, and left him, except for those, entirely to God. She had loved Frederick too deeply to be able now to do anything but pray for him. He had no idea that he never went out of the house without her blessing going with him too, hovering, like a little echo of finished love, round that once dear head. She didn't dare think of him as he used to be, as he had seemed to her to be in those marvelous first days of their lovemaking, of their marriage. Her child had died; she had nothing, nobody of her own to lavish herself on. The poor became her children, and God the object of her love. What could be happier than such a life, she sometimes asked herself; but her face, and particularly her eyes, continued sad.

"Perhaps when we're old . . . perhaps when we are both quite old . . ." she would think wistfully.

CHAPTER 3

The owner of the mediaeval castle was an Englishman, a Mr. Briggs, who was in London at the moment and wrote that it had beds enough for eight people, exclusive of servants, three sitting-rooms, battlements, dungeons, and electric light. The rent was £60 for the month, the servants' wages were extra, and he wanted references—he wanted assurances that the second half of his rent would be paid, the first half being paid in advance, and he wanted assurances of respectability from a solicitor, or a doctor, or a clergyman. He was very polite in his letter, explaining that his desire for references was what was usual and should be regarded as a mere formality.

Mrs. Arbuthnot and Mrs. Wilkins had not thought of references, and they had not dreamed a rent could be so high. In their minds had floated sums like three guineas a week; or less, seeing that the place was small and old.

Sixty pounds for a single month.

It staggered them.

Before Mrs. Arbuthnot's eyes rose up boots: endless vistas, all the stout boots that sixty pounds would buy; and besides the rent there would be the servants' wages, and the food, and the railway journeys out and home. While as for references, these did indeed seem a stumbling-block; it did seem impossible to give any without making their plan more public than they had intended.

They had both—even Mrs. Arbuthnot, lured for once away from perfect candor by the realization of the great saving of trouble and criticism an imperfect explanation would produce—they had both thought it would be a good plan to give out, each to her own circle, their circles being luckily distinct, that each was going to stay with a friend who had a house in Italy. It would be true as far as it went—Mrs. Wilkins asserted that it would be quite true, but Mrs. Arbuthnot thought it wouldn't be quite—and it was the only way, Mrs. Wilkins said, to keep Mellersh even approximately quiet. To spend any of her money just on the mere getting to Italy would cause him indignation; what he would say if he knew she was renting part of a mediaeval castle on her own account Mrs. Wilkins preferred not to think. It would take him days to say it all; and this although it was her very own money, and not a penny of it had ever been his.

"But I expect," she said, "your husband is just the same. I expect all husbands are alike in the long run."

Mrs. Arbuthnot said nothing, because her reason for not wanting Frederick to know was the exactly opposite one—Frederick would be only too pleased for her to go, he would not mind it in the very least; indeed, he would hail such a manifestation of self-indulgence and worldliness with an amusement that would hurt, and urge her to have a good time and not to hurry home with a crushing detachment. Far better, she thought, to be missed by Mellersh than to be sped by Frederick. To be missed, to be needed, from whatever motive, was, she thought, better than the complete loneliness of not being missed or needed at all.

She therefore said nothing, and allowed Mrs. Wilkins to leap at her conclusions unchecked. But they did, both of them, for a whole day feel that the only thing to be done was to renounce the mediaeval castle; and it was in arriving at this bitter decision that they really realized how acute had been their longing for it.

Then Mrs. Arbuthnot, whose mind was trained in the finding of ways out of difficulties, found a way out of the reference difficulty; and simultaneously Mrs. Wilkins had a vision revealing to her how to reduce the rent.

Mrs. Arbuthnot's plan was simple, and completely successful. She took the whole of the rent in person to the owner, drawing it out of her Savings Bank—again she looked furtive and apologetic, as if the clerk must know the money was wanted for purposes of self-indulgence—and, going up with the six ten pound notes in her hand-bag to the address near the Brompton Oratory where the owner lived, presented them to him, waiving her right to pay only half. And when he saw her, and her parted hair and soft dark eyes and sober apparel, and heard her grave voice, he told her not to bother about writing round for those references.

"It'll be all right," he said, scribbling a receipt for the rent. "Do sit down, won't you? Nasty day, isn't it? You'll find the old castle has lots of sunshine, whatever else it hasn't got. Husband going?"

Mrs. Arbuthnot, unused to anything but candor, looked troubled at this question and began to murmur inarticulately, and the owner at once concluded that she was a widow—a war one, of course, for other widows were old—and that he had been a fool not to guess it.

"Oh, I'm sorry," he said, turning red right up to his fair hair. "I didn't mean—h'm, h'm, h'm—"

He ran his eye over the receipt he had written. "Yes, I think that's all right," he said, getting up and giving it to her. "Now," he added, taking the six notes she held out and smiling, for Mrs. Arbuthnot was agreeable to look at, "I'm richer, and you're happier. I've got money, and you've got San Salvatore. I wonder which is best."

"I think you know," said Mrs. Arbuthnot with her sweet smile.

He laughed and opened the door for her. It was a pity the interview was over. He would have liked to ask her to lunch with him. She made him think of his mother, of his nurse, of all things kind and comforting, besides having the attraction of not being his mother or his nurse.

"I hope you'll like the old place," he said, holding her hand a minute at the door. The very feel of her hand, even through its glove, was reassuring; it was the sort of hand, he thought, that children would like to hold in the dark. "In April, you know, it's simply a mass of flowers. And then there's the sea. You must wear white. You'll fit in very well. There are several portraits of you there."

"Portraits?"

"Madonnas, you know. There's one on the stairs really exactly like you."

Mrs. Arbuthnot smiled and said good-bye and thanked him. Without the least trouble and at once she had got him placed in his proper category: he was an artist and of an effervescent temperament.

She shook hands and left, and he wished she hadn't. After she was gone he supposed that he ought to have asked for those references, if only because she would think him so unbusiness-like not to, but he could as soon have insisted on references from a saint in a nimbus as from that grave, sweet lady.

Rose Arbuthnot.

Her letter, making the appointment, lay on the table.

Pretty name.

That difficulty, then, was overcome. But there still remained the other one, the really annihilating effect of the expense on the nest-eggs, and especially on Mrs. Wilkins's, which was in size, compared with Mrs. Arbuthnot's, as the egg of the plover to that of the duck; and this in its turn was overcome by the vision vouchsafed to Mrs. Wilkins, revealing to her the steps to be taken for its overcoming. Having got San Salvatore—the beautiful, the religious name, fascinated them—they in their turn would advertise in the Agony Column of *The Times*, and would inquire after two more ladies, of similar desires to their own, to join them and share the expenses.

At once the strain of the nest-eggs would be reduced from half to a quarter. Mrs. Wilkins was prepared to fling her entire egg into the adventure, but she realized that if it were to cost even sixpence over her ninety pounds her position would be terrible. Imagine going to Mellersh and saying, "I owe." It would be awful enough if some day circumstances forced her to say, "I have no nest-egg," but at least she would be supported in such a case by the knowledge that the egg had been her own. She therefore, though prepared to fling her last penny into the adventure, was not prepared to fling into it a single farthing that was not demonstrably her own; and she felt that if her share of the rent was reduced to fifteen pounds only, she would have a safe margin for the other expenses. Also they might economize very much on food—gather olives off their own trees and eat them, for instance, and perhaps catch fish.

Of course, as they pointed out to each other, they could reduce the rent to an almost negligible sum by increasing the number of sharers; they could have six more ladies instead of two if they wanted to, seeing that there were eight beds. But supposing the eight beds were distributed in couples in four rooms, it would not be altogether what they wanted, to find themselves shut up at night with a stranger. Besides, they thought that perhaps having so many would not be quite so peaceful. After all, they were going to San Salvatore for peace and rest and joy, and six more ladies, especially if they got into one's bedroom, might a little interfere with that.

However, there seemed to be only two ladies in England at that moment who had any wish to join them, for they had only two answers to their advertisement.

"Well, we only want two," said Mrs. Wilkins, quickly recovering, for she had imagined a great rush.

"I think a choice would have been a good thing," said Mrs. Arbuthnot.

"You mean because then we needn't have had Lady Caroline Dester."

"I didn't say that," gently protested Mrs. Arbuthnot.

"We needn't have her," said Mrs. Wilkins. "Just one more person would help us a great deal with the rent. We're not obliged to have two."

"But why should we not have her? She seems really quite what we want."

"Yes—she does from her letter," said Mrs. Wilkins doubtfully.

She felt she would be terribly shy of Lady Caroline. Incredible as it may seem, seeing how they get into everything, Mrs. Wilkins had never come across any members of the aristocracy.

They interviewed Lady Caroline, and they interviewed the other applicant, a Mrs. Fisher.

Lady Caroline came to the club in Shaftesbury Avenue, and appeared to be wholly taken up by one great longing, a longing to get away from everybody she had ever known. When she saw the club, and Mrs. Arbuthnot, and Mrs. Wilkins, she was sure that here was exactly what she wanted. She would be in Italy—a place she adored; she would not be in hotels—places she loathed; she would not be staying with friends—persons she disliked; and she would be in the company of strangers who would never mention a single person she knew, for the simple reason that they had not, could not have, and would not come across them. She asked a few questions about the fourth woman, and was satisfied with the answers. Mrs. Fisher, of Prince of Wales Terrace. A widow. She too would be unacquainted with any of her friends. Lady Caroline did not even know where Prince of Wales Terrace was.

"It's in London," said Mrs. Arbuthnot.

"Is it?" said Lady Caroline.

It all seemed most restful.

Mrs. Fisher was unable to come to the club because, she explained by letter, she could not walk without a stick; therefore Mrs. Arbuthnot and Mrs. Wilkins went to her.

"But if she can't come to the club how can she go to Italy?" wondered Mrs. Wilkins, aloud.

"We shall hear that from her own lips," said Mrs. Arbuthnot.

From Mrs. Fisher's lips they merely heard, in reply to delicate questioning, that sitting in trains was not walking about; and they knew that already. Except for the stick, however, she appeared to be a most desirable fourth—quiet, educated, elderly. She was much older than they or Lady Caroline—Lady Caroline had informed them she was twenty-eight—but not so old as to have ceased to be active-minded. She was very respectable indeed, and still wore a complete suit of black though her husband had died, she told them, eleven years before. Her house was full of signed photographs of illustrious Victorian dead, all of whom she said she had known when she was little. Her father had been an eminent critic, and in his house she had seen practically everybody who was anybody in letters and art. Carlyle had scowled at her; Matthew Arnold had held her on his knee; Tennyson had sonorously rallied her on the length of her pig-tail. She animatedly showed them the photographs, hung everywhere on her walls, pointing out the signatures with her stick, and she neither gave any information about her own husband nor asked for any about the husbands of her visitors; which was the greatest comfort. Indeed, she seemed to think that they also were widows, for on inquiring who the fourth lady was to be, and being told it was a Lady Caroline Dester, she said, "Is she a widow too?" And on their explaining that she was not, because she had not yet been married, observed with abstracted amiability, "All in good time."

But Mrs. Fisher's very abstractedness—and she seemed to be absorbed chiefly in the interesting people she used to know and in their memorial photographs, and quite a good part of the interview was taken up by reminiscent anecdote of Carlyle, Meredith, Matthew Arnold, Tennyson, and a host of others—her very abstractedness was a recommendation. She only asked, she said, to be allowed to sit quiet in the sun and remember. That was all Mrs. Arbuthnot and Mrs. Wilkins asked of their sharers. It was their idea of a perfect sharer that she should sit quiet in the sun and remember, rousing herself on Saturday evenings sufficiently to pay her share. Mrs. Fisher was very fond, too, she said, of flowers, and once when she was spending a week-end with her father at Box Hill—

"Who lived at Box Hill?" interrupted Mrs. Wilkins, who hung on Mrs. Fisher's reminiscences, intensely excited by meeting somebody who had actually been familiar with all the really and truly and undoubtedly great—actually seen them, heard them talking, touched them.

Mrs. Fisher looked at her over the top of her glasses in some surprise. Mrs. Wilkins, in her eagerness to tear the heart out quickly of Mrs. Fisher's reminiscences, afraid that at any moment Mrs. Arbuthnot would take her away and she wouldn't have heard half, had already interrupted several times with questions which appeared ignorant to Mrs. Fisher.

"Meredith of course," said Mrs. Fisher rather shortly. "I remember a particular week-end"—she continued. "My father often took me, but I always remember this week-end particularly—"

"Did you know Keats?" eagerly interrupted Mrs. Wilkins.

Mrs. Fisher, after a pause, said with sub-acid reserve that she had been unacquainted with both Keats and Shakespeare.

"Oh, of course—how ridiculous of me!" cried Mrs. Wilkins, flushing scarlet. "It's because"—she floundered—"it's because the immortals somehow still seem alive, don't they—as if they were here, going to walk into the room in another minute—and one forgets they are dead. In fact one knows perfectly well that they're not dead—not nearly so dead as you and I even now," she assured Mrs. Fisher, who observed her over the top of her glasses.

"I thought I *saw* Keats the other day," Mrs. Wilkins incoherently proceeded, driven on by Mrs. Fisher's look over the top of her glasses. "In Hampstead—crossing the road in front of that house—you know—the house where he lived—"

Mrs. Arbuthnot said they must be going.

Mrs. Fisher did nothing to prevent them.

"I *really* thought I saw him," protested Mrs. Wilkins, appealing for belief first to one and then to the other while waves of color passed over her face, and totally unable to stop because of Mrs. Fisher's glasses and the steady eyes looking at her over their tops. "I believe I *did* see him—he was dressed in a—"

Even Mrs. Arbuthnot looked at her now, and in her gentlest voice said they would be late for lunch.

It was at this point that Mrs. Fisher asked for references. She had no wish to find herself shut up for four weeks with somebody who saw things. It is true that there were three sitting-rooms, besides the garden and the battlements at San Salvatore, so that there would be opportunities of withdrawal from Mrs. Wilkins; but it would be disagreeable to Mrs. Fisher, for instance, if Mrs. Wilkins were suddenly to assert that she saw Mr. Fisher. Mr. Fisher was dead; let him remain so. She had no wish to be told he was walking about the garden. The only reference she really wanted, for she was much too old and firmly seated in her place in the world for questionable associates to matter to her, was one with regard to Mrs. Wilkins's health. Was her health quite normal? Was she an ordinary, everyday, sensible woman? Mrs. Fisher felt that if she were given even one address she would be able to find out what she needed. So she asked for references, and her visitors appeared to be so much taken aback—Mrs. Wilkins, indeed, was instantly sobered—that she added, "It is usual."

Mrs. Wilkins found her speech first. "But," she said, "aren't we the ones who ought to ask for some from you?"

And this seemed to Mrs. Arbuthnot too the right attitude. Surely it was they who were taking Mrs. Fisher into their party, and not Mrs. Fisher who was taking them into it?

For answer Mrs. Fisher, leaning on her stick, went to the writing-table and in a firm hand wrote down three names and offered them to Mrs. Wilkins, and the names were so respectable, more, they were so momentous, they were so nearly august, that just to read them was enough. The President of the Royal Academy, the Archbishop of Canterbury, and the Governor of the Bank of England—who would dare disturb such personages in their meditations with inquiries as to whether a female friend of theirs was all she should be?

"They have known me since I was little," said Mrs. Fisher—everybody seemed to have known Mrs. Fisher since or when she was little.

"I don't think references are nice things at all between—between ordinary decent women," burst out Mrs. Wilkins, made courageous by being, as she felt, at bay; for she very well knew that the only reference she could give without getting into trouble was Shoolbred, and she had little confidence in that, as it would be entirely based on Mellersh's fish. "We're not business people. We needn't distrust each other—"

And Mrs. Arbuthnot said, with a dignity that yet was sweet, "I'm afraid references do bring an atmosphere into our holiday plan that isn't quite what we want, and I don't think we'll take yours up or give you any ourselves. So that I suppose you won't wish to join us."

And she held out her hand in good-bye.

Then Mrs. Fisher, her gaze diverted to Mrs. Arbuthnot, who inspired trust and liking even in Tube officials, felt that she would be idiotic to lose the opportunity of being in Italy in the particular conditions offered, and that she and this calm-browed woman between them would certainly be able to curb the other one when she had her attacks. So she said, taking Mrs. Arbuthnot's offered hand, "Very well. I waive references."

She waived references.

The two as they walked to the station in Kensington High Street could not help thinking that this way of putting it was lofty. Even Mrs. Arbuthnot, spendthrift of excuses for lapses, thought Mrs. Fisher might have used other words; and Mrs. Wilkins, by the time she got to the station, and the walk and the struggle on the crowded pavement with other people's umbrellas had warmed her blood, actually suggested waiving Mrs. Fisher.

"If there is any waiving to be done, do let us be the ones who waive," she said eagerly.

But Mrs. Arbuthnot, as usual, held on to Mrs. Wilkins; and presently, having cooled down in the train, Mrs. Wilkins announced that at San Salvatore Mrs. Fisher would find her level. "I *see* her finding her level there," she said, her eyes very bright.

Whereupon Mrs. Arbuthnot, sitting with her quiet hands folded, turned over in her mind how best she could help Mrs. Wilkins not to see quite so much; or at least, if she must see, to see in silence.

CHAPTER 4

It had been arranged that Mrs. Arbuthnot and Mrs. Wilkins, traveling together, should arrive at San Salvatore on the evening of March 31st—the owner, who told them how to get there, appreciated their disinclination to begin their time in it on April 1st—and Lady Caroline and Mrs. Fisher, as yet unacquainted and therefore under no obligations to bore each other on the journey, for only towards the end would they find out by a process of sifting who they were, were to arrive on the morning of April 2nd. In this way everything would be got nicely ready for the two who seemed, in spite of the equality of the sharing, yet to have something about them of guests.

There were disagreeable incidents towards the end of March, when Mrs. Wilkins, her heart in her mouth and her face a mixture of guilt, terror, and determination, told her husband that she had been invited to Italy, and he declined to believe it. Of course he declined to believe it. Nobody had ever invited his wife to Italy before. There was no precedent. He required proofs. The only proof was Mrs. Arbuthnot, and Mrs. Wilkins had produced her; but after what entreaties, what passionate persuading! Mrs. Arbuthnot had not imagined she would have to face Mr. Wilkins and say things to him that were short of the truth, and it brought home to her what she had for some time suspected, that she was slipping more and more away from God.

Indeed, the whole of March was filled with unpleasant, anxious moments. It was an uneasy month. Mrs. Arbuthnot's conscience, made super-sensitive by years of pampering, could not reconcile what she was doing with its own high standard of what was right. It gave her little peace. It nudged her at her prayers. It punctuated her entreaties for divine guidance with disconcerting questions, such as, "Are you not a hypocrite? Do you really mean that? Would you not, frankly, be disappointed if that prayer were granted?"

The prolonged wet, raw weather was on the side too of her conscience, producing far more sickness than usual among the poor. They had bronchitis; they had fevers; there was no end to the distress. And here she was going off, spending precious money on going off, simply and solely to be happy. One woman. One woman being happy, and these piteous multitudes . . .

She was unable to look the vicar in the face. He did not know, nobody knew, what she was going to do, and from the very beginning she was unable to look anybody in the face. She excused herself from making speeches appealing for money. How could she stand up and ask people for money when she herself was spending so much on her own selfish pleasure? Nor did it help her or quiet her that, having actually told Frederick, in her desire to make up for what she was squandering, that she would be grateful if he would let her have some money, he instantly gave her a check for £100. He asked no questions. She was scarlet. He looked at her a moment and then looked away. It was a relief to Frederick that she should take some money. She gave it all immediately to the organization she worked with, and found herself more tangled in doubts than ever.

Mrs. Wilkins, on the contrary, had no doubts. She was quite certain that it was a most proper thing to have a holiday, and altogether right and beautiful to spend one's own hard-collected savings on being happy.

"Think how much nicer we shall be when we come back," she said to Mrs. Arbuthnot, encouraging that pale lady.

No, Mrs. Wilkins had no doubts, but she had fears; and March was for her too an anxious month, with the unconscious Mr. Wilkins coming back daily to his dinner and eating his fish in the silence of imagined security.

Also things happen so awkwardly. It really is astonishing, how awkwardly they happen. Mrs. Wilkins, who was very careful all this month to give Mellersh only the food he liked, buying it and hovering over its cooking with a zeal more than common, succeeded so well that Mellersh was pleased; definitely pleased; so much pleased that he began to think that he might, after all, have married the right wife instead of, as he had frequently suspected, the wrong one. The result was that on the third Sunday in the month—Mrs. Wilkins had made up her trembling mind that on the fourth Sunday, there being five in that March and it being on the fifth of them that she and Mrs. Arbuthnot were to start, she would tell Mellersh of her invitation—on the third Sunday, then, after a very well-cooked lunch in which the Yorkshire pudding had melted in his mouth and the apricot tart had been so perfect that he ate it all, Mellersh, smoking his cigar by the brightly burning fire the while hail gusts banged on the window, said: "I am thinking of taking you to Italy for Easter." And paused for her astounded and grateful ecstasy.

None came. The silence in the room, except for the hail hitting the windows and the gay roar of the fire, was complete. Mrs. Wilkins could not speak. She was dumbfounded. The next Sunday was the day she had meant to break her news to him, and she had not yet even prepared the form of words in which she would break it.

Mr. Wilkins, who had not been abroad since before the war, and was noticing with increasing disgust, as week followed week of wind and rain, the peculiar persistent vileness of the weather, had slowly conceived a desire to get away from England for Easter. He was doing very well in his business. He could afford a trip. Switzerland was useless in April. There was a familiar sound about Easter in Italy. To Italy he would go; and as it would cause comment if he did not take his wife, take her he must—besides, she would be useful; a second person was always useful in a country whose language one did not speak for holding things, for waiting with the luggage.

He had expected an explosion of gratitude and excitement. The absence of it was incredible. She could not, he concluded, have heard. Probably she was absorbed in some foolish day-dream. It was regrettable how childish she remained.

He turned his head—their chairs were in front of the fire—and looked at her. She was staring straight into the fire, and it was no doubt the fire that made her face so red.

"I am thinking," he repeated, raising his clear, cultivated voice and speaking with acerbity, for inattention at such a moment was deplorable, "of taking you to Italy for Easter. Did you not hear me?"

Yes, she had heard him, and she had been wondering at the extraordinary coincidence—really most extraordinary—she was just going to tell him how—how she had been invited—a friend had invited her—Easter, too—Easter was in April, wasn't it?—her friend had a—had a house there.

In fact Mrs. Wilkins, driven by terror, guilt, and surprise, had been more incoherent if possible than usual.

It was a dreadful afternoon. Mellersh, profoundly indignant, besides having his intended treat coming back on him like a blessing to roost, cross-examined her with the utmost severity. He demanded that she refuse the invitation. He demanded that, since she had so outrageously accepted it without consulting him, she should write and cancel her acceptance. Finding himself up against an unsuspected, shocking rock of obstinacy in her, he then declined to believe she had been invited to Italy at all. He declined to believe in this Mrs. Arbuthnot, of whom till that moment he had never heard; and it was only when the gentle creature was brought round—with such difficulty, with such a desire on her part to throw the whole thing up rather than tell Mr. Wilkins less than the truth—and herself endorsed his wife's statements that he was able to give them credence. He could not but believe Mrs. Arbuthnot. She produced the precise effect on him that she did on Tube officials. She hardly needed to say anything. But that made no difference to her conscience, which knew and would not let her forget that she had given him an incomplete impression. "Do you," asked her conscience, "see any real difference between an incomplete impression and a completely stated lie? God sees none."

The remainder of March was a confused bad dream. Both Mrs. Arbuthnot and Mrs. Wilkins were shattered; try as they would not to, both felt extraordinarily guilty; and when on the morning of the 30th they did finally get off there was no exhilaration about the departure, no holiday feeling at all.

"We've been too good—much *too* good," Mrs. Wilkins kept on murmuring as they walked up and down the platform at Victoria, having arrived there an hour before they need have, "and that's why we feel as though we're doing wrong. We're brow-beaten—we're not any longer real human beings. Real human beings aren't ever as good as we've been. Oh"—she clenched her thin hands—"to *think* that we ought to be so happy now, here on the very station, actually starting, and we're not, and it's being spoilt for us just simply because we've spoilt *them!* What have we done—what have we done, I should like to know," she inquired of Mrs. Arbuthnot indignantly, "except for once want to go away by ourselves and have a little rest from *them?*"

Mrs. Arbuthnot, patiently pacing, did not ask who she meant by *them*, because she knew. Mrs. Wilkins meant their husbands, persisting in her assumption that Frederick was as indignant as Mellersh over the departure of his wife, whereas Frederick did not even know his wife had gone.

Mrs. Arbuthnot, always silent about him, had said nothing of this to Mrs. Wilkins. Frederick went too deep into her heart for her to talk about him. He was having an extra bout of work finishing another of those dreadful books, and had been away practically continually the last few weeks, and was away when she left. Why should she tell him beforehand? Sure as she so miserably was that he would have no objection to anything she did, she merely wrote him a note and put it on the hall-table ready for him if and when he should come home. She said she was going for a month's holiday as she needed a rest and she had not had one for so long, and that Gladys, the efficient parlormaid, had orders to see to his comforts. She did not say where she was going; there was no reason why she should; he would not be interested, he would not care.

The day was wretched, blustering and wet; the crossing was atrocious, and they were very sick. But after having been very sick, just to arrive at Calais and not be sick was happiness, and it was there that the real splendor of what they were doing first began to warm their benumbed spirits. It got hold of Mrs. Wilkins first, and spread from her like a rose-colored flame over her pale companion. Mellersh at Calais, where they restored themselves with soles because of Mrs. Wilkins's desire to eat a sole Mellersh wasn't having—Mellersh at Calais had already begun to dwindle and seem less important. None of the French porters knew him; not a single official at Calais cared a fig for Mellersh. In Paris there was no time to think of him because their train was late and they only just caught the Turin train at the Gare de Lyons; and by the afternoon of the next day when they got into Italy, England, Frederick, Mellersh, the vicar, the poor, Hampstead, the club, Shoolbred, everybody and everything, the whole inflamed sore dreariness, had faded to the dimness of a dream.

CHAPTER 5

It was cloudy in Italy, which surprised them. They had expected brilliant sunshine. But never mind: it was Italy, and the very clouds looked fat. Neither of them had ever been there before. Both gazed out of the windows with rapt faces. The hours flew as long as it was daylight, and after that there was the excitement of getting nearer, getting quite near, getting there. At Genoa it had begun to rain—Genoa! Imagine actually being at Genoa, seeing its name written up in the station just like any other name—at Nervi it was pouring, and when at last towards midnight, for again the train was late, they got to Mezzago, the rain was coming down in what seemed solid sheets. But it was Italy. Nothing it did could be bad. The very rain was different—straight rain, falling properly on to one's umbrella; not that violently blowing English stuff that got in everywhere. And it did leave off; and when it did, behold the earth would be strewn with roses.

Mr. Briggs, San Salvatore's owner, had said, "You get out at Mezzago, and then you drive." But he had forgotten what he amply knew, that trains in Italy are sometimes late, and he had imagined his tenants arriving at Mezzago at eight o'clock and finding a string of flys to choose from.

The train was four hours late, and when Mrs. Arbuthnot and Mrs. Wilkins scrambled down the ladder-like high steps of their carriage into the black downpour, their skirts sweeping off great pools of sooty wet because their hands were full of suit-cases, if it had not been for the vigilance of Domenico, the gardener at San Salvatore, they would have found nothing for them to drive in. All ordinary flys had long since gone home. Domenico, foreseeing this, had sent his aunt's fly, driven by her son his cousin; and his aunt and her fly lived in Castagneto, the village crouching at the feet of San Salvatore, and therefore, however late the train was, the fly would not dare come home without containing that which it had been sent to fetch.

Domenico's cousin's name was Beppo, and he presently emerged out of the dark where Mrs. Arbuthnot and Mrs. Wilkins stood, uncertain what to do next after the train had gone on, for they could see no porter and they thought from the feel of it that they were standing not so much on a platform as in the middle of the permanent way.

Beppo, who had been searching for them, emerged from the dark with a kind of pounce and talked Italian to them vociferously. Beppo was a most respectable young man, but he did not look as if he were, especially not in the dark, and he had a dripping hat slouched over one eye. They did not like the way he seized their suit-cases. He could not be, they thought, a porter. However, they presently from out of his streaming talk discerned the words San Salvatore, and after that they kept on saying them to him, for it was the only Italian they knew, as they hurried after him, unwilling to lose sight of their suit-cases, stumbling across rails and through puddles out to where in the road a small, high fly stood.

Its hood was up, and its horse was in an attitude of thought. They climbed in, and the minute they were in—Mrs. Wilkins, indeed, could hardly be called in—the horse awoke with a start from its reverie and immediately began going home rapidly; without Beppo; without the suit-cases.

Beppo darted after him, making the night ring with his shouts, and caught the hanging reins just in time. He explained proudly, and as it seemed to him with perfect clearness, that the horse always did that, being a fine animal full of corn and blood, and cared for by him, Beppo, as if he were his own son, and the ladies must not be alarmed—he had noticed they were clutching each other; but clear, and loud, and profuse of words though he was, they only looked at him blankly.

He went on talking, however, while he piled the suit-cases up round them, sure that sooner or later they must understand him, especially as he was careful to talk very loud and illustrate everything he said with the simplest elucidatory gestures, but they both continued only to look at him. They both, he noticed sympathetically, had white faces, fatigued faces, and they both had big eyes, fatigued eyes. They were beautiful ladies, he thought, and their eyes, looking at him over the tops of the suit-cases watching his every movement—there were no trunks, only numbers of suit-cases—were like the eyes of the Mother of God. The only thing the ladies said, and they repeated it at regular intervals, even after they had started, gently prodding him as he sat on his box to call his attention to it, was, "San Salvatore?"

And each time he answered vociferously, encouragingly, "*Sì, sì*—San Salvatore."

"We don't *know* of course if he's taking us there," said Mrs. Arbuthnot at last in a low voice, after they had been driving as it seemed to them a long while, and had got off the paving-stones of the sleep-shrouded town and were out on a winding road with what they could just see was a low wall on their left beyond which was a great black emptiness and the sound of the sea. On their right was something close and steep and high and black—rocks, they whispered to each other; huge rocks.

"No—we don't *know*," agreed Mrs. Wilkins, a slight coldness passing down her spine.

They felt very uncomfortable. It was so late. It was so dark. The road was so lonely. Suppose a wheel came off. Suppose they met Fascisti, or the opposite of Fascisti. How sorry they were now that they had not slept at Genoa and come on the next morning in daylight.

"But that would have been the first of April," said Mrs. Wilkins, in a low voice.

"It is that now," said Mrs. Arbuthnot beneath her breath.

"So it is," murmured Mrs. Wilkins.

They were silent.

Beppo turned round on his box—a disquieting habit already noticed, for surely his horse ought to be carefully watched—and again addressed them with what he was convinced was lucidity—no *patois*, and the clearest explanatory movements.

How much they wished their mothers had made them learn Italian when they were little. If only now they could have said, "Please sit round the right way and look after the horse." They did not even know what horse was in Italian. It was contemptible to be so ignorant.

In their anxiety, for the road twisted round great jutting rocks, and on their left was only the low wall to keep them out of the sea should anything happen, they too began to gesticulate, waving their hands at Beppo, pointing ahead. They wanted him to turn round again and face his horse, that was all. He thought they wanted him to drive faster; and there followed a terrifying ten minutes during which, as he supposed, he was gratifying them. He was proud of his horse, and it could go very fast. He rose in his seat, the whip cracked, the horse rushed forward, the rocks leaped towards them, the little fly swayed, the suit-cases heaved, Mrs. Arbuthnot and Mrs. Wilkins clung. In this way they continued, swaying, heaving, clattering, clinging, till at a point near Castagneto there was a rise in the road, and on reaching the foot of the rise the horse, who knew every inch of the way, stopped suddenly, throwing everything in the fly into a heap, and then proceeded up at the slowest of walks.

Beppo twisted himself round to receive their admiration, laughing with pride in his horse.

There was no answering laugh from the beautiful ladies. Their eyes, fixed on him, seemed bigger than ever, and their faces against the black of the night showed milky.

But here at least, once they were up the slope, were houses. The rocks left off, and there were houses; the low wall left off, and there were houses; the sea shrunk away, and the sound of it ceased, and the loneliness of the road was finished. No lights anywhere, of course, nobody to see them pass; and yet Beppo, when the houses began, after looking over his shoulder and shouting "Castagneto" at the ladies, once more stood up and cracked his whip and once more made his horse dash forward.

"We shall be there in a minute," Mrs. Arbuthnot said to herself, holding on.

"We shall soon stop now," Mrs. Wilkins said to herself, holding on. They said nothing aloud, because nothing would have been heard above the whip-cracking and the wheel-clattering and the boisterous inciting noises Beppo was making at his horse.

Anxiously they strained their eyes for any sight of the beginning of San Salvatore.

They had supposed and hoped that after a reasonable amount of village a mediaeval archway would loom upon them, and through it they would drive into a garden and draw up at an open, welcoming door, with light streaming from it and those servants standing in it who, according to the advertisement, remained.

Instead the fly suddenly stopped.

Peering out they could see they were still in the village street, with small dark houses each side; and Beppo, throwing the reins over the horse's back as if completely confident this time that he would not go any farther, got down off his box. At the same moment, springing as it seemed out of nothing, a man and several half-grown boys appeared on each side of the fly and began dragging out the suit-cases.

"No, no—San Salvatore, San Salvatore"—exclaimed Mrs. Wilkins, trying to hold on to what suit-cases she could.

"*Sì, sì*—San Salvatore," they all shouted, pulling.

"This *can't* be San Salvatore," said Mrs. Wilkins, turning to Mrs. Arbuthnot, who sat quite still watching her suit-cases being taken from her with the same patience she applied to lesser evils. She knew she could do nothing if these men were wicked men determined to have her suit-cases.

"I don't think it can be," she admitted, and could not refrain from a moment's wonder at the ways of God. Had she really been brought here, she and poor Mrs. Wilkins, after so much trouble in arranging it, so much difficulty and worry, along such devious paths of prevarication and deceit, only to be—

She checked her thoughts, and gently said to Mrs. Wilkins, while the ragged youths disappeared with the suit-cases into the night and the man with the lantern helped Beppo pull the rug off her, that they were both in God's hands; and for the first time on hearing this, Mrs. Wilkins was afraid.

There was nothing for it but to get out. Useless to try to go on sitting in the fly repeating San Salvatore. Every time they said it, and their voices each time were fainter, Beppo and the other man merely echoed it in a series of loud shouts. If only they had learned Italian when they were little. If only they could have said, "We wish to be driven to the door." But they did not even know what door was in Italian. Such ignorance was not only contemptible, it was, they now saw, definitely dangerous. Useless, however, to lament it now. Useless to put off whatever it was that was going to happen to them by trying to go on sitting in the fly. They therefore got out.

The two men opened their umbrellas for them and handed them to them. From this they received a faint encouragement, because they could not believe that if these men were wicked they would pause to open umbrellas. The man with the lantern then made signs to them to follow him, talking loud and quickly, and Beppo, they noticed, remained behind. Ought they to pay him? Not, they thought, if they were going to be robbed and perhaps murdered. Surely on such an occasion one did not pay. Besides, he had not after all brought them to San Salvatore. Where they had got to was evidently somewhere else. Also, he did not show the least wish to be paid; he let them go away into the night with no clamor at all. This, they could not help thinking, was a bad sign. He asked for nothing because presently he was to get so much.

They came to some steps. The road ended abruptly in a church and some descending steps. The man held the lantern low for them to see the steps.

"San Salvatore?" said Mrs. Wilkins once again, very faintly, before committing herself to the steps. It was useless to mention it now, of course, but she could not go down steps in complete silence. No mediaeval castle, she was sure, was ever built at the bottom of steps.

Again, however, came the echoing shout—"*Sì, sì*—San Salvatore."

They descended gingerly, holding up their skirts just as if they would be wanting them another time and had not in all probability finished with skirts for ever.

The steps ended in a steeply sloping path with flat stone slabs down the middle. They slipped a good deal on these wet slabs, and the man with the lantern, talking loud and quickly, held them up. His way of holding them up was polite.

"Perhaps," said Mrs. Wilkins in a low voice to Mrs. Arbuthnot, "it is all right after all."

"We're in God's hands," said Mrs. Arbuthnot again; and again Mrs. Wilkins was afraid.

They reached the bottom of the sloping path, and the light of the lantern flickered over an open space with houses round three sides. The sea was the fourth side, lazily washing backwards and forwards on pebbles.

"San Salvatore," said the man pointing with his lantern to a black mass curved round the water like an arm flung about it.

They strained their eyes. They saw the black mass, and on the top of it a light.

"San Salvatore?" they both repeated incredulously, for where were the suit-cases, and why had they been forced to get out of the fly?

"*Sì, sì*—San Salvatore."

They went along what seemed to be a quay, right on the edge of the water. There was not even a low wall here—nothing to prevent the man with the lantern tipping them in if he wanted to. He did not, however, tip them in. Perhaps it was all right after all, Mrs. Wilkins again suggested to Mrs. Arbuthnot on noticing this, who this time was herself beginning to think that it might be, and said no more about God's hands.

The flicker of the lantern danced along, reflected in the wet pavement of the quay. Out to the left, in the darkness and evidently at the end of a jetty, was a red light. They came to an archway with a heavy iron gate. The man with the lantern pushed the gate open. This time they went up steps instead of down, and at the top of them was a little path that wound upwards among flowers. They could not see the flowers, but the whole place was evidently full of them.

It here dawned on Mrs. Wilkins that perhaps the reason why the fly had not driven them up to the door was that there was no road, only a footpath. That also would explain the disappearance of the suit-cases. She began to feel confident that they would find their suit-cases waiting for them when they got up to the top. San Salvatore was, it seemed, on the top of a hill, as a mediaeval castle should be.

At a turn of the path they saw above them, much nearer now and shining more brightly, the light they had seen from the quay. She told Mrs. Arbuthnot of her dawning belief, and Mrs. Arbuthnot agreed that it was very likely a true one.

Once more, but this time in a tone of real hopefulness, Mrs. Wilkins said, pointing upwards at the black outline against the only slightly less black sky, "San Salvatore?" And once more, but this time comfortingly, encouragingly, came back the assurance, "*Sì, sì*—San Salvatore."

They crossed a little bridge, over what was apparently a ravine, and then came a flat bit with long grass at the sides and more flowers. They felt the grass flicking wet against their stockings, and the invisible flowers were everywhere. Then up again through trees, along a zigzag path with the smell all the way of the flowers they could not see. The warm rain was bringing out all the sweetness. Higher and higher they went in this sweet darkness, and the red light on the jetty dropped farther and farther below them.

The path wound round to the other side of what appeared to be a little peninsula; the jetty and the red light disappeared; across the emptiness on their left were distant lights.

"Mezzago," said the man, waving his lantern at the lights.

"*Sì, sì*," they answered, for they had by now learned "*sì, sì*." Upon which the man congratulated them in a great flow of polite words, not one of which they understood, on their magnificent Italian; for this was Domenico, the vigilant and accomplished gardener of San Salvatore, the prop and stay of the establishment, the resourceful, the gifted, the eloquent, the courteous, the intelligent Domenico. Only they did not know that yet; and he did in the dark, and even sometimes in the light, look, with his knife-sharp swarthy features and swift, panther movements, very like somebody wicked.

They passed along another flat bit of path, with a black shape like a high wall towering above them on their right, and then the path went up again under trellises, and trailing sprays of scented things caught at them and shook raindrops on them, and the light of the lantern flickered over lilies, and then came a flight of ancient steps worn with centuries, and then another iron gate, and then they were inside, though still climbing a twisting flight of stone steps with old walls on either side like the walls of dungeons, and with a vaulted roof.

At the top was a wrought-iron door, and through it shone a flood of electric light.

"Ecco," said Domenico, lithely running up the last few steps ahead and pushing the door open.

And there they were, arrived; and it was San Salvatore; and their suit-cases were waiting for them; and they had not been murdered.

They looked at each other's white faces and blinking eyes very solemnly.

It was a great, a wonderful moment. Here they were, in their mediaeval castle at last. Their feet touched its stones.

Mrs. Wilkins put her arm round Mrs. Arbuthnot's neck and kissed her.

"The first thing to happen in this house," she said softly, solemnly, "shall be a kiss."

"Dear Lotty," said Mrs. Arbuthnot.

"Dear Rose," said Mrs. Wilkins, her eyes brimming with gladness.

Domenico was delighted. He liked to see beautiful ladies kiss. He made them a most appreciative speech of welcome, and they stood arm in arm, holding each other up, for they were very tired, blinking smilingly at him, and not understanding a word.

CHAPTER 6

When Mrs. Wilkins woke next morning she lay in bed a few minutes before getting up and opening the shutters. What would she see out of her window? A shining world, or a world of rain? But it would be beautiful; whatever it was would be beautiful.

She was in a little bedroom with bare white walls and a stone floor and sparse old furniture. The beds—there were two—were made of iron, enameled black and painted with bunches of gay flowers. She lay putting off the great moment of going to the window as one puts off opening a precious letter, gloating over it. She had no idea what time it was; she had forgotten to wind up her watch ever since, centuries ago, she last went to bed in Hampstead. No sounds were to be heard in the house, so she supposed it was very early, yet she felt as if she had slept a long while—so completely rested, so perfectly content. She lay with her arms clasped round her head thinking how happy she was, her lips curved upwards in a delighted smile. In bed by herself: adorable condition. She had not been in a bed without Mellersh once now for five whole years; and the cool roominess of it, the freedom of one's movements, the sense of recklessness, of audacity, in giving the blankets a pull if one wanted to, or twitching the pillows more comfortably! It was like the discovery of an entirely new joy.

Mrs. Wilkins longed to get up and open the shutters, but where she was was really so very delicious. She gave a sigh of contentment, and went on lying there looking round her, taking in everything in her room, her own little room, her very own to arrange just as she pleased for this one blessed month, her room bought with her own savings, the fruit of her careful denials, whose door she could bolt if she wanted to, and nobody had the right to come in. It was such a strange little room, so different from any she had known, and so sweet. It was like a cell. Except for the two beds, it suggested a happy austerity. "And the name of the chamber," she thought, quoting and smiling round at it, "was Peace."

Well, this was delicious, to lie there thinking how happy she was, but outside those shutters it was more delicious still. She jumped up, pulled on her slippers, for there was nothing on the stone floor but one small rug, ran to the window and threw open the shutters.

"*Oh!*" cried Mrs. Wilkins.

All the radiance of April in Italy lay gathered together at her feet. The sun poured in on her. The sea lay asleep in it, hardly stirring. Across the bay the lovely mountains, exquisitely different in color, were asleep too in the light; and underneath her window, at the bottom of the flower-starred grass slope from which the wall of the castle rose up, was a great cypress, cutting through the delicate blues and violets and rose-colors of the mountains and the sea like a great black sword.

She stared. Such beauty; and she there to see it. Such beauty; and she alive to feel it. Her face was bathed in light. Lovely scents came up to the window and caressed her. A tiny breeze gently lifted her hair. Far out in the bay a cluster of almost motionless fishing boats hovered like a flock of white birds on the tranquil sea. How beautiful, how beautiful. Not to have died before this . . . to have been allowed to see, breathe, feel this. . . . She stared, her lips parted. Happy? Poor, ordinary, everyday word. But what could one say, how could one describe it? It was as though she could hardly stay inside herself, it was as though she were too small to hold so much of joy, it was as though she were washed through with light. And how astonishing to feel this sheer bliss, for here she was, not doing and not going to do a single unselfish thing, not going to do a thing she didn't want to do. According to everybody she had ever come across she ought at least to have twinges. She had not one twinge. Something was wrong somewhere. Wonderful that at home she should have been so good, so terribly good, and merely felt tormented. Twinges of every sort had there been her portion; aches, hurts, discouragements, and she the whole time being steadily unselfish. Now she had taken off all her goodness and left it behind her like a heap of rain-sodden clothes, and she only felt joy. She was naked of goodness, and was rejoicing in being naked. She was stripped, and exulting. And there, away in the dim mugginess of Hampstead, was Mellersh being angry.

She tried to visualize Mellersh, she tried to see him having breakfast and thinking bitter things about her; and lo, Mellersh himself began to shimmer, became rose-color, became delicate violet, became an enchanting blue, became formless, became iridescent. Actually Mellersh, after quivering a minute, was lost in light.

"*Well*," thought Mrs. Wilkins, staring, as it were, after him. How extraordinary not to be able to visualize Mellersh; and she who used to know every feature, every expression of his by heart. She simply could not see him as he was. She could only see him resolved into beauty, melted into harmony with everything else. The familiar words of the General Thanksgiving came quite naturally into her mind, and she found herself blessing God for her creation, preservation, and all the blessings of this life, but above all for His inestimable Love; out loud; in a burst of acknowledgment. While Mellersh, at that moment angrily pulling on his boots before going out into the dripping streets, was indeed thinking bitter things about her.

She began to dress, choosing clean white clothes in honor of the summer's day, unpacking her suit-cases, tidying her adorable little room. She moved about with quick, purposeful steps, her long thin body held up straight, her small face, so much puckered at home with effort and fear, smoothed out. All she had been and done before this morning, all she had felt and worried about, was gone. Each of her worries behaved as the image of Mellersh had behaved, and dissolved into color and light. And she noticed things she had not noticed for years—when she was doing her hair in front of the glass she noticed it, and thought, "Why, what pretty stuff." For years she had forgotten she had such a thing as hair, plaiting it in the evening and unplaiting it in the morning with the same hurry and indifference with which she laced and unlaced her shoes. Now she suddenly saw it, and she twisted it round her fingers before the glass, and was glad it was so pretty. Mellersh couldn't have seen it either, for he had never said a word about it. Well, when she got home she would draw his attention to it. "Mellersh," she would say, "look at my hair. Aren't you pleased you've got a wife with hair like curly honey?"

She laughed. She had never said anything like that to Mellersh yet, and the idea of it amused her. But why had she not? Oh yes—she used to be afraid of him. Funny to be afraid of anybody; and especially of one's husband, whom one saw in his more simplified moments, such as asleep, and not breathing properly through his nose.

When she was ready she opened her door to go across to see if Rose, who had been put the night before by a sleepy maidservant into a cell opposite, were awake. She would say good-morning to her, and then she would run down and stay with that cypress tree till breakfast was ready, and after breakfast she wouldn't so much as look out of a window till she had helped Rose get everything ready for Lady Caroline and Mrs. Fisher. There was much to be done that day, settling in, arranging the rooms; she mustn't leave Rose to do it alone. They would make it all so lovely for the two to come, have such an entrancing vision ready for them of little cells bright with flowers. She remembered she had wanted Lady Caroline not to come; fancy wanting to shut some one out of heaven because she thought she would be shy of her! And as though it mattered if she were, and as though she would be anything so self-conscious as shy. Besides, what a reason. She could not accuse herself of goodness over that. And she remembered she had wanted not to have Mrs. Fisher either, because she had seemed lofty. How funny of her. So funny to worry about such little things, making them important.

The bedrooms and two of the sitting-rooms at San Salvatore were on the top floor, and opened into a roomy hall with a wide glass window at the north end. San Salvatore was rich in small gardens in different parts and on different levels. The garden this window looked down on was made on the highest part of the walls, and could only be reached through the corresponding spacious hall on the floor below. When Mrs. Wilkins came out of her room this window stood wide open, and beyond it in the sun was a Judas tree in full flower. There was no sign of anybody, no sound of voices or feet. Tubs of arum lilies stood about on the stone floor, and on a table flamed a huge bunch of fierce nasturtiums. Spacious, flowery, silent, with the wide window at the end opening into the garden, and the Judas tree absurdly beautiful in the sunshine, it seemed to Mrs. Wilkins, arrested on her way across to Mrs. Arbuthnot, too good to be true. Was she really going to live in this for a whole month? Up to now she had had to take what beauty she could as she went along, snatching at little bits of it when she came across it—a patch of daisies on a fine day in a Hampstead field, a flash of sunset between two chimney pots. She had never been in definitely, completely beautiful places. She had never been even in a venerable house; and such a thing as a profusion of flowers in her rooms was unattainable to her. Sometimes in the spring she had bought six tulips at Shoolbred's, unable to resist them, conscious that Mellersh if he knew what they had cost would think it inexcusable; but they had soon died, and then there were no more. As for the Judas tree, she hadn't an idea what it was, and gazed at it out there against the sky with the rapt expression of one who sees a heavenly vision.

Mrs. Arbuthnot, coming out of her room, found her there like that, standing in the middle of the hall staring.

"Now what does she think she sees now?" thought Mrs. Arbuthnot.

"We *are* in God's hands," said Mrs. Wilkins, turning to her, speaking with extreme conviction.

"Oh!" said Mrs. Arbuthnot quickly, her face, which had been covered with smiles when she came out of her room, falling. "Why, what has happened?"

For Mrs. Arbuthnot had woken up with such a delightful feeling of security, of relief, and she did not want to find she had not after all escaped from the need of refuge. She had not even dreamed of Frederick. For the first time for years she had been spared the nightly dream that he was with her, that they were heart to heart, and its miserable awakening. She had slept like a baby, and had woken up confident; she had found there was nothing she wished to say in her morning prayer except Thank you. It was disconcerting to be told she was after all in God's hands.

"I hope nothing has happened?" she asked anxiously.

Mrs. Wilkins looked at her a moment, and laughed. "How funny," she said, kissing her.

"What is funny?" asked Mrs. Arbuthnot, her face clearing because Mrs. Wilkins laughed.

"We are. This is. Everything. It's all so wonderful. It's so funny and so adorable that we should be in it. I daresay when we finally reach heaven—the one they talk about so much—we shan't find it a bit more beautiful."

Mrs. Arbuthnot relaxed to smiling security again. "Isn't it divine?" she said.

"Were you ever, ever in your life so happy?" asked Mrs. Wilkins, catching her by the arm.

"No," said Mrs. Arbuthnot. Nor had she been; not ever; not even in her first love-days with Frederick. Because always pain had been close at hand in that other happiness, ready to torture with doubts, to torture even with the very excess of her love; while this was the simple happiness of complete harmony with her surroundings, the happiness that asks for nothing, that just accepts, just breathes, just is.

"Let's go and look at that tree close," said Mrs. Wilkins. "I don't believe it can only be a tree."

And arm in arm they went along the hall, and their husbands would not have known them their faces were so young with eagerness, and together they stood at the open window, and when their eyes, having feasted on the marvelous pink thing, wandered farther among the beauties of the garden, they saw sitting on the low wall at the east edge of it, gazing out over the bay, her feet in lilies, Lady Caroline.

They were astonished. They said nothing in their astonishment, but stood quite still, arm in arm, staring down at her.

She too had on a white frock, and her head was bare. They had had no idea that day in London, when her hat was down to her nose and her furs were up to her ears, that she was so pretty. They had merely thought her different from the other women in the club, and so had the other women themselves, and so had all the waitresses, eyeing her sideways and eyeing her again as they passed the corner where she sat talking; but they had had no idea she was so pretty. She was exceedingly pretty. Everything about her was very much that which it was. Her fair hair was very fair, her lovely gray eyes were very lovely and gray, her dark eyelashes were very dark, her white skin was very white, her red mouth was very red. She was extravagantly slender—the merest thread of a girl, though not without little curves beneath her thin frock where little curves should be. She was looking out across the bay, and was sharply defined against the background of empty blue. She was full in the sun. Her feet dangled among the leaves and flowers of the lilies just as if it did not matter that they should be bent or bruised.

"She ought to have a headache," whispered Mrs. Arbuthnot at last, "sitting there in the sun like that."

"She ought to have a hat," whispered Mrs. Wilkins.

"She's treading on lilies."

"But they're hers as much as ours."

"Only one-fourth of them."

Lady Caroline turned her head. She looked up at them a moment, surprised to see them so much younger than they had seemed that day at the club, and so much less unattractive. Indeed, they were really almost quite attractive, if any one could ever be really quite attractive in the wrong clothes. Her eyes, swiftly glancing over them, took in every inch of each of them in the half second before she smiled and waved her hand and called out good-morning. There was nothing, she saw at once, to be hoped for in the way of interest from their clothes. She did not consciously think this, for she was having a violent reaction against beautiful clothes and the slavery they impose on one, her experience being that the instant one had got them they took one in hand and gave one no peace till they had been everywhere and been seen by everybody. You didn't take your clothes to parties; they took you. It was quite a mistake to think that a woman, a really well-dressed woman, wore out her clothes; it was the clothes that wore out the woman—dragging her about at all hours of the day and night. No wonder men stayed young longer. Just new trousers couldn't excite them. She couldn't suppose that even the newest trousers ever behaved like that, taking the bit between their teeth. Her images were disorderly, but she thought as she chose, she used what images she liked. As she got off the wall and came towards the window, it seemed a restful thing to know she was going to spend an entire month with people in dresses made as she dimly remembered dresses used to be made five summers ago.

"I got here yesterday morning," she said, looking up at them and smiling. She really was bewitching. She had everything, even a dimple.

"It's a great pity," said Mrs. Arbuthnot, smiling back, "because we were going to choose the nicest room for you."

"Oh, but I've done that," said Lady Caroline. "At least, I think it's the nicest. It looks two ways—I adore a room that looks two ways, don't you? Over the sea to the west, and over this Judas tree to the north."

"And we had meant to make it pretty for you with flowers," said Mrs. Wilkins.

"Oh, Domenico did that. I told him to directly I got here. He's the gardener. He's wonderful."

"It's a good thing, of course," said Mrs. Arbuthnot a little hesitatingly, "to be independent, and to know exactly what one wants."

"Yes, it saves trouble," agreed Lady Caroline.

"But one shouldn't be so independent," said Mrs. Wilkins, "as to leave no opportunity for other people to exercise their benevolences on one."

Lady Caroline, who had been looking at Mrs. Arbuthnot, now looked at Mrs. Wilkins. That day at that queer club she had had merely a blurred impression of Mrs. Wilkins, for it was the other one who did all the talking, and her impression had been of somebody so shy, so awkward that it was best to take no notice of her. She had not even been able to say good-bye properly, doing it in an agony, turning red, turning damp. Therefore she now looked at her in some surprise; and she was still more surprised when Mrs. Wilkins added, gazing at her with the most obvious sincere admiration, speaking indeed with a conviction that refused to remain unuttered, "I didn't realize you were *so* pretty."

She stared at Mrs. Wilkins. She was not usually told this quite so immediately and roundly. Abundantly as she was used to it—impossible not to be after twenty-eight solid years—it surprised her to be told it with such bluntness, and by a woman.

"It's very kind of you to think so," she said.

"Why, you're lovely," said Mrs. Wilkins. "Quite, quite lovely."

"I hope," said Mrs. Arbuthnot pleasantly, "you make the most of it."

Lady Caroline then stared at Mrs. Arbuthnot. "Oh yes," she said. "I make the most of it. I've been doing that ever since I can remember."

"Because," said Mrs. Arbuthnot, smiling and raising a warning forefinger, "it won't last."

Then Lady Caroline began to be afraid these two were originals. If so, she would be bored. Nothing bored her so much as people who insisted on being original, who came and buttonholed her and kept her waiting while they were being original. And the one who admired her—it would be tiresome if she dogged her about in order to look at her. What she wanted of this holiday was complete escape from all she had had before, she wanted the rest of complete contrast. Being admired, being dogged, wasn't contrast, it was repetition; and as for originals, to find herself shut up with two on the top of a precipitous hill in a mediaeval castle built for the express purpose of preventing easy goings out and in, would not, she was afraid, be especially restful. Perhaps she had better be a little less encouraging. They had seemed such timid creatures, even the dark one—she couldn't remember their names—that day at the club, that she had felt it quite safe to be very friendly. Here they had come out of their shells; already; indeed, at once. There was no sign of timidity about either of them here. If they had got out of their shells so immediately, at the very first contact, unless she checked them they would soon begin to press upon her, and then good-bye to her dream of thirty restful, silent days, lying unmolested in the sun, getting her feathers smooth again, not being spoken to, not waited on, not grabbed at and monopolized, but just recovering from the fatigue, the deep and melancholy fatigue, of the too much.

Besides, there was Mrs. Fisher. She too must be checked. Lady Caroline had started two days earlier than had been arranged for two reasons: first, because she wished to arrive before the others in order to pick out the room or rooms she preferred, and second, because she judged it likely that otherwise she would have to travel with Mrs. Fisher. She did not want to travel with Mrs. Fisher. She did not want to arrive with Mrs. Fisher. She saw no reason whatever why for a single moment she should have to have anything at all to do with Mrs. Fisher.

But unfortunately Mrs. Fisher also was filled with a desire to get to San Salvatore first and pick out the room or rooms she preferred, and she and Lady Caroline had after all traveled together. As early as Calais they began to suspect it; in Paris they feared it; at Modane they knew it; at Mezzago they concealed it, driving out to Castagneto in two separate flys, the nose of the one almost touching the back of the other the whole way. But when the road suddenly left off at the church and the steps, further evasion was impossible; and faced by this abrupt and difficult finish to their journey there was nothing for it but to amalgamate.

Because of Mrs. Fisher's stick Lady Caroline had to see about everything. Mrs. Fisher's intentions, she explained from her fly when the situation had become plain to her, were active, but her stick prevented their being carried out. The two drivers told Lady Caroline boys would have to carry the luggage up to the castle, and she went in search of some, while Mrs. Fisher waited in the fly because of her stick. Mrs. Fisher could speak Italian, but only, she explained, the Italian of Dante, which Matthew Arnold used to read with her when she was a girl, and she thought this might be above the heads of boys. Therefore Lady Caroline, who spoke ordinary Italian very well, was obviously the one to go and do things.

"I am in your hands," said Mrs. Fisher, sitting firmly in her fly. "You must please regard me as merely an old woman with a stick."

And presently, down the steps and cobbles to the piazza, and along the quay, and up the zigzag path, Lady Caroline found herself as much obliged to walk slowly with Mrs. Fisher as if she were her own grandmother.

"It's my stick," Mrs. Fisher complacently remarked at intervals.

And when they rested at those bends of the zigzag path where seats were, and Lady Caroline, who would have liked to run on and get to the top quickly, was forced in common humanity to remain with Mrs. Fisher because of her stick, Mrs. Fisher told her how she had been on a zigzag path once with Tennyson.

"Isn't his cricket wonderful?" said Lady Caroline absently.

"*The* Tennyson," said Mrs. Fisher, turning her head and observing her a moment over her spectacles.

"Isn't he?" said Lady Caroline.

"I am speaking," said Mrs. Fisher, "of Alfred."

"Oh," said Lady Caroline.

"And it was a path, too," Mrs. Fisher went on severely, "curiously like this. No eucalyptus tree, of course, but otherwise curiously like this. And at one of the bends he turned and said to me—I see him now turning and saying to me—"

Yes, Mrs. Fisher would have to be checked. And so would these two up at the window. She had better begin at once. She was sorry she had got off the wall. All she need have done was to have waved her hand, and waited till they came down and out into the garden to her.

So she ignored Mrs. Arbuthnot's remark and raised forefinger, and said with marked coldness—at least, she tried to make it sound marked—that she supposed they would be going to breakfast, and that she had had hers; but it was her fate that however coldly she sent forth her words they came out sounding quite warm and agreeable. That was because she had a sympathetic and delightful voice, due entirely to some special formation of her throat and the roof of her mouth, and having nothing whatever to do with what she was feeling. Nobody in consequence ever believed they were being snubbed. It was most tiresome. And if she stared icily it did not look icy at all, because her eyes, lovely to begin with, had the added loveliness of very long, soft, dark eyelashes. No icy stare could come out of eyes like that; it got caught and lost in the soft eyelashes, and the persons stared at merely thought they were being regarded with a flattering and exquisite attentiveness. And if ever she was out of humor or definitely cross—and who would not be sometimes in such a world?—she only looked so pathetic that people all rushed to comfort her, if possible by means of kissing. It was more than tiresome, it was maddening. Nature was determined that she should look and sound angelic. She could never be disagreeable or rude without being completely misunderstood.

"I had my breakfast in my room," she said, trying her utmost to sound curt. "Perhaps I'll see you later."

And she nodded, and went back to where she had been sitting on the wall, with the lilies being nice and cool round her feet.

CHAPTER 7

Their eyes followed her admiringly. They had no idea they had been snubbed. It was a disappointment, of course, to find she had forestalled them and that they were not to have the happiness of preparing for her, of watching her face when she arrived and first saw everything, but there was still Mrs. Fisher. They would concentrate on Mrs. Fisher, and would watch her face instead; only, like everybody else, they would have preferred to watch Lady Caroline's.

Perhaps, then, as Lady Caroline had talked of breakfast, they had better begin by going and having it, for there was too much to be done that day to spend any more time gazing at the scenery—servants to be interviewed, the house to be gone through and examined, and finally Mrs. Fisher's room to be got ready and adorned.

They waved their hands gaily at Lady Caroline, who seemed absorbed in what she saw and took no notice, and turning away found the maidservant of the night before had come up silently behind them in cloth slippers with string soles.

She was Francesca, the elderly parlormaid, who had been with the owner, he had said, for years, and whose presence made inventories unnecessary; and after wishing them good-morning and hoping they had slept well, she told them breakfast was ready in the dining-room on the floor below, and if they would follow her she would lead.

They did not understand a single word of the very many in which Francesca succeeded in clothing this simple information, but they followed her, for it at least was clear that they were to follow, and going down the stairs, and along the broad hall like the one above except for glass doors at the end instead of a window opening into the garden, they were shown into the dining-room; where, sitting at the head of the table having her breakfast, was Mrs. Fisher.

This time they exclaimed. Even Mrs. Arbuthnot exclaimed, though her exclamation was only "Oh."

Mrs. Wilkins exclaimed at greater length. "Why, but it's like having the bread taken out of one's mouth!" exclaimed Mrs. Wilkins.

"How do you do," said Mrs. Fisher. "I can't get up because of my stick." And she stretched out her hand across the table.

They advanced and shook it.

"We had no idea you were here," said Mrs. Arbuthnot.

"Yes," said Mrs. Fisher, resuming her breakfast. "Yes. I am here." And with composure she removed the top of her egg.

"It's a great disappointment," said Mrs. Wilkins. "We had meant to give you *such* a welcome."

This was the one, Mrs. Fisher remembered, briefly glancing at her, who when she came to Prince of Wales Terrace said she had seen Keats. She must be careful with this one—curb her from the beginning.

She therefore ignored Mrs. Wilkins and said gravely, with a downward face of impenetrable calm bent on her egg, "Yes. I arrived yesterday with Lady Caroline."

"It's really dreadful," said Mrs. Wilkins, exactly as if she had not been ignored. "There's nobody left to get anything ready for now. I feel thwarted. I feel as if the bread had been taken out of my mouth just when I was going to be happy swallowing it."

"Where will you sit?" asked Mrs. Fisher of Mrs. Arbuthnot—markedly of Mrs. Arbuthnot; the comparison with the bread seemed to her most unpleasant.

"Oh, thank you—" said Mrs. Arbuthnot, sitting down rather suddenly next to her.

There were only two places she could sit down in, the places laid on either side of Mrs. Fisher. She therefore sat down in one, and Mrs. Wilkins sat down opposite her in the other.

Mrs. Fisher was at the head of the table. Round her was grouped the coffee and the tea. Of course they were all sharing San Salvatore equally, but it was she herself and Lotty, Mrs. Arbuthnot mildly reflected, who had found it, who had had the work of getting it, who had chosen to admit Mrs. Fisher into it. Without them, she could not help thinking, Mrs. Fisher would not have been there. Morally Mrs. Fisher was a guest. There was no hostess in this party, but supposing there had been a hostess it would not have been Mrs. Fisher, nor Lady Caroline, it would have been either herself or Lotty. Mrs. Arbuthnot could not help feeling this as she sat down, and Mrs. Fisher, the hand which Ruskin had wrung suspended over the pots before her, inquired, "Tea or coffee?" She could not help feeling it even more definitely when Mrs. Fisher touched a small gong on the table beside her as though she had been used to that gong and that table ever since she was little, and, on Francesca's appearing, bade her in the language of Dante bring more milk. There was a curious air about Mrs. Fisher, thought Mrs. Arbuthnot, of being in possession; and if she herself had not been so happy she would have perhaps minded.

Mrs. Wilkins noticed it too, but it only made her discursive brain think of cuckoos. She would no doubt immediately have begun to talk of cuckoos, incoherently, unrestrainably and deplorably, if she had been in the condition of nerves and shyness she was in last time she saw Mrs. Fisher. But happiness had done away with shyness—she was very serene; she could control her conversation; she did not have, horrified, to listen to herself saying things she had no idea of saying when she began; she was quite at her ease, and completely natural. The disappointment of not going to be able to prepare a welcome for Mrs. Fisher had evaporated at once, for it was impossible to go on being disappointed in heaven. Nor did she mind her behaving as hostess. What did it matter? You did not mind things in heaven. She and Mrs. Arbuthnot, therefore, sat down more willingly than they otherwise would have done, one on either side of Mrs. Fisher, and the sun, pouring through the two windows facing east across the bay, flooded the room, and there was an open door leading into the garden, and the garden was full of many lovely things, especially freesias.

The delicate and delicious fragrance of the freesias came in through the door and floated round Mrs. Wilkins's enraptured nostrils. Freesias in London were quite beyond her. Occasionally she went into a shop and asked what they cost, so as just to have an excuse for lifting up a bunch and smelling them, well knowing that it was something awful like a shilling for about three flowers. Here they were everywhere—bursting out of every corner and carpeting the rose beds. Imagine it—having freesias to pick in armsful if you wanted to, and with glorious sunshine flooding the room, and in your summer frock, and its being only the first of April!

"I suppose you realize, don't you, that we've got to heaven?" she said, beaming at Mrs. Fisher with all the familiarity of a fellow-angel.

"They are considerably younger than I had supposed," thought Mrs. Fisher, "and not nearly so plain." And she mused a moment, while she took no notice of Mrs. Wilkins's exuberance, on their instant and agitated refusal that day at Prince of Wales Terrace to have anything to do with the giving or the taking of references.

Nothing could affect her, of course; nothing that anybody did. She was far too solidly seated in respectability. At her back stood massively in a tremendous row those three great names she had offered, and they were not the only ones she could turn to for support and countenance. Even if these young women—she had no grounds for believing the one out in the garden to be really Lady Caroline Dester, she had merely been told she was—even if these young women should all turn out to be what Browning used to call—how well she remembered his amusing and delightful way of putting things—Fly-by-Nights, what could it possibly, or in any way matter to her? Let them fly by night if they wished. One was not sixty-five for nothing. In any case there would only be four weeks of it, at the end of which she would see no more of them. And in the meanwhile there were plenty of places where she could sit quietly away from them and remember. Also there was her own sitting-room, a charming room, all honey-colored furniture and pictures, with windows to the sea towards Genoa, and a door opening on to the battlements. The house possessed two sitting-rooms, and she had explained to that pretty creature Lady Caroline—certainly a pretty creature, whatever else she was; Tennyson would have enjoyed taking her for blows on the downs—who had seemed inclined to appropriate the honey-colored one, that she needed some little refuge entirely to herself because of her stick.

"Nobody wants to see an old woman hobbling about everywhere," she had said. "I shall be quite content to spend much of my time by myself in here or sitting out on these convenient battlements."

And she had a very nice bedroom, too; it looked two ways, across the bay to the morning sun—she liked the morning sun—and onto the garden. There were only two of these bedrooms with cross-views in the house, she and Lady Caroline had discovered, and they were by far the airiest. They each had two beds in them, and she and Lady Caroline had had the extra beds taken out at once and put into two of the other rooms. In this way there was much more space and comfort. Lady Caroline, indeed, had turned hers into a bed-sitting-room, with the sofa out of the bigger drawing-room and the writing-table and the most comfortable chair, but she herself had not had to do that because she had her own sitting-room, equipped with what was necessary. Lady Caroline had thought at first of taking the bigger sitting-room entirely for her own, because the dining-room on the floor below could quite well be used between meals to sit in by the two others, and was a very pleasant room with nice chairs, but she had not liked the bigger sitting-room's shape—it was a round room in the tower, with deep slit windows pierced through the massive walls, and a domed and ribbed ceiling arranged to look like an open umbrella, and it seemed a little dark. Undoubtedly Lady Caroline had cast covetous glances at the honey-colored room, and if she, Mrs. Fisher, had been less firm would have installed herself in it. Which would have been absurd.

"I hope," said Mrs. Arbuthnot, smilingly making an attempt to convey to Mrs. Fisher that though she, Mrs. Fisher, might not be exactly a guest she certainly was not in the very least a hostess, "your room is comfortable."

"Quite," said Mrs. Fisher. "Will you have some more coffee?"

"No, thank you. Will you?"

"No, thank you. There were two beds in my bedroom, filling it up unnecessarily, and I had one taken out. It has made it much more convenient."

"Oh, *that's* why I've got two beds in my room!" exclaimed Mrs. Wilkins, illuminated; the second bed in her little cell had seemed an unnatural and inappropriate object from the moment she saw it.

"I gave no directions," said Mrs. Fisher, addressing Mrs. Arbuthnot. "I merely asked Francesca to remove it."

"I have two in my room as well," said Mrs. Arbuthnot.

"Your second one must be Lady Caroline's. She had hers removed too," said Mrs. Fisher. "It seems foolish to have more beds in a room than there are occupiers."

"But *we* haven't got any husbands here either," said Mrs. Wilkins, "and I don't see any use in extra beds in one's room if one hasn't got husbands to put in them. Can't we have them taken away too?"

"Beds," said Mrs. Fisher coldly, "cannot be removed from one room after another. They must remain somewhere."

Mrs. Wilkins's remarks seemed to Mrs. Fisher persistently unfortunate. Each time she opened her mouth she said something best left unsaid. Loose talk about husbands had never in Mrs. Fisher's circle been encouraged. In the 'eighties, when she chiefly flourished, husbands were taken seriously, as the only real obstacles to sin. Beds too, if they had to be mentioned, were approached with caution; and a decent reserve prevented them and husbands ever being spoken of in the same breath.

She turned more markedly than ever to Mrs. Arbuthnot. "Do let me give you a little more coffee," she said.

"No, thank you. But won't you have some more?"

"No indeed. I never have more than two cups at breakfast. Would you like an orange?"

"No, thank you. Would you?"

"No, I don't eat fruit at breakfast. It is an American fashion which I am too old now to adopt. Have you had all you want?"

"Quite. Have you?"

Mrs. Fisher paused before replying. Was this a habit, this trick of answering a simple question with the same question? If so it must be curbed, for no one could live for four weeks in any real comfort with somebody who had a habit.

She glanced at Mrs. Arbuthnot, and her parted hair and gentle brow reassured her. No; it was accident, not habit, that had produced those echoes. She could as soon imagine a dove having tiresome habits as Mrs. Arbuthnot. Considering her, she thought what a splendid wife she would have been for poor Carlyle. So much better than that horrid clever Jane. She would have soothed him.

"Then shall we go?" she suggested.

"Let me help you up," said Mrs. Arbuthnot, all consideration.

"Oh, thank you—I can manage perfectly. It's only sometimes that my stick prevents me—"

Mrs. Fisher got up quite easily; Mrs. Arbuthnot had hovered over her for nothing.

"*I'm* going to have one of these gorgeous oranges," said Mrs. Wilkins, staying where she was and reaching across to a black bowl piled with them. "Rose, how can you resist them. Look—have this one. Do have this beauty—" And she held out a big one.

"No, I'm going to see to my duties," said Mrs. Arbuthnot, moving towards the door. "You'll forgive me for leaving you, won't you," she added politely to Mrs. Fisher.

Mrs. Fisher moved towards the door too; quite easily; almost quickly; her stick did not hinder her at all. She had no intention of being left with Mrs. Wilkins.

"What time would you like to have lunch?" Mrs. Arbuthnot asked her, trying to keep her head as at least a non-guest, if not precisely a hostess, above water.

"Lunch," said Mrs. Fisher, "is at half-past twelve."

"You shall have it at half-past twelve then," said Mrs. Arbuthnot. "I'll tell the cook. It will be a great struggle," she continued, smiling, "but I've brought a little dictionary—"

"The cook," said Mrs. Fisher, "knows."

"Oh?" said Mrs. Arbuthnot.

"Lady Caroline has already told her," said Mrs. Fisher.

"Oh?" said Mrs. Arbuthnot again.

"Yes. Lady Caroline speaks the kind of Italian cooks understand. I am prevented going into the kitchen because of my stick. And even if I were able to go, I fear I shouldn't be understood."

"But—" began Mrs. Arbuthnot.

"But it's *too* wonderful," Mrs. Wilkins finished for her from the table, delighted with these unexpected simplifications in her and Rose's lives. "Why, we've got positively nothing to do here, either of us, except just be happy. You wouldn't believe," she said, turning her head and speaking straight to Mrs. Fisher, portions of orange in either hand, "how terribly good Rose and I have been for years without stopping, and how much now we need a perfect rest."

And Mrs. Fisher, going without answering her out of the room, said to herself, "She must, she shall be curbed."

CHAPTER 8

Presently, when Mrs. Wilkins and Mrs. Arbuthnot, unhampered by any duties, wandered out and down the worn stone steps and under the pergola into the lower garden, Mrs. Wilkins said to Mrs. Arbuthnot, who seemed pensive, "Don't you see that if somebody else does the ordering it frees us?"

Mrs. Arbuthnot said she did see, but nevertheless she thought it rather silly to have everything taken out of their hands.

"I love things to be taken out of my hands," said Mrs. Wilkins.

"But we found San Salvatore," said Mrs. Arbuthnot, "and it is rather silly that Mrs. Fisher should behave as if it belonged only to her."

"What is rather silly," said Mrs. Wilkins with much serenity, "is to mind. I can't see the least point in being in authority at the price of one's liberty."

Mrs. Arbuthnot said nothing to that for two reasons—first, because she was struck by the remarkable and growing calm of the hitherto incoherent and excited Lotty, and secondly because what she was looking at was so very beautiful.

All down the stone steps on either side were periwinkles in full flower, and she could now see what it was that had caught at her the night before and brushed, wet and scented, across her face. It was wistaria. *Wistaria and sunshine* . . . she remembered the advertisement. Here indeed were both in profusion. The wistaria was tumbling over itself in its excess of life, its prodigality of flowering;

and where the pergola ended the sun blazed on scarlet geraniums, bushes of them, and nasturtiums in great heaps, and marigolds so brilliant that they seemed to be burning, and red and pink snapdragons, all outdoing each other in bright, fierce color. The ground behind these flaming things dropped away in terraces to the sea, each terrace a little orchard, where among the olives grew vines on trellises, and fig-trees, and peach-trees, and cherry-trees. The cherry-trees and peach-trees were in blossom—lovely showers of white and deep rose-color among the trembling delicacy of the olives; the fig-leaves were just big enough to smell of figs, the vine-buds were only beginning to show. And beneath these trees were groups of blue and purple irises, and bushes of lavender, and gray, sharp cactuses, and the grass was thick with dandelions and daisies, and right down at the bottom was the sea. Color seemed flung down anyhow, anywhere; every sort of color, piled up in heaps, pouring along in rivers—the periwinkles looked exactly as if they were being poured down each side of the steps—and flowers that grow only in borders in England, proud flowers keeping themselves to themselves over there, such as the great blue irises and the lavender, were being jostled by small, shining common things like dandelions and daisies and the white bells of the wild onion, and only seemed the better and the more exuberant for it.

They stood looking at this crowd of loveliness, this happy jumble, in silence. No, it didn't matter what Mrs. Fisher did; not here; not in such beauty. Mrs. Arbuthnot's discomposure melted out of her. In the warmth and light of what she was looking at, of what to her was a manifestation, an entirely new side of God, how could one be discomposed? If only Frederick were with her, seeing it too, seeing as he would have seen it when first they were lovers, in the days when he saw what she saw and loved what she loved . . .

She sighed.

"You mustn't sigh in heaven," said Mrs. Wilkins. "One doesn't."

"I was thinking how one longs to share this with those one loves," said Mrs. Arbuthnot.

"You mustn't long in heaven," said Mrs. Wilkins. "You're supposed to be quite complete there. And it is heaven, isn't it, Rose? See how everything has been let in together—the dandelions and the irises, the vulgar and the superior, me and Mrs. Fisher—all welcome, all mixed up anyhow, and all so visibly happy and enjoying ourselves."

"Mrs. Fisher doesn't seem happy—not visibly, anyhow," said Mrs. Arbuthnot, smiling.

"She'll begin soon, you'll see."

Mrs. Arbuthnot said she didn't believe that after a certain age people began anything.

Mrs. Wilkins said she was sure no one, however old and tough, could resist the effects of perfect beauty. Before many days, perhaps only hours, they would see Mrs. Fisher bursting out into every kind of exuberance. "I'm quite sure," said Mrs. Wilkins, "that we've got to heaven, and once Mrs. Fisher realizes that that's where she is, she's bound to be different. You'll see. She'll leave off being ossified, and go all soft and able to stretch, and we shall get quite—why, I shouldn't be surprised if we get quite fond of her."

The idea of Mrs. Fisher bursting out into anything, she who seemed so particularly firmly fixed inside her buttons, made Mrs. Arbuthnot laugh. She condoned Lotty's loose way of talking of heaven, because in such a place, on such a morning, condonation was in the very air. Besides, what an excuse there was.

And Lady Caroline, sitting where they had left her before breakfast on the wall, peeped over when she heard laughter, and saw them standing on the path below, and thought what a mercy it was they were laughing down there and had not come up and done it round her. She disliked jokes at all times, but in the morning she hated them; especially close up; especially crowding in her ears. She hoped the originals were on their way out for a walk, and not on their way back from one. They were laughing more and more. What could they possibly find to laugh at?

She looked down on the tops of their heads with a very serious face, for the thought of spending a month with laughers was a grave one, and they, as though they felt her eyes, turned suddenly and looked up.

The dreadful geniality of those women . . .

She shrank away from their smiles and wavings, but she could not shrink out of sight without falling into the lilies. She neither smiled nor waved back, and turning her eyes to the more distant mountains surveyed them carefully till the two, tired of waving, moved away along the path and turned the corner and disappeared.

This time they both did notice that they had been met with, at least, unresponsiveness.

"If we weren't in heaven," said Mrs. Wilkins serenely, "I should say we had been snubbed, but as nobody snubs anybody there of course we can't have been."

"Perhaps she is unhappy," said Mrs. Arbuthnot.

"Whatever it is she is she'll get over it here," said Mrs. Wilkins with conviction.

"We must try and help her," said Mrs. Arbuthnot.

"Oh, but nobody helps anybody in heaven. That's finished with. You don't try to be, or do. You simply *are*."

Well, Mrs. Arbuthnot wouldn't go into that—not here, not to-day. The vicar, she knew, would have called Lotty's talk levity, if not profanity. How old he seemed from here; an old, old vicar.

They left the path, and clambered down the olive terraces, down and down, to where at the bottom the warm, sleepy sea heaved gently among the rocks. There a pine-tree grew close to the water, and they sat under it, and a few yards away was a fishing boat lying motionless and green-bellied on the water. The ripples of the sea made little gurgling noises at their feet. They screwed up their eyes to be able to look into the blaze of light beyond the shade of their tree. The hot smell from the pine-needles and from the cushions of wild thyme that padded the spaces between the rocks, and sometimes a smell of pure honey from a clump of warm irises up behind them in the sun, puffed across their faces. Very soon Mrs. Wilkins took her shoes and stockings off, and let her feet hang in the water. After watching her a minute Mrs. Arbuthnot did the same. Their happiness was then complete. Their husbands would not have known them. They left off talking. They ceased to mention heaven. They were just cups of acceptance.

Meanwhile Lady Caroline, on her wall, was considering her position. The garden on the top of the wall was a delicious garden, but its situation made it insecure and exposed to interruptions. At any moment the others might come and want to use it, because both the hall and the dining-room had doors opening straight into it. Perhaps, thought Lady Caroline, she could arrange that it should be solely hers. Mrs. Fisher had the battlements, delightful with flowers, and a watch-tower all to herself, besides having snatched the one really nice room in the house. There were plenty of places the originals could go to—she had herself seen at least two other little gardens, while the hill the castle stood on was itself a garden, with walks and seats. Why should not this one spot be kept exclusively for her? She liked it; she liked it best of all. It had the Judas tree and an umbrella pine, it had the freesias and the lilies, it had a tamarisk beginning to flush pink, it had the convenient low wall to sit on, it had from each of its three sides the most amazing views—to the east the bay and mountains, to the north the village across the tranquil clear green water of the little harbor and the hills dotted with white houses and orange groves, and to the west was the thin thread of land by which San Salvatore was tied to the mainland, and then the open sea and the coast line beyond Genoa reaching away into the blue dimness of

France. Yes, she would say she wanted to have this entirely to herself. How obviously sensible if each of them had their own special place to sit in apart. It was essential to her comfort that she should be able to be apart, left alone, not talked to. The others ought to like it best too. Why herd? One had enough of that in England, with one's relations and friends—oh, the numbers of them!—pressing on one continually. Having successfully escaped them for four weeks why continue, and with persons having no earthly claim on one, to herd?

She lit a cigarette. She began to feel secure. Those two had gone for a walk. There was no sign of Mrs. Fisher. How very pleasant this was.

Somebody came out through the glass doors, just as she was drawing a deep breath of security. Surely it couldn't be Mrs. Fisher, wanting to sit with her? Mrs. Fisher had her battlements. She ought to stay on them, having snatched them. It would be too tiresome if she wouldn't, and wanted not only to have them and her sitting-room but to establish herself in this garden as well.

No; it wasn't Mrs. Fisher, it was the cook.

She frowned. Was she going to have to go on ordering the food? Surely one or other of those two waving women would do that now.

The cook, who had been waiting in increasing agitation in the kitchen, watching the clock getting nearer to lunch-time while she still was without knowledge of what lunch was to consist of, had gone at last to Mrs. Fisher, who had immediately waved her away. She then wandered about the house seeking a mistress, any mistress, who would tell her what to cook, and finding none; and at last, directed by Francesca, who always knew where everybody was, came out to Lady Caroline.

Domenico had provided this cook. She was Costanza, the sister of that one of his cousins who kept a restaurant down on the piazza. She helped her brother in his cooking when she had no other job, and knew every sort of fat, mysterious Italian dish such as the workmen of Castagneto, who crowded the restaurant at midday, and the inhabitants of Mezzago when they came over on Sundays, loved to eat. She was a fleshless spinster of fifty, gray-haired, nimble, rich of speech, and thought Lady Caroline more beautiful than anyone she had ever seen; and so did Domenico; and so did the boy Giuseppe who helped Domenico and was, besides, his nephew; and so did the girl Angela who helped Francesca and was, besides, Domenico's niece; and so did Francesca herself. Domenico and Francesca, the only two who had seen them, thought the two ladies who arrived last very beautiful, but compared to the fair young lady who arrived first they were as candles to the electric light that had lately been installed, and as the tin tubs in the bedrooms to the wonderful new bathroom their master had had arranged on his last visit.

Lady Caroline scowled at the cook. The scowl, as usual, was transformed on the way into what appeared to be an intent and beautiful gravity, and Costanza threw up her hands and took the saints aloud to witness that here was the very picture of the Mother of God.

Lady Caroline asked her crossly what she wanted, and Costanza's head went on one side with delight at the sheer music of her voice. She said, after waiting a moment in case the music was going to continue, for she didn't wish to miss any of it, that she wanted orders; she had been to the Signorina's mother, but in vain.

"She is not my mother," repudiated Lady Caroline angrily; and her anger sounded like the regretful wail of a melodious orphan.

Costanza poured forth pity. She too, she explained, had no mother—

Lady Caroline interrupted with the curt information that her mother was alive and in London.

Costanza praised God and the saints that the young lady did not yet know what it was like to be without a mother. Quickly enough did misfortunes overtake one; no doubt the young lady already had a husband.

"No," said Lady Caroline icily. Worse than jokes in the morning did she hate the idea of husbands. And everybody was always trying to press them on her—all her relations, all her friends, all the evening papers. After all, she could only marry one, anyhow; but you would think from the way everybody talked, and especially those persons who wanted to be husbands, that she could marry at least a dozen.

Her soft, pathetic "No" made Costanza, who was standing close to her, well with sympathy.

"Poor little one," said Costanza, moved actually to pat her encouragingly on the shoulder, "take hope. There is still time."

"For lunch," said Lady Caroline freezingly, marveling as she spoke that she should be patted, she who had taken so much trouble to come to a place, remote and hidden, where she could be sure that among other things of a like oppressive nature pattings also were not, "we will have—"

Costanza became business-like. She interrupted with suggestions, and her suggestions were all admirable and all expensive.

Lady Caroline did not know they were expensive, and fell in with them at once. They sounded very nice. Every sort of young vegetables and fruits came into them, and much butter and a great deal of cream and incredible numbers of eggs. Costanza said enthusiastically at the end, as a tribute to this acquiescence, that of the many ladies and gentlemen she had worked for on temporary jobs such as this she preferred the English ladies and gentlemen. She more than preferred them—they roused devotion in her. For they knew what to order; they did not skimp; they refrained from grinding down the faces of the poor.

From this Lady Caroline concluded that she had been extravagant, and promptly countermanded the cream.

Costanza's face fell, for she had a cousin who had a cow, and the cream was to have come from them both.

"And perhaps we had better not have chickens," said Lady Caroline.

Costanza's face fell more, for her brother at the restaurant kept chickens in his back-yard, and many of them were ready for killing.

"Also do not order strawberries till I have consulted with the other ladies," said Lady Caroline, remembering that it was only the first of April, and that perhaps people who lived in Hampstead might be poor; indeed, must be poor, or why live in Hampstead? "It is not I who am mistress here."

"Is it the old one?" asked Costanza, her face very long.

"No," said Lady Caroline.

"Which of the other two ladies is it?"

"Neither," said Lady Caroline.

Then Costanza's smiles returned, for the young lady was having fun with her and making jokes. She told her so, in her friendly Italian way, and was genuinely delighted.

"I never make jokes," said Lady Caroline briefly. "You had better go, or lunch will certainly not be ready by half-past twelve."

And these curt words came out sounding so sweet that Costanza felt as if kind compliments were being paid her, and forgot her disappointment about the cream and the chickens, and went away all gratitude and smiles.

"This," thought Lady Caroline, "will never do. I haven't come here to housekeep, and I won't."

She called Costanza back. Costanza came running. The sound of her name in that voice enchanted her.

"I have ordered the lunch for to-day," said Lady Caroline, with the serious angel face that was hers when she was annoyed, "and I have also ordered the dinner, but from now on you will go to one of the other ladies for orders. I give no more."

The idea that she would go on giving orders was too absurd. She never gave orders at home. Nobody there dreamed of asking her to do anything. That such a very tiresome activity should be thrust upon her here, simply because she happened to be able to talk Italian, was ridiculous. Let the originals give orders if Mrs. Fisher refused to. Mrs. Fisher, of course, was the one Nature intended for such a purpose. She had the very air of a competent housekeeper. Her clothes were the clothes of a housekeeper, and so was the way she did her hair.

Having delivered herself of her ultimatum with an acerbity that turned sweet on the way, and accompanied it by a peremptory gesture of dismissal that had the grace and loving-kindness of a benediction, it was annoying that Costanza should only stand still with her head on one side gazing at her in obvious delight.

"Oh, go away!" exclaimed Lady Caroline in English, suddenly exasperated.

There had been a fly in her bedroom that morning which had stuck just as Costanza was sticking; only one, but it might have been a myriad it was so tiresome from daylight on. It was determined to settle on her face, and she was determined it should not. Its persistence was uncanny. It woke her, and would not let her go to sleep again. She hit at it, and it eluded her without fuss or effort and with an almost visible blandness, and she had only hit herself. It came back again instantly, and with a loud buzz alighted on her cheek. She hit at it again and hurt herself, while it skimmed gracefully away. She lost her temper, and sat up in bed and waited, watching to hit at it and kill it. She kept on hitting at it at last with fury and with all her strength, as if it were a real enemy deliberately trying to madden her; and it elegantly skimmed in and out of her blows, not even angry, to be back again the next instant. It succeeded every time in getting on to her face, and was quite indifferent how often it was driven away. That was why she had dressed and come out so early. Francesca had already been told to put a net over her bed, for she was not going to allow herself to be annoyed twice like that. People were exactly like flies. She wished there were nets for keeping them off too. She hit at them with words and frowns, and like the fly they slipped between her blows and were untouched. Worse than the fly, they seemed unaware that she had even tried to hit them. The fly at least did for a moment go away. With human beings the only way to get rid of them was to go away herself. That was what, so tired, she had done this April; and having got here, having got close up to the details of life at San Salvatore, it appeared that here, too, she was not to be let alone.

Viewed from London there had seemed to be no details. San Salvatore from there seemed to be an empty, a delicious blank. Yet, after only twenty-four hours of it, she was discovering that it was not a blank at all, and that she was having to ward off as actively as ever. Already she had been much stuck to. Mrs. Fisher had stuck nearly the whole of the day before, and this morning there had been no peace, not ten minutes uninterruptedly alone.

Costanza of course had finally to go because she had to cook, but hardly had she gone before Domenico came. He came to water and tie up. That was natural, since he was the gardener, but he watered and tied up all the things that were nearest to her; he hovered closer and closer; he watered to excess; he tied plants that were as straight and steady as arrows. Well, at least he was a man, and therefore not quite so annoying, and his smiling good-morning was received with an answering smile; upon which Domenico forgot his family, his wife, his mother, his grown-up children and all his duties, and only wanted to kiss the young lady's feet.

He could not do that, unfortunately, but he could talk while he worked, and talk he did; voluminously; pouring out every kind of information, illustrating what he said with gestures so lively that he had to put down the watering-pot, and thus delay the end of the watering.

Lady Caroline bore it for a time but presently was unable to bear it, and as he would not go, and she could not tell him to, seeing that he was engaged in his proper work, once again it was she who had to.

She got off the wall and moved to the other side of the garden, where in a wooden shed were some comfortable low cane chairs. All she wanted was to turn one of these round with its back to Domenico and its front to the sea towards Genoa. Such a little thing to want. One would have thought she might have been allowed to do that unmolested. But he, who watched her every movement, when he saw her approaching the chairs darted after her and seized one and asked to be told where to put it.

Would she never get away from being waited on, being made comfortable, being asked where she wanted things put, having to say thank you? She was short with Domenico, who instantly concluded the sun had given her a headache, and ran in and fetched her a sunshade and a cushion and a footstool, and was skillful, and was wonderful, and was one of Nature's gentlemen.

She shut her eyes in a heavy resignation. She could not be unkind to Domenico. She could not get up and walk indoors as she would have done if it had been one of the others. Domenico was intelligent and very competent. She had at once discovered that it was he who really ran the house, who really did everything. And his manners were definitely delightful, and he undoubtedly was a charming person. It was only that she did so much long to be let alone. If only, only she could be left quite quiet for this one month, she felt that she might perhaps make something of herself after all.

She kept her eyes shut, because then he would think she wanted to sleep and would go away.

Domenico's romantic Italian soul melted within him at the sight, for having her eyes shut was extraordinarily becoming to her. He stood entranced, quite still, and she thought he had stolen away, so she opened them again.

No; there he was, staring at her. Even he. There was no getting away from being stared at.

"I have a headache," she said, shutting them again.

"It is the sun," said Domenico, "and sitting on the wall without a hat."

"I wish to sleep."

"*Sì, signorina*," he said sympathetically; and went softly away.

She opened her eyes with a sigh of relief. The gentle closing of the glass doors showed her that he had not only gone quite away but had shut her out in the garden so that she should be undisturbed. Now perhaps she would be alone till lunch-time.

It was very curious, and no one in the world could have been more surprised than she herself, but she wanted to think. She had never wanted to do that before. Everything else that it is possible to do without too much inconvenience she had either wanted to do or had done at one period or another of her life, but not before had she wanted to think. She had come to San Salvatore with the single intention of lying comatose for four weeks in the sun, somewhere where her parents and friends were not, lapped in forgetfulness, stirring herself only to be fed, and she had not been there more than a few hours when this strange new desire took hold of her.

There had been wonderful stars the evening before, and she had gone out into the top garden after dinner, leaving Mrs. Fisher alone over her nuts and wine, and, sitting on the wall at the place where the lilies crowded their ghost heads, she had looked out into the gulf of the night, and it had suddenly seemed as if her life had been a noise all about nothing.

She had been intensely surprised. She knew stars and darkness did produce unusual emotions because, in others, she had seen them being produced, but they had not before done it in herself. A noise all about nothing. Could she be quite well? She had wondered. For a long while past she had been aware that her life was a noise, but it had seemed to be very much about something; a noise, indeed, about so much that she felt she must get out of earshot for a little or she would be completely, and perhaps permanently, deafened. But suppose it was only a noise about nothing?

She had not had a question like that in her mind before. It had made her feel lonely. She wanted to be alone, but not lonely. That was very different; that was something that ached and hurt dreadfully right inside one. It was what one dreaded most. It was what made one go to so many parties; and lately even the parties had seemed once or twice not to be a perfectly certain protection. Was it possible that loneliness had nothing to do with circumstances, but only with the way one met them? Perhaps, she had thought, she had better go to bed. She couldn't be very well.

She went to bed; and in the morning, after she had escaped the fly and had her breakfast and got out again into the garden, there was this same feeling again, and in broad daylight. Once more she had that really rather disgusting suspicion that her life till now had not only been loud but empty. Well, if that were so, and if her first twenty-eight years—the best ones—had gone just in meaningless noise, she had better stop a moment and look round her, pause, as they said in tiresome novels, and consider. She hadn't got many sets of twenty-eight years. One more would see her growing very like Mrs. Fisher. Two more— She averted her eyes.

Her mother would have been concerned if she had known. Her mother doted. Her father would have been concerned too, for he also doted. Everybody doted. And when, melodiously obstinate, she had insisted on going off to entomb herself in Italy for a whole month with queer people she had got out of an advertisement, refusing even to take her maid, the only explanation her friends could imagine was that poor Scrap—such was her name among them—had overdone it and was feeling a little nervy.

Her mother had been distressed at her departure. It was such an odd thing to do, such a sign of disappointment. She encouraged the general idea of the verge of a nervous breakdown. If she could have seen her adored Scrap, more delightful to look upon than any other mother's daughter had ever yet been, the object of her utmost pride, the source of all her fondest hopes, sitting staring at the empty noon-day Mediterranean considering her three possible sets of twenty-eight years, she would have been miserable. To go away alone was bad; to think was worse. No good could come out of the thinking of a beautiful young woman. Complications could come out of it in profusion, but no good. The thinking of the beautiful was bound to result in hesitations, in reluctances, in unhappiness all round. And here, if she could have seen her, sat her Scrap thinking quite hard. And such things. Such old things. Things nobody ever began to think till they were at least forty.

CHAPTER 9

That one of the two sitting-rooms which Mrs. Fisher had taken for her own was a room of charm and character. She surveyed it with satisfaction on going into it after breakfast, and was glad it was hers. It had a tiled floor, and walls the color of pale honey, and inlaid furniture the color of amber, and mellow books, many in ivory or lemon-colored covers. There was a big window overlooking the sea towards Genoa, and a glass door through which she could proceed out on to the battlements and walk along past the quaint and attractive watch-tower, in itself a room with chairs and a writing table, to where on the other side of the tower the battlements ended in a marble seat, and one could see the western bay and the point round which began the Gulf of Spezia. Her south view, between these two stretches of sea, was another hill, higher than San Salvatore, the last of the little peninsula, with the bland turrets of a smaller and uninhabited castle on the top, on which the setting sun still shone when everything else was sunk in shadow. Yes, she was very comfortably established here; and receptacles—Mrs. Fisher did not examine their nature closely, but they seemed to be small stone troughs, or perhaps little sarcophagi—ringed round the battlements with flowers.

These battlements, she thought, considering them, would have been a perfect place for her to pace up and down gently in moments when she least felt the need of her stick, or to sit in on the marble seat, having first put a cushion on it, if there had not unfortunately been a second glass door opening on to them, destroying their complete privacy, spoiling her feeling that the place was only for her. The second door belonged to the round drawing-room, which both she and Lady Caroline had rejected as too dark. That room would probably be sat in by the women from Hampstead, and she was afraid they would not confine themselves to sitting in it, but would come out through the glass door and invade her battlements. This would ruin the battlements. It would ruin them as far as she was concerned if they were to be overrun; or even if, not actually overrun, they were liable to be raked by the eyes of persons inside the room. No one could be perfectly at ease if they were being watched and knew it. What she wanted, what she surely had a right to, was privacy. She had no wish to intrude on the others; why then should they intrude on her? And she could always relax her privacy if, when she became better acquainted with her companions, she should think it worth while, but she doubted whether any of the three would so develop as to make her think it worth while.

Hardly anything was really worth while, reflected Mrs. Fisher, except the past. It was astonishing, it was simply amazing, the superiority of the past to the present. Those friends of hers in London, solid persons of her own age, knew the same past that she knew, could talk about it with her, could compare it as she did with the tinkling present, and in remembering great men forget for a moment the trivial and barren young people who still, in spite of the war, seemed to litter the world in such numbers. She had not come away from these friends, these conversable ripe friends, in order to spend her time in Italy chatting with three persons of another generation and defective experience; she had come away merely to avoid the treacheries of a London April. It was true what she had told the two who came to Prince of Wales Terrace, that all she wished to do at San Salvatore was to sit by herself in the sun and remember. They knew this, for she had told them. It had been plainly expressed and clearly understood. Therefore she had a right to expect them to stay inside the round drawing-room and not to emerge interruptingly on to her battlements.

But would they? The doubt spoilt her morning. It was only towards lunch-time that she saw a way to be quite safe, and ringing for Francesca, bade her, in slow and majestic Italian, shut the shutters of the glass door of the round drawing-room, and then, going with her into the room, which had become darker than ever in consequence, but also, Mrs. Fisher observed to Francesca, who was being voluble, would because of this very darkness remain agreeably cool, and after all there were the numerous slit-windows in the walls to let in light and it was nothing to do with her if they did not let it in, she directed the placing of a cabinet of curios across the door on its inside.

This would discourage egress.

Then she rang for Domenico, and caused him to move one of the flower-filled sarcophagi across the door on its outside.

This would discourage ingress.

"No one," said Domenico, hesitating, "will be able to use the door."

"No one," said Mrs. Fisher firmly, "will wish to."

She then retired to her sitting-room, and from a chair placed where she could look straight on to them, gazed at her battlements, secured to her now completely, with calm pleasure.

Being here, she reflected placidly, was much cheaper than being in an hotel and, if she could keep off the others, immeasurably more agreeable. She was paying for her rooms—extremely pleasant rooms, now that she was arranged in them—£3 a week, which came to about eight shillings a day, battlements, watch-tower, and all. Where else abroad could she live as well for so little, and have as many baths as she liked, for eight shillings a day? Of course she did not yet know what her food would cost, but she would insist on carefulness over that, though she would also insist on its being carefulness combined with excellence. The two were perfectly compatible if the caterer took pains. The servants' wages, she had ascertained, were negligible, owing to the advantageous exchange, so that there was only the food to cause her anxiety. If she saw signs of extravagance she would propose that they each hand over a reasonable sum every week to Lady Caroline which should cover the bills, any of it that was not used to be returned, and if it were exceeded the loss to be borne by the caterer.

Mrs. Fisher was well off and had the desire for comforts proper to her age, but she disliked expenses. So well off was she that, had she so chosen, she could have lived in an opulent part of London and driven from it and to it in a Rolls-Royce. She had no such wish. It needed more vitality than went with true comfort to deal with a house in an opulent spot and a Rolls-Royce. Worries attended such possessions, worries of every kind, crowned by bills. In the sober gloom of Prince of Wales Terrace she could obscurely enjoy inexpensive yet real comfort, without being snatched at by predatory men-servants or collectors for charities, and a taxi stand was at the end of the road. Her annual outlay was small. The house was inherited. Death had furnished it for her. She trod in the dining-room on the Turkey carpet of her fathers; she regulated her day by the excellent black marble clock on the mantelpiece which she remembered from childhood; her walls were entirely covered by the photographs her illustrious deceased friends had given either herself or her father, with their own handwriting across the lower parts of their bodies, and the windows, shrouded by the maroon curtains of all her life, were decorated besides with the selfsame aquariums to which she owed her first lessons in sealore, and in which still swam slowly the goldfishes of her youth.

Were they the same goldfish? She did not know. Perhaps, like carp, they outlived everybody. Perhaps, on the other hand, behind the deep-sea vegetation provided for them at the bottom, they had from time to time as the years went by withdrawn and replaced themselves. Were they or were they not, she sometimes wondered, contemplating them between the courses of her solitary meals, the same goldfish that had that day been there when Carlyle—how well she remembered it—angrily strode up to them in the middle of some argument with her father that had grown heated, and striking the glass smartly with his fist had put them to flight, shouting as they fled, "Och, ye deaf deevils! Och, ye lucky deaf deevils! Ye can't hear anything of the blasted, blethering, doddering, glaikit fool-stuff yer maister talks, can ye?" Or words to that effect.

Dear, great-souled Carlyle. Such natural gushings forth; such true freshness; such real grandeur. Rugged, if you will—yes, undoubtedly sometimes rugged, and startling in a drawing-room, but magnificent. Who was there now to put beside him? Who was there to mention in the same breath? Her father, than whom no one had had more *flair*, said: "Thomas is immortal." And here was this generation, this generation of puniness, raising its little voice in doubts, or, still worse, not giving itself the trouble to raise it at all, not—it was incredible, but it had been thus reported to her—even reading him. Mrs. Fisher did not read him either, but that was different. She had read him; she had certainly read him. Of course she had read him. There was Teufelsdrock—she quite well remembered a tailor called Teufelsdröck. So like Carlyle to call him that. Yes, she must have read him, though naturally details escaped her.

The gong sounded. Lost in reminiscence Mrs. Fisher had forgotten time, and hastened to her bedroom to wash her hands and smooth her hair. She did not wish to be late and set a bad example, and perhaps find her seat at the head of the table taken. One could put no trust in the manners of the younger generation; especially not in those of that Mrs. Wilkins.

She was, however, the first to arrive in the dining-room. Francesca in a white apron stood ready with an enormous dish of smoking hot, glistening macaroni, but nobody was there to eat it.

Mrs. Fisher sat down, looking stern. Lax, lax.

"Serve me," she said to Francesca, who showed a disposition to wait for the others.

Francesca served her. Of the party she liked Mrs. Fisher least, in fact she did not like her at all. She was the only one of the four ladies who had not yet smiled. True she was old, true she was unbeautiful, true she therefore had no reason to smile, but kind ladies smiled, reason or no. They smiled, not because they were happy but because they wished to make happy. This one of the four ladies could not then, Francesca decided, be kind; so she handed her the macaroni, being unable to hide any of her feelings, morosely.

It was very well cooked, but Mrs. Fisher had never cared for macaroni, especially not this long, worm-shaped variety. She found it difficult to eat—slippery, wriggling off her fork, making her look, she felt, undignified when, having got it as she supposed into her mouth, ends of it yet hung out. Always, too, when she ate it she was reminded of Mr. Fisher. He had during their married life behaved very much like macaroni. He had slipped, he had wriggled, he had made her feel undignified, and when at last she had got him safe, as she thought, there had invariably been little bits of him that still, as it were, hung out.

Francesca from the sideboard watched Mrs. Fisher's way with macaroni gloomily, and her gloom deepened when she saw her at last take her knife to it and chop it small.

Mrs. Fisher really did not know how else to get hold of the stuff. She was aware that knives in this connection were improper, but one did finally lose patience. Macaroni was never allowed to appear on her table in London. Apart from its tiresomeness she did not even like it, and she would tell Lady Caroline not to order it again. Years of practice, reflected Mrs. Fisher, chopping it up, years of actual living in Italy, would be necessary to learn the exact trick. Browning managed macaroni wonderfully. She remembered watching him one day when he came to lunch with her father, and a dish of it had been ordered as a compliment to his connection with Italy. Fascinating, the way it went in. No chasing round the plate, no slidings off the fork, no subsequent protrusions of loose ends—just one dig, one whisk, one thrust, one gulp, and lo, yet another poet had been nourished.

"Shall I go and seek the young lady?" asked Francesca, unable any longer to look on a good macaroni being cut with a knife.

Mrs. Fisher came out of her reminiscent reflections with difficulty. "She knows lunch is at half-past twelve," she said. "They all know."

"She may be asleep," said Francesca. "The other ladies are further away, but this one is not far away."

"Beat the gong again then," said Mrs. Fisher.

What manners, she thought; what, what manners. It was not an hotel, and considerations were due. She must say she was surprised at Mrs. Arbuthnot, who had not looked like somebody unpunctual. Lady Caroline, too—she had seemed amiable and courteous, whatever else she might be. From the other one, of course, she expected nothing.

Francesca fetched the gong, and took it out into the garden and advanced, beating it as she advanced, close up to Lady Caroline, who, still stretched in her low chair, waited till she had done, and then turned her head and in the sweetest tones poured forth what appeared to be music but was really invective.

Francesca did not recognize the liquid flow as invective; how was she to, when it came out sounding like that? And with her face all smiles, for she could not but smile when she looked at this young lady, she told her the macaroni was getting cold.

"When I do not come to meals it is because I do not wish to come to meals," said the irritated Scrap, "and you will not in future disturb me."

"Is she ill?" asked Francesca, sympathetic but unable to stop smiling. Never, never had she seen hair so beautiful. Like pure flax;

like the hair of northern babes. On such a little head only blessing could rest, on such a little head the nimbus of the holiest saints could fitly be placed.

Scrap shut her eyes and refused to answer. In this she was injudicious, for its effect was to convince Francesca, who hurried away full of concern to tell Mrs. Fisher, that she was indisposed. And Mrs. Fisher, being prevented, she explained, from going out to Lady Caroline herself because of her stick, sent the two others instead, who had come in at that moment heated and breathless and full of excuses, while she herself proceeded to the next course, which was a very well-made omelette, bursting most agreeably at both its ends with young green peas.

"Serve me," she directed Francesca, who again showed a disposition to wait for the others.

"*Oh*, why won't they leave me alone?—oh, why *won't* they leave me alone?" Scrap asked herself when she heard more scrunchings on the little pebbles which took the place of grass, and therefore knew some one else was approaching.

She kept her eyes tight shut this time. Why should she go in to lunch if she didn't want to? This wasn't a private house; she was in no way tangled up in duties towards a tiresome hostess. For all practical purposes San Salvatore was an hotel, and she ought to be let alone to eat or not to eat exactly as if she really had been in an hotel.

But the unfortunate Scrap could not just sit still and close her eyes without rousing that desire to stroke and pet in her beholders with which she was only too familiar. Even the cook had patted her. And now a gentle hand—how well she knew and how much she dreaded gentle hands—was placed on her forehead.

"I'm afraid you're not well," said a voice that was not Mrs. Fisher's, and therefore must belong to one of the originals.

"I have a headache," murmured Scrap. Perhaps it was best to say that; perhaps it was the shortest cut to peace.

"I'm so sorry," said Mrs. Arbuthnot softly, for it was her hand being gentle.

"And I," said Scrap to herself, "who thought if I came here I would escape mothers."

"Don't you think some tea would do you good?" asked Mrs. Arbuthnot tenderly.

Tea? The idea was abhorrent to Scrap. In this heat to be drinking tea in the middle of the day . . .

"No," she murmured.

"I expect what would really be best for her," said another voice, "is to be left quiet."

How sensible, thought Scrap; and raised the eye-lashes of one eye just enough to peep through and see who was speaking.

It was the freckled original. The dark one, then, was the one with the hand. The freckled one rose in her esteem.

"But I can't bear to think of you with a headache and nothing being done for it," said Mrs. Arbuthnot. "Would a cup of strong black coffee—?"

Scrap said no more. She waited, motionless and dumb, till Mrs. Arbuthnot should remove her hand. After all, she couldn't stand there all day, and when she went away she would have to take her hand with her.

"I do think," said the freckled one, "that she wants nothing except quiet."

And perhaps the freckled one pulled the one with the hand by the sleeve, for the hold on Scrap's forehead relaxed, and after a minute's silence, during which no doubt she was being contemplated—she was always being contemplated—the footsteps began to scrunch the pebbles again, and grew fainter, and were gone.

"Lady Caroline has a headache," said Mrs. Arbuthnot, re-entering the dining-room and sitting down in her place next to Mrs. Fisher. "I can't persuade her to have even a little tea, or some black coffee. Do you know what aspirin is in Italian?"

"The proper remedy for headaches," said Mrs. Fisher firmly, "is castor oil."

"But she hasn't got a headache," said Mrs. Wilkins.

"Carlyle," said Mrs. Fisher, who had finished her omelette and had leisure, while she waited for the next course, to talk, "suffered at one period terribly from headaches, and he constantly took castor oil as a remedy. He took it, I should say, almost to excess, and called it, I remember, in his interesting way the oil of sorrow. My father said it colored for a time his whole attitude to life, his whole philosophy. But that was because he took too much. What Lady Caroline wants is one dose, and one only. It is a mistake to keep on taking castor oil."

"Do you know the Italian for it?" asked Mrs. Arbuthnot.

"Ah, that I'm afraid I don't. However, she would know. You can ask her."

"But she hasn't got a headache," repeated Mrs. Wilkins, who was struggling with the macaroni. "She only wants to be let alone."

They both looked at her. The word shovel crossed Mrs. Fisher's mind in connection with Mrs. Wilkins's actions at that moment.

"Then why should she say she has?" asked Mrs. Arbuthnot.

"Because she is still trying to be polite. Soon she won't try, when the place has got more into her—she'll really be it. Without trying. Naturally."

"Lotty, you see," explained Mrs. Arbuthnot, smiling to Mrs. Fisher, who sat waiting with a stony patience for her next course, delayed because Mrs. Wilkins would go on trying to eat the macaroni, which must be less worth eating than ever now that it was cold; "Lotty, you see, has a theory about this place—"

But Mrs. Fisher had no wish to hear any theory of Mrs. Wilkins's.

"I am sure I don't know," she interrupted, looking severely at Mrs. Wilkins, "why you should assume Lady Caroline is not telling the truth."

"I don't assume—I know," said Mrs. Wilkins.

"And pray how do you know?" asked Mrs. Fisher icily, for Mrs. Wilkins was actually helping herself to more macaroni, offered her officiously and unnecessarily a second time by Francesca.

"When I was out there just now I saw inside her."

Well, Mrs. Fisher wasn't going to say anything to that; she wasn't going to trouble to reply to downright idiocy. Instead she sharply rapped the little table-gong by her side, though there was Francesca standing at the sideboard, and said, for she would wait no longer for her next course, "Serve me."

And Francesca—it must have been willful—offered her the macaroni again.

CHAPTER 10

There was no way of getting into or out of the top garden at San Salvatore except through the two glass doors, unfortunately side by side, of the dining-room and the hall. A person in the garden who wished to escape unseen could not, for the person to be escaped from would be met on the way. It was a small, oblong garden, and concealment was impossible. What trees there were—the Judas tree, the tamarisk, the umbrella-pine—grew close to the low parapets. Rose bushes gave no real cover; one step to right or left of them, and the person wishing to be private was discovered. Only the north-west corner was a little place jutting out from the great wall, a kind of excrescence or loop, no doubt used in the old distrustful days for observation, where it was possible to sit really unseen, because between it and the house was a thick clump of daphne.

Scrap, after glancing round to see that no one was looking, got up and carried her chair into this place, stealing away as carefully on tiptoe as those steal whose purpose is sin. There was another excrescence on the walls just like it at the north-east corner, but this, though the view from it was almost more beautiful, for from it you could see the bay and the lovely mountains behind Mezzago, was exposed. No bushes grew near it, nor had it any shade. The north-west loop then was where she would sit, and she settled into it, and nestling her head in her cushion and putting her feet comfortably on the parapet, from whence they appeared to the villagers on the piazza below as two white doves, thought that now indeed she would be safe.

Mrs. Fisher found her there, guided by the smell of her cigarette. The incautious Scrap had not thought of that. Mrs. Fisher did not smoke herself, and all the more distinctly could she smell the smoke of others. The virile smell met her directly she went out into the garden from the dining-room after lunch in order to have her coffee. She had bidden Francesca set the coffee in the shade of the house just outside the glass door, and when Mrs. Wilkins, seeing a table being carried there, reminded her, very officiously and tactlessly Mrs. Fisher considered, that Lady Caroline wanted to be alone, she retorted—and with what propriety—that the garden was for everybody.

Into it accordingly she went, and was immediately aware that Lady Caroline was smoking. She said to herself, "These modern young women," and proceeded to find her; her stick, now that lunch was over, being no longer the hindrance to action that it was before her meal had been securely, as Browning once said—surely it was Browning? Yes, she remembered how much diverted she had been—roped in.

Nobody diverted her now, reflected Mrs. Fisher, making straight for the clump of daphne; the world had grown very dull, and had entirely lost its sense of humor. Probably they still had their jokes, these people in fact she knew they did, for *Punch* still went on; but how differently it went on, and what jokes. Thackeray, in his inimitable way, would have made mincemeat of this generation. Of how much it needed the tonic properties of that astringent pen it was of course unaware. It no longer even held him—at least, so she had been informed—in any particular esteem. Well, she could not give it eyes to see and ears to hear and a heart to understand, but she could and would give it, represented and united in the form of Lady Caroline, a good dose of honest medicine.

"I hear you are not well," she said, standing in the narrow entrance of the loop and looking down with the inflexible face of one who is determined to do good at the motionless and apparently sleeping Scrap.

Mrs. Fisher had a deep voice, very like a man's, for she had been overtaken by that strange masculinity that sometimes pursues a woman during the last laps of her life.

Scrap tried to pretend that she was asleep, but if she had been her cigarette would not have been held in her fingers but would have been lying on the ground.

She forgot this. Mrs. Fisher did not, and coming inside the loop, sat down on a narrow stone seat built out of the wall. For a little she could sit on it; for a little, till the chill began to penetrate.

She contemplated the figure before her. Undoubtedly a pretty creature, and one that would have had a success at Farringford. Strange how easily even the greatest men were moved by exteriors. She had seen with her own eyes Tennyson turn away from everybody—turn, positively, his back on a crowd of eminent people assembled to do him honor, and withdraw to the window with a young person nobody had ever heard of, who had been brought there by accident and whose one and only merit—if it be a merit, that which is conferred by chance—was beauty. Beauty! All over before you can turn round. An affair, one might almost say, of minutes. Well, while it lasted it did seem able to do what it liked with men. Even husbands were not immune. There had been passages in the life of Mr. Fisher . . .

"I expect the journey has upset you," she said in her deep voice. "What you want is a good dose of some simple medicine. I shall ask Domenico if there is such a thing in the village as castor oil."

Scrap opened her eyes and looked straight at Mrs. Fisher.

"Ah," said Mrs. Fisher, "I knew you were not asleep. If you had been you would have let your cigarette fall to the ground."

Scrap threw the cigarette over the parapet.

"Waste," said Mrs. Fisher. "I don't like smoking for women, but I still less like waste."

"What *does* one do with people like this?" Scrap asked herself, her eyes fixed on Mrs. Fisher in what felt to her an indignant stare but appeared to Mrs. Fisher as really charming docility.

"Now you'll take my advice," said Mrs. Fisher, touched, "and not neglect what may very well turn into an illness. We are in Italy, you know, and one has to be careful. You ought, to begin with, to go to bed."

"I never go to bed," snapped Scrap; and it sounded as moving, as forlorn, as that line spoken years and years ago by an actress playing the part of Poor Jo in a dramatized version of *Bleak House*—"I'm always moving on," said Poor Jo in this play, urged to do so by a policeman; and Mrs. Fisher, then a girl, had laid her head on the red velvet parapet of the front row of the dress circle and wept aloud.

It was wonderful, Scrap's voice. It had given her, in the ten years since she came out, all the triumphs that intelligence and wit can have, because it made whatever she said seem memorable. She ought, with a throat formation like that, to have been a singer, but in every kind of music Scrap was dumb except this one music of the speaking voice; and what a fascination, what a spell lay in that. Such was the loveliness of her face and the beauty of her coloring that there was not a man into whose eyes at the sight of her there did not leap a flame of intensest interest; but, when he heard her voice, the flame in that man's eyes was caught and fixed. It was the same with every man, educated and uneducated, old, young, desirable themselves or undesirable, men of her own world and bus-conductors, generals and Tommies—during the war she had had a perplexing time—bishops equally with vergers—round about her confirmation startling occurrences had taken place—wholesome and unwholesome, rich and penniless, brilliant or idiotic; and it made no difference at all what they were, or how long and securely married; into the eyes of every one of them, when they saw her, leapt this flame, and when they heard her it stayed there.

Scrap had had enough of this look. It only led to difficulties. At first it had delighted her. She had been excited, triumphant. To be apparently incapable of doing or saying the wrong thing, to be applauded, listened to, petted, adored wherever she went, and when she came home to find nothing there either but the most indulgent proud fondness—why, how extremely pleasant. And so easy, too. No preparation necessary for this achievement, no hard work, nothing to learn. She need take no trouble. She had only to appear, and presently say something.

But gradually experiences gathered round her. After all, she had to take trouble, she had to make efforts, because, she discovered with astonishment and rage, she had to defend herself. That look, that leaping look, meant that she was going to be grabbed at. Some of those who had it were more humble than others, especially if they were young, but they all, according to their several ability, grabbed; and she who had entered the world so jauntily, with her head in the air and the completest confidence in anybody whose hair was gray, began to distrust, and then to dislike, and soon to shrink away from, and presently to be indignant. Sometimes it was just as if she didn't belong to herself, wasn't her own at all, but was regarded as a universal thing, a sort of beauty-of-all-work. Really men . . . And she found herself involved in queer, vague quarrels, being curiously hated. Really women . . . And when the war came, and she flung herself into it along with everybody else, it finished her. Really generals . . .

The war finished Scrap. It killed the one man she felt safe with, whom she would have married, and it finally disgusted her with love. Since then she had been embittered. She was struggling as angrily in the sweet stuff of life as a wasp got caught in honey.

Just as desperately did she try to unstick her wings. It gave her no pleasure to outdo other women; she didn't want their tiresome men. What could one do with men when one had got them? None of them would talk to her of anything but the things of love, and how foolish and fatiguing that became after a bit. It was as though a healthy person with a normal hunger was given nothing whatever to eat but sugar. Love, love . . . the very word made her want to slap somebody. "*Why* should I love you? *Why* should I?" she would ask amazed sometimes when somebody was trying—somebody was always trying—to propose to her. But she never got a real answer, only further incoherence.

A deep cynicism took hold of the unhappy Scrap. Her inside grew hoary with disillusionment, while her gracious and charming outside continued to make the world more beautiful. What had the future in it for her? She would not be able, after such a preparation, to take hold of it. She was fit for nothing; she had wasted all this time being beautiful. Presently she wouldn't be beautiful, and what then? Scrap didn't know what then, it appalled her to wonder even. Tired as she was of being conspicuous she was at least used to that, she had never known anything else; and to become inconspicuous, to fade, to grow shabby and dim, would probably be most painful. And once she began, what years and years of it there would be! Imagine, thought Scrap, having most of one's life at the wrong end. Imagine being old for two or three times as long as being young. Stupid, stupid. Everything was stupid. There wasn't a thing she wanted to do. There were thousands of things she didn't want to do. Avoidance, silence, invisibility, if possible unconsciousness—these negations were all she asked for at the moment; and here, even here, she was not allowed a minute's peace, and this absurd woman must come pretending, merely because she wanted to exercise power and make her go to bed and make her—hideous—drink castor oil, that she thought she was ill.

“I’m sure,” said Mrs. Fisher, who felt the cold of the stone beginning to come through and knew she could not sit much longer, “you’ll do what is reasonable. Your mother would wish—have you a mother?”

A faint wonder came into Scrap’s eyes. Have you a mother? If ever anybody had a mother it was Scrap. It had not occurred to her that there could be people who had never heard of her mother. She was one of the major marchionesses—there being, as no one knew better than Scrap, marchionesses and marchionesses—and had held high positions at Court. Her father, too, in his day had been most prominent. His day was a little over, poor dear, because in the war he had made some important mistakes, and besides he was now grown old; still, there he was, an excessively well-known person. How restful, how extraordinarily restful to have found some one who had never heard of any of her lot, or at least had not yet connected her with them.

She began to like Mrs. Fisher. Perhaps the originals didn’t know anything about her either. When she first wrote to them and signed her name, that great name of Dester which twisted in and out of English history like a bloody thread, for its bearers constantly killed, she had taken it for granted that they would know who she was; and at the interview in Shaftesbury Avenue she was sure they did know, because they hadn’t asked, as they otherwise would have, for references.

Scrap began to cheer up. If nobody at San Salvatore had ever heard of her, if for a whole month she could shed herself, get right away from everything connected with herself, be allowed really to forget the clinging and the clogging and all the noise, why, perhaps she might make something of herself after all. She might really think; really clear up her mind; really come to some conclusion.

“What I want to do here,” she said, leaning forward in her chair and clasping her hands round her knees and looking up at Mrs.

Fisher, whose seat was higher than hers, almost with animation, so much pleased was she that Mrs. Fisher knew nothing about her, "is to come to a conclusion. That's all. It isn't much to want, is it? Just that."

She gazed at Mrs. Fisher, and thought that almost any conclusion would do; the great thing was to get hold of something, catch something tight, cease to drift.

Mrs. Fisher's little eyes surveyed her. "I should say," she said, "that what a young woman like you wants is a husband and children."

"Well, that's one of the things I'm going to consider," said Scrap amiably. "But I don't think it would be a conclusion."

"And meanwhile," said Mrs. Fisher, getting up, for the cold of the stone was now through, "I shouldn't trouble my head if I were you with considerings and conclusions. Women's heads weren't made for thinking, I assure you. I should go to bed and get well."

"I am well," said Scrap.

"Then why did you send a message that you were ill?"

"I didn't."

"Then I've had all the trouble of coming out here for nothing."

"But wouldn't you prefer coming out and finding me well than coming out and finding me ill?" asked Scrap, smiling.

Even Mrs. Fisher was caught by the smile.

"Well, you're a pretty creature," she said forgivingly. "It's a pity you weren't born fifty years ago. My friends would have liked looking at you."

"I'm very glad I wasn't," said Scrap. "I dislike being looked at."

"Absurd," said Mrs. Fisher, growing stern again. "That's what you are made for, young women like you. For what else, pray? And I assure you that if my friends had looked at you, you would have been looked at by some very great people."

"I dislike very great people," said Scrap, frowning. There had been an incident quite recently—really potentates. . .

"What *I* dislike," said Mrs. Fisher, now as cold as the stone she had got up from, "is the pose of the modern young woman. It seems to me pitiful, positively pitiful, in its silliness."

And, her stick crunching the pebbles, she walked away.

"That's all right," Scrap said to herself, dropping back into her comfortable position with her head in the cushion and her feet on the parapet; if only people would go away she didn't in the least mind why they went.

"Don't you think darling Scrap is growing a little, just a little, peculiar?" her mother had asked her father a short time before that latest peculiarity of the flight to San Salvatore, uncomfortably struck by the very odd things Scrap said and the way she had taken to slinking out of reach whenever she could and avoiding everybody except—such a sign of age—quite young men, almost boys.

"Eh? What? Peculiar? Well, let her be peculiar if she likes. A woman with her looks can be any damned thing she pleases," was the infatuated answer.

"I do let her," said her mother meekly; and indeed if she did not, what difference would it make?

Mrs. Fisher was sorry she had bothered about Lady Caroline. She went along the hall towards her private sitting-room, and her stick as she went struck the stone floor with a vigor in harmony with her feelings. Sheer silliness, these poses. She had no patience with them. Unable to be or do anything of themselves, the young of the present generation tried to achieve a reputation for cleverness by decrying all that was obviously great and obviously good and by praising everything, however obviously bad, that was different. Apes, thought Mrs. Fisher, roused. Apes. Apes. And in her sitting-room she found more apes, or what seemed to her in her present mood more, for there was Mrs. Arbuthnot placidly drinking coffee, while at the writing-table, the writing-table she already looked upon as sacred, using her pen, her own pen brought for her hand alone from Prince of Wales Terrace, sat Mrs. Wilkins writing; at the table; in her room; with her pen.

"Isn't this a delightful place?" said Mrs. Arbuthnot cordially. "We have just discovered it."

"I'm writing to Mellersh," said Mrs. Wilkins, turning her head and also cordially—as though, Mrs. Fisher thought, she cared a straw who she was writing to and anyhow knew who the person she called Mellersh was. "He'll want to know," said Mrs. Wilkins, optimism induced by her surroundings, "that I've got here safely."

CHAPTER 11

The sweet smells that were everywhere in San Salvatore were alone enough to produce concord. They came into the sitting-room from the flowers on the battlements, and met the ones from the flowers inside the room, and almost, thought Mrs. Wilkins, could be seen greeting each other with a holy kiss. Who could be angry in the middle of such gentlenesses? Who could be acquisitive, selfish, in the old rasped London way, in the presence of this bounteous beauty?

Yet Mrs. Fisher seemed to be all three of these things.

There was so much beauty, so much more than enough for every one, that it did appear to be a vain activity to try and make a corner in it.

Yet Mrs. Fisher was trying to make a corner in it, and had railed off a portion for her exclusive use.

Well, she would get over that presently; she would get over it inevitably, Mrs. Wilkins was sure, after a day or two in the extraordinary atmosphere of peace in that place.

Meanwhile she obviously hadn't even begun to get over it. She stood looking at her and Rose with an expression that appeared to be one of anger. Anger. Fancy. Silly old nerve-racked London feelings, thought Mrs. Wilkins, whose eyes saw the room full of kisses, and everybody in it being kissed, Mrs. Fisher as copiously as she herself and Rose.

"You don't like us being in here," said Mrs. Wilkins, getting up and at once, after her manner, fixing on the truth. "Why?"

"I should have thought," said Mrs. Fisher, leaning on her stick, "you could have seen that it is my room."

"You mean because of the photographs," said Mrs. Wilkins.

Mrs. Arbuthnot, who was a little red and surprised, got up too.

"And the notepaper," said Mrs. Fisher. "Notepaper with my London address on it. That pen—"

She pointed. It was still in Mrs. Wilkins's hand.

"Is yours. I'm very sorry," said Mrs. Wilkins, laying it on the table. And she added, smiling, that it had just been writing some very amiable things.

"But why," asked Mrs. Arbuthnot, who found herself unable to acquiesce in Mrs. Fisher's arrangements without at least a gentle struggle, "ought we not to be here? It's a sitting-room."

"There is another one," said Mrs. Fisher. "You and your friend cannot sit in two rooms at once, and if I have no wish to disturb you in yours I am unable to see why you should wish to disturb me in mine."

"But why—" began Mrs. Arbuthnot again.

"It's quite natural," Mrs. Wilkins interrupted, for Rose was looking stubborn; and turning to Mrs. Fisher she said that although sharing things with friends was pleasant she could understand that Mrs. Fisher, still steeped in the Prince of Wales Terrace attitude to life, did not yet want to, but that she would get rid of that after a bit and feel quite different. "Soon you'll *want* us to share," said Mrs. Wilkins reassuringly. "Why, you may even get so far as *asking* me to use your pen if you knew I hadn't got one."

Mrs. Fisher was moved almost beyond control by this speech. To have a ramshackle young woman from Hampstead patting her on the back as it were, in breezy certitude that quite soon she would improve, stirred her more deeply than anything had stirred her since her first discovery that Mr. Fisher was not what he seemed. Mrs. Wilkins must certainly be curbed. But how? There was a curious imperviousness about her. At that moment, for instance, she was smiling as pleasantly and with as unclouded a face as if she were saying nothing in the least impertinent. Would she know she was being curbed? If she didn't know, if she were too tough to feel it, then what? Nothing, except avoidance; except, precisely, one's own private sitting-room.

"I'm an old woman," said Mrs. Fisher, "and I need a room to myself. I cannot get about, because of my stick. As I cannot get about I have to sit. Why should I not sit quietly and undisturbed, as I told you in London I intended to? If people are to come in and out all day long, chattering and leaving doors open, you will have broken the agreement, which was that I was to be quiet."

"But we haven't the least wish—" began Mrs. Arbuthnot, who was again cut short by Mrs. Wilkins.

"We're only too glad," said Mrs. Wilkins, "for you to have this room if it makes you happy. We didn't know about it, that's all. We wouldn't have come in if we had—not till you invited us, anyhow. I expect," she finished looking down cheerfully at Mrs. Fisher, "you soon will." And picking up her letter she took Mrs. Arbuthnot's hand and drew her towards the door.

Mrs. Arbuthnot did not want to go. She, the mildest of women, was filled with a curious and surely unchristian desire to stay and fight. Not, of course, really, nor even with any definitely aggressive words. No; she only wanted to reason with Mrs. Fisher, and to reason patiently. But she did feel that something ought to be said, and that she ought not to allow herself to be rated and turned out as if she were a schoolgirl caught in ill behavior by Authority.

Mrs. Wilkins, however, drew her firmly to and through the door, and once again Rose wondered at Lotty, at her balance, her sweet and equable temper—she who in England had been such a thing of gusts. From the moment they got into Italy it was Lotty who seemed the elder. She certainly was very happy; blissful, in fact. Did happiness so completely protect one? Did it make one so untouchable, so wise? Rose was happy herself, but not anything like *so* happy. Evidently not, for not only did she want to fight Mrs. Fisher but she wanted something else, something more than this lovely place, something to complete it; she wanted Frederick. For the first time in her life she was surrounded by perfect beauty, and her one thought was to show it to him, to share it with him. She wanted Frederick. She yearned for Frederick. Ah, if only, only Frederick . . .

"Poor old thing," said Mrs. Wilkins, shutting the door gently on Mrs. Fisher and her triumph. "Fancy on a day like this."

"She's a very rude old thing," said Mrs. Arbuthnot.

"She'll get over that. I'm sorry we chose just her room to go and sit in."

"It's much the nicest," said Mrs. Arbuthnot. "And it isn't hers."

"Oh, but there are lots of other places, and she's such a poor old thing. Let her have the room. Whatever does it matter?"

And Mrs. Wilkins said she was going down to the village to find out where the post-office was and post her letter to Mellersh, and would Rose go too.

"I've been thinking about Mellersh," said Mrs. Wilkins as they walked, one behind the other, down the narrow zigzag path up which they had climbed in the rain the night before.

She went first. Mrs. Arbuthnot, quite naturally now, followed. In England it had been the other way about—Lotty, timid, hesitating, except when she burst out so awkwardly, getting behind the calm and reasonable Rose whenever she could.

"I've been thinking about Mellersh," repeated Mrs. Wilkins over her shoulder, as Rose seemed not to have heard.

"Have you?" said Rose, a faint distaste in her voice, for her experiences with Mellersh had not been of a kind to make her enjoy remembering him. She had deceived Mellersh; therefore she didn't like him. She was unconscious that this was the reason of her dislike, and thought it was that there didn't seem to be much, if any, of the grace of God about him. And yet how wrong to feel that, she rebuked herself, and how presumptuous. No doubt Lotty's husband was far, far nearer to God than she herself was ever likely to be. Still, she didn't like him.

"I've been a mean dog," said Mrs. Wilkins.

"A what?" asked Mrs. Arbuthnot, incredulous of her hearing.

"All this coming away and leaving him in that dreary place while I rollick in heaven. He had planned to take me to Italy for Easter himself. Did I tell you?"

"No," said Mrs. Arbuthnot; and indeed she had discouraged talk about husbands. Whenever Lotty had begun to blurt out things she had swiftly changed the conversation. One husband led to another, in conversation as well as in life, she felt, and she could not, she would not, talk of Frederick. Beyond the bare fact that he was there, he had not been mentioned. Mellersh had had to be mentioned, because of his obstructiveness, but she had carefully kept him from overflowing outside the limits of necessity.

"Well, he did," said Mrs. Wilkins. "He had never done such a thing in his life before, and I was horrified. Fancy—just as I had planned to come to it myself."

She paused on the path and looked up at Rose.

"Yes," said Rose, trying to think of something else to talk about.

"Now you see why I say I've been a mean dog. *He* had planned a holiday in Italy with me, and *I* had planned a holiday in Italy leaving him at home. I think," she went on, her eyes fixed on Rose's face, "Mellersh has every reason to be both angry and hurt."

Mrs. Arbuthnot was astonished. The extraordinary quickness with which, hour by hour, under her very eyes, Lotty became more selfless, disconcerted her. She was turning into something surprisingly like a saint. Here she was now being affectionate about Mellersh—Mellersh, who only that morning, while they hung their feet into the sea, had seemed a mere iridescence, Lotty had told her, a thing of gauze. That was only that morning; and by the time they had had lunch Lotty had developed so far as to have got him solid enough again to write to, and to write to at length. And now, a few minutes later, she was announcing that he had every reason to be angry with her and hurt, and that she herself had been—the language was unusual, but it did express real penitence—a mean dog.

Rose stared at her astonished. If she went on like this, soon a nimbus might be expected round her head, was there already, if one didn't know it was the sun through the tree-trunks catching her sandy hair.

A great desire to love and be friends, to love everybody, to be friends with everybody, seemed to be invading Lotty—a desire for sheer goodness. Rose's own experience was that goodness, the state of being good, was only reached with difficulty and pain. It took a long time to get to it; in fact one never did get to it, or, if for a flashing instant one did, it was only for a flashing instant. Desperate perseverance was needed to struggle along its path, and all the way was dotted with doubts. Lotty simply flew along. She had certainly, thought Rose, not got rid of her impetuousness. It had merely taken another direction. She was now impetuously becoming a saint. Could one really attain goodness so violently? Wouldn't there be an equally violent reaction?

"I shouldn't," said Rose with caution, looking down into Lotty's bright eyes—the path was steep, so that Lotty was well below her—"I shouldn't be sure of that too quickly."

"But I am sure of it, and I've written and told him so."

Rose stared. "Why, but only this morning—" she began.

"It's all in this," interrupted Lotty, tapping the envelope and looking pleased.

"What—everything?"

"You mean about the advertisement and my savings being spent? Oh no—not yet. But I'll tell him all that when he comes."

"When he comes?" repeated Rose.

"I've invited him to come and stay with us."

Rose could only go on staring.

"It's the least I could do. Besides—look at this." Lotty waved her hand. "Disgusting not to share it. I was a mean dog to go off and leave him, but no dog I've ever heard of was ever as mean as I'd be if I didn't try and persuade Mellersh to come out and enjoy this too. It's barest decency that he should have some of the fun out of my nest-egg. After all, he has housed me and fed me for years. One shouldn't be churlish."

"But—do you think he'll come?"

"Oh, I *hope* so," said Lotty with the utmost earnestness; and added, "Poor lamb."

At that Rose felt she would like to sit down. Mellersh a poor lamb? That same Mellersh who a few hours before was mere shimmer? There was a seat at the bend of the path, and Rose went to it and sat down. She wished to get her breath, gain time. If she had time she might perhaps be able to catch up to the leaping Lotty, and perhaps be able to stop her before she committed herself to what she probably presently would be sorry for. Mellersh at San Salvatore? Mellersh, from whom Lotty had taken such pains so recently to escape?

"I *see* him here," said Lotty, as if in answer to her thoughts.

Rose looked at her with real concern: for every time Lotty said in that convinced voice, "I *see*," what she saw came true. Then it was to be supposed that Mr. Wilkins too would presently come true.

"I wish," said Rose anxiously, "I understood you."

"Don't try," said Lotty, smiling.

"But I must, because I love you."

"Dear Rose," said Lotty, swiftly bending down and kissing her.

"You're so quick," said Rose. "I can't follow your developments. I can't keep touch. It was what happened with Freder—"

She broke off and looked frightened.

"The whole idea of our coming here," she went on again, as Lotty didn't seem to have noticed, "was to get away, wasn't it? Well, we've got away. And now, after only a single day of it, you want to write to the very people—"

She stopped.

"The very people we were getting away from," finished Lotty. "It's quite true. It seems idiotically illogical. But I'm so happy, I'm so well, I feel so fearfully wholesome. This place—why, it makes me feel *flooded* with love."

And she stared down at Rose in a kind of radiant surprise.

Rose was silent a moment. Then she said, "And do you think it will have the same effect on Mr. Wilkins?"

Lotty laughed. "I don't know," she said. "But even if it doesn't, there's enough love about to flood fifty Mr. Wilkinses, as you call him. The great thing is to have lots of love *about*. I don't see," she went on, "at least I don't see here, though I did at home, that it matters who loves as long as somebody does. I was a stingy beast at home, and used to measure and count. I had a queer obsession about justice. As though justice mattered. As though justice can really be distinguished from vengeance. It's only love that's any good. At home I wouldn't love Mellersh unless he loved me back, exactly as much, absolute fairness. Did you ever. And as he didn't, neither did I, and the *aridity* of that house! The *aridity* . . ."

Rose said nothing. She was bewildered by Lotty. One odd effect of San Salvatore on her rapidly developing friend was her sudden free use of robust words. She had not used them in Hampstead. Beast and dog were more robust than Hampstead cared about. In words, too, Lotty had come unchained.

But how she wished, oh how Rose wished, that she too could write to her husband and say "Come." The Wilkins *ménage*, however pompous Mellersh might be, and he had seemed to Rose pompous, was on a healthier, more natural footing than hers. Lotty could write to Mellersh and would get an answer. She couldn't write to Frederick, for only too well did she know he wouldn't answer. At least, he might answer—a hurried scribble, showing how much bored he was at doing it, with perfunctory thanks for her letter. But that would be worse than no answer at all; for his handwriting, her name on an envelope addressed by him, stabbed her heart. Too acutely did it bring back the letters of their beginnings together, the letters from him so desolate with separation, so aching with love and longing. To see apparently one of these very same letters arrive, and open it and find:

> Dear Rose—Thanks for letter. Glad you're having a good time. Don't hurry back. Say if you want any money. Everything going splendidly here.—Yours,
>
> Frederick

—no, it couldn't be borne.

"I don't think I'll come down to the village with you to-day," she said, looking up at Lotty with eyes suddenly gone dim. "I think I want to think."

"All right," said Lotty, at once starting off briskly down the path. "But don't think too long," she called back over her shoulder. "Write and invite him at once."

"Invite whom?" asked Rose, startled.

"Your husband."

CHAPTER 12

At the evening meal, which was the first time the whole four sat round the dining-room table together, Scrap appeared.

She appeared quite punctually, and in one of those wrappers or tea-gowns which are sometimes described as ravishing. This one really was ravishing. It certainly ravished Mrs. Wilkins, who could not take her eyes off the enchanting figure opposite. It was a shell-pink garment, and clung to the adorable Scrap as though it, too, loved her.

"What a beautiful dress!" exclaimed Mrs. Wilkins eagerly.

"What—this old rag?" said Scrap, glancing down at it as if to see which one she had got on. "I've had it a hundred years." And she concentrated on her soup.

"You must be very cold in it," said Mrs. Fisher, thin-lipped; for it showed a great deal of Scrap—the whole of her arms, for instance, and even where it covered her up it was so thin that you still saw her.

"Who—me?" said Scrap, looking up a moment. "Oh, no."

And she continued her soup.

"You mustn't catch a chill, you know," said Mrs. Arbuthnot, feeling that such loveliness must at all costs be preserved unharmed. "There's a great difference here when the sun goes down."

"I'm quite warm," said Scrap, industriously eating her soup.

"You look as if you had nothing at all on underneath," said Mrs. Fisher.

"I haven't. At least, hardly anything," said Scrap, finishing her soup.

"How very imprudent," said Mrs. Fisher, "and how highly improper."

Whereupon Scrap stared at her.

Mrs. Fisher had arrived at dinner feeling friendly towards Lady Caroline. She at least had not intruded into her room and sat at her table and written with her pen. She did, Mrs. Fisher had supposed, know how to behave. Now it appeared that she did not know, for was this behaving, to come dressed—no, undressed—like that to a meal? Such behavior was not only exceedingly improper but also most inconsiderate, for the indelicate creature would certainly catch a chill, and then infect the entire party. Mrs. Fisher had a great objection to other people's chills. They were always the fruit of folly; and then they were handed on to her, who had done nothing at all to deserve them.

"Bird-brained," thought Mrs. Fisher, sternly contemplating Lady Caroline. "Not an idea in her head except vanity."

"But there are no men here," said Mrs. Wilkins, "so how can it be improper? Have you noticed," she inquired of Mrs. Fisher, who endeavored to pretend she did not hear, "how difficult it is to be improper without men?"

Mrs. Fisher neither answered her nor looked at her; but Scrap looked at her, and did that with her mouth which in any other mouth would have been a faint grin. Seen from without, across the bowl of nasturtiums, it was the most beautiful of brief and dimpled smiles.

She had a very alive sort of face, that one, thought Scrap, observing Mrs. Wilkins with a dawn of interest. It was rather like a field of corn swept by lights and shadows. Both she and the dark one, Scrap noticed, had changed their clothes, but only in order to put on silk jumpers. The same amount of trouble would have been enough

to dress them properly, reflected Scrap. Naturally they looked like nothing on earth in the jumpers. It didn't matter what Mrs. Fisher wore; indeed, the only thing for her, short of plumes and ermine, was what she did wear. But these others were quite young still, and quite attractive. They really definitely had faces. How different life would be for them if they made the most of themselves instead of the least. And yet—Scrap was suddenly bored, and turned away her thoughts and absently ate toast. What did it matter? If you did make the best of yourself, you only collected people round you who ended by wanting to grab.

"I've had the most wonderful day," began Mrs. Wilkins, her eyes shining.

Scrap lowered hers. "Oh," she thought, "she's going to gush."

"As though anybody were interested in her day," thought Mrs. Fisher, lowering hers also.

In fact, whenever Mrs. Wilkins spoke Mrs. Fisher deliberately cast down her eyes. Thus would she mark her disapproval. Besides, it seemed the only safe thing to do with her eyes, for no one could tell what the uncurbed creature would say next. That which she had just said, for instance, about men—addressed, too, to her—what could she mean? Better not conjecture, thought Mrs. Fisher; and her eyes, though cast down, yet saw Lady Caroline stretch out her hand to the Chianti flask and fill her glass again.

Again. She had done it once already, and the fish was only just going out of the room. Mrs. Fisher could see that the other respectable member of the party, Mrs. Arbuthnot, was noticing it too. Mrs. Arbuthnot was, she hoped and believed, respectable and well-meaning. It is true she also had invaded her sitting-room, but no doubt she had been dragged there by the other one, and Mrs. Fisher had little if anything against Mrs. Arbuthnot, and observed with approval that she only drank water. That was as it should be. So, indeed, to give her her dues, did the freckled one; and very right at their age. She herself drank wine, but with what moderation: one meal, one glass. And she was sixty-five, and might properly, and even beneficially, have had at least two.

"That," she said to Lady Caroline, cutting right across what Mrs. Wilkins was telling them about her wonderful day and indicating the wine-glass, "is very bad for you."

Lady Caroline, however, could not have heard, for she continued to sip, her elbow on the table, and listen to what Mrs. Wilkins was saying.

And what was it she was saying? She had invited somebody to come and stay? A man?

Mrs. Fisher could not credit her ears. Yet it evidently was a man, for she spoke of the person as he.

Suddenly and for the first time—but then this was most important—Mrs. Fisher addressed Mrs. Wilkins directly. She was sixty-five, and cared very little what sorts of women she happened to be with for a month, but if the women were to be mixed with men it was a different proposition altogether. She was not going to be made a cat's-paw of. She had not come out there to sanction by her presence what used in her day to be called fast behavior. Nothing had been said at the interview in London about men; if there had been she would have declined, of course, to come.

"What is his name?" asked Mrs. Fisher, abruptly interposing.

Mrs. Wilkins turned to her with a slight surprise. "Wilkins," she said.

"Wilkins?"

"Yes."

"Your name?"

"And his."

"A relation?"

"Not blood."

"A connection?"

"A husband."

Mrs. Fisher once more cast down her eyes. She could not talk to Mrs. Wilkins. There was something about the things she said . . . "A husband." Suggesting one of many. Always that unseemly twist to everything. Why could she not say "My husband"? Besides, Mrs. Fisher had, she herself knew not for what reason, taken both the Hampstead young women for widows. War ones. There had been an absence of mention of husbands at the interview which would not, she considered, be natural if such persons did after all exist. And if a husband was not a relation, who was? "Not blood." What a way to talk. Why, a husband was the first of all relations. How well she remembered Ruskin—no, it was not Ruskin, it was the Bible that said a man should leave his father and mother and cleave only to his wife; showing that she became by marriage an even more than blood relation. And if the husband's father and mother were to be nothing to him compared to his wife, how much less than nothing ought the wife's father and mother be to her compared to her husband. She herself had been unable to leave her father and mother in order to cleave to Mr. Fisher because they were no longer, when she married, alive, but she certainly would have left them if they had been there to leave. Not blood, indeed. Silly talk.

The dinner was very good. Succulence succeeded succulence. Costanza had determined to do as she chose in the matter of cream and eggs the first week, and see what happened at the end of it when the bills had to be paid. Her experience of the English was that they were quiet about bills. They were shy of words. They believed readily. Besides, who was the mistress here? In the absence of a definite one, it occurred to Costanza that she might as well be the mistress herself. So she did as she chose about the dinner, and it was very good.

The four, however, were so much preoccupied by their own conversation that they ate it without noticing how good it was. Even

Mrs. Fisher, she who in such matters was manly, did not notice. The entire excellent cooking was to her as though it were not; which shows how much she must have been stirred.

She was stirred. It was that Mrs. Wilkins. She was enough to stir anybody. And she was undoubtedly encouraged by Lady Caroline, who, in her turn, was no doubt influenced by the Chianti.

Mrs. Fisher was very glad there were no men present, for they certainly would have been foolish about Lady Caroline. She was precisely the sort of young woman to unbalance them; especially, Mrs. Fisher recognized, at that moment. Perhaps it was the Chianti momentarily intensifying her personality, but she was undeniably most attractive; and there were few things Mrs. Fisher disliked more than having to look on while sensible, intelligent men, who the moment before were talking seriously and interestingly about real matters, became merely foolish and simpering—she had seen them actually simpering—just because in walked a bit of bird-brained beauty. Even Mr. Gladstone, that great wise statesman, whose hand had once rested for an unforgettable moment solemnly on her head, would have, she felt, on perceiving Lady Caroline left off talking sense and horribly embarked on badinage.

"You see," Mrs. Wilkins said—a silly trick that, with which she mostly began her sentences; Mrs. Fisher each time wished to say, "Pardon me—I do not see, I hear"—but why trouble?—"You see," said Mrs. Wilkins, leaning across towards Lady Caroline, "we arranged, didn't we, in London that if any of us wanted to we could each invite one guest. So now I'm doing it."

"I don't remember that," said Mrs. Fisher, her eyes on her plate.

"Oh yes, we did—didn't we, Rose?"

"Yes—I remember," said Lady Caroline. "Only it seemed so incredible that one could ever want to. One's whole idea was to get away from one's friends."

"And one's husbands."

Again that unseemly plural. But how altogether unseemly, thought Mrs. Fisher. Such implications. Mrs. Arbuthnot clearly thought so too, for she had turned red.

"And family affection," said Lady Caroline—or was it the Chianti speaking? Surely it was the Chianti.

"And the want of family affection," said Mrs. Wilkins—what a light she was throwing on her home life and real character.

"That wouldn't be so bad," said Lady Caroline. "I'd stay with that. It would give one room."

"Oh no, no—it's dreadful," cried Mrs. Wilkins. "It's as if one had no clothes on."

"But I like that," said Lady Caroline.

"Really—" said Mrs. Fisher.

"It's a divine feeling, getting rid of things," said Lady Caroline, who was talking altogether to Mrs. Wilkins and paid no attention to the other two.

"Oh, but in a bitter wind to have nothing on and know there never will be anything on and you going to get colder and colder till at last you die of it—that's what it was like, living with somebody who didn't love one."

These confidences, thought Mrs. Fisher . . . and no excuse whatever for Mrs. Wilkins, who was making them entirely on plain water. Mrs. Arbuthnot, judging from her face, quite shared Mrs. Fisher's disapproval; she was fidgeting.

"But didn't he?" asked Lady Caroline—every bit as shamelessly unreticent as Mrs. Wilkins.

"Mellersh? He showed no signs of it."

"Delicious," murmured Lady Caroline.

"Really—" said Mrs. Fisher.

"I didn't think it was at all delicious. I was miserable. And now, since I've been here, I simply stare at myself being miserable. As miserable as that. And about Mellersh."

"You mean he wasn't worth it."

"Really—" said Mrs. Fisher.

"No, I don't. I mean I've suddenly got well."

Lady Caroline, slowly twisting the stem of her glass in her fingers, scrutinized the lit-up face opposite.

"And now I'm well I find I can't sit here and gloat all to myself. I can't be happy, shutting him out. I must share. I understand exactly what the Blessed Damozel felt like."

"What was the Blessed Damozel?" asked Scrap.

"Really—" said Mrs. Fisher; and with such emphasis this time that Lady Caroline turned to her.

"Ought I to know?" she asked. "I don't know any natural history. It sounds like a bird."

"It is a poem," said Mrs. Fisher with extraordinary frost.

"Oh," said Scrap.

"I'll lend it to you," said Mrs. Wilkins, over whose face laughter rippled.

"No," said Scrap.

"And its author," said Mrs. Fisher icily, "though not perhaps quite what one would have wished him to be, was frequently at my father's table."

"What a bore for you," said Scrap. "That's what mother's always doing—inviting authors. I hate authors. I wouldn't mind them so much if they didn't write books. Go on about Mellersh," she said, turning to Mrs. Wilkins.

"Really—" said Mrs. Fisher.

"All those empty beds," said Mrs. Wilkins.

"What empty beds?" asked Scrap.

"The ones in this house. Why, of course they each ought to have somebody happy inside them. Eight beds, and only four people. It's dreadful, dreadful to be so greedy and keep everything just for oneself. I want Rose to ask her husband out too. You and Mrs. Fisher haven't got husbands, but why not give some friend a glorious time?"

Rose bit her lip. She turned red, she turned pale. If only Lotty would keep quiet, she thought. It was all very well to have suddenly become a saint and want to love everybody, but need she be so tactless? Rose felt that all her poor sore places were being danced on. If only Lotty would keep quiet . . .

And Mrs. Fisher, with even greater frostiness than that with which she had received Lady Caroline's ignorance of the Blessed Damozel, said, "There is only one unoccupied bedroom in this house."

"Only one?" echoed Mrs. Wilkins, astonished. "Then who are in all the others?"

"We are," said Mrs. Fisher.

"But we're not in all the bedrooms. There must be at least six. That leaves two over, and the owner told us there were eight beds—didn't he, Rose?"

"There are six bedrooms," said Mrs. Fisher; for both she and Lady Caroline had thoroughly searched the house on arriving, in order to see which part of it they would be most comfortable in, and they both knew that there were six bedrooms, two of which were very small, and in one of these small ones Francesca slept in the company of a chair and a chest of drawers, and the other, similarly furnished, was empty.

Mrs. Wilkins and Mrs. Arbuthnot had hardly looked at the house, having spent most of their time out of doors gaping at the scenery, and had, in the agitated inattentiveness of their minds when first they began negotiating for San Salvatore, got into their heads that the eight beds of which the owner spoke were the same as eight bedrooms; which they were not. There were indeed eight beds, but four of them were in Mrs. Wilkins's and Mrs. Arbuthnot's rooms.

"There are six bedrooms," repeated Mrs. Fisher. "We have four, Francesca has the fifth, and the sixth is empty."

"So that," said Scrap, "however kind we feel we would be if we could, we can't. Isn't it fortunate?"

"But then there's only room for one?" said Mrs. Wilkins, looking round at the three faces.

"Yes—and you've got him," said Scrap.

Mrs. Wilkins was taken aback. This question of the beds was unexpected. In inviting Mellersh she had intended to put him in one of the four spare-rooms that she imagined were there. When there were plenty of rooms and enough servants there was no reason why they should, as they did in their small, two-servanted house at home, share the same one. Love, even universal love, the kind of love with which she felt herself flooded, should not be tried. Much patience and self-effacement were needed for successful married sleep. Placidity; a steady faith; these too were needed. She was sure she would be much fonder of Mellersh, and he not mind her nearly so much, if they were not shut up together at night, if in the morning they could meet with the cheery affection of friends between whom lies no shadow of differences about the window or the washing arrangements, or of absurd little choked-down resentments at something that had seemed to one of them unfair. Her happiness, she felt, and her ability to be friends with everybody, was the result of her sudden new freedom and its peace. Would there be that sense of freedom, that peace, after a night shut up with Mellersh? Would she be able in the morning to be full towards him, as she was at that moment full, of nothing at all but loving-kindness? After all, she hadn't been very long in heaven. Suppose she hadn't been in it long enough for her to have become fixed in blandness? And only that morning what an extraordinary joy it had been to find herself alone when she woke, and able to pull the bed-clothes any way she liked!

Francesca had to nudge her. She was so much absorbed that she did not notice the pudding.

"If," thought Mrs. Wilkins, distractedly helping herself, "I share my room with Mellersh I risk losing all I now feel about him. If on the other hand I put him in the one spare-room, I prevent Mrs. Fisher and Lady Caroline from giving somebody a treat. True they don't seem to want to at present, but at any moment in this place one or the other of them may be seized with a desire to make somebody happy, and then they wouldn't be able to because of Mellersh."

"What a problem," she said aloud, her eyebrows puckered.

"What is?" asked Scrap.

"Where to put Mellersh."

Scrap stared. "Why, isn't one room enough for him?" she asked.

"Oh yes, quite. But then there won't be any room left at all—any room for somebody you may want to invite."

"I shan't want to," said Scrap.

"Or *you*," said Mrs. Wilkins to Mrs. Fisher. "Rose, of course, doesn't count. I'm sure she would like sharing her room with her husband. It's written all over her."

"Really—" said Mrs. Fisher.

"Really what?" asked Mrs. Wilkins, turning hopefully to her, for she thought the word this time was the preliminary to a helpful suggestion.

It was not. It stood by itself. It was, as before, mere frost.

Challenged, however, Mrs. Fisher did fasten it on to a sentence. "Really am I to understand," she asked, "that you propose to reserve the one spare-room for the exclusive use of your own family?"

"He isn't my own family," said Mrs. Wilkins. "He's my husband. You see—"

"I see nothing," Mrs. Fisher could not this time refrain from interrupting—for what an intolerable trick. "At the most I hear, and that reluctantly."

But Mrs. Wilkins, as impervious to rebuke as Mrs. Fisher had feared, immediately repeated the tiresome formula and launched out into a long and excessively indelicate speech about the best place for the person she called Mellersh to sleep in.

Mellersh—Mrs. Fisher, remembering the Thomases and Johns and Alfreds and Roberts of her day, plain names that yet had all become glorious, thought it sheer affectation to be christened Mellersh—was, it seemed, Mrs. Wilkins's husband, and therefore his place was clearly indicated. Why this talk? She herself, as if foreseeing his arrival, had had a second bed put in Mrs. Wilkins's room. There were certain things in life which were never talked about but only done. Most things connected with husbands were not talked about; and to have a whole dinner-table taken up with a discussion as to where one of them should sleep was an affront to the decencies. How and where husbands slept should be known only to their wives. Sometimes it was not known to them, and then the marriage had less happy moments; but these moments were not talked about either; the decencies continued to be preserved. At least, it was so in her day. To have to hear whether Mr. Wilkins should or should not sleep with Mrs. Wilkins, and the reasons why he should and the reasons why he shouldn't, was both uninteresting and indelicate.

She might have succeeded in imposing propriety and changing the conversation if it had not been for Lady Caroline. Lady Caroline encouraged Mrs. Wilkins, and threw herself into the discussion with every bit as much unreserve as Mrs. Wilkins herself. No doubt she was impelled on this occasion by Chianti, but whatever the reason there it was. And, characteristically, Lady Caroline was all for Mr. Wilkins being given the solitary spare-room. She took that for granted. Any other arrangement would be impossible, she said; her expression was, "Barbarous." Had she never read her Bible, Mrs. Fisher was tempted to inquire—*And they two shall be one flesh?* Clearly also, then, one room. But Mrs. Fisher did not inquire. She did not care even to allude to such texts to some one unmarried.

However, there was one way she could force Mr. Wilkins into his proper place and save the situation: she could say she herself intended to invite a friend. It was her right. They had all said so. Apart from propriety, it was monstrous that Mrs. Wilkins should want to monopolize the one spare-room, when in her own room was everything necessary for her husband. Perhaps she really would invite somebody—not invite, but suggest coming. There was Kate Lumley, for instance. Kate could perfectly afford to come and pay her share; and she was of her own period and knew, and had known, most of the people she herself knew and had known. Kate, of course, had only been on the fringe; she used to be asked only to the big parties, not to the small ones, and she still was only on the fringe. There were some people who never got off the fringe, and Kate was one. Often, however, such people were more permanently agreeable to be with than the others, in that they remained grateful.

Yes; she might really consider Kate. The poor soul had never married, but then everybody could not expect to marry, and she was quite comfortably off—not too comfortably, but just comfortably enough to pay her own expenses if she came and yet be grateful. Yes; Kate was the solution. If she came, at one stroke, Mrs. Fisher saw, would the Wilkinses be regularized and Mrs. Wilkins be prevented from having more than her share of the rooms. Also, Mrs. Fisher would save herself from isolation; spiritual isolation. She desired physical isolation between meals, but she disliked that isolation which is of the spirit. Such isolation would, she feared, certainly be hers with these three alien-minded young women. Even Mrs. Arbuthnot was, owing to her friendship with Mrs. Wilkins, necessarily alien-minded. In Kate she would have a support. Kate, without intruding on her sitting-room, for Kate was tractable, would be there at meals to support her.

Mrs. Fisher said nothing at the moment; but presently in the drawing-room, when they were gathered round the wood fire—she had discovered there was no fireplace in her own sitting-room, and therefore she would after all be forced, so long as the evenings remained cool, to spend them in the other room—presently, while Francesca was handing coffee round and Lady Caroline was poisoning the air with smoke, Mrs. Wilkins, looking relieved and pleased, said: "Well, if nobody really wants that room, and wouldn't use it anyhow, I shall be very glad if Mellersh may have it."

"Of course he must have it," said Lady Caroline.

Then Mrs. Fisher spoke.

"I have a friend," she said in her deep voice; and sudden silence fell upon the others.

"Kate Lumley," said Mrs. Fisher.

Nobody spoke.

"Perhaps," continued Mrs. Fisher, addressing Lady Caroline, "you know her?"

No, Lady Caroline did not know Kate Lumley; and Mrs. Fisher, without asking the others if they did, for she was sure they knew no one, proceeded. "I wish to invite her to join me," said Mrs. Fisher.

Complete silence.

Then Scrap said, turning to Mrs. Wilkins, "That settles Mellersh, then."

"It settles the question of Mr. Wilkins," said Mrs. Fisher, "although I am unable to understand that there should ever have been a question, in the only way that is right."

"I'm afraid you're in for it, then," said Lady Caroline, again to Mrs. Wilkins. "Unless," she added, "he can't come."

But Mrs. Wilkins, her brow perturbed—for suppose after all she were not yet quite stable in heaven?—could only say, a little uneasily, "I *see* him here."

CHAPTER 13

The uneventful days—only outwardly uneventful—slipped by in floods of sunshine, and the servants, watching the four ladies, came to the conclusion there was very little life in them.

To the servants San Salvatore seemed asleep. No one came to tea, nor did the ladies go anywhere to tea. Other tenants in other springs had been far more active. There had been stir and enterprise; the boat had been used; excursions had been made; Beppo's fly was ordered; people from Mezzago came over and spent the day; the house rang with voices; even sometimes champagne had been drunk. Life was varied, life was interesting. But this? What was this? The servants were not even scolded. They were left completely to themselves. They yawned.

Perplexing, too, was the entire absence of gentlemen. How could gentlemen keep away from so much beauty? For, added up, and even after the subtraction of the old one, the three younger ladies produced a formidable total of that which gentlemen usually sought.

Also the evident desire of each lady to spend long hours separated from the other ladies puzzled the servants. The result was a deathly stillness in the house, except at meal-times. It might have been as empty as it had been all the winter, for any sounds of life there were. The old lady sat in her room, alone; the dark-eyed lady wandered off alone, loitering, so Domenico told them, who sometimes came across her in the course of his duties, incomprehensibly among the rocks; the very beautiful fair lady lay in her low chair in the top garden, alone; the less, but still beautiful fair lady went up the hills and stayed up them for hours, alone; and every day the sun blazed slowly round the house, and disappeared at evening into the sea, and nothing at all had happened.

The servants yawned.

Yet the four visitors, while their bodies sat—that was Mrs. Fisher's—or lay—that was Lady Caroline's—or loitered—that was Mrs. Arbuthnot's—or went in solitude up into the hills—that was Mrs. Wilkins's—were anything but torpid really. Their minds were unusually busy. Even at night their minds were busy, and the dreams they had were clear, thin, quick things, entirely different from the heavy dreams of home. There was that in the atmosphere of San Salvatore which produced active-mindedness in all except the natives. They, as before, whatever the beauty around them, whatever the prodigal seasons did, remained immune from thoughts other than those they were accustomed to. All their lives they had seen, year by year, the amazing recurrent spectacle of April in the gardens, and custom had made it invisible to them. They were as blind to it, as unconscious of it, as Domenico's dog asleep in the sun.

The visitors could not be blind to it—it was too arresting after London in a particularly wet and gloomy March. Suddenly to be transported to that place where the air was so still that it held its breath, where the light was so golden that the most ordinary things were transfigured—to be transported into that delicate warmth, that caressing fragrance, and to have the old gray castle as the setting, and, in the distance, the serene clear hills of Perugini's backgrounds, was an astonishing contrast. Even Lady Caroline, used all her life to beauty, who had been everywhere and seen everything, felt the surprise of it. It was, that year, a particularly wonderful spring, and of all the months at San Salvatore, April, if the weather was fine, was best. May scorched and withered; March was restless, and could be hard and cold in its brightness; but April came along softly like a blessing, and if it were a fine April it was so beautiful that it was impossible not to feel different, not to feel stirred and touched.

Mrs. Wilkins, we have seen, responded to it instantly. She, so to speak, at once flung off all her garments and dived straight into glory, unhesitatingly, with a cry of rapture.

Mrs. Arbuthnot was stirred and touched, but differently. She had odd sensations—presently to be described.

Mrs. Fisher, being old, was of a closer, more impermeable texture, and offered more resistance; but she too had odd sensations, also in their place to be described.

Lady Caroline, already amply acquainted with beautiful houses and climates, to whom they could not come quite with the same surprise, yet was very nearly as quick to react as Mrs. Wilkins. The place had an almost instantaneous influence on her as well, and of one part of this influence she was aware: it had made her, beginning on the very first evening, want to think, and acted on her curiously like a conscience. What this conscience seemed to press upon her notice with an insistence that startled her—Lady Caroline hesitated to accept the word, but it would keep on coming into her head—was that she was tawdry.

Tawdry. She. Fancy.

She must think that out.

The morning after the first dinner together, she woke up in a condition of regret that she should have been so talkative to Mrs. Wilkins the night before. What had made her be, she wondered. Now, of course, Mrs. Wilkins would want to grab, she would want to be inseparable; and the thought of a grabbing and an inseparableness that should last four weeks made Scrap's spirit swoon within her. No doubt the encouraged Mrs. Wilkins would be lurking in the top garden waiting to waylay her when she went out, and would hail her with morning cheerfulness. How much she hated being hailed with morning cheerfulness—or indeed, hailed at all. She oughtn't to have encouraged Mrs. Wilkins the night before. Fatal to encourage. It was bad enough not to encourage, for just sitting there and saying nothing seemed usually to involve her, but actively to encourage was suicidal. What on earth had made her? Now she would have to waste all the precious time, the precious, lovely time for thinking in, for getting square with herself, in shaking Mrs. Wilkins off.

With great caution and on the tips of her toes, balancing herself carefully lest the pebbles should scrunch, she stole out when she was dressed to her corner; but the garden was empty. No shaking off was necessary. Neither Mrs. Wilkins nor anybody else was to be seen. She had it entirely to herself. Except for Domenico, who presently came and hovered, watering his plants, again especially all the plants that were nearest her, no one came out at all; and when, after a long while of following up thoughts which seemed to escape her just as she had got them, and dropping off exhausted to sleep in the intervals of this chase, she felt hungry and looked at her watch and saw that it was past three, she realized that nobody had even bothered to call her in to lunch. So that, Scrap could not but remark, if any one was shaken off it was she herself.

Well, but how delightful, and how very new. Now she would really be able to think, uninterruptedly. Delicious to be forgotten.

Still, she was hungry; and Mrs. Wilkins, after that excessive friendliness the night before, might at least have told her lunch was ready. And she had really been excessively friendly—so nice about Mellersh's sleeping arrangements, wanting him to have the spare-room and all. She wasn't usually interested in arrangements, in fact she wasn't ever interested in them; so that Scrap considered she might be said almost to have gone out of her way to be agreeable to Mrs. Wilkins. And, in return, Mrs. Wilkins didn't even bother whether or not she had any lunch.

Fortunately, though she was hungry, she didn't mind missing a meal. Life was full of meals. They took up an enormous proportion of one's time; and Mrs. Fisher was, she was afraid, one of those persons who at meals linger. Twice now had she dined with Mrs. Fisher, and each time she had been difficult at the end to dislodge, lingering on slowly cracking innumerable nuts and slowly drinking a glass of wine that seemed as if it would never be finished. Probably it would be a good thing to make a habit of missing lunch, and as it was quite easy to have tea brought out to her, and as she breakfasted in her room, only once a day would she have to sit at the dining-room table and endure the nuts.

Scrap burrowed her head comfortably in the cushions, and with her feet crossed on the low parapet gave herself up to more thought. She said to herself, as she had said at intervals throughout the morning: Now I'm going to think. But, never having thought out anything in her life, it was difficult. Extraordinary how one's attention wouldn't stay fixed; extraordinary how one's mind slipped sideways. Settling herself down to a review of her past as a preliminary to the consideration of her future, and hunting in it to begin with for any justification of that distressing word tawdry, the next thing she knew was that she wasn't thinking about this at all, but had somehow switched on to Mr. Wilkins.

Well, Mr. Wilkins was quite easy to think about, though not pleasant. She viewed his approach with misgivings. For not only was it a profound and unexpected bore to have a man added to the party, and a man, too, of the kind she was sure Mr. Wilkins must be, but she was afraid—and her fear was the result of a drearily unvarying experience—that he might wish to hang about her.

This possibility had evidently not yet occurred to Mrs. Wilkins, and it was not one to which she could very well draw her attention; not, that is, without being too fatuous to live. She tried to hope that Mr. Wilkins would be a wonderful exception to the dreadful rule. If only he were, she would be so much obliged to him that she believed she might really quite like him.

But—she had misgivings. Suppose he hung about her so that she was driven from her lovely top garden; suppose the light in Mrs. Wilkins's funny, flickering face was blown out. Scrap felt she would particularly dislike this to happen to Mrs. Wilkins's face, yet she had never in her life met any wives, not any at all, who had been able to understand that she didn't in the least want their husbands. Often she had met wives who didn't want their husbands either, but that made them none the less indignant if they thought somebody else did, and none the less sure, when they saw them hanging round Scrap, that she was trying to get them. Trying to get them! The bare thought, the bare recollection of these situations, filled her with a boredom so extreme that it instantly sent her to sleep again.

When she woke up she went on with Mr. Wilkins.

Now if, thought Scrap, Mr. Wilkins were not an exception and behaved in the usual way, would Mrs. Wilkins understand, or would it just simply spoil her holiday? She seemed quick, but would she be quick about just this? She seemed to understand and see inside one, but would she understand and see inside one when it came to Mr. Wilkins?

The experienced Scrap was full of doubts. She shifted her feet on the parapet; she jerked a cushion straight. Perhaps she had better try and explain to Mrs. Wilkins, during the days still remaining before the arrival—explain in a general way, rather vague and talking at large—her attitude towards such things. She might also expound to her her peculiar dislike of people's husbands, and her profound craving to be, at least for this one month, let alone.

But Scrap had her doubts about this too. Such talk meant a certain familiarity, meant embarking on a friendship with Mrs. Wilkins; and if, after having embarked on it and faced the peril it contained of too much Mrs. Wilkins, Mr. Wilkins should turn out to be artful—and people did get very artful when they were set on anything—and manage after all to slip through into the top garden, Mrs. Wilkins might easily believe she had been taken in, and that she, Scrap, was deceitful. Deceitful! And about Mr. Wilkins. Wives were really pathetic.

At half-past four she heard sounds of saucers on the other side of the daphne bushes. Was tea being sent out to her?

No; the sounds came no closer, they stopped near the house. Tea was to be in the garden, in her garden. Scrap considered she might at least have been asked if she minded being disturbed. They all knew she sat there.

Perhaps some one would bring hers to her in her corner.

No; nobody brought anything.

Well, she was too hungry not to go and have it with the others to-day, but she would give Francesca strict orders for the future.

She got up, and walked with that slow grace which was another of her outrageous number of attractions towards the sounds of tea. She was conscious not only of being very hungry but of wanting to talk to Mrs. Wilkins again. Mrs. Wilkins had not grabbed, she had left her quite free all day in spite of the *rapprochement* the night before. Of course she was an original, and put on a silk jumper for dinner, but she hadn't grabbed. This was a great thing. Scrap went towards the tea-table quite looking forward to Mrs. Wilkins; and when she came in sight of it she saw only Mrs. Fisher and Mrs. Arbuthnot.

Mrs. Fisher was pouring out the tea, and Mrs. Arbuthnot was offering Mrs. Fisher macaroons. Every time Mrs. Fisher offered Mrs. Arbuthnot anything—her cup, or milk, or sugar—Mrs. Arbuthnot offered her macaroons—pressed them on her with an odd assiduousness, almost with obstinacy. "Was it a game?" Scrap wondered, sitting down and seizing a macaroon.

"Where is Mrs. Wilkins?" asked Scrap.

They did not know. At least, Mrs. Arbuthnot, on Scrap's inquiry, did not know; Mrs. Fisher's face, at the name, became elaborately uninterested.

It appeared that Mrs. Wilkins had not been seen since breakfast. Mrs. Arbuthnot thought she had probably gone for a picnic. Scrap missed her. She ate the enormous macaroons, the best and biggest she had ever come across, in silence. Tea without Mrs. Wilkins was dull; and Mrs. Arbuthnot had that fatal flavor of motherliness about her, of wanting to pet one, to make one very comfortable, coaxing one to eat—coaxing her, who was already so frankly, so even excessively, eating—that seemed to have dogged Scrap's steps through life. Couldn't people leave one alone? She was perfectly able to eat what she wanted unincited. She tried to quench Mrs. Arbuthnot's zeal by being short with her. Useless. The shortness was not apparent. It remained, as all Scrap's evil feelings remained, covered up by the impenetrable veil of her loveliness.

Mrs. Fisher sat monumentally, and took no notice of either of them. She had had a curious day, and was a little worried. She had been quite alone, for none of the three had come to lunch, and none of them had taken the trouble to let her know they were not coming; and Mrs. Arbuthnot, drifting casually into tea, had behaved oddly till Lady Caroline joined them and distracted her attention.

Mrs. Fisher was prepared not to dislike Mrs. Arbuthnot, whose parted hair and mild expression seemed very decent and womanly, but she certainly had habits that were difficult to like. Her habit of instantly echoing any offer made her of food or drink, of throwing the offer back on one, as it were, was not somehow what one expected of her. "Will you have some more tea?" was surely a question to which the answer was simply yes or no; but Mrs. Arbuthnot persisted in the trick she had exhibited the day before at breakfast, of adding to her yes or no the words, "Will *you?*" She had done it again that morning at breakfast and here she was doing it at tea—the two meals at which Mrs. Fisher presided and poured out. Why did she do it? Mrs. Fisher failed to understand.

But this was not what was worrying her; this was merely by the way. What was worrying her was that she had been quite unable that day to settle to anything, and had done nothing but wander restlessly from her sitting-room to her battlements and back again. It had been a wasted day, and how much she disliked waste. She had tried to read, and she had tried to write to Kate Lumley; but no—a few words read, a few lines written, and up she got again and went out on to the battlements and stared at the sea.

It did not matter that the letter to Kate Lumley should not be written. There was time enough for that. Let the others suppose her coming was definitely fixed. All the better. So would Mr. Wilkins be kept out of the spare-room and put where he belonged. Kate would keep. She could be held in reserve. Kate in reserve was just as potent as Kate in actuality, and there were points about Kate in reserve which might be missing from Kate in actuality. For instance, if Mrs. Fisher were going to be restless, she would rather Kate were not there to see. There was a want of dignity about restlessness, about trotting backwards and forwards. But it did matter that she could not read a sentence of any of her great dead friends' writings; no, not even of Browning's, who had been so much in Italy, nor of Ruskin's, whose *Stones of Venice* she had brought with her to re-read so nearly on the very spot; nor even a sentence of a really interesting book like the one she had found in her sitting-room about the home life of the German Emperor, poor man—written in the nineties, when he had not yet begun to be more sinned against than sinning, which was, she was firmly convinced, what was the matter with him now, and full of exciting things about his birth and his right arm and *accoucheurs*—without having to put it down and go and stare at the sea.

Reading was very important; the proper exercise and development of one's mind was a paramount duty. How could one read if one were constantly trotting in and out? Curious, this restlessness. Was she going to be ill? No, she felt well; indeed, unusually well, and she went in and out quite quickly—trotted, in fact—and without her stick. Very odd that she shouldn't be able to sit still, she thought, frowning across the tops of some purple hyacinths at the Gulf of Spezia glittering beyond a headland; very odd that she, who walked so slowly, with such dependence on her stick, should suddenly trot.

It would be interesting to talk to some one about it, she felt. Not to Kate—to a stranger. Kate would only look at her and suggest a cup of tea. Kate always suggested cups of tea. Besides, Kate had a flat face. That Mrs. Wilkins, now—annoying as she was, loose-tongued as she was, impertinent, objectionable, would probably understand, and perhaps know what was making her be like this. But she could say nothing to Mrs. Wilkins. She was the last person to whom one would admit sensations. Dignity alone forbade it. Confide in Mrs. Wilkins? Never.

And Mrs. Arbuthnot, while she wistfully mothered the obstructive Scrap at tea, felt too that she had had a curious day. Like Mrs. Fisher's, it had been active, but, unlike Mrs. Fisher's, only active in mind. Her body had been quite still; her mind had not been still at all, it had been excessively active. For years she had taken care to have no time to think. Her scheduled life in the parish had prevented memories and desires from intruding on her. That day they had crowded. She went back to tea feeling dejected, and that she should feel dejected in such a place with everything about her to make her rejoice, only dejected her the more. But how could she rejoice alone? How could anybody rejoice and enjoy and appreciate, really appreciate, alone? Except Lotty. Lotty seemed able to. She had gone off down the hill directly after breakfast, alone yet obviously rejoicing, for she had not suggested that Rose should go too, and she was singing as she went.

Rose had spent the day by herself, sitting with her hands clasping her knees, staring straight in front of her. What she was staring at were the gray swords of the agaves, and, on their tall stalks, the pale irises that grew in the remote place she had found, while beyond them, between the gray leaves and the blue flowers, she saw the sea. The place she had found was a hidden corner where the sun-baked stones were padded with thyme, and nobody was likely to come. It was out of sight and sound of the house; it was off any path; it was near the end of the promontory. She sat so quiet that presently lizards darted over her feet, and some tiny birds like finches, frightened away at first, came back again and flitted among the bushes round her just as if she hadn't been there. How beautiful it was. And what was the good of it with no one there, no one who loved being with one, who belonged to one, to whom one could say, "Look." And wouldn't one say, "Look—*dearest?*" Yes, one would say *dearest*, and the sweet word, just to say it to somebody who loved one, would make one happy.

She sat quite still, staring straight in front of her. Strange that in this place she did not want to pray. She who had prayed so constantly at home didn't seem able to do it here at all. The first morning she had merely thrown up a brief thank you to heaven on getting out of bed, and had gone straight to the window to see what everything looked like—thrown up the thank you as carelessly as a ball, and thought no more about it. That morning, remembering this and ashamed, she had knelt down with determination; but perhaps determination was bad for prayers, for she had been unable to think of a thing to say. And as for her bedtime prayers, on neither of the nights had she said a single one. She had forgotten them. She had been so much absorbed in other thoughts that she had forgotten them; and, once in bed, she was asleep and whirling along among bright, thin, swift dreams before she had so much time as to stretch herself out.

What had come over her? Why had she let go the anchor of prayer? And she had difficulty, too, in remembering her poor, in remembering even that there were such things as poor. Holidays, of course, were good, and were recognized by everybody as good, but ought they so completely to blot out, to make such havoc of, the realities? Perhaps it was healthy to forget her poor; with all the greater gusto would she go back to them. But it couldn't be healthy to forget her prayers, and still less could it be healthy not to mind.

Rose did not mind. She knew she did not mind. And, even worse, she knew she did not mind not minding. In this place she was indifferent to both the things that had filled her life and made it seem as if it were happy for years. Well, if only she could rejoice in her wonderful new surroundings, have that much at least to set against the indifference, the letting go—but she could not. She had no work; she did not pray; she was left empty.

Lotty had spoilt her day that day, as she had spoilt her day the day before—Lotty, with her invitation to her husband, with her suggestion that she too should invite hers. Having flung Frederick into her mind again the day before, Lotty had left her; for the whole afternoon she had left her alone with her thoughts. Since then they had been all of Frederick. Where at Hampstead he came to her only in her dreams, here he left her dreams free and was with her during the day instead. And again that morning, as she was struggling not to think of him, Lotty had asked her, just before disappearing singing down the path, if she had written yet and invited him, and again he was flung into her mind and she wasn't able to get him out.

How could she invite him? It had gone on so long, their estrangement, such years; she would hardly know what words to use; and besides, he would not come. Why should he come? He didn't care about being with her. What could they talk about? Between them was the barrier of his work and her religion. She could not—how could she, believing as she did in purity, in responsibility for the effect of one's actions on others—bear his work, bear living by it; and he, she knew, had at first resented and then been merely bored by her religion. He had let her slip away; he had given her up; he no longer minded; he accepted her religion indifferently, as a settled fact. Both it and she—Rose's mind, becoming more luminous in the clear light of April at San Salvatore, suddenly saw the truth—bored him.

Naturally when she saw this, when that morning it flashed upon her for the first time, she did not like it; she liked it so little that for a space the whole beauty of Italy was blotted out. What was to be done about it? She could not give up believing in good and not liking evil, and it must be evil to live entirely on the proceeds of adulteries, however dead and distinguished they were. Besides, if she did, if she sacrificed her whole past, her bringing up, her work for the last ten years, would she bore him less? Rose felt right down at her very roots that if you have once thoroughly bored somebody it is next to impossible to unbore him. Once a bore always a bore—certainly, she thought, to the person originally bored.

Then, thought she, looking out to sea through eyes grown misty, better cling to her religion. It was better—she hardly noticed the reprehensibleness of her thought—than nothing. But oh, she wanted to cling to something tangible, to love something living, something that one could hold against one's heart, that one could see and touch and do things for. If her poor baby hadn't died . . . babies didn't get bored with one, it took them a long while to grow up and find one out. And perhaps one's baby never did find one out; perhaps one would always be to it, however old and bearded it grew, somebody special, somebody different from every one else, and if for no other reason, precious in that one could never be repeated.

Sitting with dim eyes looking out to sea she felt an extraordinary yearning to hold something of her very own tight to her bosom.

Rose was slender, and as reserved in figure as in character, yet she felt a queer sensation of—how could she describe it?—bosom. There was something about San Salvatore that made her feel all bosom. She wanted to gather to her bosom, to comfort and protect, soothing the dear head that should lie on it with softest strokings and murmurs of love. Frederick, Frederick's child—come to her, pillowed on her, because they were unhappy, because they had been hurt . . . They would need her then, if they had been hurt; they would let themselves be loved then, if they were unhappy.

Well, the child was gone, would never come now; but perhaps Frederick—some day—when he was old and tired . . .

Such were Mrs. Arbuthnot's reflections and emotions that first day at San Salvatore by herself. She went back to tea dejected as she had not been for years. San Salvatore had taken her carefully built-up semblance of happiness away from her, and given her nothing in exchange. Yes—it had given her yearnings in exchange, this ache and longing, this queer feeling of bosom; but that was worse than nothing. And she who had learned balance, who never at home was irritated but always able to be kind, could not, even in her dejection, that afternoon endure Mrs. Fisher's assumption of the position as hostess at tea.

One would have supposed that such a little thing would not have touched her, but it did. Was her nature changing? Was she to be not only thrown back on long-stifled yearnings after Frederick, but also turned into somebody who wanted to fight over little things? After tea, when both Mrs. Fisher and Lady Caroline had disappeared again—it was quite evident that nobody wanted her—she was more dejected than ever, overwhelmed by the discrepancy between the splendor outside her, the warm, teeming beauty and self-sufficiency of nature, and the blank emptiness of her heart.

Then came Lotty, back to dinner, incredibly more freckled, exuding the sunshine she had been collecting all day, talking, laughing, being tactless, being unwise, being without reticence; and Lady Caroline, so quiet at tea, woke up to animation, and Mrs. Fisher was not so noticeable, and Rose was beginning to revive a little, for Lotty's spirits were contagious as she described the delights of her day, a day which might easily to any one else have had nothing in it but a very long and very hot walk and sandwiches, when she suddenly said, catching Rose's eye, "Letter gone?"

Rose flushed. This tactlessness . . .

"What letter?" asked Scrap, interested. Both her elbows were on the table and her chin was supported in her hands, for the nut-stage had been reached, and there was nothing for it but to wait in as comfortable a position as possible till Mrs. Fisher had finished cracking.

"Asking her husband here," said Lotty.

Mrs. Fisher looked up. Another husband? Was there to be no end to them? Nor was this one, then, a widow either; but her husband was no doubt a decent, respectable man, following a decent, respectable calling. She had little hope of Mr. Wilkins; so little, that she had refrained from inquiring what he did.

"Has it?" persisted Lotty, as Rose said nothing.

"No," said Rose.

"Oh, well—to-morrow then," said Lotty.

Rose wanted to say no again to this. Lotty would have in her place, and would, besides, have expounded all her reasons. But she could not turn herself inside out like that and invite any and everybody to come and look. How was it that Lotty, who saw so many things, didn't see stuck on her heart, and seeing keep quiet about it, the sore place that was Frederick?

"Who is your husband?" asked Mrs. Fisher, carefully adjusting another nut between the crackers.

"Who should he be," said Rose quickly, roused at once by Mrs. Fisher to irritation, "except *Mr.* Arbuthnot?"

"I mean, of course, what is Mr. Arbuthnot?"

And Rose, gone painfully red at this, said after a tiny pause, "My husband."

Naturally, Mrs. Fisher was incensed. She couldn't have believed it of this one, with her decent hair and gentle voice, that she too should be impertinent.

CHAPTER 14

That first week the wistaria began to fade, and the flowers of the Judas tree and peach-trees fell off and carpeted the ground with rose-color. Then all the freesias disappeared, and the irises grew scarce. And then, while these were clearing themselves away, the double banksia roses came out, and the big summer roses suddenly flaunted gorgeously on the walls and trellises. Fortune's Yellow was one of them; a very beautiful rose. Presently the tamarisk and the daphnes were at their best, and the lilies at their tallest. By the end of the week the fig-trees were giving shade, the plum-blossom was out among the olives, the modest weigelias appeared in their fresh pink clothes, and on the rocks sprawled masses of thick-leaved, star-shaped flowers, some vivid purple and some a clear, pale lemon.

By the end of the week, too, Mr. Wilkins arrived; even as his wife had foreseen he would, so he did. And there were signs almost of eagerness about his acceptance of her suggestion, for he had not waited to write a letter in answer to hers, but had telegraphed.

That, surely, was eager. It showed, Scrap thought, a definite wish for reunion; and watching his wife's happy face, and aware of her desire that Mellersh should enjoy his holiday, she told herself that he would be a very unusual fool should he waste his time bothering about anybody else. "If he isn't nice to her," Scrap thought, "he shall be taken to the battlements and tipped over." For, by the end of the week, she and Mrs. Wilkins had become Caroline and Lotty to each other, and were friends.

Mrs. Wilkins had always been friends, but Scrap had struggled not to be. She had tried hard to be cautious, but how difficult was caution with Mrs. Wilkins! Free herself from every vestige of it, she was so entirely unreserved, so completely expansive, that soon Scrap, almost before she knew what she was doing, was being unreserved too. And nobody could be more unreserved than Scrap, once she let herself go.

The only difficulty about Lotty was that she was nearly always somewhere else. You couldn't catch her; you couldn't pin her down to come and talk. Scrap's fears that she would grab seemed grotesque in retrospect. Why, there was no grab in her. At dinner and after dinner were the only times one really saw her. All day long she was invisible, and would come back in the late afternoon looking a perfect sight, her hair full of bits of moss, and her freckles worse than ever. Perhaps she was making the most of her time before Mellersh arrived to do all the things she wanted to do, and meant to devote herself afterwards to going about with him, tidy and in her best clothes.

Scrap watched her, interested in spite of herself, because it seemed so extraordinary to be as happy as all that on so little. San Salvatore was beautiful, and the weather was divine; but scenery and weather had never been enough for Scrap, and how could they be enough for somebody who would have to leave them quite soon and go back to life in Hampstead? Also, there was the imminence of Mellersh, of that Mellersh from whom Lotty had so lately run. It was all very well to feel one ought to share, and to make a *beau geste* and do it, but the *beaux gestes* Scrap had known hadn't made anybody happy. Nobody really liked being the object of one, and it always meant an effort on the part of the maker. Still, she had to admit there was no effort about Lotty; it was quite plain that everything she did and said was effortless, and that she was just simply, completely happy.

And so Mrs. Wilkins was; for her doubts as to whether she had had time to become steady enough in serenity to go on being serene in Mellersh's company when she had it uninterruptedly right round the clock, had gone by the middle of the week, and she felt that nothing now could shake her. She was ready for anything. She was firmly grafted, rooted, built into heaven. Whatever Mellersh said or did, she would not budge an inch out of heaven, would not rouse herself a single instant to come outside it and be cross. On the contrary, she was going to pull him up into it beside her, and they would sit comfortably together, suffused in light, and laugh at how much afraid of him she used to be in Hampstead, and at how deceitful her afraidness had made her. But he wouldn't need much pulling. He would come in quite naturally after a day or two, irresistibly wafted on the scented breezes of that divine air; and there he would sit arrayed in stars, thought Mrs. Wilkins, in whose mind, among much other *débris*, floated occasional bright shreds of poetry. She laughed to herself a little at the picture of Mellersh, that top-hatted, black-coated, respectable family solicitor, arrayed in stars, but she laughed affectionately, almost with a maternal pride in how splendid he would look in such fine clothes. "Poor lamb," she murmured to herself affectionately. And added, "What he wants is a thorough airing."

This was during the first half of the week. By the beginning of the last half, at the end of which Mr. Wilkins arrived, she left off even assuring herself that she was unshakeable, that she was permeated beyond altering by the atmosphere, she no longer thought of it or noticed it; she took it for granted. If one may say so, and she certainly said so, not only to herself but also to Lady Caroline, she had found her celestial legs.

Contrary to Mrs. Fisher's idea of the seemly—but of course contrary; what else would one expect of Mrs. Wilkins?—she did not go to meet her husband at Mezzago, but merely walked down to the point where Beppo's fly would leave him and his luggage in the street of Castagneto. Mrs. Fisher disliked the arrival of Mr. Wilkins, and was sure that anybody who could have married Mrs. Wilkins must be at least of an injudicious disposition, but a husband, whatever his disposition, should be properly met. Mr. Fisher had always been properly met. Never once in his married life had he gone unmet at a station, nor had he ever not been seen off. These observances, these courtesies, strengthened the bonds of marriage, and made the husband feel he could rely on his wife's being always there. Always being there was the essential secret for a wife. What would have become of Mr. Fisher if she had neglected to act on this principle she preferred not to think. Enough things became of him as it was; for whatever one's care in stopping up, married life yet seemed to contain chinks.

But Mrs. Wilkins took no pains. She just walked down the hill singing—Mrs. Fisher could hear her—and picked up her husband in the street as casually as if he were a pin. The three others, still in bed, for it was not nearly time to get up, heard her as she passed beneath their windows down the zigzag path to meet Mr. Wilkins, who was coming by the morning train, and Scrap smiled, and Rose sighed, and Mrs. Fisher rang her bell and desired Francesca to bring her her breakfast in her room. All three had breakfast that day in their rooms, moved by a common instinct to take cover.

Scrap always breakfasted in bed, but she had the same instinct for cover, and during breakfast she made plans for spending the whole day where she was. Perhaps, though, it wouldn't be as necessary that day as the next. That day, Scrap calculated, Mellersh would be provided for. He would want to have a bath, and having a bath at San Salvatore was an elaborate business, a real adventure if one had a hot one in the bathroom, and it took a lot of time. It involved the attendance of the entire staff—Domenico and the boy Giuseppe coaxing the patent stove to burn, restraining it when it burnt too fiercely, using the bellows to it when it threatened to go out, relighting it when it did go out; Francesca anxiously hovering over the tap regulating its trickle, because if it were turned on too full the water instantly ran cold, and if not full enough the stove blew up inside and mysteriously flooded the house; and Costanza and Angela running up and down bringing pails of hot water from the kitchen to eke out what the tap did.

This bath had been put in lately, and was at once the pride and the terror of the servants. It was very patent. Nobody quite understood it. There were long printed instructions as to its right treatment hanging on the wall, in which the word *pericoloso* recurred. When Mrs. Fisher, proceeding on her arrival to the bathroom, saw this word, she went back to her room again and ordered a sponge-bath instead; and when the others found what using the bathroom meant, and how reluctant the servants were to leave them alone with the stove, and how Francesca positively refused to, and stayed with her back turned watching the tap, and how the remaining servants waited anxiously outside the door till the bather came safely out again, they too had sponge-baths brought into their rooms instead.

Mr. Wilkins, however, was a man, and would be sure to want a big bath. Having it, Scrap calculated, would keep him busy for a long while. Then he would unpack, and then, after his night in the train, he would probably sleep till the evening. So would he be provided for the whole of that day, and not be let loose on them till dinner.

Therefore Scrap came to the conclusion she would be quite safe in the garden that day, and got up as usual after breakfast, and dawdled as usual through her dressing, listening with a slightly cocked ear to the sounds of Mr. Wilkins's arrival, of his luggage being carried into Lotty's room on the other side of the landing, of his educated voice as he inquired of Lotty, first, "Do I give this fellow anything?" and immediately afterwards, "Can I have a hot bath?"—of Lotty's voice cheerfully assuring him that he needn't give the fellow anything because he was the gardener, and that yes, he could have a hot bath; and soon after this the landing was filled with the familiar noises of wood being brought, of water being brought, of feet running, of tongues vociferating—in fact, with the preparation of the bath.

Scrap finished dressing, and then loitered at her window, waiting till she should hear Mr. Wilkins go into the bathroom. When he was safely there she would slip out and settle herself in her garden and resume her inquiries into the probable meaning of her life. She was getting on with her inquiries. She dozed much less frequently, and was beginning to be inclined to agree that tawdry was the word to apply to her past. Also she was afraid that her future looked black.

There—she could hear Mr. Wilkins's educated voice again. Lotty's door had opened, and he was coming out of it asking his way to the bathroom.

"It's where you see the crowd," Lotty's voice answered—still a cheerful voice, Scrap was glad to notice.

His steps went along the landing, and Lotty's steps seemed to go downstairs, and then there seemed to be a brief altercation at the bathroom door—hardly so much an altercation as a chorus of vociferations on one side and a wordless determination, Scrap judged, to have a bath by oneself on the other.

Mr. Wilkins knew no Italian, and the expression *pericoloso* left him precisely as it found him—or would have if he had seen it, but naturally he took no notice of the printed matter on the wall. He firmly closed the door on the servants, resisting Domenico, who tried to the last to press through, and locked himself in as a man should for his bath, judicially considering, as he made his simple preparations for getting in, the singular standard of behavior of these foreigners who, both male and female, apparently wished to stay with him while he bathed. In Finland, he had heard, the female natives not only were present on such occasions but actually washed the bath-taking traveler. He had not heard, however, that this was true too of Italy, which somehow seemed much nearer civilization—perhaps because one went there, and did not go to Finland.

Impartially examining this reflection, and carefully balancing the claims to civilization of Italy and Finland, Mr. Wilkins got into the bath and turned off the tap. Naturally he turned off the tap. It was what one did. But on the instructions, printed in red letters, was a paragraph saying that the tap should not be turned off as long as there was still fire in the stove. It should be left on—not much on, but on—until the fire was quite out; otherwise, and here again was the word *pericoloso*, the stove would blow up.

Mr. Wilkins got into the bath, turned off the tap, and the stove blew up, exactly as the printed instructions said it would. It blew up, fortunately, only in its inside, but it blew up with a terrific noise, and Mr. Wilkins leapt out of the bath and rushed to the door, and only the instinct born of years of training made him snatch up a towel as he rushed.

Scrap, half-way across the landing on her way out of doors, heard the explosion.

"Good heavens," she thought, remembering the instructions, "there goes Mr. Wilkins!"

And she ran toward the head of the stairs to call the servants, and as she ran, out ran Mr. Wilkins clutching his towel, and they ran into each other.

"That damned bath!" cried Mr. Wilkins, perhaps for the only time in his life forgetting himself; but he was upset.

Here was an introduction. Mr Wilkins, imperfectly concealed in his towel, his shoulders exposed at one end and his legs at the other, and Lady Caroline Dester, to meet whom he had swallowed all his anger with his wife and come out to Italy.

For Lotty in her letter had told him who was at San Salvatore besides herself and Mrs. Arbuthnot, and Mr. Wilkins at once had perceived that this was an opportunity which might never recur. Lotty had merely said, "There are two other women here, Mrs. Fisher and Lady Caroline Dester," but that was enough. He knew all about the Droitwiches, their wealth, their connections, their place in history, and the power they had, should they choose to exert it, of making yet another solicitor happy by adding him to those they already employed. Some people employed one solicitor for one branch of their affairs, and another for another. The affairs of the Droitwiches must have many branches. He had also heard—for it was, he considered, part of his business to hear, and having heard to remember—of the beauty of their only daughter. Even if the Droitwiches themselves did not need his services, their daughter might. Beauty led one into strange situations; advice could never come amiss. And should none of them, neither parents nor daughter nor any of their brilliant sons, need him in his professional capacity, it yet was obviously a most valuable acquaintance to make. It opened up vistas. It swelled with possibilities. He might go on living in Hampstead for years, and not again come across such another chance.

Directly his wife's letter reached him he telegraphed and packed. This was business. He was not a man to lose time when it came to business; nor was he a man to jeopardize a chance by neglecting to be amiable. He met his wife perfectly amiably, aware that amiability under such circumstances was wisdom. Besides, he actually felt amiable—very. For once, Lotty was really helping him. He kissed her affectionately on getting out of Beppo's fly, and was afraid she must have got up extremely early; he made no complaints of the steepness of the walk up; he told her pleasantly of his journey, and when called upon, obediently admired the views. It was all neatly mapped out in his mind, what he was going to do that first day—have a shave, have a bath, put on clean clothes, sleep a while, and then would come lunch and the introduction to Lady Caroline.

In the train he had selected the words of his greeting, going over them with care—some slight expression of his gratification in meeting one of whom he, in common with the whole world, had heard—but of course put delicately, very delicately; some slight reference to her distinguished parents and the part her family had played in the history of England—made, of course, with proper tact; a sentence or two about her eldest brother Lord Winchcombe, who had won his V.C. in the late war under circumstances which could only cause—he might or might not add this—every Englishman's heart to beat higher than ever with pride, and the first steps towards what might well be the turning-point in his career would have been taken.

And here he was . . . no, it was too terrible, what could be more terrible? Only a towel on, water running off his legs, and that exclamation. He knew at once the lady was Lady Caroline—the minute the exclamation was out he knew it. Rarely did Mr. Wilkins use that word, and never, never in the presence of a lady or a client. While as for the towel—why had he come? Why had he not stayed in Hampstead? It would be impossible to live this down.

But Mr. Wilkins was reckoning without Scrap. She, indeed, screwed up her face at the first flash of him on her astonished sight in an enormous effort not to laugh, and having choked the laughter down and got her face serious again, she said as composedly as if he had had all his clothes on, "How do you do."

What perfect tact. Mr. Wilkins could have worshipped her. This exquisite ignoring. Blue blood, of course, coming out.

Overwhelmed with gratitude he took her offered hand and said "How do you do," in his turn, and merely to repeat the ordinary words seemed magically to restore the situation to the normal. Indeed, he was so much relieved, and it was so natural to be shaking hands, to be conventionally greeting, that he forgot he had only a towel on and his professional manner came back to him. He forgot what he was looking like, but he did not forget that this was Lady Caroline Dester, the lady he had come all the way to Italy to see, and he did not forget that it was in her face, her lovely and important face, that he had flung his terrible exclamation. He must at once entreat her forgiveness. To say such a word to a lady—to any lady, but of all ladies to just this one . . .

"I'm afraid I used unpardonable language," began Mr. Wilkins very earnestly, as earnestly and ceremoniously as if he had had his clothes on.

"I thought it most appropriate," said Scrap, who was used to damns.

Mr. Wilkins was incredibly relieved and soothed by this answer. No offence, then, taken. Blue blood again. Only blue blood could afford such a liberal, such an understanding attitude.

"It is Lady Caroline Dester, is it not, to whom I am speaking?" he asked, his voice sounding even more carefully cultivated than usual, for he had to restrain too much pleasure, too much relief, too much of the joy of the pardoned and the shriven from getting into it.

"Yes," said Scrap; and for the life of her she couldn't help smiling. She couldn't help it. She hadn't meant to smile at Mr. Wilkins, not ever; but really he looked—and then his voice on the top of the rest of him, oblivious of the towel and his legs, and talking just like a church.

"Allow me to introduce myself," said Mr. Wilkins, with the ceremony of the drawing-room. "My name is Mellersh-Wilkins."

And he instinctively held out his hand a second time at the words.

"I thought perhaps it was," said Scrap, a second time having hers shaken and a second time unable not to smile.

He was about to proceed to the first of the graceful tributes he had prepared in the train, oblivious, as he could not see himself, that he was without his clothes, when the servants came running up the stairs and, simultaneously, Mrs. Fisher appeared in the doorway of her sitting-room. For all this had happened very quickly, and the servants away in the kitchen, and Mrs. Fisher pacing her battlements, had not had time on hearing the noise to appear before the second handshake.

The servants when they heard the dreaded noise knew at once what had happened, and rushed straight into the bathroom to try and staunch the flood, taking no notice of the figure on the landing in the towel, but Mrs. Fisher did not know what the noise could be, and coming out of her room to inquire stood rooted on the door-sill.

It was enough to root anybody. Lady Caroline shaking hands with what evidently, if he had had clothes on, would have been Mrs. Wilkins's husband, and both of them conversing just as if—

Then Scrap became aware of Mrs. Fisher. She turned to her at once. "Do let me," she said gracefully, "introduce Mr. Mellersh-Wilkins. He has just come. This," she added, turning to Mr. Wilkins, "is Mrs. Fisher."

And Mr. Wilkins, nothing if not courteous, reacted at once to the conventional formula. First he bowed to the elderly lady in the doorway, then he crossed over to her, his wet feet leaving footprints as he went, and having got to her he politely held out his hand.

"It is a pleasure," said Mr. Wilkins in his carefully modulated voice, "to meet a friend of my wife's."

Scrap melted away down into the garden.

CHAPTER 15

The strange effect of this incident was that when they met that evening at dinner both Mrs. Fisher and Lady Caroline had a singular feeling of secret understanding with Mr. Wilkins. He could not be to them as other men. He could not be to them as he would have been if they had met him in his clothes. There was a sense of broken ice; they felt at once intimate and indulgent; almost they felt to him as nurses do—as those feel who have assisted either patients or young children at their baths. They were acquainted with Mr. Wilkins's legs.

What Mrs. Fisher said to him that morning in her first shock will never be known, but what Mr. Wilkins said to her in reply, when reminded by what she was saying of his condition, was so handsome in its apology, so proper in its confusion, that she had ended by being quite sorry for him and completely placated. After all, it was an accident, and nobody could help accidents. And when she saw him next at dinner, dressed, polished, spotless as to linen and sleek as to hair, she felt this singular sensation of a secret understanding with him and, added to it, of a kind of almost personal pride in his appearance, now that he was dressed, which presently extended in some subtle way to an almost personal pride in everything he said.

There was no doubt whatever in Mrs. Fisher's mind that a man was infinitely preferable as a companion to a woman. Mr. Wilkins's presence and conversation at once raised the standard of the dinner-table from that of a bear garden—yes, a bear garden—to that of a civilized social gathering. He talked as men talk, about interesting subjects, and, though most courteous to Lady Caroline, showed no traces of dissolving into simpers and idiocy whenever he addressed her. He was, indeed, precisely as courteous to Mrs. Fisher herself; and when for the first time at that table politics were introduced, he listened to her with the proper seriousness on her exhibiting a desire to speak, and treated her opinions with the attention they deserved. He appeared to think much as she did about Lloyd George, and in regard to literature he was equally sound. In fact there was real conversation, and he liked nuts. How he could have married Mrs. Wilkins was a mystery.

Lotty, for her part, looked on with round eyes. She had expected Mellersh to take at least two days before he got to this stage, but the San Salvatore spell had worked instantly. It was not only that he was pleasant at dinner, for she had always seen him pleasant at dinners with other people, but he had been pleasant all day privately—so pleasant that he had complimented her on her looks while she was brushing out her hair, and kissed her. Kissed her! And it was neither good-morning nor good-night.

Well, this being so, she would put off telling him the truth about her nest-egg, and about Rose not being his hostess after all, till next day. Pity to spoil things. She had been going to blurt it out as soon as he had had a rest, but it did seem a pity to disturb such a very beautiful frame of mind as that of Mellersh this first day. Let him too get more firmly fixed in heaven. Once fixed he wouldn't mind anything.

Her face sparkled with delight at the instantaneous effect of San Salvatore. Even the catastrophe of the bath, of which she had been told when she came in from the garden, had not shaken him. Of course all that he had needed was a holiday. What a brute she had been to him when he wanted to take her himself to Italy. But this arrangement, as it happened, was ever so much better, though not through any merit of hers. She talked and laughed gaily, not a shred of fear of him left in her, and even when she said, struck by his spotlessness, that he looked so clean that one could eat one's dinner off him, and Scrap laughed, Mellersh laughed too. He would have minded that at home, supposing that at home she had had the spirit to say it.

It was a successful evening. Scrap, whenever she looked at Mr. Wilkins, saw him in his towel, dripping water, and felt indulgent. Mrs. Fisher was delighted with him. Rose was a dignified hostess in Mr. Wilkins's eyes, quiet and dignified, and he admired the way she waived her right to preside at the head of the table—as a graceful compliment, of course, to Mrs. Fisher's age. Mrs. Arbuthnot was, opined Mr. Wilkins, naturally retiring. She was the most retiring of the three ladies. He had met her before dinner alone for a moment in the drawing-room, and had expressed in appropriate language his sense of her kindness in wishing him to join her party, and she had been retiring. Was she shy? Probably. She had blushed, and murmured as if in deprecation, and then the others had come in. At dinner she talked least. He would, of course, become better acquainted with her during the next few days, and it would be a pleasure, he was sure.

Meanwhile Lady Caroline was all and more than all Mr. Wilkins had imagined, and had received his speeches, worked in skillfully between the courses, graciously; Mrs. Fisher was the exact old lady he had been hoping to come across all his professional life; and Lotty had not only immensely improved, but was obviously *au mieux*—Mr. Wilkins knew what was necessary in French—with Lady Caroline. He had been much tormented during the day by the thought of how he had stood conversing with Lady Caroline forgetful of his not being dressed, and had at last written her a note most deeply apologizing, and beseeching her to overlook his amazing, his incomprehensible obliviousness, to which she had replied in pencil on the back of the envelope, "Don't worry." And he had obeyed her commands, and had put it from him. The result was he was now in great contentment. Before going to sleep that night he pinched his wife's ear. She was amazed. These endearments . . .

What is more, the morning brought no relapse in Mr. Wilkins, and he kept up to this high level throughout the day, in spite of its being the first day of the second week, and therefore pay day.

Its being pay day precipitated Lotty's confession, which she had, when it came to the point, been inclined to put off a little longer. She was not afraid, she dared anything, but Mellersh was in such an admirable humor—why risk clouding it just yet? When, however, soon after breakfast Costanza appeared with a pile of very dirty little bits of paper covered with sums in pencil, and having knocked at Mrs. Fisher's door and been sent away, and at Lady Caroline's door and been sent away, and at Rose's door and had no answer because Rose had gone out, she waylaid Lotty, who was showing Mellersh over the house, and pointed to the bits of paper and talked very rapidly and loud, and shrugged her shoulders a great deal, and kept on pointing at the bits of paper, Lotty remembered that a week had passed without anybody paying anything to anyone, and that the moment had come to settle up.

"Does this good lady want something?" inquired Mr. Wilkins mellifluously.

"Money," said Lotty.

"Money?"

"It's the housekeeping bills."

"Well, you have nothing to do with those," said Mr. Wilkins serenely.

"Oh yes, I have—"

And the confession was precipitated.

It was wonderful how Mellersh took it. One would have imagined that his sole idea about the nest-egg had always been that it should be lavished on just this. He did not, as he would have done at home, cross-examine her; he accepted everything as it came pouring out, about her fibs and all, and when she had finished and said, "You have every right to be angry, I think, but I hope you won't be and will forgive me instead," he merely asked, "What can be more beneficial than such a holiday?"

Whereupon she put her arm through his and held it tight and said, "Oh, Mellersh, you really are too sweet!"—her face red with pride in him.

That he should so quickly assimilate the atmosphere, that he should at once become nothing but kindness, showed surely what a real affinity he had with good and beautiful things. He belonged quite naturally in this place of heavenly calm. He was—extraordinary how she had misjudged him—by nature a child of light. Fancy not minding the dreadful fibs she had gone in for before leaving home; fancy passing even those over without comment. Wonderful. Yet not wonderful, for wasn't he in heaven? In heaven nobody minded any of those done-with things, one didn't even trouble to forgive and forget, one was much too happy. She pressed his arm tight in her gratitude and appreciation; and though he did not withdraw his, neither did he respond to her pressure. Mr. Wilkins was of a cool habit, and rarely had any real wish to press.

Meanwhile, Costanza, perceiving that she had lost the Wilkinses' ear had gone back to Mrs. Fisher, who at least understood Italian, besides being clearly in the servants' eyes the one of the party marked down by age and appearance to pay the bills; and to her, while Mrs. Fisher put the final touches to her toilette, for she was preparing, by means of putting on a hat and veil and feather boa and gloves, to go for her first stroll in the lower garden—positively her first since her arrival—she explained that unless she was given money to pay the last week's bills the shops of Castagneto would refuse credit for the current week's food. Not even credit would they give, affirmed Costanza, who had been spending a great deal and was anxious to pay all her relations what was owed them and also to find out how her mistresses took it, for that day's meals. Soon it would be the hour of *colazione*, and how could there be *colazione* without meat, without fish, without eggs, without—

Mrs. Fisher took the bills out of her hand and looked at the total; and she was so much astonished by its size, so much horrified by the extravagance to which it testified, that she sat down at her writing-table to go into the thing thoroughly.

Costanza had a very bad half-hour. She had not supposed it was in the English to be so mercenary. And then *la Vecchia*, as she was called in the kitchen, knew so much Italian, and with a doggedness that filled Costanza with shame on her behalf, for such conduct was the last one expected from the noble English, she went through item after item, requiring and persisting till she got them, explanations.

There were no explanations, except that Costanza had had one glorious week of doing exactly as she chose, of splendid unbridled license, and that this was the result.

Costanza, having no explanations, wept. It was miserable to think she would have to cook from now on under watchfulness, under suspicion; and what would her relations say when they found the orders they received were whittled down? They would say she had no influence; they would despise her.

Costanza wept, but Mrs. Fisher was unmoved. In slow and splendid Italian, with the roll of the cantos of the *Inferno*, she informed her that she would pay no bills till the following week, and that meanwhile the food was to be precisely as good as ever, and at a quarter the cost.

Costanza threw up her hands.

Next week, proceeded Mrs. Fisher unmoved, if she found this had been so she would pay the whole. Otherwise—she paused; for what she would do otherwise she did not know herself. But she paused and looked impenetrable, majestic and menacing, and Costanza was cowed.

Then Mrs. Fisher, having dismissed her with a gesture, went in search of Lady Caroline to complain. She had been under the impression that Lady Caroline ordered the meals and therefore was responsible for the prices, but now it appeared that the cook had been left to do exactly as she pleased ever since they got there, which of course was simply disgraceful.

Scrap was not in her bedroom, but the room, on Mrs. Fisher's opening the door, for she suspected her of being in it and only pretending not to hear the knock, was still flowerlike from her presence.

"Scent," sniffed Mrs. Fisher, shutting it again; and she wished Carlyle could have had five minutes' straight talk with this young woman. And yet—perhaps even he—

She went downstairs to go into the garden in search of her, and in the hall encountered Mr. Wilkins. He had his hat on, and was lighting a cigar.

Indulgent as Mrs. Fisher felt towards Mr. Wilkins, and peculiarly and even mystically related after the previous morning's encounter, she yet could not like a cigar in the house. Out of doors she endured it, but it was not necessary, when out of doors was such a big place, to indulge the habit indoors. Even Mr. Fisher, who had been, she should say, a man originally tenacious of habits, had quite soon after marriage got out of this one.

However, Mr. Wilkins, snatching off his hat on seeing her, instantly threw the cigar away. He threw it into the water a great jar of arum lilies presumably contained, and Mrs. Fisher, aware of the value men attach to their newly lit cigars, could not but be impressed by this immediate and magnificent *amende honorable*.

But the cigar did not reach the water. It got caught in the lilies, and smoked on by itself among them, a strange and depraved-looking object.

"Where are you going to, my prett—" began Mr. Wilkins, advancing towards Mrs. Fisher; but he broke off just in time.

Was it morning spirits impelling him to address Mrs. Fisher in the terms of a nursery rhyme? He wasn't even aware that he knew the thing. Most strange. What could have put it, at such a moment, into his self-possessed head? He felt great respect for Mrs. Fisher, and would not for the world have insulted her by addressing her as a maid, pretty or otherwise. He wished to stand well with her. She was a woman of parts, and also, he suspected, of property. At breakfast they had been most pleasant together, and he had been struck by her apparent intimacy with well-known persons. Victorians, of course; but it was restful to talk about them after the strain of his brother-in-law's Georgian parties on Hampstead Heath. He and she were getting on famously, he felt. She already showed all the symptoms of presently wishing to become a client. Not for the world would he offend her. He turned a little cold at the narrowness of his escape.

She had not, however, noticed.

"You are going out," he said very politely, all readiness should she confirm his assumption to accompany her.

"I want to find Lady Caroline," said Mrs. Fisher, going towards the glass door leading into the top garden.

"An agreeable quest," remarked Mr. Wilkins. "May I assist in the search? Allow me—" he added, opening the door for her.

"She usually sits over in that corner behind the bushes," said Mrs. Fisher. "And I don't know about it being an agreeable quest. She has been letting the bills run up in the most terrible fashion, and needs a good scolding."

"Lady Caroline?" said Mr. Wilkins, unable to follow such an attitude. "What has Lady Caroline, if I may inquire, to do with the bills here?"

"The housekeeping was left to her, and as we all share alike it ought to have been a matter of honor with her—"

“But—Lady Caroline housekeeping for the party here? A party which includes my wife? My dear lady, you render me speechless. Do you not know she is the daughter of the Droitwiches?”

“Oh, is that who she is,” said Mrs. Fisher, scrunching heavily over the pebbles towards the hidden corner. “Well, that accounts for it. The muddle that man Droitwich made in his department in the war was a national scandal. It amounted to misappropriation of the public funds.”

“But it is impossible, I assure you, to expect the daughter of the Droitwiches—” began Mr. Wilkins earnestly.

“The Droitwiches,” interrupted Mrs. Fisher, “are neither here nor there. Duties undertaken should be performed. I don’t intend my money to be squandered for the sake of any Droitwiches.”

A headstrong old lady. Perhaps not so easy to deal with as he had hoped. But how wealthy. Only the consciousness of great wealth would make her snap her fingers in this manner at the Droitwiches. Lotty, on being questioned, had been vague about her circumstances, and had described her house as a mausoleum with goldfish swimming about in it; but now he was sure she was more than very well off. Still, he wished he had not joined her at this moment, for he had no sort of desire to be present at such a spectacle as the scolding of Lady Caroline Dester.

Again, however, he was reckoning without Scrap. Whatever she felt when she looked up and beheld Mr. Wilkins discovering her corner on the very first morning, nothing but angelicness appeared on her face. She took her feet off the parapet on Mrs. Fisher’s sitting down on it, and listening gravely to her opening remarks as to her not having any money to fling about in reckless and uncontrolled household expenditure, interrupted her flow by pulling one of the cushions from behind her head and offering it to her.

“Sit on this,” said Scrap, holding it out. “You’ll be more comfortable.”

Mr. Wilkins leapt to relieve her of it.

"Oh, thanks," said Mrs. Fisher, interrupted.

It was difficult to get into the swing again. Mr. Wilkins inserted the cushion solicitously between the slightly raised Mrs. Fisher and the stone of the parapet, and again she had to say "Thanks." It was interrupted. Besides, Lady Caroline said nothing in her defense; she only looked at her, and listened with the face of an attentive angel.

It seemed to Mr. Wilkins that it must be difficult to scold a Dester who looked like that and so exquisitely said nothing. Mrs. Fisher, he was glad to see, gradually found it difficult herself, for her severity slackened, and she ended by saying lamely, "You ought to have told me you were not doing it."

"I didn't know you thought I was," said the lovely voice.

"I would now like to know," said Mrs. Fisher, "what you propose to do for the rest of the time here."

"Nothing," said Scrap, smiling.

"Nothing? Do you mean to say—"

"If I may be allowed, ladies," interposed Mr. Wilkins in his suavest professional manner, "to make a suggestion"—they both looked at him, and remembering him as they first saw him felt indulgent—"I would advise you not to spoil a delightful holiday with worries over housekeeping."

"Exactly," said Mrs. Fisher. "It is what I intend to avoid."

"Most sensible," said Mr. Wilkins. "Why not, then," he continued, "allow the cook—an excellent cook, by the way—so much a head *per diem*"—Mr. Wilkins knew what was necessary in Latin—"and tell her that for this sum she must cater for you, and not only cater but cater as well as ever? One could easily reckon it out. The charges of a moderate hotel, for instance, would do as a basis, halved, or perhaps even quartered."

"And this week that has just passed?" asked Mrs. Fisher. "The terrible bills of this first week? What about them?"

"They shall be my present to San Salvatore," said Scrap, who didn't like the idea of Lotty's nest-egg being reduced so much beyond what she was prepared for.

There was a silence. The ground was cut from under Mrs. Fisher's feet.

"Of course if you choose to throw your money about—" she said at last, disapproving but immensely relieved, while Mr. Wilkins was rapt in the contemplation of the precious qualities of blue blood. This readiness, for instance, not to trouble about money, this free-handedness—it was not only what one admired in others, admired in others perhaps more than anything else, but it was extraordinarily useful to the professional classes. When met with it should be encouraged by warmth of reception. Mrs. Fisher was not warm. She accepted—from which he deduced that with her wealth went closeness—but she accepted grudgingly. Presents were presents, and one did not look them in this manner in the mouth, he felt; and if Lady Caroline found her pleasure in presenting his wife and Mrs. Fisher with their entire food for a week, it was their part to accept gracefully. One should not discourage gifts.

On behalf of his wife, then, Mr. Wilkins expressed what she would wish to express, and remarking to Lady Caroline—with a touch of lightness, for so should gifts be accepted in order to avoid embarrassing the donor—that she had in that case been his wife's hostess since her arrival, he turned almost gaily to Mrs. Fisher and pointed out that she and his wife must now jointly write Lady Caroline the customary letter of thanks for hospitality. "A Collins," said Mr. Wilkins, who knew what was necessary in literature. "I prefer the name Collins for such a letter to either that of Board and Lodging or Bread and Butter. Let us call it a Collins."

Scrap smiled, and held out her cigarette case. Mrs. Fisher could not help being mollified. A way out of waste was going to be found, thanks to Mr. Wilkins, and she hated waste quite as much as having to pay for it; also a way was found out of housekeeping. For a moment she had thought that if everybody tried to force her into housekeeping on her brief holiday by their own indifference (Lady Caroline), or inability to speak Italian (the other two), she would have to send for Kate Lumley after all. Kate could do it. Kate and she had learnt Italian together. Kate would only be allowed to come on condition that she did do it.

But this was much better, this way of Mr. Wilkins's. Really a most superior man. There was nothing like an intelligent, not too young man for profitable and pleasurable companionship. And when she got up, the business for which she had come being settled, and said she now intended to take a little stroll before lunch, Mr. Wilkins did not stay with Lady Caroline, as most of the men she had known would, she was afraid, have wanted to—he asked to be permitted to go and stroll with her; so that he evidently definitely preferred conversation to faces. A sensible, companionable man. A clever, well-read man. A man of the world. A man. She was very glad indeed she had not written to Kate the other day. What did she want with Kate? She had found a better companion.

But Mr. Wilkins did not go with Mrs. Fisher because of her conversation, but because, when she got up and he got up because she got up, intending merely to bow her out of the recess, Lady Caroline had put her feet up on the parapet again, and arranging her head sideways in the cushions had shut her eyes.

The daughter of the Droitwiches desired to go to sleep.

It was not for him, by remaining, to prevent her.

CHAPTER 16

And so the second week began, and all was harmony. The arrival of Mr. Wilkins, instead of, as three of the party had feared and the fourth had only been protected from fearing by her burning faith in the effect on him of San Salvatore, disturbing such harmony as there was, increased it. He fitted in. He was determined to please, and he did please. He was most amiable to his wife—not only in public, which she was used to, but in private, when he certainly wouldn't have been if he hadn't wanted to. He did want to. He was so much obliged to her, so much pleased with her, for making him acquainted with Lady Caroline, that he felt really fond of her. Also proud; for there must be, he reflected, a good deal more in her than he had supposed, for Lady Caroline to have become so intimate with her and so affectionate. And the more he treated her as though she were really very nice, the more Lotty expanded and became really very nice, and the more he, affected in his turn, became really very nice himself; so that they went round and round, not in a vicious but in a highly virtuous circle.

Positively, for him, Mellersh petted her. There was at no time much pet in Mellersh, because he was by nature a cool man; yet such was the influence on him of, as Lotty supposed, San Salvatore, that in this second week he sometimes pinched both her ears, one after the other, instead of only one; and Lotty, marveling at such rapidly developing affectionateness, wondered what he would do, should he continue at this rate, in the third week, when her supply of ears would have come to an end.

He was particularly nice about the washstand, and genuinely desirous of not taking up too much of the space in the small bedroom. Quick to respond, Lotty was even more desirous not to be in his way; and the room became the scene of many an affectionate *combat de générosité*, each of which left them more pleased with each other than ever. He did not again have a bath in the bathroom, though it was mended and ready for him, but got up and went down every morning to the sea, and in spite of the cool nights making the water cold early had his dip as a man should, and came up to breakfast rubbing his hands and feeling, as he told Mrs. Fisher, prepared for anything.

Lotty's belief in the irresistible influence of the heavenly atmosphere of San Salvatore being thus obviously justified, and Mr. Wilkins, whom Rose knew as alarming and Scrap had pictured as icily unkind, being so evidently a changed man, both Rose and Scrap began to think there might after all be something in what Lotty insisted on, and that San Salvatore did work purgingly on the character.

They were the more inclined to think so in that they too felt a working going on inside themselves: they felt more cleared, both of them, that second week—Scrap in her thoughts, many of which were now quite nice thoughts, real amiable ones about her parents and relations, with a glimmer in them of recognition of the extraordinary benefits she had received at the hands of—what? Fate? Providence?—anyhow of something, and of how, having received them, she had misused them by failing to be happy; and Rose in her bosom, which though it still yearned, yearned to some purpose, for she was reaching the conclusion that merely inactively to yearn was no use at all, and that she must either by some means stop her yearning or give it at least a chance—remote, but still a chance—of being quieted by writing to Frederick and asking him to come out.

If Mr. Wilkins could be changed, thought Rose, why not Frederick? How wonderful it would be, how too wonderful, if the place worked on him too and were able to make them even a little understand each other, even a little be friends. Rose, so far had loosening and disintegration gone on in her character, now was beginning to think her obstinate strait-lacedness about his books and her austere absorption in good works had been foolish and perhaps even wrong. He was her husband, and she had frightened him away. She had frightened love away, precious love, and that couldn't be good. Was not Lotty right when she said the other day that nothing at all except love mattered? Nothing certainly seemed much use unless it was built up on love. But once frightened away, could it ever come back? Yes, it might in that beauty, it might in the atmosphere of happiness Lotty and San Salvatore seemed between them to spread round like some divine infection.

She had, however, to get him there first, and he certainly couldn't be got there if she didn't write and tell him where she was.

She would write. She must write; for if she did there was at least a chance of his coming, and if she didn't there was manifestly none. And then, once here in this loveliness, with everything so soft and kind and sweet all round, it would be easier to tell him, to try and explain, to ask for something different, for at least an attempt at something different in their lives in the future, instead of the blankness of separation, the cold—oh, the cold—of nothing at all but the great windiness of faith, the great bleakness of works. Why, one person in the world, one single person belonging to one, of one's very own, to talk to, to take care of, to love, to be interested in, was worth more than all the speeches on platforms and the compliments of chairmen in the world. It was also worth more—Rose couldn't help it, the thought would come—than all the prayers.

These thoughts were not head thoughts, like Scrap's, who was altogether free from yearnings, but bosom thoughts. They lodged in the bosom; it was in the bosom that Rose ached, and felt so dreadfully lonely. And when her courage failed her, as it did on most days, and it seemed impossible to write to Frederick, she would look at Mr. Wilkins and revive.

There he was, a changed man. There he was, going into that small, uncomfortable room every night, that room whose proximities had been Lotty's only misgiving, and coming out of it in the morning, and Lotty coming out of it too, both of them as unclouded and as nice to each other as when they went in. And hadn't he, so critical at home, Lotty had told her, of the least thing going wrong, emerged from the bath catastrophe as untouched in spirit as Shadrach, Meshach, and Abednego were untouched in body when they emerged from the fire? Miracles were happening in this place. If they could happen to Mr. Wilkins, why not to Frederick?

She got up quickly. Yes, she would write. She would go and write to him at once.

But suppose—

She paused. Suppose he didn't answer. Suppose he didn't even answer.

And she sat down again to think a little longer.

In these hesitations did Rose spend most of the second week.

Then there was Mrs. Fisher. Her restlessness increased that second week. It increased to such an extent that she might just as well not have had her private sitting-room at all, for she could no longer sit. Not for ten minutes together could Mrs. Fisher sit. And added to the restlessness, as the days of the second week proceeded on their way, she had a curious sensation, which worried her, of rising sap. She knew the feeling, because she had sometimes had it in childhood in specially swift springs, when the lilacs and the syringas seemed to rush out into blossom in a single night, but it was strange to have it again after over fifty years. She would have liked to remark on the sensation to some one, but she was ashamed. It was such an absurd sensation at her age. Yet oftener and oftener, and every day more and more, did Mrs. Fisher have a ridiculous feeling as if she were presently going to burgeon.

Sternly she tried to frown the unseemly sensation down. Burgeon, indeed. She had heard of dried staffs, pieces of mere dead wood, suddenly putting forth fresh leaves, but only in legend. She was not in legend. She knew perfectly what was due to herself. Dignity demanded that she should have nothing to do with fresh leaves at her age; and yet there it was—the feeling that presently, that at any moment now, she might crop out all green.

Mrs. Fisher was upset. There were many things she disliked more than anything else, and one was when the elderly imagined they felt young and behaved accordingly. Of course they only imagined it, they were only deceiving themselves; but how deplorable were the results. She herself had grown old as people should grow old—steadily and firmly. No interruptions, no belated after-glows and spasmodic returns. If, after all these years, she were now going to be deluded into some sort of unsuitable breaking-out, how humiliating.

Indeed she was thankful, that second week, that Kate Lumley was not there. It would be most unpleasant, should anything different occur in her behavior, to have Kate looking on. Kate had known her all her life. She felt she could let herself go—here Mrs. Fisher frowned at the book she was vainly trying to concentrate on, for where did that expression come from?—much less painfully before strangers than before an old friend. Old friends, reflected Mrs. Fisher, who hoped she was reading, compare one constantly with what one used to be. They are always doing it if one develops. They are surprised at development. They hark back; they expect motionlessness after, say, fifty, to the end of one's days.

That, thought Mrs. Fisher, her eyes going steadily line by line down the page and not a word of it getting through into her consciousness, is foolish of friends. It is condemning one to a premature death. One should continue (of course with dignity) to develop, however old one may be. She had nothing against developing, against further ripeness, because as long as one was alive one was not dead—obviously, decided Mrs. Fisher; and development, change, ripening, were life. What she would dislike would be unripening, going back to something green. She would dislike it intensely; and this is what she felt she was on the brink of doing.

Naturally it made her very uneasy, and only in constant movement could she find distraction. Increasingly restless and no longer able to confine herself to her battlements, she wandered more and more frequently, and also aimlessly, in and out of the top garden, to the growing surprise of Scrap, especially when she found that all Mrs. Fisher did was to stare for a few minutes at the view, pick a few dead leaves off the rose-bushes, and go away again.

In Mr. Wilkins's conversation she found temporary relief, but though he joined her whenever he could he was not always there, for he spread his attentions judiciously among the three ladies, and when he was somewhere else she had to face and manage her thoughts as best she could by herself. Perhaps it was the excess of light and color at San Salvatore which made every other place seem dark and black; and Prince of Wales Terrace did seem a very dark black spot to have to go back to—a dark, narrow street, and her house dark and narrow as the street, with nothing really living or young in it. The goldfish could hardly be called living, or at most not more than half living, and were certainly not young, and except for them there were only the maids, and they were dusty old things.

Dusty old things. Mrs. Fisher paused in her thoughts, arrested by the strange expression. Where had it come from? How was it possible for it to come at all? It might have been one of Mrs. Wilkins's, in its levity, its almost slang. Perhaps it was one of hers, and she had heard her say it and unconsciously caught it from her.

If so, this was both serious and disgusting. That the foolish creature should penetrate into Mrs. Fisher's very mind and establish her personality there, the personality which was still, in spite of the harmony apparently existing between her and her intelligent husband, so alien to Mrs. Fisher's own, so far removed from what she understood and liked, and infect her with her undesirable phrases, was most disturbing. Never in her life before had such a sentence come into Mrs. Fisher's head. Never in her life before had she thought of her maids, or of anybody else, as dusty old things. Her maids were not dusty old things; they were most respectable, neat women, who were allowed the use of the bathroom every Saturday night. Elderly, certainly, but then so was she, so was her house, so was her furniture, so were her goldfish. They were all elderly, as they should be, together. But there was a great difference between being elderly and being a dusty old thing.

How true it was what Ruskin said, that evil communications corrupt good manners. But did Ruskin say it? On second thoughts she was not sure, but it was just the sort of thing he would have said if he had said it, and in any case it was true. Merely hearing Mrs. Wilkins's evil communications at meals—she did not listen, she avoided listening, yet it was evident she had heard—those communications which, in that they so often were at once vulgar, indelicate, and profane, and always, she was sorry to say, laughed at by Lady Caroline, must be classed as evil, was spoiling her own mental manners. Soon she might not only think but say. How terrible that would be. If that were the form her breaking-out was going to take, the form of unseemly speech, Mrs. Fisher was afraid she would hardly with any degree of composure be able to bear it.

At this stage Mrs. Fisher wished more than ever that she were able to talk over her strange feelings with some one who would understand. There was, however, no one who would understand except Mrs. Wilkins herself. She would. She would know at once,

Mrs. Fisher was sure, what she felt like. But this was impossible. It would be as abject as begging the very microbe that was infecting one for protection against its disease.

She continued, accordingly, to bear her sensations in silence, and was driven by them into that frequent aimless appearing in the top garden which presently roused even Scrap's attention.

Scrap had noticed it, and vaguely wondered at it, for some time before Mr. Wilkins inquired of her one morning as he arranged her cushions for her—he had established the daily assisting of Lady Caroline into her chair as his special privilege—whether there was anything the matter with Mrs. Fisher.

At that moment Mrs. Fisher was standing by the eastern parapet, shading her eyes and carefully scrutinizing the distant white houses of Mezzago. They could see her through the branches of the daphnes.

"I don't know," said Scrap.

"She is a lady, I take it," said Mr. Wilkins, "who would be unlikely to have anything on her mind?"

"I should imagine so," said Scrap, smiling.

"If she has, and her restlessness appears to suggest it, I should be more than glad to assist her with advice."

"I am sure you would be most kind."

"Of course she has her own legal adviser, but he is not on the spot. I am. And a lawyer on the spot," said Mr. Wilkins, who endeavored to make his conversation when he talked to Lady Caroline light, aware that one must be light with young ladies, "is worth two in—we won't be ordinary and complete the proverb, but say London."

"You should ask her."

"Ask her if she needs assistance? Would you advise it? Would it not be a little—a little delicate to touch on such a question, the question whether or no a lady has something on her mind?"

"Perhaps she will tell you if you go and talk to her. I think it must be lonely to be Mrs. Fisher."

"You are all thoughtfulness and consideration," declared Mr. Wilkins, wishing, for the first time in his life, that he were a foreigner so that he might respectfully kiss her hand on withdrawing to go obediently and relieve Mrs. Fisher's loneliness.

It was wonderful what a variety of exits from her corner Scrap contrived for Mr. Wilkins. Each morning she found a different one, which sent him off pleased after he had arranged her cushions for her. She allowed him to arrange the cushions because she instantly had discovered, the very first five minutes of the very first evening, that her fears lest he should cling to her and stare in dreadful admiration were baseless. Mr. Wilkins did not admire like that. It was not only, she instinctively felt, not in him, but if it had been he would not have dared to in her case. He was all respectfulness. She could direct his movements in regard to herself with the raising of an eyelash. His one concern was to obey. She had been prepared to like him if he would only be so obliging as not to admire her, and she did like him. She did not forget his moving defenselessness the first morning in his towel, and he amused her, and he was kind to Lotty. It is true she liked him most when he wasn't there, but then she usually liked everybody most when they weren't there. Certainly he did seem to be one of those men, rare in her experience, who never looked at a woman from the predatory angle. The comfort of this, the simplification it brought into the relations of the party, was immense. From this point of view Mr. Wilkins was simply ideal; he was unique and precious. Whenever she thought of him, and was perhaps inclined to dwell on the aspects of him that were a little boring, she remembered this and murmured, "But what a treasure."

Indeed it was Mr. Wilkins's one aim during his stay at San Salvatore to be a treasure. At all costs the three ladies who were not his wife must like him and trust him. Then presently when trouble arose in their lives—and in what lives did not trouble sooner or later arise?—they would recollect how reliable he was and how sympathetic, and turn to him for advice. Ladies with something on their minds were exactly what he wanted. Lady Caroline, he judged, had nothing on hers at the moment, but so much beauty—for he could not but see what was evident—must have had its difficulties in the past and would have more of them before it had done. In the past he had not been at hand; in the future he hoped to be. And meanwhile the behavior of Mrs. Fisher, the next in importance of the ladies from the professional point of view, showed definite promise. It was almost certain that Mrs. Fisher had something on her mind. He had been observing her attentively, and it was almost certain.

With the third, with Mrs. Arbuthnot, he had up to this made least headway, for she was so very retiring and quiet. But might not this very retiringness, this tendency to avoid the others and spend her time alone, indicate that she too was troubled? If so, he was her man. He would cultivate her. He would follow her and sit with her, and encourage her to tell him about herself. Arbuthnot, he understood from Lotty, was a British Museum official—nothing specially important at present, but Mr. Wilkins regarded it as his business to know all sorts and kinds. Besides, there was promotion. Arbuthnot, promoted, might become very much worth while.

As for Lotty, she was charming. She really had all the qualities he had credited her with during his courtship, and they had been, it appeared, merely in abeyance since. His early impressions of her were now being endorsed by the affection and even admiration Lady Caroline showed for her. Lady Caroline Dester was the last person, he was sure, to be mistaken on such a subject. Her knowledge of the world, her constant association with only the best, must make her quite unerring. Lotty was evidently, then, that which before marriage he had believed her to be—she was valuable. She certainly had been most valuable in introducing him to Lady Caroline and

Mrs. Fisher. A man in his profession could be immensely helped by a clever and attractive wife. Why had she not been attractive sooner? Why this sudden flowering?

Mr. Wilkins began too to believe there was something peculiar, as Lotty had almost at once informed him, in the atmosphere of San Salvatore. It promoted expansion. It brought out dormant qualities. And feeling more and more pleased, and even charmed, by his wife, and very content with the progress he was making with the two others, and hopeful of progress to be made with the retiring third, Mr. Wilkins could not remember ever having had such an agreeable holiday. The only thing that might perhaps be bettered was the way they would call him Mr. Wilkins. Nobody said Mr. Mellersh-Wilkins. Yet he had introduced himself to Lady Caroline—he flinched a little on remembering the circumstances—as Mellersh-Wilkins.

Still, this was a small matter, not enough to worry about. He would be foolish if in such a place and such society he worried about anything. He was not even worrying about what the holiday was costing, and had made up his mind to pay not only his own expenses but his wife's as well, and surprise her at the end by presenting her with her nest-egg as intact as when she started; and just the knowledge that he was preparing a happy surprise for her made him feel warmer than ever towards her.

In fact Mr. Wilkins, who had begun by being consciously and according to plan on his best behavior, remained on it unconsciously, and with no effort at all.

And meanwhile the beautiful golden days were dropping gently from the second week one by one, equal in beauty with those of the first, and the scent of beanfields in flower on the hillside behind the village came across to San Salvatore whenever the air moved. In the garden that second week the poet's narcissus disappeared out of the long grass at the edge of the zigzag path, and wild gladiolus, slender and rose-colored, came in their stead, white pinks bloomed in the borders, filling the whole place with their smoky-sweet smell, and a bush nobody had noticed burst into glory and fragrance, and it was a purple lilac bush. Such a jumble of spring and summer was not to be believed in, except by those who dwelt in those gardens. Everything seemed to be out together—all the things crowded into one month which in England are spread penuriously over six. Even primroses were found one day by Mrs. Wilkins in a cold corner up in the hills; and when she brought them down to the geraniums and heliotrope of San Salvatore they looked quite shy.

CHAPTER 17

On the first day of the third week Rose wrote to Frederick.

In case she should again hesitate and not post the letter, she gave it to Domenico to post; for if she did not write now there would be no time left at all. Half the month at San Salvatore was over. Even if Frederick started directly he got the letter, which of course he wouldn't be able to do, what with packing and passport, besides not being in a hurry to come, he couldn't arrive for five days.

Having done it, Rose wished she hadn't. He wouldn't come. He wouldn't bother to answer. And if he did answer, it would just be giving some reason which was not true, and about being too busy to get away; and all that had been got by writing to him would be that she would be more unhappy than before.

What things one did when one was idle. This resurrection of Frederick, or rather this attempt to resurrect him, what was it but the result of having nothing whatever to do? She wished she had never come away on a holiday. What did she want with holidays? Work was her salvation; work was the only thing that protected one, that kept one steady and one's values true. At home in Hampstead, absorbed and busy, she had managed to get over Frederick, thinking of him latterly only with the gentle melancholy with which one thinks of some one once loved but long since dead; and now this place, idleness in this soft place, had thrown her back to the wretched state she had climbed so carefully out of years ago. Why, if Frederick did come she would only bore him. Hadn't she seen in a flash quite soon after getting to San Salvatore that that was really what kept him away from her? And why should she suppose that now, after such a long estrangement, she would be able not to bore him, be able to do anything but stand before him like a tongue-tied idiot, with all the fingers of her spirit turned into thumbs? Besides, what a hopeless position, to have as it were to beseech: Please wait a little—please don't be impatient—I think perhaps I shan't be a bore presently.

A thousand times a day Rose wished she had let Frederick alone. Lotty, who asked her every evening whether she had sent her letter yet, exclaimed with delight when the answer at last was yes, and threw her arms round her. "Now we shall be *completely* happy!" cried the enthusiastic Lotty.

But nothing seemed less certain to Rose, and her expression became more and more the expression of one who has something on her mind.

Mr. Wilkins, wanting to find out what it was, strolled in the sun in his Panama hat, and began to meet her accidentally.

"I did not know," said Mr. Wilkins the first time, courteously raising his hat, "that you too liked this particular spot." And he sat down beside her.

In the afternoon she chose another spot; and she had not been in it half an hour before Mr. Wilkins, lightly swinging his cane, came round the corner.

"We are destined to meet in our rambles," said Mr. Wilkins pleasantly. And he sat down beside her.

Mr. Wilkins was very kind, and she had, she saw, misjudged him in Hampstead, and this was the real man, ripened like fruit by the beneficent sun of San Salvatore, but Rose did want to be alone. Still, she was grateful to him for proving to her that though she might bore Frederick she did not bore everybody; if she had, he would not have sat talking to her on each occasion till it was time to go in.

True he bored her, but that wasn't anything like so dreadful as if she bored him. Then indeed her vanity would have been sadly ruffled. For now that Rose was not able to say her prayers she was being assailed by every sort of weakness: vanity, sensitiveness, irritability, pugnacity—strange, unfamiliar devils to have coming crowding on one and taking possession of one's swept and empty heart. She had never been vain or irritable or pugnacious in her life before. Could it be that San Salvatore was capable of opposite effects, and the same sun that ripened Mr. Wilkins made her go acid?

The next morning, so as to be sure of being alone, she went down, while Mr. Wilkins was still lingering pleasantly with Mrs. Fisher over breakfast, to the rocks by the water's edge where she and Lotty had sat the first day. Frederick by now had got her letter. To-day, if he were like Mr. Wilkins, she might get a telegram from him.

She tried to silence the absurd hope by jeering at it. Yet—if Mr. Wilkins had telegraphed, why not Frederick? The spell of San Salvatore lurked even, it seemed, in notepaper. Lotty had not dreamed of getting a telegram, and when she came in at lunch-time there it was. It would be too wonderful if when she went back at lunch-time she found one there for her too . . .

Rose clasped her hands tight round her knees. How passionately she longed to be important to somebody again—not important on platforms, not important as an asset in an organization, but privately important, just to one other person, quite privately, nobody else to know or notice. It didn't seem much to ask in a world so crowded with people, just to have one of them, only one out of all the millions, to oneself. Somebody who needed one, who thought of one, who was eager to come to one—oh, *oh* how dreadfully one wanted to be precious!

All the morning she sat beneath the pine-tree by the sea. Nobody came near her. The great hours passed slowly; they seemed enormous. But she wouldn't go up before lunch, she would give the telegram time to arrive . . .

That day Scrap, egged on by Lotty's persuasions and also thinking that perhaps she had sat long enough, had arisen from her chair and cushions and gone off with Lotty and sandwiches up into the hills till evening. Mr. Wilkins, who wished to go with them, stayed on Lady Caroline's advice with Mrs. Fisher in order to cheer her solitude, and though he left off cheering her about eleven to go and look for Mrs. Arbuthnot, so as for a space to cheer her too, thus dividing himself impartially between these solitary ladies, he came back again presently mopping his forehead and continued with Mrs. Fisher where he had left off, for this time Mrs. Arbuthnot had hidden successfully. There was a telegram, too, for her he noticed when he came in. Pity he did not know where she was.

"Ought we to open it?" he said to Mrs. Fisher.

"No," said Mrs. Fisher.

"It may require an answer."

"I don't approve of tampering with other people's correspondence."

"Tampering! My dear lady—"

Mr. Wilkins was shocked. Such a word. Tampering. He had the greatest possible esteem for Mrs. Fisher, but he did at times find her a little difficult. She liked him, he was sure, and she was in a fair way, he felt, to become a client, but he feared she would be a headstrong and secretive client. She was certainly secretive, for though he had been skillful and sympathetic for a whole week, she had as yet given him no inkling of what was so evidently worrying her.

"Poor old thing," said Lotty, on his asking her if she perhaps could throw light on Mrs. Fisher's troubles. "She hasn't got love."

"Love?" Mr. Wilkins could only echo, genuinely scandalized. "But surely, my dear—at her age—"

"*Any* love," said Lotty.

That very morning he had asked his wife, for he now sought and respected her opinion, if she could tell him what was the matter with Mrs. Arbuthnot, for she too, though he had done his best to thaw her into confidences, had remained persistently retiring.

"She wants her husband," said Lotty.

"Ah," said Mr. Wilkins, a new light shed on Mrs. Arbuthnot's shy and modest melancholy. And he added, "Very proper."

And Lotty said, smiling at him, "One does."

And Mr. Wilkins said, smiling at her, "Does one?"

And Lotty said, smiling at him, "Of course."

And Mr. Wilkins, much pleased with her, though it was still quite early in the day, a time when caresses are sluggish, pinched her ear.

Just before half-past twelve Rose came slowly up through the pergola and between the camellias ranged on either side of the old stone steps. The rivulets of periwinkles that flowed down them when first she arrived were gone, and now there were these bushes, incredibly rosetted. Pink, white, red, striped—she fingered and smelt them one after the other, so as not to get to her disappointment too quickly. As long as she hadn't seen for herself, seen the table in the hall quite empty except for its bowl of flowers, she still could hope, she still could have the joy of imagining the telegram lying on it waiting for her. But there is no smell in a camellia, as Mr. Wilkins, who was standing in the doorway on the look-out for her and knew what was necessary in horticulture, reminded her.

She started at his voice and looked up.

"A telegram has come for you," said Mr. Wilkins.

She stared at him, her mouth open.

"I searched for you everywhere, but failed—"

Of course. She knew it. She had been sure of it all the time. Bright and burning, Youth in that instant flashed down again on Rose. She flew up the steps, red as the camellia she had just been fingering, and was in the hall and tearing open the telegram before Mr.

Wilkins had finished his sentence. Why, but if things could happen like this—why, but there was no end to—why, she and Frederick—they were going to be—again—at last—

"No bad news, I trust?" said Mr. Wilkins who had followed her, for when she had read the telegram she stood staring at it and her face went slowly white. Curious to watch how her face went slowly white.

She turned and looked at Mr. Wilkins as if trying to remember him. "Oh no. On the contrary—"

She managed to smile. "I'm going to have a visitor," she said, holding out the telegram; and when he had taken it she walked away towards the dining-room, murmuring something about lunch being ready.

Mr. Wilkins read the telegram. It had been sent that morning from Mezzago, and was:

> Am passing through on way to Rome.
> May I pay my respects this afternoon?
> Thomas Briggs

Why should such a telegram make the interesting lady turn pale? For her pallor on reading it had been so striking as to convince Mr. Wilkins she was receiving a blow.

"Who is Thomas Briggs?" he asked, following her into the dining-room.

She looked at him vaguely. "Who is—?" she repeated, getting her thoughts together again.

"Thomas Briggs."

"Oh. Yes. He is the owner. This is his house. He is very nice. He is coming this afternoon."

Thomas Briggs was at that very moment coming. He was jogging along the road between Mezzago and Castagneto in a fly, sincerely hoping that the dark-eyed lady would grasp that all he wanted was to see her, and not at all to see if his house were still there. He felt that an owner of delicacy did not intrude on a tenant. But—he had been thinking so much of her since that day. Rose Arbuthnot. Such a pretty name. And such a pretty creature—mild, milky, mothery in the best sense; the best sense being that she wasn't his mother and couldn't have been if she had tried, for parents were the only things impossible to have younger than oneself. Also, he was passing so near. It seemed absurd not just to look in and see if she were comfortable. He longed to see her in his house. He longed to see it as her background, to see her sitting in his chairs, drinking out of his cups, using all his things. Did she put the big crimson brocade cushion in the drawing-room behind her little dark head? Her hair and the whiteness of her skin would look lovely against it. Had she seen the portrait of herself on the stairs? He wondered if she liked it. He would explain it to her. If she didn't paint, and she had said nothing to suggest it, she wouldn't perhaps notice how exactly the molding of the eyebrows and the slight hollow of the cheek—

He told the fly to wait in Castagneto, and crossed the piazza, hailed by children and dogs, who all knew him and sprang up suddenly from nowhere, and walking quickly up the zigzag path, for he was an active young man not much more than thirty, he pulled the ancient chain that rang the bell, and waited decorously on the proper side of the open door to be allowed to come in.

At the sight of him Francesca flung up every bit of her that would fling up—eyebrows, eyelids, and hands, and volubly assured him that all was in perfect order and that she was doing her duty.

"Of course, of course," said Briggs, cutting her short. "No one doubts it."

And he asked her to take in his card to her mistress.

"Which mistress?" asked Francesca.

"Which mistress?"

"There are four," said Francesca, scenting an irregularity on the part of the tenants, for her master looked surprised; and she felt pleased, for life was dull and irregularities helped it along at least a little.

"Four?" he repeated, surprised. "Well, take it to the lot then," he said, recovering himself, for he noticed her expression.

Coffee was being drunk in the top garden in the shade of the umbrella pine. Only Mrs. Fisher and Mr. Wilkins were drinking it, for Mrs. Arbuthnot, after eating nothing and being completely silent during lunch, had disappeared immediately afterwards.

While Francesca went away into the garden with his card, her master stood examining the picture on the staircase of that Madonna by an early Italian painter, name unknown, picked up by him at Orvieto, who was so much like his tenant. It really was remarkable, the likeness. Of course his tenant that day in London had had her hat on, but he was pretty sure her hair grew just like that off her forehead. The expression of the eyes, grave and sweet, was exactly the same. He rejoiced to think that he would always have her portrait.

He looked up at the sound of footsteps, and there she was, coming down the stairs just as he had imagined her in that place, dressed in white.

She was astonished to see him so soon. She had supposed he would come about tea-time, and till then she had meant to sit somewhere out of doors where she could be by herself.

He watched her coming down the stairs with the utmost eager interest. In a moment she would be level with her portrait.

"It really is extraordinary," said Briggs.

"How do you do," said Rose, intent only on a decent show of welcome.

She did not welcome him. He was here, she felt, the telegram bitter in her heart, instead of Frederick, doing what she had longed Frederick would do, taking his place.

"Just stand still a moment—"

She obeyed automatically.

"Yes—quite astonishing. Do you mind taking off your hat?"

Rose, surprised, took it off obediently.

"Yes—I thought so—I just wanted to make sure. And look—have you noticed—"

He began to make odd swift passes with his hand over the face in the picture, measuring it, looking from it to her.

Rose's surprise became amusement, and she could not help smiling. "Have you come to compare me with my original?" she asked.

"You do see how extraordinarily alike—"

"I didn't know I looked so solemn."

"You don't. Not now. You did a minute ago, quite as solemn. Oh yes—how do you do," he finished suddenly, noticing her outstretched hand. And he laughed and shook it, flushing—a trick of his—to the roots of his fair hair.

Francesca came back. "The Signora Fisher," she said, "will be pleased to see him."

"Who is the Signora Fisher?" he asked Rose.

"One of the four who are sharing your house."

"Then there are four of you?"

"Yes. My friend and I found we couldn't afford it by ourselves."

"Oh, I say—" began Briggs in confusion, for he would best have liked Rose Arbuthnot—pretty name—not to have to afford anything, but to stay at San Salvatore as long as she liked as his guest.

"Mrs. Fisher is having coffee in the top garden," said Rose. "I'll take you to her and introduce you."

"I don't want to go. You've got your hat on, so you were going for a walk. Mayn't I come too? I'd immensely like being shown round by you."

"But Mrs. Fisher is waiting for you."

"Won't she keep?"

"Yes," said Rose, with the smile that had so much attracted him the first day. "I think she will keep quite well till tea."

"Do you speak Italian?"

"No," said Rose. "Why?"

On that he turned to Francesca, and told her at a great rate, for in Italian he was glib, to go back to the Signora in the top garden and tell her he had encountered his old friend the Signora Arbuthnot, and was going for a walk with her and would present himself to her later.

"Do you invite me to tea?" he asked Rose, when Francesca had gone.

"Of course. It's your house."

"It isn't. It's yours."

"Till Monday week," she smiled.

"Come and show me all the views," he said eagerly; and it was plain, even to the self-depreciatory Rose, that she did not bore Mr. Briggs.

CHAPTER 18

They had a very pleasant walk, with a great deal of sitting down in warm, thyme-fragrant corners, and if anything could have helped Rose to recover from the bitter disappointment of the morning it would have been the company and conversation of Mr. Briggs. He did help her to recover, and the same process took place as that which Lotty had undergone with her husband, and the more Mr. Briggs thought Rose charming the more charming she became.

Briggs was a man incapable of concealments, who never lost time if he could help it. They had not got to the end of the headland where the lighthouse is—Briggs asked her to show him the lighthouse, because the path to it, he knew, was wide enough for two to walk abreast and fairly level—before he had told her of the impression she had made on him in London.

Since even the most religious, sober women like to know they have made an impression, particularly the kind that has nothing to do with character or merits, Rose was pleased. Being pleased, she smiled. Smiling, she was more attractive than ever. Color came into her cheeks, and brightness into her eyes. She heard herself saying things that really sounded quite interesting and even amusing. If Frederick were listening now, she thought, perhaps he would see that she couldn't after all be such a hopeless bore; for here was a man, nice-looking, young, and surely clever—he seemed clever, and she hoped he was, for then the compliment would be still greater—who was evidently quite happy to spend the afternoon just talking to her.

And indeed Mr. Briggs seemed very much interested. He wanted to hear all about everything she had been doing from the moment she got there. He asked her if she had seen this, that, and the other in the house, what she liked best, which room she had, if she were comfortable, if Francesca was behaving, if Domenico took care of her, and whether she didn't enjoy using the yellow sitting-room—the one that got all the sun and looked out towards Genoa.

Rose was ashamed how little she had noticed in the house, and how few of the things he spoke of as curious or beautiful in it she had even seen. Swamped in thoughts of Frederick, she appeared to have lived in San Salvatore blindly, and more than half the time had gone, and what had been the good of it? She might just as well have been sitting hankering on Hampstead Heath. No, she mightn't; through all her hankerings she had been conscious that she was at least in the very heart of beauty; and indeed it was this beauty, this longing to share it, that had first started her off hankering.

Mr. Briggs, however, was too much alive for her to be able to spare any attention at this moment for Frederick, and she praised the servants in answer to his questions, and praised the yellow sitting-room without telling him she had only been in it once and then was ignominiously ejected, and she told him she knew hardly anything about art and curiosities, but thought perhaps if somebody would tell her about them she would know more, and she said she had spent every day since her arrival out of doors, because out of doors there was so very wonderful and different from anything she had ever seen.

Briggs walked by her side along his paths that were yet so happily for the moment her paths, and felt all the innocent glows of family life. He was an orphan and an only child, and had a warm, domestic disposition. He would have adored a sister and spoilt a mother, and was beginning at this time to think of marrying; for though he had been very happy with his various loves, each of whom, contrary to the usual experience, turned ultimately into his devoted friend, he was fond of children and thought he had perhaps now got to the age of settling if he did not wish to be too old by the time his eldest son was twenty. San Salvatore had latterly seemed a little forlorn. He fancied it echoed when he walked about it. He had felt lonely there; so lonely that he had preferred this year to miss out a spring and let it. It wanted a wife in it. It wanted that final touch of warmth and beauty, for he never thought of his wife except in terms of warmth and beauty—she would of course be beautiful and kind. It amused him how much in love with this vague wife he was already.

At such a rate was he making friends with the lady with the sweet name as he walked along the path towards the lighthouse, that he was sure presently he would be telling her everything about himself and his past doings and his future hopes; and the thought of such a swiftly developing confidence made him laugh.

"Why are you laughing?" she asked, looking at him and smiling.

"It's so like coming home," he said.

"But it is coming home for you to come here."

"I mean *really* like coming home. To one's—one's family. I never had a family. I'm an orphan."

"Oh, are you?" said Rose with the proper sympathy. "I hope you've not been one very long. No—I mean I hope you have been one very long. No—I don't know what I mean, except that I'm sorry."

He laughed again. "Oh, I'm used to it. I haven't anybody. No sisters or brothers."

"Then you're an only child," she observed intelligently.

"Yes. And there's something about you that's exactly my idea of a—of a family."

She was amused.

"So—cozy," he said, looking at her and searching for a word.

"You wouldn't think so if you saw my house in Hampstead," she said, a vision of that austere and hard-seated dwelling presenting itself to her mind, with nothing soft in it except the shunned and neglected Du Barri sofa. No wonder, she thought, for a moment clear-brained, that Frederick avoided it. There was nothing cozy about *his* family.

"I don't believe any place you lived in could be anything but exactly like you," he said.

"You're not going to pretend San Salvatore is like me?"

"Indeed I do pretend it. Surely you admit that it is beautiful?"

He said several things like that. She enjoyed her walk. She could not recollect any walk so pleasant since her courting days.

She came back to tea, bringing Mr. Briggs, and looking quite different, Mr. Wilkins noticed, from what she had looked till then. Trouble here, trouble here, thought Mr. Wilkins, mentally rubbing his professional hands. He could see himself being called in presently to advise. On the one hand there was Arbuthnot, on the other hand here was Briggs. Trouble brewing, trouble sooner or later. But why had Briggs's telegram acted on the lady like a blow? If she had turned pale from excess of joy, then trouble was nearer than he had supposed. She was not pale now; she was more like her name than he had yet seen her. Well, he was the man for trouble. He regretted, of course, that people should get into it, but being in he was their man.

And Mr. Wilkins, invigorated by these thoughts, his career being very precious to him, proceeded to assist in doing the honors to Mr. Briggs, both in his quality of sharer in the temporary ownership of San Salvatore and of probable helper out of difficulties, with great hospitality, and pointed out the various features of the place to him, and led him to the parapet and showed him Mezzago across the bay.

Mrs. Fisher too was gracious. This was this young man's house. He was a man of property. She liked property, and she liked men of property. Also there seemed a peculiar merit in being a man of property so young. Inheritance, of course; and inheritance was more respectable than acquisition. It did indicate fathers; and in an age where most people appeared neither to have them nor to want them she liked this too.

Accordingly it was a pleasant meal, with everybody amiable and pleased. Briggs thought Mrs. Fisher a dear old lady, and showed he thought so; and again the magic worked, and she became a dear old lady. She developed benignity with him, and a kind of benignity which was almost playful—actually before tea was over including in some observation she made him the words "My dear boy."

Strange words in Mrs. Fisher's mouth. It is doubtful whether in her life she had used them before. Rose was astonished. How nice people really were. When would she leave off making mistakes about them? She hadn't suspected this side of Mrs. Fisher, and she began to wonder whether those other sides of her with which alone she was acquainted had not perhaps after all been the effect of her own militant and irritating behavior. Probably they were. How horrid, then, she must have been. She felt very penitent when she saw Mrs. Fisher beneath her eyes blossoming out into real amiability the moment some one came along who was charming to her, and she could have sunk into the ground with shame when Mrs. Fisher presently laughed, and she realized by the shock it gave her that the sound was entirely new. Not once before had she or any one else there heard Mrs. Fisher laugh. What an indictment of the lot of them! For they had all laughed, the others, some more and some less, at one time or another since their arrival, and only Mrs. Fisher had not. Clearly, since she could enjoy herself as she was now enjoying herself, she had not enjoyed herself before. Nobody had cared whether she did or not, except perhaps Lotty. Yes; Lotty had cared, and had wanted her to be happy; but Lotty seemed to produce a bad effect on Mrs. Fisher, while as for Rose herself she had never been with her for five minutes without wanting, really wanting, to provoke and oppose her.

How very horrid she had been. She had behaved unpardonably. Her penitence showed itself in a shy and deferential solicitude towards Mrs. Fisher which made the observant Briggs think her still more angelic, and wish for a moment that he were an old lady himself in order to be behaved to by Rose Arbuthnot just like that. There was evidently no end, he thought, to the things she could do sweetly. He would even not mind taking medicine, really nasty medicine, if it were Rose Arbuthnot bending over him with the dose.

She felt his bright blue eyes, the brighter because he was so sunburnt, fixed on her with a twinkle in them, and smiling asked him what he was thinking about.

But he couldn't very well tell her that, he said; and added, "Some day."

"Trouble, trouble," thought Mr. Wilkins at this, again mentally rubbing his hands. "Well, I'm their man."

"I'm sure," said Mrs. Fisher benignly, "you have no thoughts we may not hear."

"I'm sure," said Briggs, "I would be telling you every one of my secrets in a week."

"You would be telling somebody very safe, then," said Mrs. Fisher benevolently—just such a son would she have liked to have had "And in return," she went on, "I daresay I would tell you mine."

"Ah no," said Mr. Wilkins, adapting himself to this tone of easy *badinage*, "I must protest. I really must. I have a prior claim, I am the older friend. I have known Mrs. Fisher ten days, and you, Briggs, have not yet known her one. I assert my right to be told her secrets first. That is," he added, bowing gallantly, "if she has any—which I beg leave to doubt."

"Oh, haven't I!" exclaimed Mrs. Fisher, thinking of those green leaves. That she should exclaim at all was surprising, but that she should do it with gaiety was miraculous. Rose could only watch her in wonder.

"Then I shall worm them out," said Briggs with equal gaiety.

"They won't need much worming out," said Mrs. Fisher. "My difficulty is to keep them from bursting out."

It might have been Lotty talking. Mr. Wilkins adjusted the single eyeglass he carried with him for occasions like this, and examined Mrs. Fisher carefully. Rose looked on, unable not to smile too since Mrs. Fisher seemed so much amused, though Rose did not quite know why, and her smile was a little uncertain, for Mrs. Fisher amused was a new sight, not without its awe-inspiring aspects, and had to be got accustomed to.

What Mrs. Fisher was thinking was how much surprised they would be if she told them of her very odd and exciting sensation of going to come out all over buds. They would think she was an extremely silly old woman, and so would she have thought as lately as two days ago; but the bud idea was becoming familiar to her, she was more *apprivoisée* now, as dear Matthew Arnold used to say, and though it would undoubtedly be best if one's appearance and sensations matched, yet supposing they did not—and one couldn't have everything—was it not better to feel young somewhere rather than old everywhere? Time enough to be old everywhere again, inside as well as out, when she got back to her sarcophagus in Prince of Wales Terrace.

Yet it is probable that without the arrival of Briggs Mrs. Fisher would have gone on secretly fermenting in her shell. The others only knew her as severe. It would have been more than her dignity could bear suddenly to relax—especially towards the three young women. But now came the stranger Briggs, a stranger who at once took to her as no young man had taken to her in her life, and it was the coming of Briggs and his real and manifest appreciation—for just such a grandmother, thought Briggs, hungry for home life and its concomitants, would he have liked to have—that released Mrs. Fisher from her shell; and here she was at last, as Lotty had predicted, pleased, good-humored, and benevolent.

Lotty, coming back half an hour later from her picnic, and following the sound of voices into the top garden in the hope of still finding tea, saw at once what had happened, for Mrs. Fisher at that very moment was laughing.

"She's burst her cocoon," thought Lotty; and swift as she was in all her movements, and impulsive, and also without any sense of propriety to worry and delay her, she bent over the back of Mrs. Fisher's chair and kissed her.

"Good gracious!" cried Mrs. Fisher, starting violently, for such a thing had not happened to her since Mr. Fisher's earlier days, and then only gingerly. This kiss was a real kiss, and rested on Mrs. Fisher's cheek a moment with a strange, soft sweetness.

When she saw whose it was, a deep flush spread over her face. Mrs. Wilkins kissing her and the kiss feeling so affectionate. . . . Even if she had wanted to she could not in the presence of the appreciative Mr. Briggs resume her cast-off severity and begin rebuking again; but she did not want to. Was it possible Mrs. Wilkins liked her—had liked her all this time, while she had been so much disliking her herself? A queer little trickle of warmth filtered through the frozen defenses of Mrs. Fisher's heart. Somebody young kissing her—somebody young *wanting* to kiss her. . . . Very much flushed, she watched the strange creature, apparently quite unconscious she had done anything extraordinary, shaking hands with Mr. Briggs, on her husband's introducing him, and immediately embarking on the friendliest conversation with him, exactly as if she had known him all her life. What a strange creature; what a very strange creature. It was natural, she being so strange, that one should have, perhaps, misjudged her. . .

"I'm sure you want some tea," said Briggs with eager hospitality to Lotty. He thought her delightful,—freckles, picnic-untidiness and all. Just such a sister would he—

"This is cold," he said, feeling the teapot. "I'll tell Francesca to make you some fresh—"

He broke off and blushed. "Aren't I forgetting myself," he said, laughing and looking round at them.

"Very natural, very natural," Mr. Wilkins reassured him.

"I'll go and tell Francesca," said Rose, getting up.

"No, no," said Briggs. "Don't go away." And he put his hands to his mouth and shouted.

"Francesca!" shouted Briggs.

She came running. No summons in their experience had been answered by her with such celerity.

"'Her master's voice,'" remarked Mr. Wilkins; aptly, he considered.

"Make fresh tea," ordered Briggs in Italian. "Quick—quick—" And then remembering himself he blushed again, and begged everybody's pardon.

"Very natural, very natural," Mr. Wilkins reassured him.

Briggs then explained to Lotty what he had explained twice already, once to Rose and once to the other two, that he was on his way to Rome and thought he would get out at Mezzago and just look in to see if they were comfortable and continue his journey the next day, staying the night in an hotel at Mezzago.

"But how ridiculous," said Lotty. "Of course you must stay here. It's your house. There's Kate Lumley's room," she added, turning to Mrs. Fisher. "You wouldn't mind Mr. Briggs having it for one night? Kate Lumley isn't in it, you know," she said, turning to Briggs again and laughing.

And Mrs. Fisher to her immense surprise laughed too. She knew that at any other time this remark would have struck her as excessively unseemly, and yet now she only thought it funny.

No indeed, she assured Briggs, Kate Lumley was not in that room. Very fortunately, for she was an excessively wide person and the room was excessively narrow. Kate Lumley might get into it, but that was about all. Once in, she would fit it so tightly that probably she would never be able to get out again. It was entirely at Mr. Briggs's disposal, and she hoped he would do nothing so absurd as go to an hotel—he, the owner of the whole place.

Rose listened to this speech wide-eyed with amazement. Mrs. Fisher laughed very much as she made it. Lotty laughed very much too, and at the end of it bent down and kissed her again—kissed her several times.

"So you see, my dear boy," said Mrs. Fisher, "you must stay here and give us all a great deal of pleasure."

"A great deal indeed," corroborated Mr. Wilkins heartily.

"A very great deal," repeated Mrs. Fisher, looking exactly like a pleased mother.

"Do," said Rose, on Briggs's turning inquiringly to her.

"How kind of you all," he said, his face broad with smiles. "I'd love to be a guest here. What a new sensation. And with three such—"

He broke off and looked round. "I say," he asked, "oughtn't I to have a fourth hostess? Francesca said she had four mistresses."

"Yes. There's Lady Caroline," said Lotty.

"Then hadn't we better find out first if she invites me too?"

"Oh, but she's sure—" began Lotty.

"The daughter of the Droitwiches, Briggs," said Mr. Wilkins, "is not likely to be wanting in the proper hospitable impulses."

"The daughter of the—" repeated Briggs; but he stopped dead, for there in the doorway was the daughter of the Droitwiches herself; or rather, coming towards him out of the dark doorway into the brightness of the sunset, was that which he had not in his life yet seen but only dreamed of, his ideal of absolute loveliness.

CHAPTER 19

And then when she spoke . . . what chance was there for poor Briggs? He was undone. All Scrap said was, "How do you do," on Mr. Wilkins presenting him, but it was enough; it undid Briggs.

From a cheerful, chatty, happy young man, overflowing with life and friendliness, he became silent, solemn, and with little beads on his temples. Also he became clumsy, dropping the teaspoon as he handed her her cup, mismanaging the macaroons, so that one rolled on the ground. His eyes could not keep off the enchanting face for a moment; and when Mr. Wilkins, elucidating him, for he failed to elucidate himself, informed Lady Caroline that in Mr. Briggs she beheld the owner of San Salvatore, who was on his way to Rome, but had got out at Mezzago, etc., etc., and that the other three ladies had invited him to spend the night in what was to all intents and purposes his own house rather than an hotel, and Mr. Briggs was only waiting for the seal of her approval to this invitation, she being the fourth hostess—when Mr. Wilkins, balancing his sentences and being admirably clear and enjoying the sound of his own cultured voice, explained the position in this manner to Lady Caroline, Briggs sat and said never a word.

A deep melancholy invaded Scrap. The symptoms of the incipient grabber were all there and only too familiar, and she knew that if Briggs stayed her rest-cure might be regarded as over.

Then Kate Lumley occurred to her. She caught at Kate as at a straw.

"It would have been delightful," she said, faintly smiling at Briggs—she could not in decency not smile, at least a little, but even a little betrayed the dimple, and Briggs's eyes became more fixed than ever—"I'm only wondering if there is room."

"Yes, there is," said Lotty. "There's Kate Lumley's room."

"I thought," said Scrap to Mrs. Fisher, and it seemed to Briggs that he had never heard music till now, "your friend was expected immediately."

"Oh no," said Mrs. Fisher—with an odd placidness, Scrap thought.

"Miss Lumley," said Mr. Wilkins, "—or should I," he inquired of Mrs. Fisher, "say Mrs.?"

"Nobody has ever married Kate," said Mrs. Fisher complacently.

"Quite so. Miss Lumley does not arrive to-day in any case, Lady Caroline, and Mr. Briggs has—unfortunately, if I may say so—to continue his journey to-morrow, so that his staying would in no way interfere with Miss Lumley's possible movements."

"Then of course I join in the invitation," said Scrap, with what was to Briggs the most divine cordiality.

He stammered something, flushing scarlet, and Scrap thought, "*Oh*," and turned her head away; but that merely made Briggs acquainted with her profile, and if there existed anything more lovely than Scrap's full face it was her profile.

Well, it was only for this one afternoon and evening. He would leave, no doubt, the first thing in the morning. It took hours to get to Rome. Awful if he hung on till the night train. She had a feeling that the principal express to Rome passed through at night. Why hadn't that woman Kate Lumley arrived yet? She had forgotten all about her, but now she remembered she was to have been invited a fortnight ago. What had become of her? This man, once let in, would come and see her in London, would haunt the places she was likely to go to. He had the makings, her experienced eye could see, of a passionately persistent grabber.

"If," thought Mr. Wilkins, observing Briggs's face and sudden silence, "any understanding existed between this young fellow and Mrs. Arbuthnot, there is now going to be trouble. Trouble of a different nature from the kind I feared, in which Arbuthnot would have played a leading part, in fact the part of petitioner, but trouble that may need help and advice none the less for its not being publicly scandalous. Briggs, impelled by his passions and her beauty, will aspire to the daughter of the Droitwiches. She, naturally and properly, will repel him. Mrs. Arbuthnot, left in the cold, will be upset and show it. Arbuthnot on his arrival will find his wife in enigmatic tears. Inquiring into their cause, he will be met with an icy reserve. More trouble may then be expected, and in me they will seek and find their adviser. When Lotty said Mrs. Arbuthnot wanted her husband, she was wrong. What Mrs. Arbuthnot wants is Briggs, and it looks uncommonly as if she were not going to get him. Well, I'm their man."

"Where are your things, Mr. Briggs?" asked Mrs. Fisher, her voice round with motherliness. "Oughtn't they to be fetched?" For the sun was nearly in the sea now, and the sweet-smelling April dampness that followed immediately on its disappearance was beginning to steal into the garden.

Briggs started. "My things?" he repeated. "Oh yes—I must fetch them. They're in Mezzago. I'll send Domenico. My fly is waiting in the village. He can go back in it. I'll go and tell him."

He got up. To whom was he talking? To Mrs. Fisher, ostensibly, yet his eyes were fixed on Scrap, who said nothing and looked at no one.

Then, recollecting himself, he stammered, "I'm awfully sorry—I keep on forgetting—I'll go down and fetch them myself."

"We can easily send Domenico," said Rose; and at her gentle voice he turned his head.

Why, there was his friend, the sweet-named lady—but how had she not in this short interval changed! Was it the failing light making her so colorless, so vague-featured, so dim, so much like a ghost? A nice good ghost, of course, and still with a pretty name, but only a ghost.

He turned from her to Scrap again, and forgot Rose Arbuthnot's existence. How was it possible for him to bother about anybody or anything else in this first moment of being face to face with his dream come true?

Briggs had not supposed or hoped that any one as beautiful as his dream of beauty existed. He had never till now met even an approximation. Pretty women, charming women by the score he had met and properly appreciated, but never the real, the godlike thing itself. He used to think, "If ever I saw a perfectly beautiful woman I should die"; and though, having now met what to his ideas was a perfectly beautiful woman, he did not die, he became very nearly as incapable of managing his own affairs as if he had.

The others were obliged to arrange everything for him. By questions they extracted from him that his luggage was in the station cloakroom at Mezzago, and they sent for Domenico, and, urged and prompted by everybody except Scrap, who sat in silence and looked at no one, Briggs was induced to give him the necessary instructions for going back in the fly and bringing out his things.

It was a sad sight to see the collapse of Briggs. Everybody noticed it, even Rose.

"Upon my word," thought Mrs. Fisher, "the way one pretty face can turn a delightful man into an idiot is past all patience."

And feeling the air getting chilly, and the sight of the enthralled Briggs painful, she went in to order his room to be got ready, regretting now that she had pressed the poor boy to stay. She had forgotten

Lady Caroline's kill-joy face for the moment, and the more completely owing to the absence of any ill effects produced by it on Mr. Wilkins. Poor boy. Such a charming boy too, left to himself. It was true she could not accuse Lady Caroline of not leaving him to himself, for she was taking no notice of him at all, but that did not help. Exactly like foolish moths did men, in other respects intelligent, flutter round the impassive lighted candle of a pretty face. She had seen them doing it. She had looked on only too often. Almost she laid a motherly hand on Briggs's fair head as she passed him. Poor boy.

Then Scrap, having finished her cigarette, got up and went indoors too. She saw no reason why she should sit there in order to gratify Mr. Briggs's desire to stare. She would have liked to stay out longer, to go to her corner behind the daphne bushes and look at the sunset sky and watch the lights coming out one by one in the village below and smell the sweet moistness of the evening, but if she did Mr. Briggs would certainly follow her.

The old familiar tyranny had begun again. Her holiday of peace and liberation was interrupted—perhaps over, for who knew if he would go away, after all, to-morrow? He might leave the house, driven out of it by Kate Lumley, but there was nothing to prevent his taking rooms in the village and coming up every day. This tyranny of one person over another! And she was so miserably constructed that she wouldn't even be able to frown him down without being misunderstood.

Scrap, who loved this time of the evening in her corner, felt indignant with Mr. Briggs who was doing her out of it, and she turned her back on the garden and him and went towards the house without a look or a word. But Briggs, when he realized her intention, leapt to his feet, snatched chairs which were not in her way out of it, kicked a footstool which was not in her path on one side, hurried to the door, which stood wide open, in order to hold it open, and followed her through it, walking by her side along the hall.

What was to be done with Mr. Briggs? Well, it was his hall; she couldn't prevent his walking along it.

"I hope," he said, not able while walking to take his eyes off her, so that he knocked against several things he would otherwise have avoided—the corner of a bookcase, an ancient carved cupboard, the table with the flowers on it, shaking the water over—"that you are quite comfortable here? If you're not I'll—I'll flay them alive."

His voice vibrated. What was to be done with Mr. Briggs? She could of course stay in her room the whole time, say she was ill, not appear at dinner; but again, the tyranny of this . . .

"I'm very comfortable indeed," said Scrap.

"If I had dreamed you were coming—" he began.

"It's a wonderful old place," said Scrap, doing her utmost to sound detached and forbidding, but with little hope of success.

The kitchen was on this floor, and passing its door, which was open a crack, they were observed by the servants, whose thoughts, communicated to each other by looks, may be roughly reproduced by such rude symbols as Aha and Oho—symbols which represented and included their appreciation of the inevitable, their foreknowledge of the inevitable, and their complete understanding and approval.

"Are you going upstairs?" asked Briggs, as she paused at the foot of them.

"Yes."

"Which room do you sit in? The drawing-room, or the small yellow room?"

"In my own room."

So then he couldn't go up with her; so then all he could do was to wait till she came out again.

He longed to ask her which was her own room—it thrilled him to hear her call any room in his house her own room—that he might picture her in it. He longed to know if by any happy chance it was his room, for ever after to be filled with her wonder;

but he didn't dare. He would find that out later from some one else—Francesca, anybody.

"Then I shan't see you again till dinner?"

"Dinner is at eight," was Scrap's evasive answer as she went upstairs.

He watched her go.

She passed the Madonna, the portrait of Rose Arbuthnot, and the dark-eyed figure he had thought so sweet seemed to turn pale, to shrivel into insignificance as she passed.

She turned the bend of the stairs, and the setting sun, shining through the west window a moment on her face, turned her to glory.

She disappeared, and the sun went out too, and the stairs were dark and empty.

He listened till her footsteps were silent, trying to tell from the sound of the shutting door which room she had gone into, then wandered aimlessly away through the hall again, and found himself back in the top garden.

Scrap from her window saw him there. She saw Lotty and Rose sitting on the end parapet, where she would have liked to have been, and she saw Mr. Wilkins buttonholing Briggs and evidently telling him the story of the oleander tree in the middle of the garden.

Briggs was listening with a patience she thought rather nice, seeing that it was his oleander and his own father's story. She knew Mr. Wilkins was telling him the story by his gestures. Domenico had told it her soon after her arrival, and he had also told Mrs. Fisher, who had told Mr. Wilkins. Mrs. Fisher thought highly of this story, and often spoke of it. It was about a cherrywood walking-stick. Briggs's father had thrust this stick into the ground at that spot, and said to Domenico's father, who was then the gardener, "Here we will have an oleander." And Briggs's father left the stick in the ground as a reminder to Domenico's father, and presently—how long afterwards nobody remembered—the stick began to sprout, and it was an oleander.

There stood poor Mr. Briggs being told all about it, and listening with patience to the story he must have known from infancy.

Probably he was thinking of something else. She was afraid he was. How unfortunate, how extremely unfortunate, the determination that seized people to get hold of and engulf other people. If only they could be induced to stand more on their own feet. Why couldn't Mr. Briggs be more like Lotty, who never wanted anything of anybody, but was complete in herself and respected other people's completeness? One loved being with Lotty. With her one was free, and yet befriended. Mr. Briggs looked so really nice, too. She thought she might like him if only he wouldn't so excessively like her.

Scrap felt melancholy. Here she was shut up in her bedroom, which was stuffy from the afternoon sun that had been pouring into it, instead of out in the cool garden, and all because of Mr. Briggs.

Intolerable tyranny, she thought, flaring up. She wouldn't endure it; she would go out all the same; she would run downstairs while Mr. Wilkins—really that man was a treasure—held Mr. Briggs down telling him about the oleander, and get out of the house by the front door, and take cover in the shadows of the zigzag path. Nobody could see her there; nobody would think of looking for her there.

She snatched up a wrap, for she did not mean to come back for a long while, perhaps not even to dinner—it would be all Mr. Briggs's fault if she went dinnerless and hungry—and with another glance out of the window to see if she were still safe, she stole out and got away to the sheltering trees of the zigzag path, and there sat down on one of the seats placed at each bend to assist the upward journey of those who were breathless.

Ah, this was lovely, thought Scrap with a sigh of relief. How cool. How good it smelt. She could see the quiet water of the little harbor through the pine trunks, and the lights coming out in the houses on the other side, and all round her the green dusk was splashed by the rose-pink of the gladioluses in the grass and the white of the crowding daisies.

Ah, this was lovely. So still. Nothing moving—not a leaf, not a stalk. The only sound was a dog barking, far away somewhere up on the hills, or when the door of the little restaurant in the piazza below was opened and there was a burst of voices, silenced again immediately by the swinging to of the door.

She drew in a deep breath of pleasure. Ah, this was—

Her deep breath was arrested in the middle. What was that?

She leaned forward listening, her body tense.

Footsteps. On the zigzag path. Briggs. Finding her out.

Should she run?

No—the footsteps were coming up, not down. Some one from the village. Perhaps Angelo, with provisions.

She relaxed again. But the steps were not the steps of Angelo, that swift and springy youth; they were slow and considered, and they kept on pausing.

"Some one who isn't used to hills," thought Scrap.

The idea of going back to the house did not occur to her. She was afraid of nothing in life except love. Brigands or murderers as such held no terrors for the daughter of the Droitwiches; she only would have been afraid of them if they left off being brigands and murderers and began instead to try and make love.

The next moment the footsteps turned the corner of her bit of path, and stood still.

"Getting his wind," thought Scrap, not looking round.

Then as he—from the sounds of the steps she took them to belong to a man—did not move, she turned her head, and beheld with astonishment a person she had seen a good deal of lately in London, the well-known writer of amusing memoirs, Mr. Ferdinand Arundel.

She stared. Nothing in the way of being followed surprised her any more, but that he should have discovered where she was surprised her. Her mother had promised faithfully to tell no one.

"You?" she said, feeling betrayed. "Here?"

He came up to her and took off his hat. His forehead beneath the hat was wet with the beads of unaccustomed climbing. He looked ashamed and entreating, like a guilty but devoted dog.

"You must forgive me," he said. "Lady Droitwich told me where you were, and as I happened to be passing through on my way to Rome I thought I would get out at Mezzago and just look in and see how you were."

"But—didn't my mother tell you I was doing a rest-cure?"

"Yes. She did. And that's why I haven't intruded on you earlier in the day. I thought you would probably sleep all day, and wake up about now so as to be fed."

"But—"

"I know. I've got nothing to say in excuse. I couldn't help myself."

"This," thought Scrap, "comes of mother insisting on having authors to lunch, and me being so much more amiable in appearance than I really am."

She had been amiable to Ferdinand Arundel; she liked him or rather she did not dislike him. He seemed a jovial, simple man, and had the eyes of a nice dog. Also, though it was evident that he admired her, he had not in London grabbed. There he had merely been a good-natured, harmless person of entertaining conversation, who helped to make luncheons agreeable. Now it appeared that he too was a grabber. Fancy following her out there—daring to. Nobody else had. Perhaps her mother had given him the address because she considered him so absolutely harmless, and thought he might be useful and see her home.

Well, whatever he was he couldn't possibly give her the trouble an active young man like Mr. Briggs might give her. Mr. Briggs, infatuated, would be reckless, she felt, would stick at nothing, would lose his head publicly. She could imagine Mr. Briggs doing things with rope-ladders, and singing all night under her window—being really difficult and uncomfortable. Mr. Arundel hadn't the figure for any kind of recklessness. He had lived too long and too well. She was sure he couldn't sing, and wouldn't want to. He must be at least forty. How many good dinners could not a man have eaten by the time he was forty? And if during that time instead of taking exercise he had sat writing books, he would quite naturally acquire the figure Mr. Arundel had in fact acquired—the figure rather for conversation than adventure.

Scrap, who had become melancholy at the sight of Briggs, became philosophical at the sight of Arundel. Here he was. She couldn't send him away till after dinner. He must be nourished.

This being so, she had better make the best of it, and do that with a good grace which anyhow wasn't to be avoided. Besides, he would be a temporary shelter from Mr. Briggs. She was at least acquainted with Ferdinand Arundel, and could hear news from him of her mother and her friends, and such talk would put up a defensive barrier at dinner between herself and the approaches of the other one. And it was only for one dinner, and he couldn't eat *her*.

She therefore prepared herself for friendliness. "I'm to be fed," she said, ignoring his last remark, "at eight, and you must come up and be fed too. Sit down and get cool and tell me how everybody is."

"May I really dine with you? In these traveling things?" he said, wiping his forehead before sitting down beside her.

She was too lovely to be true, he thought. Just to look at her for an hour, just to hear her voice, was enough reward for his journey and his fears.

"Of course. I suppose you've left your fly in the village, and will be going on from Mezzago by the night train."

"Or stay in Mezzago in an hotel and go on to-morrow. But tell me," he said, gazing at the adorable profile, "about yourself. London has been extraordinarily dull and empty. Lady Droitwich said you were with people here she didn't know. I hope they've been kind to you? You look—well, as if your cure had done everything a cure should."

"They've been very kind," said Scrap. "I got them out of an advertisement."

"An advertisement?"

"It's a good way, I find, to get friends. I'm fonder of one of these than I've been of anybody in years."

"Really? Who is it?"

"You shall guess which of them it is when you see them. Tell me about mother. When did you see her last? We arranged not to write to each other unless there was something special. I wanted to have a month that was perfectly blank."

"And now I've come and interrupted. I can't tell you how ashamed I am—both of having done it and of not having been able to help it."

"Oh, but," said Scrap quickly, for he could not have come on a better day, when up there waiting and watching for her was, she knew, the enamored Briggs, "I'm really very glad indeed to see you. Tell me about mother."

CHAPTER 20

Scrap wanted to know so much about her mother that Arundel had presently to invent. He would talk about anything she wished if only he might be with her for a while and see her and hear her, but he knew very little of the Droitwiches and their friends really—beyond meeting them at those bigger functions where literature is also represented, and amusing them at luncheons and dinners, he knew very little of them really. To them he had always remained Mr. Arundel; no one called him Ferdinand; and he only knew the gossip also available to the evening papers and the frequenters of clubs. But he was, however, good at inventing; and as soon as he had come to an end of first-hand knowledge, in order to answer her inquiries and keep her there to himself he proceeded to invent. It was quite easy to fasten some of the entertaining things he was constantly thinking on to other people and pretend they were theirs. Scrap, who had that affection for her parents which warms in absence, was athirst for news, and became more and more interested by the news he gradually imparted.

At first it was ordinary news. He had met her mother here, and seen her there. She looked very well; she said so and so. But presently the things Lady Droitwich had said took on an unusual quality: they became amusing.

"Mother said *that?*" Scrap interrupted, surprised.

And presently Lady Droitwich began to do amusing things as well as say them.

"*Mother* did that?" Scrap inquired, wide-eyed.

Arundel warmed to his work. He fathered some of the most entertaining ideas he had lately had on to Lady Droitwich, and also any charming funny things that had been done—or might have been done, for he could imagine almost anything.

Scrap's eyes grew round with wonder and affectionate pride in her mother. Why, but how funny—fancy mother. What an old darling. Did she really do that? How perfectly adorable of her. And did she really say—but how wonderful of her to think of it. What sort of a face did Lloyd George make?

She laughed and laughed, and had a great longing to hug her mother, and the time flew, and it grew quite dusk, and it grew nearly dark, and Mr. Arundel still went on amusing her, and it was a quarter to eight before she suddenly remembered dinner.

"Oh, good heavens!" she exclaimed, jumping up.

"Yes. It's late," said Arundel.

"I'll go on quickly and send the maid to you. I must run, or I'll never be ready in time—"

And she was gone up the path with the swiftness of a young, slender deer.

Arundel followed. He did not wish to arrive too hot, so had to go slowly. Fortunately he was near the top, and Francesca came down the pergola to pilot him indoors, and having shown him where he could wash she put him in the empty drawing-room to cool himself by the crackling wood fire.

He got as far away from the fire as he could, and stood in one of the deep window-recesses looking out at the distant lights of Mezzago. The drawing-room door was open, and the house was quiet with the hush that precedes dinner, when the inhabitants are all shut up in their rooms dressing. Briggs in his room was throwing away spoilt tie after spoilt tie; Scrap in hers was hurrying into a black frock with a vague notion that Mr. Briggs wouldn't be able to see her so clearly in black; Mrs. Fisher was fastening the lace shawl, which nightly transformed her day dress into her evening dress, with the brooch Ruskin had given her on her marriage, formed of two pearl lilies tied together by a blue enamel ribbon on which was written in gold letters *Esto perpetua*; Mr. Wilkins was sitting on the edge of his bed brushing his wife's hair—thus far in this third week had he progressed in demonstrativeness—while she, for her part, sitting on a chair in front of him, put his studs in a clean shirt; and Rose, ready dressed, sat at her window considering her day.

Rose was quite aware of what had happened to Mr. Briggs. If she had had any difficulty about it, Lotty would have removed it by the frank comments she made while she and Rose sat together after tea on the wall. Lotty was delighted at more love being introduced into San Salvatore, even if it were only one-sided, and said that when once Rose's husband was there she didn't suppose, now that Mrs. Fisher too had at last come unglued—Rose protested at the expression, and Lotty retorted that it was in Keats—there would be another place in the world more swarming with happiness than San Salvatore.

"Your husband," said Lotty, swinging her feet, "might be here quite soon, perhaps to-morrow evening if he starts at once, and there'll be a glorious final few days before we all go home refreshed for life. I don't believe any of us will ever be the same again—and I wouldn't be a bit surprised if Caroline doesn't end by getting fond of the young man Briggs. It's in the air. You *have* to get fond of people here."

Rose sat at her window thinking of these things. Lotty's optimism . . . yet it had been justified by Mr. Wilkins; and look, too, at Mrs. Fisher. If only it would come true as well about Frederick! For Rose, who between lunch and tea had left off thinking about Frederick, was now, between tea and dinner, thinking of him harder than ever.

It had been funny and delightful, that little interlude of admiration, but of course it couldn't go on once Caroline appeared. Rose knew her place. She could see as well as any one the unusual, the unique loveliness of Lady Caroline. How warm, though, things like admiration and appreciation made one feel, how capable of really deserving them, how different, how glowing. They seemed to quicken unsuspected faculties into life. She was sure she had been a thoroughly amusing woman between lunch and tea, and a pretty one too. She was quite certain she had been pretty; she saw it in Mr. Briggs's eyes as clearly as in a looking-glass. For a brief space, she thought, she had been like a torpid fly brought back to gay buzzing by the lighting of a fire in a wintry room. She still buzzed, she still tingled, just at the remembrance. What fun it had been, having an admirer even for that little while. No wonder people liked admirers. They seemed, in some strange way, to make one come alive.

Although it was all over she still glowed with it and felt more exhilarated, more optimistic, more as Lotty probably constantly felt, than she had done since she was a girl. She dressed with care, though she knew Mr. Briggs would no longer see her, but it gave her pleasure to see how pretty, while she was about it, she could make herself look; and very nearly she stuck a crimson camellia in her hair down by her ear. She did hold it there for a minute, and it looked almost sinfully attractive and was exactly the color of her mouth, but she took it out again with a smile and a sigh and put it in the proper place for flowers, which is water. She mustn't be silly, she thought. Think of the poor. Soon she would be back with them again, and what would a camellia behind her ear seem like then? Simply fantastic.

But on one thing she was determined: the first thing she would do when she got home would be to have it out with Frederick. If he didn't come to San Salvatore that is what she would do—the very first thing. Long ago she ought to have done this, but always she had been handicapped, when she tried to, by being so dreadfully fond of him and so much afraid that fresh wounds were going to be given her wretched, soft heart. But now let him wound her as much as he chose, as much as he possibly could, she would still have it out with him. Not that he ever intentionally wounded her; she knew he never meant to, she knew he often had no idea of having done it. For a person who wrote books, thought Rose, Frederick didn't seem to have much imagination. Anyhow, she said to herself, getting up from the dressing-table, things couldn't go on like this. She would have it out with him. This separate life, this freezing loneliness, she had had enough of it. Why shouldn't she too be happy? Why on earth—the energetic expression matched her mood of rebelliousness—shouldn't she too be loved and allowed to love?

She looked at her little clock. Still ten minutes before dinner. Tired of staying in her bedroom she thought she would go on to Mrs. Fisher's battlements, which would be empty at this hour, and watch the moon rise out of the sea.

She went into the deserted upper hall with this intention, but was attracted on her way along it by the firelight shining through the open door of the drawing-room.

How gay it looked. The fire transformed the room. A dark, ugly room in the daytime, it was transformed just as she had been transformed by the warmth of—no, she wouldn't be silly; she would think of the poor; the thought of them always brought her down to sobriety at once.

She peeped in. Firelight and flowers; and outside the deep slits of windows hung the blue curtain of the night. How pretty. What a sweet place San Salvatore was. And that gorgeous lilac on the table—she must go and put her face in it . . .

But she never got to the lilac. She went one step towards it, and then stood still, for she had seen the figure looking out of the window in the farthest corner, and it was Frederick.

All the blood in Rose's body rushed to her heart and seemed to stop its beating.

Frederick. Come.

She stood quite still. He had not heard her. He did not turn round. She stood looking at him. The miracle had happened, and he had come.

She stood holding her breath. So he needed her, for he had come instantly. So he too must have been thinking, longing . . .

Her heart, which had seemed to stop beating, was suffocating her now, the way it raced along. Frederick did love her then—he must love her, or why had he come? Something, perhaps her absence, had made him turn to her, want her . . . and now the understanding she had made up her mind to have with him would be quite—would be quite—easy—

Her thoughts wouldn't go on. Her mind stammered. She couldn't think. She could only see and feel. She didn't know how it had happened. It was a miracle. God could do miracles. God had done this one. God could—God could—could—

Her mind stammered again, and broke off.

"Frederick—" she tried to say; but no sound came, or if it did the crackling of the fire covered it up.

She must go nearer. She began to creep towards him—softly, softly.

He did not move. He had not heard.

She stole nearer and nearer, and the fire crackled and he heard nothing.

She stopped a moment, unable to breathe. She was afraid. Suppose he—suppose he—oh, but he had come, he had come.

She went on again, close up to him, and her heart beat so loud that she thought he must hear it. And couldn't he feel—didn't he know—

"Frederick," she whispered, hardly able even to whisper, choked by the beating of her heart.

He spun round on his heels.

"Rose!" he exclaimed, staring blankly.

But she did not see his stare, for her arms were round his neck, and her cheek was against his, and she was murmuring, her lips on his ear, "I knew you would come—in my very heart I always, always knew you would come—"

CHAPTER 21

Now Frederick was not the man to hurt anything if he could help it; besides, he was completely bewildered. Not only was his wife here—here, of all places in the world—but she was clinging to him as she had not clung for years, and murmuring love, and welcoming him. If she welcomed him she must have been expecting him. Strange as this was, it was the only thing in the situation which was evident—that, and the softness of her cheek against his, and the long-forgotten sweet smell of her.

Frederick was bewildered. But not being the man to hurt anything if he could help it he too put his arms round her, and having put them round her he also kissed her; and presently he was kissing her almost as tenderly as she was kissing him; and presently he was kissing her quite as tenderly; and again presently he was kissing her more tenderly, and just as if he had never left off.

He was bewildered, but he still could kiss. It seemed curiously natural to be doing it. It made him feel as if he were thirty again instead of forty, and Rose were his Rose of twenty, the Rose he had so much adored before she began to weigh what he did with her idea of right, and the balance went against him, and she had turned strange, and stony, and more and more shocked, and oh, so lamentable. He couldn't get at her in those days at all; she wouldn't, she couldn't understand. She kept on referring everything to what she called God's eyes—in God's eyes it couldn't be right, it wasn't right. Her miserable face—whatever her principles did for her they didn't make her happy—her little miserable face, twisted with effort to be patient, had been at last more than he could bear to see, and he had kept away as much as he could. She never ought to have been the daughter of a low-church rector—narrow devil; she was quite unfitted to stand up against such an upbringing.

What had happened, why she was here, why she was his Rose again, passed his comprehension; and meanwhile, and until such time as he understood, he still could kiss. In fact he could not stop kissing; and it was he now who began to murmur, to say love things in her ear under the hair that smelt so sweet and tickled him just as he remembered it used to tickle him.

And as he held her close to his heart and her arms were soft round his neck, he felt stealing over him a delicious sense of—at first he didn't know what it was, this delicate, pervading warmth, and then he recognized it as security. Yes; security. No need now to be ashamed of his figure, and to make jokes about it so as to forestall other people's and show he didn't mind it; no need now to be ashamed of getting hot going up hills, or to torment himself with pictures of how he probably appeared to beautiful young women—how middle-aged, how absurd in his inability to keep away from them. Rose cared nothing for such things. With her he was safe. To her he was her lover, as he used to be; and she would never notice or mind any of the ignoble changes that getting older had made in him and would go on making more and more.

Frederick continued, therefore, with greater and greater warmth and growing delight to kiss his wife, and the mere holding of her in his arms caused him to forget everything else. How could he, for instance, remember or think of Lady Caroline, to mention only one of the complications with which his situation bristled, when here was his sweet wife, miraculously restored to him, whispering with her cheek against his in the dearest, most romantic words how much she loved him, how terribly she had missed him? He did for one brief instant, for even in moments of love there are brief instants of lucid thought, recognize the immense power of the woman present and being actually held compared to that of the woman, however beautiful, who is somewhere else, but that is as far as he got towards remembering Scrap; no farther. She was like a dream, fleeing before the morning light.

"When did you start?" murmured Rose, her mouth on his ear. She couldn't let him go; not even to talk she couldn't let him go.

"Yesterday morning," murmured Frederick, holding her close. He couldn't let her go either.

"Oh—the very instant then," murmured Rose.

This was cryptic, but Frederick said, "Yes, the very instant," and kissed her neck.

"How quickly my letter got to you," murmured Rose, whose eyes were shut in the excess of her happiness.

"Didn't it," said Frederick, who felt like shutting his eyes himself.

So there had been a letter. Soon, no doubt, light would be vouchsafed him, and meanwhile this was so strangely, touchingly sweet, this holding his Rose to his heart again after all the years, that he couldn't bother to try to guess anything. Oh, he had been happy during these years, because it was not in him to be unhappy; besides, how many interests life had had to offer him, how many friends, how much success, how many women only too willing to help him to blot out the thought of the altered, petrified, pitiful little wife at home who wouldn't spend his money, who was appalled by his books, who drifted away and away from him, and always if he tried to have it out with her asked him with patient obstinacy what he thought the things he wrote and lived by looked in the eyes of God. "No one," she said once, "should ever write a book God wouldn't like to read. That is the test, Frederick." And he had laughed hysterically, burst into a great shriek of laughter, and rushed out of the house, away from her solemn little face—away from her pathetic, solemn little face . . .

But this Rose was his youth again, the best part of his life, the part of it that had had all the visions in it and all the hopes. How they had dreamed together, he and she, before he struck that vein of memoirs; how they had planned, and laughed, and loved. They had lived for a while in the very heart of poetry. After the happy days came the happy nights, the happy, happy nights, with her asleep close against his heart, with her when he woke in the morning still close against his heart, for they hardly moved in their deep, happy sleep. It was wonderful to have it all come back to him at the touch of her, at the feel of her face against his—wonderful that she should be able to give him back his youth.

"Sweetheart—sweetheart," he murmured, overcome by remembrance, clinging to her now in his turn.

"Beloved husband," she breathed—the bliss of it—the sheer bliss . . .

Briggs, coming in a few minutes before the gong went on the chance that Lady Caroline might be there, was much astonished. He had supposed Rose Arbuthnot was a widow, and he still supposed it; so that he was much astonished.

"Well, I'm damned," thought Briggs, quite clearly and distinctly, for the shock of what he saw in the window startled him so much that for a moment he was shaken free of his own confused absorption.

Aloud he said, very red, "Oh, I say—I beg your pardon"—and then stood hesitating, and wondering whether he oughtn't to go back to his bedroom again.

If he had said nothing they would not have noticed he was there, but when he begged their pardon Rose turned and looked at him as one looks who is trying to remember, and Frederick looked at him too without at first quite seeing him.

They didn't seem, thought Briggs, to mind or to be at all embarrassed. He couldn't be her brother; no brother ever brought that look into a woman's face. It was very awkward. If they didn't mind, he did. It upset him to come across his Madonna forgetting herself.

"Is this one of your friends?" Frederick was able after an instant to ask Rose, who made no attempt to introduce the young man standing awkwardly in front of them but continued to gaze at him with a kind of abstracted, radiant goodwill.

"It's Mr. Briggs," said Rose, recognizing him. "This is my husband," she added.

And Briggs, shaking hands, just had time to think how surprising it was to have a husband when you were a widow before the gong sounded, and Lady Caroline would be there in a minute, and he ceased to be able to think at all, and merely became a thing with its eyes fixed on the door.

Through the door immediately entered, in what seemed to him an endless procession, first Mrs. Fisher, very stately in her evening lace shawl and brooch, who when she saw him at once relaxed into smiles and benignity, only to stiffen, however, when she caught sight of the stranger; then Mr. Wilkins, cleaner and neater and more carefully dressed and brushed than any man on earth; and then, tying something hurriedly as she came, Mrs. Wilkins; and then nobody.

Lady Caroline was late. Where was she? Had she heard the gong? Oughtn't it to be beaten again? Suppose she didn't come to dinner after all . . .

Briggs went cold.

"Introduce me," said Frederick on Mrs. Fisher's entrance, touching Rose's elbow.

"My husband," said Rose, holding him by the hand, her face exquisite.

"This," thought Mrs. Fisher, "must now be the last of the husbands, unless Lady Caroline produces one from up her sleeve."

But she received him graciously, for he certainly looked exactly like a husband, not at all like one of those people who go about abroad pretending they are husbands when they are not, and said she supposed he had come to accompany his wife home at the end of the month, and remarked that now the house would be completely full. "So that," she added, smiling at Briggs, "we shall at last really be getting our money's worth."

Briggs grinned automatically, because he was just able to realize that somebody was being playful with him, but he had not heard her and he did not look at her. Not only were his eyes fixed on the door but his whole body was concentrated on it.

Introduced in his turn, Mr. Wilkins was most hospitable and called Frederick "sir."

"Well, sir," said Mr. Wilkins heartily, "here we are, here we are"—and having gripped his hand with an understanding that only wasn't mutual because Arbuthnot did not yet know what he was in for in the way of trouble, he looked at him as a man should, squarely in the eyes, and allowed his look to convey as plainly as a look can that in him would be found staunchness, integrity, reliability—in fact a friend in need. Mrs. Arbuthnot was very much flushed, Mr. Wilkins noticed. He had not seen her flushed like that before. "Well, I'm their man," he thought.

Lotty's greeting was effusive. It was done with both hands. "Didn't I tell you?" she laughed to Rose over her shoulder while Frederick was shaking her hands in both his.

"What did you tell her?" asked Frederick, in order to say something. The way they were all welcoming him was confusing. They had evidently all expected him, not only Rose.

The sandy but agreeable young woman didn't answer his question, but looked extraordinarily pleased to see him. Why should she be extraordinarily pleased to see him?

"What a delightful place this is," said Frederick, confused, and making the first remark that occurred to him.

"It's a tub of love," said the sandy young woman earnestly; which confused him more than ever.

And his confusion became excessive at the next words he heard—spoken, these, by the old lady, who said: "We won't wait. Lady Caroline is always late"—for he only then, on hearing her name, really and properly remembered Lady Caroline, and the thought of her confused him to excess.

He went into the dining-room like a man in a dream. He had come out to this place to see Lady Caroline, and had told her so. He had even told her in his fatuousness—it was true, but how fatuous—that he hadn't been able to help coming. She didn't know he was married. She thought his name was Arundel. Everybody in London thought his name was Arundel. He had used it and written under it so long that he almost thought it was himself. In the short time since she had left him on the seat in the garden, where he told her he had come because he couldn't help it, he had found Rose again, had passionately embraced and been embraced, and had forgotten Lady Caroline. It would be an extraordinary piece of good fortune if Lady Caroline's being late meant she was tired or bored and would not come to dinner at all. Then he could—no, he couldn't. He turned a deeper red even than usual, he being a man of full habit and red anyhow, at the thought of such cowardice. No, he couldn't go away after dinner and catch his train and disappear to Rome; not unless, that is, Rose came with him. But even so, what a running away. No, he couldn't.

When they got to the dining-room Mrs. Fisher went to the head of the table—was this Mrs. Fisher's house? he asked himself. He didn't know; he didn't know anything—and Rose, who in her earlier days of defying Mrs. Fisher had taken the other end as her place, for after all no one could say by looking at a table which was its top and which its bottom, led Frederick to the seat next to her. If only, he thought, he could have been alone with Rose; just five minutes more alone with Rose, so that he could have asked her—

But probably he wouldn't have asked her anything, and only gone on kissing her.

He looked round. The sandy young woman was telling the man they called Briggs to go and sit beside Mrs. Fisher—was the house, then, the sandy young woman's and not Mrs. Fisher's? He didn't know; he didn't know anything—and she herself sat down on Rose's other side, so that she was opposite him, Frederick, and next to the genial man who had said "Here we are," when it was only too evident that there they were indeed.

Next to Frederick, and between him and Briggs, was an empty chair: Lady Caroline's. No more than Lady Caroline knew of the presence in Frederick's life of Rose was Rose aware of the presence in Frederick's life of Lady Caroline. What would each think? He didn't know; he didn't know anything. Yes, he did know something, and that was that his wife had made it up with him—suddenly, miraculously, unaccountably, and divinely. Beyond that he knew nothing. The situation was one with which he felt he could not cope. It must lead him whither it would. He could only drift.

In silence Frederick ate his soup, and the eyes, the large expressive eyes of the young woman opposite, were on him, he could feel, with a growing look in them of inquiry. They were, he could see, very intelligent and attractive eyes, and full, apart from the inquiry, of goodwill. Probably she thought he ought to talk—but if she knew everything she wouldn't think so. Briggs didn't talk either. Briggs seemed uneasy. What was the matter with Briggs? And Rose too didn't talk, but then that was natural. She never had been a talker. She had the loveliest expression on her face. How long would it be on it after Lady Caroline's entrance? He didn't know; he didn't know anything.

But the genial man on Mrs. Fisher's left was talking enough for everybody. That fellow ought to have been a parson. Pulpits were the place for a voice like his; it would get him a bishopric in six months. He was explaining to Briggs, who shuffled about in his seat—why did Briggs shuffle about in his seat?—that he must have come out by the same train as Arbuthnot, and when Briggs, who said nothing, wriggled in apparent dissent, he undertook to prove it to him, and did prove it to him in long clear sentences.

"Who's the man with the voice?" Frederick asked Rose in a whisper; and the young woman opposite, whose ears appeared to have the quickness of hearing of wild creatures, answered, "He's my husband."

"Then by all the rules," said Frederick pleasantly, pulling himself together, "you oughtn't to be sitting next to him."

"But I want to. I like sitting next to him. I didn't before I came here."

Frederick could think of nothing to say to this, so he only smiled generally.

"It's this place," she said, nodding at him. "It makes one understand. You've no idea what a lot you'll understand before you've done here."

"I'm sure I hope so," said Frederick with real fervor.

The soup was taken away, and the fish was brought. Briggs, on the other side of the empty chair, seemed more uneasy than ever. What was the matter with Briggs? Didn't he like fish?

Frederick wondered what Briggs would do in the way of fidgets if he were in his own situation. Frederick kept on wiping his mustache, and was not able to look up from his plate, but that was as much as he showed of what he was feeling.

Though he didn't look up he felt the eyes of the young woman opposite raking him like searchlights, and Rose's eyes were on him too, he knew, but they rested on him unquestioningly, beautifully, like a benediction. How long would they go on doing that once Lady Caroline was there? He didn't know; he didn't know anything.

He wiped his mustache for the twentieth unnecessary time, and could not quite keep his hand steady, and the young woman opposite saw his hand not being quite steady, and her eyes raked him persistently. Why did her eyes rake him persistently? He didn't know; he didn't know anything.

Then Briggs leapt to his feet. What was the matter with Briggs? Oh—yes—quite: she had come.

Frederick wiped his mustache and got up too. He was in for it now. Absurd, fantastic situation. Well, whatever happened he could only drift—drift, and look like an ass to Lady Caroline, the most absolute as well as deceitful ass—an ass who was also a reptile, for she might well think he had been mocking her out in the garden when he said, no doubt in a shaking voice—fool and ass—that he had come because he couldn't help it; while as for what he would look like to his Rose—when Lady Caroline introduced him to her—when Lady Caroline introduced him as her friend whom she had invited in to dinner—well, God alone knew that.

He, therefore, as he got up wiped his mustache for the last time before the catastrophe.

But he was reckoning without Scrap.

That accomplished and experienced young woman slipped into the chair Briggs was holding for her, and on Lotty's leaning across eagerly, and saying before any one else could get a word in, "Just fancy, Caroline, how quickly Rose's husband has got here!" turned to him without so much as the faintest shadow of surprise on her face, and held out her hand, and smiled like a young angel, and said, "and me late your very first evening."

The daughter of the Droitwiches . . .

CHAPTER 22

That evening was the evening of the full moon. The garden was an enchanted place where all the flowers seemed white. The lilies, the daphnes, the orange-blossom, the white stocks, the white pinks, the white roses—you could see these as plainly as in the daytime; but the colored flowers existed only as fragrance.

The three younger women sat on the low wall at the end of the top garden after dinner, Rose a little apart from the others, and watched the enormous moon moving slowly over the place where Shelley had lived his last months just on a hundred years before. The sea quivered along the path of the moon. The stars winked and trembled. The mountains were misty blue outlines, with little clusters of lights shining through from little clusters of homes. In the garden the plants stood quite still, straight and unstirred by the smallest ruffle of air. Through the glass doors the dining-room, with its candle-lit table and brilliant flowers—nasturtiums and marigolds that night—glowed like some magic cave of color, and the three men smoking round it looked strangely animated figures seen from the silence, the huge cool calm of outside.

Mrs. Fisher had gone to the drawing-room and the fire. Scrap and Lotty, their faces upturned to the sky, said very little and in whispers. Rose said nothing. Her face too was upturned. She was looking at the umbrella pine, which had been smitten into something glorious, silhouetted against stars. Every now and then Scrap's eyes lingered on Rose; so did Lotty's. For Rose was lovely. Anywhere at that moment, among all the well-known beauties, she would have been lovely. Nobody could have put her in the shade, blown out her light that evening; she was too evidently shining.

Lotty bent close to Scrap's ear, and whispered. "Love," she whispered.

Scrap nodded. "Yes," she said, under her breath.

She was obliged to admit it. You only had to look at Rose to know that here was Love.

"There's nothing like it," whispered Lotty.

Scrap was silent.

"It's a great thing," whispered Lotty after a pause, during which they both watched Rose's upturned face, "to get on with one's loving. Perhaps you can tell me of anything else in the world that works such wonders."

But Scrap couldn't tell her; and if she could have, what a night to begin arguing in. This was a night for—

She pulled herself up. Love again. It was everywhere. There was no getting away from it. She had come to this place to get away from it, and here was everybody in its different stages. Even Mrs. Fisher seemed to have been brushed by one of the many feathers of Love's wing, and at dinner was different—full of concern because Mr. Briggs wouldn't eat, and her face when she turned to him all soft with motherliness.

Scrap looked up at the pine-tree motionless among stars. Beauty made you love, and love made you beautiful . . .

She pulled her wrap closer round her with a gesture of defense, of keeping out and off. She didn't want to grow sentimental. Difficult not to, here; the marvelous night stole in through all one's chinks, and brought in with it, whether one wanted them or not, enormous feelings—feelings one couldn't manage, great things about death and time and waste; glorious and devastating things, magnificent and bleak, at once rapture and terror and immense, heart-cleaving longing. She felt small and dreadfully alone. She felt uncovered and defenseless. Instinctively she pulled her wrap closer. With this thing of chiffon she tried to protect herself from the eternities.

"I suppose," whispered Lotty, "Rose's husband seems to you just an ordinary, good-natured, middle-aged man."

Scrap brought her gaze down from the stars and looked at Lotty a moment while she focused her mind again.

"Just a rather red, rather round man," whispered Lotty.

Scrap bowed her head.

"He isn't," whispered Lotty. "Rose sees through all that. That's mere trimmings. She sees what we can't see, because she loves him."

Always love.

Scrap got up, and winding herself very tightly in her wrap moved away to her day corner, and sat down there alone on the wall and looked out across the other sea, the sea where the sun had gone down, the sea with the far-away dim shadow stretching into it which was France.

Yes, love worked wonders, and Mr. Arundel—she couldn't at once get used to his other name—was, to Rose, Love itself; but it also worked inverted wonders, it didn't invariably, as she well knew, transfigure people into saints and angels. Grievously indeed did it sometimes do the opposite. She had had it in her life applied to her to excess. If it had let her alone, if it had at least been moderate and infrequent, she might, she thought, have turned out a quite decent, generous-minded, kindly human being. And what was she, thanks to this Love Lotty talked so much about? Scrap searched for a just description. She was a spoilt, a sour, a suspicious, and a selfish spinster.

The glass doors of the dining-room opened, and the three men came out into the garden, Mr. Wilkins's voice flowing along in front of them. He appeared to be doing all the talking; the other two were saying nothing.

Perhaps she had better go back to Lotty and Rose; it would be tiresome to be discovered and hemmed into that *cul-de-sac* by Mr. Briggs.

She got up reluctantly, for she considered it unpardonable of Mr. Briggs to force her to move about like this, to force her out of any place she wished to sit in; and she emerged from the daphne bushes feeling like some gaunt, stern figure of just resentment and wishing that she looked as gaunt and stern as she felt; so would she have struck repugnance into the soul of Mr. Briggs, and been free of him. But she knew she didn't look like that, however hard she might try. At dinner his hand shook when he drank, and he couldn't speak to her without flushing scarlet and then going pale, and Mrs. Fisher's eyes had sought hers with the entreaty of one who asks that her only son may not be hurt.

How could a human being, thought Scrap, frowning as she issued forth from her corner, how could a man made in God's image behave so; and he fitted for better things she was sure, with his youth, his attractiveness, and his brains. He had brains. She had examined him cautiously whenever at dinner Mrs. Fisher forced him to turn away to answer her, and she was sure he had brains. Also he had character; there was something noble about his head, about the shape of his forehead—noble and kind. All the more deplorable that he should allow himself to be infatuated by a mere outside, and waste any of his strength, any of his peace of mind, hanging round just a woman-thing. If only he could see right through her, see through all her skin and stuff, he would be cured, and she might go on sitting undisturbed on this wonderful night by herself.

Just beyond the daphne bushes she met Frederick, hurrying.

"I was determined to find you first," he said, "before I go to Rose." And he added quickly, "I want to kiss your shoes."

"Do you?" said Scrap, smiling. "Then I must go and put on my new ones. These aren't nearly good enough."

She felt immensely well-disposed towards Frederick. He, at least, would grab no more. His grabbing days, so sudden and so brief, were done. Nice man; agreeable man. She now definitely liked him. Clearly he had been getting into some sort of a tangle, and she was grateful to Lotty for stopping her in time at dinner from saying something hopelessly complicating. But whatever he had been getting into he was out of it now; his face and Rose's face had the same light in them.

"I shall adore you for ever now," said Frederick.

Scrap smiled. "Shall you?" she said.

"I adored you before because of your beauty. Now I adore you because you're not only as beautiful as a dream but as decent as a man."

Scrap laughed. "Am I?" she said, amused.

"When the impetuous young woman," Frederick went on, "the blessedly impetuous young woman, blurted out in the nick of time that I am Rose's husband, you behaved exactly as a man would have behaved to his friend."

"Did I?" said Scrap, her enchanting dimple very evident.

"It's the rarest, most precious of combinations," said Frederick, "to be a woman and have the loyalty of a man."

"Is it?" smiled Scrap, a little wistfully. These were indeed handsome compliments. If only she were really like that . . .

"And I want to kiss your shoes."

"Won't this save trouble?" she asked, holding out her hand.

He took it and swiftly kissed it, and was hurrying away again. "Bless you," he said as he went.

"Where is your luggage?" Scrap called after him.

"Oh, Lord, yes—" said Frederick, pausing. "It's at the station."

"I'll send for it."

He disappeared through the bushes. She went indoors to give the order; and this is how it happened that Domenico, for the second time that evening, found himself journeying into Mezzago and wondering as he went.

Then, having made the necessary arrangements for the perfect happiness of these two people, she came slowly out into the garden again, very much absorbed in thought. Love seemed to bring happiness to everybody but herself. It had certainly got hold of everybody there, in its different varieties, except herself. Poor Mr. Briggs had been got hold of by its least dignified variety. Poor Mr. Briggs. He was a disturbing problem, and his going away next day wouldn't, she was afraid, solve him.

When she reached the others Mr. Arundel—she kept on forgetting that he wasn't Mr. Arundel—was already, his arm through Rose's, going off with her, probably to the greater seclusion of the lower garden. No doubt they had a great deal to say to each other; something had gone wrong between them, and had suddenly been put right. San Salvatore, Lotty would say, San Salvatore working its spell of happiness. She could quite believe in its spell. Even she was happier there than she had been for ages and ages. The only person who would go empty away would be Mr. Briggs.

Poor Mr. Briggs. When she came in sight of the group he looked much too nice and boyish not to be happy. It seemed out of the picture that the owner of the place, the person to whom they owed all this, should be the only one to go away from it unblessed.

Compunction seized Scrap. What very pleasant days she had spent in his house, lying in his garden, enjoying his flowers, loving his views, using his things, being comfortable, being rested—recovering, in fact. She had had the most leisured, peaceful, and thoughtful time of her life; and all really thanks to him. Oh, she knew she paid him some ridiculous small sum a week, out of all proportion to the benefits she got in exchange, but what was that in the balance? And wasn't it entirely thanks to him that she had come across Lotty? Never else would she and Lotty have met; never else would she have known her.

Compunction laid its quick, warm hand on Scrap. Impulsive gratitude flooded her. She went straight up to Briggs.

"I owe you so *much*," she said, overcome by the sudden realization of all she did owe him, and ashamed of her churlishness in the afternoon and at dinner. Of course he hadn't known she was being churlish. Of course her disagreeable inside was camouflaged as usual by the chance arrangement of her outside; but she knew it. She was churlish. She had been churlish to everybody for years. Any penetrating eye, thought Scrap, any really penetrating eye, would see her for what she was—a spoilt, a sour, a suspicious, and a selfish spinster.

"I owe you so *much*," therefore said Scrap earnestly, walking straight up to Briggs, humbled by these thoughts.

He looked at her in wonder. "*You* owe *me*?" he said. "But it's I who—I who—" he stammered. To see her there in his garden . . . nothing in it, no white flower, was whiter, more exquisite.

"Please," said Scrap, still more earnestly, "won't you clear your mind of everything except just truth? You don't owe me anything. How should you?"

"I don't owe you anything?" echoed Briggs. "Why, I owe you my first sight of—of—"

"Oh, for goodness sake—for *goodness* sake," said Scrap entreatingly, "do, please, be ordinary. Don't be humble. Why should you be humble? It's ridiculous of you to be humble. You're worth fifty of me."

"Unwise," thought Mr. Wilkins, who was standing there too, while Lotty sat on the wall. He was surprised, he was concerned, he was shocked that Lady Caroline should thus encourage Briggs. "Unwise—very," thought Mr. Wilkins, shaking his head.

Briggs's condition was so bad already that the only course to take with him was to repel him utterly, Mr. Wilkins considered. No half measures were the least use with Briggs, and kindliness and familiar talk would only be misunderstood by the unhappy youth.

The daughter of the Droitwiches could not really, it was impossible to suppose it, desire to encourage him. Briggs was all very well, but Briggs was Briggs; his name alone proved that. Probably Lady Caroline did not quite appreciate the effect of her voice and face, and how between them they made otherwise ordinary words seem—well, encouraging. But these words were not quite ordinary; she had not, he feared, sufficiently pondered them. Indeed and indeed she needed an adviser—some sagacious, objective counselor like himself. There she was, standing before Briggs almost holding out her hands to him. Briggs of course ought to be thanked, for they were having a most delightful holiday in his house, but not thanked to excess and not by Lady Caroline alone. That very evening he had been considering the presentation to him next day of a round robin of collective gratitude on his departure; but he should not be thanked like this, in the moonlight, in the garden, by the lady he was so manifestly infatuated with.

Mr. Wilkins therefore, desiring to assist Lady Caroline out of this situation by swiftly applied tact, said with much heartiness: "It is most proper, Briggs, that you should be thanked. You will please allow me to add my expressions of indebtedness, and those of my wife, to Lady Caroline's. We ought to have proposed a vote of thanks to you at dinner. You should have been toasted. There certainly ought to have been some—"

But Briggs took no notice of him whatever; he simply continued to look at Lady Caroline as though she were the first woman he had ever seen. Neither, Mr. Wilkins observed, did Lady Caroline take any notice of him; she too continued to look at Briggs, and with that odd air of almost appeal. Most unwise. Most.

Lotty, on the other hand, took too much notice of him, choosing this moment when Lady Caroline needed special support and protection to get up off the wall and put her arm through his and draw him away.

"I want to tell you something, Mellersh," said Lotty at this juncture, getting up.

"Presently," said Mr. Wilkins, waving her aside.

"No—now," said Lotty; and she drew him away.

He went with extreme reluctance. Briggs should be given no rope at all—not an inch.

"Well—what is it?" he asked impatiently, as she led him towards the house. Lady Caroline ought not to be left like that, exposed to annoyance.

"Oh, but she isn't," Lotty assured him, just as if he had said this aloud, which he certainly had not. "Caroline is perfectly all right."

"Not at all all right. That young Briggs is—"

"Of course he is. What did you expect? Let's go indoors to the fire and Mrs. Fisher. She's all by herself."

"I cannot," said Mr. Wilkins, trying to draw back, "leave Lady Caroline alone in the garden."

"Don't be silly, Mellersh—she isn't alone. Besides, I want to tell you something."

"Well, tell me, then."

"Indoors."

With a reluctance that increased at every step Mr. Wilkins was taken farther and farther away from Lady Caroline. He believed in his wife now and trusted her, but on this occasion he thought she was making a terrible mistake. In the drawing-room sat Mrs. Fisher by the fire, and it certainly was to Mr. Wilkins, who preferred rooms and fires after dark to gardens and moonlight, more agreeable to be in there than out of doors if he could have brought Lady Caroline safely in with him. As it was, he went in with extreme reluctance.

Mrs. Fisher, her hands folded on her lap, was doing nothing, merely gazing fixedly into the fire. The lamp was arranged conveniently for reading, but she was not reading. Her great dead friends did not seem worth reading that night. They always said the same things now—over and over again they said the same things, and nothing new was to be got out of them any more for ever. No doubt they were greater than any one was now, but they had this immense disadvantage, that they were dead. Nothing further was to be expected of them; while of the living, what might one not still expect? She craved for the living, the developing—the crystallized and finished wearied her. She was thinking that if only she had had a son—a son like Mr. Briggs, a dear boy like that, going on, unfolding, alive, affectionate, taking care of her and loving her . . .

The look on her face gave Mrs. Wilkins's heart a little twist when she saw it. "Poor old dear," she thought, all the loneliness of age flashing upon her, the loneliness of having outstayed one's welcome in the world, of being in it only on sufferance, the complete loneliness of the old childless woman who has failed to make friends. It did seem that people could only be really happy in pairs—any sorts of pairs, not in the least necessarily lovers, but pairs of friends, pairs of mothers and children, of brothers and sisters—and where was the other half of Mrs. Fisher's pair going to be found?

Mrs. Wilkins thought she had perhaps better kiss her again. The kissing this afternoon had been a great success; she knew it, she had instantly felt Mrs. Fisher's reaction to it. So she crossed over and bent down and kissed her and said cheerfully, "We've come in—" which indeed was evident.

This time Mrs. Fisher actually put up her hand and held Mrs. Wilkins's cheek against her own—this living thing, full of affection, of warm, racing blood; and as she did this she felt safe with the strange creature, sure that she who herself did unusual things so naturally would take the action quite as a matter of course, and not embarrass her by being surprised.

Mrs. Wilkins was not at all surprised; she was delighted. "I believe *I'm* the other half of her pair," flashed into her mind. "I believe it's me, positively me, going to be fast friends with Mrs. Fisher!"

Her face when she lifted her head was full of laughter. Too extraordinary, the developments produced by San Salvatore. She and Mrs. Fisher . . . but she *saw* them being fast friends.

"Where are the others?" asked Mrs. Fisher. "Thank you—dear," she added, as Mrs. Wilkins put a footstool under her feet, a footstool obviously needed, Mrs. Fisher's legs being short.

"I see myself throughout the years," thought Mrs. Wilkins, her eyes dancing, "bringing footstools to Mrs. Fisher . . ."

"The Roses," she said, straightening herself, "have gone into the lower garden—I *think* lovemaking."

"The Roses?"

"The Fredericks, then, if you like. They're completely merged and indistinguishable."

"Why not say the Arbuthnots, my dear?" said Mr. Wilkins.

"Very well, Mellersh—the Arbuthnots. And the Carolines—"

Both Mr. Wilkins and Mrs. Fisher started. Mr. Wilkins, usually in such complete control of himself, started even more than Mrs. Fisher, and for the first time since his arrival felt angry with his wife.

"Really—" he began indignantly.

"Very well, Mellersh—the Briggses, then."

"The Briggses!" cried Mr. Wilkins, now very angry indeed; for the implication was to him a most outrageous insult to the entire race of Desters—dead Desters, living Desters, and Desters still harmless because they were yet unborn. "Really—"

"I'm sorry, Mellersh," said Mrs. Wilkins, pretending meekness, "if you don't like it."

"Like it! You've taken leave of your senses. Why, they've never set eyes on each other before to-day."

"That's true. But that's why they're able now to go ahead."

"Go ahead!" Mr. Wilkins could only echo the outrageous words.

"I'm sorry, Mellersh," said Mrs. Wilkins again, "if you don't like it, but—"

Her gray eyes shone, and her face rippled with the light and conviction that had so much surprised Rose the first time they met.

"It's useless minding," she said. "I shouldn't struggle if I were you. Because—"

She stopped, and looked first at one alarmed solemn face and then at the other, and laughter as well as light flickered and danced over her.

"I see them being the Briggses," finished Mrs. Wilkins.

That last week the syringa came out at San Salvatore, and all the acacias flowered. No one had noticed how many acacias there were till one day the garden was full of a new scent, and there were the delicate trees, the lovely successors to the wistaria, hung all over among their trembling leaves with blossom. To lie under an acacia tree that last week and look up through the branches at its frail leaves and white flowers quivering against the blue of the sky, while the least movement of the air shook down their scent, was a great happiness. Indeed, the whole garden dressed itself gradually towards the end in white, and grew more and more scented. There were the lilies, as vigorous as ever, and the white stocks and white pinks and white banksia roses, and the syringa and the jessamine, and at last the crowning fragrance of the acacias. When, on the first of May, everybody went away, even after they had got to the bottom of the hill and passed through the iron gates out into the village, they still could smell the acacias.

ELIZABETH VON ARNIM (1866–1941) was an English writer who penned a popular series of autobiographical novels. Besides *The Enchanted April*, some of her best-known works include *Vera* and *Mr. Skeffington*.

KATE FORRESTER is an illustrator and hand-lettering artist based by the sea in Brighton, England. She works predominantly in the publishing industry, adorning book covers with her intricate hand-drawn words and swirling, organic illustrations. Forrester is also known for her packaging designs, branding, patterns, and large-scale murals for international clients—mainly in the United States and Europe. She is also, of course, a hopeless romantic!